MW01253529

LIME JUICE MONEY

Jo Morey

HARPER

An Imprint of HarperCollins*Publishers*

LIME JUICE MONEY

A Novel

HarperCollins books may be purchased for educational, business, or sales promotional use. For information, please email the Special Markets Department at SPsales@harpercollins.com.

hc.com

"Voyager" from *Memling's Veil* by Mary Ruefle, 1982. Published by University of Alabama Press. Used by permission.

From *The Beach* by Alex Garland published by Penguin. Copyright © Alex Garland, 1996. Reprinted by permission of Penguin Books Limited.

Reprinted with permission of Scribner, a division of Simon & Schuster, LLC. from *The Lathe of Heaven* by Ursula K. Le Guin. Copyright © 1971, 1999 by Ursula K. Le Guin. All Rights reserved.

Excerpt from *The Mosquito Coast* by Paul Theroux. Copyright © Paul Theroux, 1981, used by permission of The Wylie Agency (UK) Limited.

Excerpt from *The Orchid Hunters* by Norman MacDonald (1939).

FIRST U.S. EDITION

Designed by Elina Cohen
Art courtesy of Shutterstock / title: Flame of life, part art: slavantonov; chapter art: Nina Shchavielieva

Library of Congress Cataloging-in-Publication Data

Names: Morey, Jo author
Title: Lime juice money : a novel / Jo Morey.
Description: First U.S. edition. | New York : Harper, 2025.
Identifiers: LCCN 2024050236 | ISBN 9780063399266 hardcover | ISBN 9780063399259 trade paperback | ISBN 9780063399273 ebook
Subjects: LCGFT: Novels
Classification: LCC PR6113.O7365 L56 2025 | DDC 823/.92—dc23/eng/20250402
LC record available at https://lccn.loc.gov/2024050236

25 26 27 28 29 LBC 5 4 3 2 1

For anyone who feels unheard
and for everyone who cares to listen.

I have become an orchid
  washed in on the salt white beach.
Memory,
  what can I make of it now
  that might please you—
  this life, already wasted
  and still strewn with
  miracles?

—Mary Ruefle, "Voyager," 1982

Nuh evrything weh gat suga sweet.
(Not everything that has sugar is sweet).

—Belizean proverb

LIME JUICE MONEY

Awakening

The jungle thrives as it has for millennia, in wild shadows, even in the basking light of day, shrouding its secrets in a tangle of leaves and roots and vines. A majesty of evergreens cast their shade, overseeing all like wise counsel: chicle trees and cacao trees and ceiba, palmettos of silver, and cohune palms. A frenetic trilling of birdsong pulses its backdrop. Frogs croak and bark and groak. Bees hum. A screech owl drills into the dusk. *Gogogogogogogo.* A fer-de-lance, camouflaged amongst leaf litter, sleeks under a log. It's an abundance of lush self-protection, teeming with life upon life upon life. But everything rots faster in the heat.

The body has lain here since Tuesday, a bloated invitation under unforgiving suns and a murmuring haunt of flies.

From the cavities of dead trees vultures soar, their wings spanning like black cloaks, their pupils eagerly searching. They circle on high, sailing the winds, surveying, until they descend into a wake. Smaller raptors scatter, arguing with breathy grunts. Birds in bishops' clothing, they gather, one by one. And wait.

They start with the eyes. The first slits in with its beak, inaugurating the feast. The second and third join in, remorselessly ripping, cleaving into skin. Rasp-like tongues tear at tendons, rip flesh from honeycomb bone. Intestines are pulled like strawberry laces, shared sweet canapés.

Grim guests keep on arriving, diving from on high, wing over wing over wing, devouring entrails of a life.

The sun bleeds into the sky as the breeze slowly dies. The jungle rouses another octave—cheeping, whirring, croaking. A final cleansing, the vultures piss down their legs before—one by one—they set off, ascending with their secrets back into the sky, back to the hollows of their skeleton trees.

The body remains, just a carcass. The bones of four fingers are curled stiff, clutching at the torn single bloom of an orchid: a bright orange *Cattleya*, its colour screaming brighter than the sun.

PART ONE
Saltwater

Cocos nucifera (*Arecaceae*). Palm, coconut tree. The most widespread fruit plant on Earth with a great capacity for natural dispersal. A perennial flowering plant found in tropical and subtropical climates, its nuts (fruit) have the capability to survive up to 120 days floating in seawater, germinating when they make landfall.

1

Laelia

When I lied to him for the first time, it sparkled off my tongue as sweet as popping candy. He didn't even know, he didn't catch it, and I hadn't planned to, not really. It just fell out of my mouth, and I wasn't sure why.

Maybe it was shame. Was it shame, or something stronger? A defensive move I'd learned—or a preemptive one—because women have that kind of sixth sense, don't they? Jacobson's organ. I read about that once, in one of Dad's *New Scientist* magazines, how females are predisposed to listen to their gut; how we can sense fear like we're about to be fed it.

Through broken clouds, the sun warmed the sea. Turquoise medicine. I breathed it all in, deep into my bones. Jet Skis wasped in the distance, irritating the flat blues beyond.

Aid lay next to me, five thousand miles of relaxed. Tattoos wrapped around his chest, his neck, his arms, commemorating untold stories with blood and pain and ink. The newest—soft black and grey roses—graced his bicep afresh below the "L.F." heart. He was resting on his elbows, his foot tapping a rhythm to the music in his ears I couldn't hear.

He'd been distracted since we got to the island. When I'd asked over breakfast if he was nervous about meeting Dad, he insisted he wasn't, got annoyed with me for asking. He barely ate any of his pancakes though, left most of his coffee. I'd wanted to tell him about the restaurant then but thought against it, deciding to wait until we were all a bit more relaxed.

Low, ebbing reggae from the beach bar drowned out my tinnitus, but on the offbeats I could still feel the buzzing electrics; they were never not there. The audiologist had told me to ignore them—the crazed sounds in my head—but it's impossible to hear nothing when you're listening for silence.

Running in and out of the waves, the kids were embroidering the sand near the jetty. The breeze kissed salty-sweet with their giggles; with my hearing aids, I could just make them out.

A soundless breeze teased the palm fronds above us, their shadows dancing grey upon the sand—grittier than I remembered it—narrower, too; the beach a gentle hem dotted with picnic benches, clam chairs, and slack hammocks. We just sat on towels.

Aid pulled the headphones from his ears. "How you feeling?" He started zincing his face. "Being back here, I mean?"

"It's fine," I said. "It's good . . . I can't wait to see the south." A pelican squawked, eyeing up the fish below as it padded along the jetty.

"Ella seems relaxed." The children seemed to simply slide into this place, leave the sludge of London behind.

"She needs a break."

"We all do, but it is weird be   again." I lost some of his words to the crawk of the pelican, but his New England accent felt stronger than usual.

Dylan was rushing up the beach towards us, kicking up the sand. "Aid, will you come back in the ea with   ?"

"Sure, little man," Aid shouted. "Le m have a quick moke, then I'll be in." He turned to me. "When   we mee ing your da ?"

I turned up my hearing aids. "I need to check with Chloe. She's got it all figured out."

"No shit." Aid pulled his tobacco pouch out of my beach bag.

"To be fair, she has organised the whole thing."

"I thought he might want to meet me first, before everyone else."

"She wants to do it like that, thinks it will be more fun . . . You sure you're not nervous?"

"Let's not stay on too long. Once we're done with the party, let's hit Placencia, like we said. Beaches are better there anyway." Aid hadn't wanted to come to Caye Caulker again, asked why we couldn't have visited Dad down in the jungle, which is what I'd wanted to do, too. But my sister had her plan, and I knew better than to mess with it. Besides, I liked the idea of being back here on the island; Aid just wasn't nostalgic like that.

"Do you want a coffee?" I asked.

He was rubbing the last of the sunscreen into his tattooed arms. "Yeah. Thanks."

I cast my eye towards the children. "Anything else?"

He grabbed me by the back of the neck, pulling me closer. "A kiss." Under the shade of passing clouds, we breathed each other in. He smelt of coconut and wood, a moreish musk I had to prise myself away from.

"I love you, Wylde," he called after me as I made my way across the sand. "Wildly." I turned to smile at him, his blue eyes tracking mine.

A young couple and their toddler beat me to the kiosk. She was beautiful, the woman. She looked Scandinavian, but they started speaking to each other in something else—German, maybe, or Dutch. Arguing with the girl about what she wanted to order, they were gesticulating back and forth between her and the faded ice-cream board. The sun so bright through the clouds, I had to squint to make out the scrawled chalk on the side of the hut: ICED COFFEE, BELIKIN, SMOOTHIES.

The girl started to whine, stomping her flip-flopped little foot. "Room-ijs, roomijs," she singsonged.

I could feel my body acclimatising—sinking into the fortnight. It felt so good to be in a bikini, to finally be away. We hadn't had the money to go abroad for so long, and now it felt even more precious. I tried not to think about what happened with Aktar and the restaurant, how we'd left things. This was pretty much paid for, so I'd enjoy it, worry about worrying when I was back home, but then, of course, I thought about Aktar, and the restaurant, and how we'd left things. Fuck. I needed to call him, needed to apologise again. And I needed to tell Aid.

He was lying flat then, deadening his cigarette butt into the sand. His body bragged incredible, even from this distance. I lost sight of it sometimes, but there was no doubt about it—people noticed him; and he liked to be noticed. Three years in, all I had to do was look at him and my head still dissolved.

A heavy grit-grey had appeared as if from nowhere on the horizon. The kids were splashing each other now, kicking the water, not too deep. Ella, even at fourteen, still enjoyed playing with Dylan. I flashed in my mind to a day when I might no longer be able to hear them, my own children—the cruellest void imaginable. I had to remember this all.

"Nee!" The blond woman shouted in front of me, side-eyeing her husband, bending towards the girl who was stamping her other foot.

Ella was in deeper now, swimming closer to the jetty, where a speedboat was coming in from the distance. She looked so much taller than last time I'd seen her in a swimsuit, her limbs impossibly long. Only a few years ago, she'd been so clingy, so wholly dependent on me; now though, she was blooming wildly—so enigmatic and ripe with possibilities.

The boat whipped close by the tip of the dock, an aftermath of waves gathering and spilling.

A woman in a red bikini got up from a nearby table, her chair pushed back. She took a final draining sup of coffee and tossed down her newspaper, the pages rustling in the gathering breeze. The title caught my eye, *Amandala*, and then the headline:

Shooting on Logwood Street. Man Dead. Police Hunt for Zabaneh.

"Rooooooooom-ijs," the toddler screamed in front of me until it pierced into my ears. The water was picking up now, cascading over the sand. Ella was up to her chest, rising and falling, defensive against the newly violent sea. I scoured the shoreline, thick grey clouds bruising the sky behind. *Where's Dylan?*

A chill riptided through me. I swept my eyes back and forth, colours blurring. I could still make out Ella, disappearing up and down in the waves. But no Dylan.

I started walking fast, gathering pace, then running, back towards the sea, "Roomijs, roomijs" still screeching out behind me. The sand felt heavy, clumpy, beneath my feet. I saw Ella clearly then, struggling in between the boat's waves, but still no Dylan.

Aid was running into the sea.

"Ella!" I yelled, throwing my wallet down like a missile. "Where's Dylan?" She couldn't hear. Hurtling, the sand thrashed up against my calves. I untied my sarong, still running, and threw myself into the water, scanning the surface.

Ella, hair stuck to her face, looked back at me blankly, and then around; she didn't know, she didn't know he was under. Aid was swimming through the water far in front. I screamed for Dylan while paddling and fighting the waves—each seeming more powerful than the one before. The boat pulled away from the dock, its engine growling like an unseen monster. New waves slapped against me in its wake. My ears pounded, the tinnitus screeching, so alive.

Grappling with Ella, I managed to grab her arm and push her towards the shore. I paddled back around. The wave above me was gathering height, swelling, starting to break. I dived down, submerging myself, a weight of water crashing over me.

As I came back up, I saw him: Dylan, floating in the water next to the jetty. Bobbing. Limp.

"There!" I pointed, shouting at Aid, who was closer. He stared back at me, eyes frozen, like he'd seen a ghost. "Aid!" I screamed. But he was just floating, treading water, deadlocked. A look of dread I'd never seen before overtook his face.

I swam nearer, fighting the waves, being pulled and dragged around like seaweed. I tugged at Dylan, flipping him over, cupping his chin like I was sure you were supposed to, but the waves were so strong, sucking us up and down, just flotsam.

I managed to scoop him into my arms, cradling him, holding him like I had all those nights. He was spluttering, pale but breathing. Aid was next to me again, swimming with us now, guiding us all back to the shore. Another push and we were into the shallows, wading. Back into the calm. I dropped to the sand, still holding Dylan.

Aid prised him off me, laid him down. "Come on, dude."

Dylan spluttered up saltwater, searching for breaths. Quick gasps.

"He's all right," Aid reassured me. "He's gonna be okay." Aid kneeled next to me, blocking out the sun. A blur of tattoos.

The distant reggae gently thumped, the same song. The *same* song.

I hugged Dylan. "Are you okay?" He smiled, a little, and nodded. "You gave us such a fright."

People were streaming towards us like bright confetti out onto the beach. Strangers' hands stroking at my back, I flinched. Unknown voices: "That boat shouldn't have been so close to the shore, not that fast." The volume alternated in and out, ringing waves of tinnitus flooding over everything. A cloud of unbearable sound.

My hearing aids had drowned in the water. I pulled them from my ears, wondering if they were still working; I couldn't tell. There were too many people. Too much noise. My muscles ached with exhaustion. Too much. Too much.

Too much.

I stumbled away from them, our little scene, back up the beach towards the towels, my ears screeching as I checked my aids which were somehow still working. The Dutch couple walked by in front of me, arm in arm, glancing down towards the sea. A few steps behind them the little blond girl followed, carrying a strawberry ice cream.

I was prepared for Chloe. After lunch, Aid had bumped into Tom by the cash machine—the only cash machine on the island—and told him about Dyl. So I knew that she knew.

"Lil, what on earth happened?" No hello. She hugged me in tight to her ponchoed breasts as we gathered by the side of their pool, and then she released me just as histrionically. I turned down my hearing aids.

We never normally hugged—really only at births, weddings, deaths. And we'd seen them only the night before, when the golf carts—laden with kids and suitcases and more kids—dropped them off at their hotel. Aid had made me promise we wouldn't have to stay with them in the same accommodation. We wanted space for lie-ins and meandering mornings. Our place was cheaper, rustic. Anyway, who needed a pool when the Caribbean Sea was right there, just footprints away?

"How are you, Dylan? You feeling okay?" Chloe ruffled Dyl's hair, as he dropped his swim fins and goggles to the tiled floor.

He shook her off and shrugged his shoulders. "Good, thanks."

A jangle of a memory. A flash of Dylan's submerged face.

I blinked it away.

"He's fine," I said. "Really." I took a seat opposite Tom, hoping I could chat to him and redirect the conversation.

"Aren't you hot wearing that?" Chloe asked Ella, pointing to her long-sleeved rashie.

"I'm good," Ella replied while I widened my eyes at Chloe and furtively shook my head.

Dylan and Ella mixed in with their cousins, the six of them dashing off in a collective cyclone to check out the starfish Edmund announced he'd found on the beach. Only Mathilda remained, stuck to her high chair, smeared in lurid sweet potato mush.

"How's your guesthouse, Laelia?" Tom asked. Thank fuck. He didn't want to keep regurgitating the morning's events either.

"It's great." I grinned, thinking of Mikel's breakfast pancakes with their banana eyes and honey smiles. "Nothing like this place, of course."

"You must have been beside yourself," Chloe went on. "I can't believe it. I mean, you can't take your eyes off them for a second, can you?" She passed me the drinks menu. "The cocktails look good. What are you having, Tom?" But she didn't wait for his reply. "You need to watch them constantly. When we were in Sanibel, when the twins were four, Flora went under and she almost didn't come back up, and that was in a pool. I don't think you can leave them alone in the sea."

I shot Aid a look, but he was pretending to be deep into the menu.

Another flash: Dylan's lifeless face in the water. Glazed brown eyes turning liquid green. I swallowed back the memory.

"It could have happened to anyone," said Tom as he signalled to the bar guy, who clocked him but carried on stacking glasses anyway. "What do you all want—beer?"

Mathilda started crying short fussy sobs as she wriggled in her chair. Chloe began searching about in her bag, one of several dumped at her pedicured, flip-flopped feet.

"What do you want, love?" Tom asked. "I don't think it's waiter service."

"Daiquiri. Extra sour." She pulled out a plush bunny rabbit and threw it onto Mathilda's tray.

"I'll come with you," said Aid, grabbing his wallet to follow Tom.

Alone now, Chloe took her real shot, half whispering in case they weren't out of range. "Weren't you watching them properly?" Her lip-sticked mouth overextended around every word, eyes widening in dramatic pleasure. "Tom said you were getting coffee when it happened."

"Of course we were watching them. The sea got rough really quickly.

The speedboat came out of nowhere. It shouldn't have been that close." I pulled the aviators I'd finally located out of my bag and put them on. "Do you remember, when you and I were here before, that old guy got caught in a rip by the Split, and the dive woman had to rescue him?"

"All the more reason to be in there swimming with them, Lil. It might look like paradise, but you've still got to keep your wits about you. Dylan's only eight, and he's not a strong swimmer."

"What's the plan tonight?" I sighed. "Are we just meeting Dad at the restaurant?"

Another blurring flash. A face. Eyes like emeralds.

"Mounia should get him there by six. I've told her we'll be waiting for them with everyone else. I've been emailing the owner, Ervin or Erin, I think he's called, and he said they're fine to sort candles. They're doing a white fruit cake or something. Apparently, it's traditional." Mathilda's cries were disintegrating into blithering wails.

"Shouldn't we meet Dad on our own first?" I asked. "Before the restaurant? It might be a bit overwhe—"

Chloe's face dropped. "Lil, this is so you. You don't do anything and then you come around now trying to change everything. It's all organised, plus we're here for a fortnight. We'll have plenty of time to catch up with Dad."

They were here for a fortnight; we could afford only ten days. I'd told them I would have to get back for work; didn't tell them we didn't have the money, or that I no longer had a job. My gut bunched like twine.

"I just figured he'd head back down south as soon as it was over." I glanced to see where our drinks had got to. "And aren't you staying up here on the cayes?" I needed alcohol. My body was exhausted. After all the jet lag and the adrenaline of the morning, I was seriously crashing.

"Yes. Aren't you? I mean, I don't think it's a good idea to take the children to the jungle. There's all sorts down there."

I really wanted to go down and see Dad's place. We'd never visited his jungle home, and I wanted to see where he lived now.

Chloe started waving the bunny in Mathilda's face, which only served to rile her further. "She's all over the place. She didn't sleep on the flight, and barely at all last night." A couple of leathery women at the next table shot Chloe pointed looks.

"Why don't you go and try putting her down?" I asked. Mathilda's wails turned back to sobs as she searched for little breaths.

Another flash of memory, or hallucination. A blur of green eyes in water. I twisted in my seat.

"There's no way I'd take the kids to Dad's," Chloe went on. "There's snakes and scorpions, and fucking tarantulas, and Christ knows what. Edmund would probably get eaten by a jaguar, and then it's holiday over. I'm not risking that." She laughed, lifting Mathilda out of her high chair. "I'm not leaving that sun lounger once I finally get to lie on it. We'll just see Dad here for a couple of days until he heads off." She started rocking back and forth, clasping Mathilda's head, willing her to quiet down. I didn't dare remind Chloe there were crocodiles and sharks all around us right here on Caye Caulker.

Tom and Aid stood at the bar, deep in forced conversation, our drinks lingering next to them. They looked so mismatched together: Tom in his Hawaiian shirt—bursting with newness—with tailored, belted chinos that made me feel uptight just looking at them, and Aid wearing only his Quiksilver board shorts and tattoos; two men with nothing in common in the entire world, apart from a beer and a Wylde woman. The poor, poor bastards.

"I'll take her for a nap," Chloe finally declared, staring over to the sunbaked women on the next table, loudly enough for them to hear and bitingly enough for them to shut up and get back to their margaritas. She began throwing nappy bags and handbags and muslins over her free shoulder. "I'll see you in a bit. Use the pool. And can you keep an eye on the kids? Tom's here so you should be fine."

She started off towards her room but managed one last snipe over her shoulder, "I don't think you should let Dylan back in the water today."

$\mathbf{D}$ad was going to loathe the paraphernalia Chloe had thrown up everywhere: endless crepe streamers, balloons, and frou-frou pompoms she'd flown over from England, all hanging expectantly from the rafters. It was like she didn't know him at all—as long as there were smiles, and laughter, and whisky, and rum, he'd be happy. He didn't need a fuss, just a good time.

"Looks great, doesn't it?" Tom asked, reaching up his arms in a sort of semi-committed hallelujah.

I glanced around, taking in the restaurant beyond the multicoloured decorations. White weathered wood, sand-filled storm lanterns, and tired seascape paintings. I was sure I'd been here before, one of the few smarter joints on the island in which to enjoy the ubiquitous lobster, fries, and beer.

"It looks really . . . colourful," I said, squeezing Aid's hand and dropping my bag on a barstool.

"Chloe's done such a good job," Tom said. "She wouldn't tell me what it cost. Can't have been cheap." I didn't bite. He was always fixating on the price of things. It was his way to wrestle back some semblance of control from Chloe, who not only won the bread in their household but kneaded it, too.

Aid took the children out onto the terrace where Edmund, Flora, and the twins were sat dressed like a double spread from the White

Company brochure. He instantly started chatting with other guests, coaxing smiles out of them, helping everyone relax.

I *did* recognise it. Aid and I had eaten at this restaurant when we first hooked up; a seafood and rum interlude to stave off the sex-after-sex induced hunger, a change from the room service that had punctuated that long, lustful day we'd spent basking in each other. It had felt so illicit stealing ourselves away behind his hotel room door, Aid hiding from his friends, me hiding from Chloe. I'd just split from Simon, and it was Chloe's idea to go on holiday. She suggested it and pretty much paid for the whole thing. She even got Tom and her nanny at the time—Ramona, was it?—to look after Ella and Dylan at their place. *A proper break*, she'd said. Mexico and Belize. Two weeks. No kids. *To get him out of your system.* Like he was a stomach bug. Still, I knew she would have been the first to disapprove, even if it was just holiday sex. A one-night-one-day stand really, at that point, but the sex was unreal. Nothing else mattered. I'd wanted Aid with every part of me. In that hotel room, I swear I could taste the sky, feel the ocean. True blue. Everything was nothing, and nothing everything.

"Oh, good, you're here," Chloe said, sauntering across the designated dance floor, Mathilda clamped to her hip. "People are arriving."

Guests started trickling in, ex-pats (or immigrants, as Aid and I told Chloe they should rightly be called)—locals from the island, Americans, Brits, and Belizeans, including a few who had managed the journey up from Stann Creek. Chloe had given everyone a clear diktat not to arrive until the night before at the earliest, so as to avoid accidentally bumping into Dad. Mounia could keep him at their hotel only so long. Caye Caulker was just five miles north to south, and a couple of blocks wide— beautiful but claustrophobic. Everyone knew everyone. Dad told me once: the whole country is the size of Massachusetts and has the same population as Coventry. I never googled it, but it was probably true.

I got why Dad didn't settle on the islands like everyone else. The incestuous ex-pat (immigrant) lifestyle. He would just dip in and out of it a little when he fancied a few days on the sand with a book ogling bikinis, or when he needed to top up his wine supplies, or tap up his contacts for cheaper imports from the States: Oreo cookies, breakfast cereals, and flour for bread making, which Dad apparently did now, as you do, when you live in the middle of nowhere in Belize. He always told us tourism is opting out of the ordinary, a search for something unreal. Living in the jungle, he considered himself enmeshed beyond gringoism, particularly as he'd found this place before any guidebook was ever even written.

The buzz in the restaurant grew louder as guests spilled in. Over swift rum and cokes I gained forgetful snippets of people's lives: Jeff and Laurie from Fort Lauderdale, who loved Belize because it's "so easy and English speaking"; Carmen from the dive school, who'd moved here from Trinidad; and—while demolishing the tomato, lime, and jalapeño sal-butes, and more rum—I chatted to Erian, Caye Caulker born and bred, hearing his tales of unimaginable hurricanes and devastated homes, fi-estas, trade winds, and Chavannes red lemonade, how he always knew Dad would rock up to this place on this day every year, and he'd have a ten-year-old Don Omario waiting "with his name on it," and I didn't even know what that was, whisky, maybe, or rum. Dad would drink it all, whatever.

"Caye Caulker used to be a fishing island with a drinking problem," Erian told me. "Now it's a drinking island with a fishing problem." He asked me what Dad was working on now, but I didn't know. Erian prob-ably knew more about his recent life than I did. Growing up, I'd always been close to my dad—more than Chloe was—but in recent years, life had entangled us all so separately.

"Still orchids," I said. It was always orchids. I glanced over at Aid, who was surrounded by a shoal of people hanging off his every word. They loved him, and he loved it. He reminded me of Dad.

"That's what brought him here, wasn't it?" Erian asked. "When he bought in Stann Creek?"

Chloe hurtled up, interrupting us. "Lil, can you try the conch frit-ters?" Erian smiled and eased himself away to another small circle of conversation. "I'm worried the sauce is too spicy." With a flick of her palm, she halted a bar guy who was threading his way through the room with a plate. "Can my sister try these?" she asked, before adding, "She's a chef. In London."

Was a chef.

I gave the guy a half smile, one that begged him to forgive me for my pained complicity.

"They're delicious," I said to him, going for another bite, the flavour puckering tart on my tongue.

Aid was flirting playfully now with the older ladies and Tom at the bar, his charisma prepossessing. I could see them falling instantly in love with his warmth and excitement. His energy attracted people like a magnet; it's what everyone always fell for. They all wanted in.

"I think they need more lime," Chloe instructed, before turning back to me. "They never normally do private functions. I had to talk Erian into it over the phone, and into making the canapés. Not easy in between client meetings." Was that another dig into how little I'd contributed to organising this thing? Probably. "Can you hear okay in here? Is it too noisy?"

"Just about."

"So have you spoken to Aid about things?"

"What things?" I grabbed some passing tortilla chips. I still needed to tell him about the restaurant.

"About not watching the kids in the water."

"Chloe, I told you, we were watching them. It was a freak accident."

"Aid told Tom you were a th coffee kios ," Chloe beamed. "So, were you . . . or not?"

"Look, it's not a big deal." I drained my glass, ice clashing against ice.

"Not a big deal?" She looked over her shoulders, checking no-one was listening. "They're your children, Laelia. You're responsible for them."

"Oh, for fuck's sake. Please don't do this."

Her face dropped. "Do what?"

"Mother me like this." I felt my chest getting tighter, the tinnitus searing through my ears. She couldn't bear that I had Aid now, someone who cared for me, looked out for me so she didn't need to anymore.

"Well,   need take responsibili y. Face up t things."

My ears screamed, grinding like metal. "Are we really doing this now?" I lowered my voice to a forced whisper. "It's Dad's birthday. You've spent so much energy organising this bloody thing, can we not just try to enjoy it?"

I turned away, the restaurant a blur. The room was crowded now, pulsing with a soup of conversation and incongruous laughter. Kids ran like butterflies, weaving in and out of skyscraping adults. I heaved a deep breath, the rum colluding with the nausea in my stomach.

Seconds after six—Chloe having updated us regularly on the time—and after several dramatic hushes and flailing hands begging us all to halt the conversations—Mounia and Dad walked in, all bright eyes and beaming smiles.

"SUR-PRIIIIISE!!" The swarm hollered and whooped in misfired unison. Still seething, I could barely mouth the words. The tinnitus volted through my ears.

Dad affected astonishment perfectly, guffawing and bear-hugging everyone in sight, raising his arms sky high, Christlike in heartfelt admiration. "My, my," he bellowed, followed by a disbelieving shake of the head, crossed palms across his heart. "You shouldn't have." He looked older, craggier, but softer somehow, too—smartly dressed, in a light-coloured shirt and linen shorts, and the Panama hat he'd taken to wearing pretty much permanently, Belize or England, rain or shine. He picked out a few faces, pointing and shifting expression with each new acquaintance he spotted.

Dad was an emperor everywhere he went, sovereign in his world. He'd always had this boundless magnetism. It emanated from him like electric current. People loved him, and loathed him, but they just couldn't keep away from him, and he liked the limelight. He'd play up to it, lean into it, like Olivier, and the curtain would never come down.

Erian placed a drink into his hand, and they all cheered. Waiting for Dad to become free, I found Aid at the bar.

"Hey." He smiled. "D'you want another?"

"Rum and ginger, please," I said to the bar guy as he placed a fresh bottle of Belikin down in front of Aid and he took a swig.

"Did you pick up my tobacco?"

I smiled, fumbling through my bag: room key, phone, Dylan's football cards, Durex. "Did you remember condoms?" Chloe had breathed into my ear at the boarding gate while the kids were sprawled on the super-shined floor, tearing open magazine bundles of plastic beneath our feet. She was always prying for details, searching for something vicarious, something exciting to cling on to—I doubted she and Tom shagged that much anymore, five kids later. Ever since we were little, she'd taunted me like this, as older sisters are inclined to, but she'd never grown out of it.

"Yes," I'd replied, thinking it was best to close her down. How was that yesterday? Was it just yesterday? It felt like the jet lag had swallowed memory, digested time. I placed my hands on Aid's tobacco and passed it to him.

"Your dad managed to look surprised . . . Bet he got wind of it somehow. He can't not have bumped into someone he knew . . . You   told me   ." Aid laughed.

"What?"

"The   ," Aid bellowed. "Remember h ?"

It was exhausting lip-reading, especially in busy settings like this. I couldn't stand these sorts of rooms now, crowded with insurmountable noise. There was no way to get the balance right, everything always out of kilter. I lost the ends of words and important bits of sentences. Life dampened by my ears. I hit the button on the back of my hearing aid, but they were already on their highest setting.

"You okay?" Aid's hand settled on my back. I couldn't stop thinking about what had happened with the shellfish, how I'd left things with Aktar.

"I'm fine. Just tired." I wanted to tell him, but this wasn't the moment, especially when I could barely hear.

"What were you   Chloe talking about? She looked   animated."

The barman placed my drink down, and I took a sip. "She won't shut up about Dylan in the water."

"Oh, Lil. Do you want me to chat t her? Tell her t ease off."

"Maybe." I pressed my lips together and put my glass back on the bar.

Aid leaned in and kissed me. "Don't worry about her. Enjoy the night."

"Hey, Aunty Laelia!" Edmund was running back in from outside, Dylan tagging behind. "Dad says you've dived the Blue Hole before . . . is tha true?"

Aid widened his eyes at me, rubbing his face.

"What's it like?" Edmund asked.

I hit Aid back with a look, but he was squeezing his eyes shut. Tom was at the bar now, too, ordering a drink and half listening in. Panicking slightly, I knew I needed to cover my back here, imagine what I might have seen that day if I hadn't spent it in a hotel room shagging Aid.

"The Blue Hole . . ." I started. "The Blue Hole is beautiful. It's like a wonder of the world . . . It's a sinkhole."

"What does it look like?" Dylan asked. Aid was turned away, gazing off into the distance.

"It's like . . ." I struggled to remember what I'd ever seen about it from documentaries and travel magazines. "It's a deep topaz circle of sea, almost perfectly round . . . erm . . . It's like the most incredible blue eye."

"An eye?" Edmund's face lit up.

The bar man joined in. "The depths haven't ever been mapped. No-one knows what's at the bottom. The Maya say it hides mysteries and unknown sea creatures . . . but there's not much oxygen down there." The kids looked mesmerised. "The Blue Hole keeps its secrets."

My mind snapped to an image of tendrils floating like seagrass, my throat tightening.

"Like people with blue eyes," said Tom, raising his brows. We all looked at him blankly. "They say they hold more secrets than people with other-coloured eyes . . ."

"Are there sharks?" asked Dylan.

"Yes!" I replied, confident in my answer to that. "So many sharks."

"Laelia," Dad's voice boomed behind me. "Baby girl."

There it was. There I was. I turned and fell into him. Tom and the kids peeled away.

"Dad . . ." His chest was warm, his paunchy stomach soft. "Happy birthday."

"Let me get a look at you." He grabbed me by the shoulders and pushed me gently away. "Belize suits you, baby girl." A ragged smile emerged over the barbs of his silvered beard. His cheeks were redder than I remembered, his nose thickening with rosacea. "You and your sister kept this well under your hats."

"Chloe did all the hard work."

"That's my Chloe." Dad laughed. "So . . . this must be Aidrian." He examined Aid up and down, not even bothering to hide it, looking back at me in between glances. I felt sixteen again.

"It's Aid." He offered his hand, his accent leaning into the British.

"Aid," Dad repeated, like it was the most basic name, like he was the actual definition of something. I knew that look. The way his eyes darted back to me, the way he curled his top lip, ever so slightly, the way he pulled his eyebrows down. "Have we met before?"

"No, we haven't met," Aid said, clutching his beer bottle.

Dad took a swig of his drink. "I don't know any other American Aidrians. It's not a popular name, is it?"

"It's a family name."

"You been to Belize before, Aid?" Dad prised his fingers into his collar, loosening the tight fabric. Sweat beads were forming tributaries above the haphazard threads of his brows.

"Well, yeah. I lived here for a while, and this is where Laelia and I met."

"That's right. Holiday romance, wasn't it?" Dad rocked back on his deck shoes, smudging at his forehead with a handkerchief.

"Something like that," I said, staring at my feet.

"Would I have met you then?" Dad asked. "I visited Caye Caulker when Laelia and Chloe were on their girls' trip here."

"No, Dad." I smiled. "I only met Aid at the end of the holiday."

"We didn't start dating until a couple of years later," Aid said. "Once I'd moved to England. To Brighton."

"That's right. Once you got divorced from Simon." Dad looked at me. "You been married before, Aid?" He was still looking at me.

"Er . . . no."

"Engaged?" Dad pushed.

Ohmygod, kill me now.

Aid took a long swig of his beer before placing it carefully back down on the counter. He picked at the corner of his beer mat and shook his head. "I'm saving myself." He smiled at me.

"Nice idea," Dad said, puffing out his chest before swigging back his drink. "Ah, here she is. Can't believe she managed to keep this a secret." Dad laughed, winking at me. Mounia sidled over from the bar, cackling at a joke she carried with her. She shocked vivid in fulsome curves, an embroidered blouse and red-violet skirt. "Mounia."

"Laelia? How you di du?" She beamed as though she knew only colossal pleasure. "I recogni you fr the photographs. It's gr to finally mee you." I furtively beeped up my hearing aids again under my hair, forgetting they were already on their highest setting.

"And this is Aidrian," Dad told her.

"I met this young man earlier. He helped me move all the chairs to make some extra dancing space." She chuckled heartily and then, pushing her tawny owl glasses up on her nose, turned just to me. "Such a kind *and* good-looking boy . . . How are you fin ing Caye Caulker?"

I leaned with my ear to listen more carefully. "It's great."

"Ellis told me you and Aidrian met here?"

"Yeah, a few years back. It's just the same." It hadn't really changed: a handful of extra bars, a new yoga café with decent iced coffee, more rusting barbecues skimming the beachfront charring chicken wings and shrimp kebabs and corn on the cob, the Caribbean colours licking fresher in places, flaking and peeling in others—walls powing with electric teals, hot pinks, and laser limes. Rum still laced the air.

"Pace slow as the waves." Mounia smiled.

Aid and my dad were finishing up their conversation. "Good to meet you, Aid," Dad said, grabbing Mounia gently by the arm, starting to turn away.

"Yeah, you, too. Happy birthday."

Dad stopped, turned back to Aid. "You say you lived here for a bit? In Belize?"

"Er, yeah . . . in San Ignacio."

"We'll catch up properly later, Laelia," Dad said, leaning in to kiss my cheek, and as he did, I thought I caught him whispering something into my ear.

"Dad?" I pulled away to look into his eyes, but he'd already turned, melting back into the room.

Aid found me later outside on the terrace. "Hey." His smile was so warm. He was brandishing a couple of daiquiris. A stubbly beard had appeared over the last few days. He hadn't had time to shave, what with all the car rides, and trains, and flights, and boats. Grizzled suited him, though.

"What's up?" he asked, passing me a cocktail. God, he looked sexy unkempt. "You seem distracted." It was he who seemed distracted, surely? Since we'd got to the island. On the beach, he couldn't relax. But more so with Dad, he wasn't himself, holding back in a way I'd never seen before. It was endearing, seeing him so nervous.

"I . . ." I had to tell him.

He rubbed his chin. "What?"

I took a breath, squeezed my bottom lip. "Aktar fired me. I think."

His face dropped. "What? Why?"

And then it came. "Tris fucked up." Sweet like sugar. "He didn't listen. He doused nam pla over the salmon . . ." I dropped my chin. "Shellfish allergy."

"Shit." Aid's eyes widened. "Were they okay?"

"We had to call an ambulance. Aktar lost it. We closed up and then he started throwing things, smashing bottles . . . It wasn't good."

"Why did he fire *you*?" Aid shook his head a little. "What about Tris?"

"My kitchen, my responsibility . . . Tris is still there. Thank God. He needs the money."

"*We* need the money."

Tears welled in my eyes, began rolling down my cheeks. "I'm sorry." I wasn't sure if I was apologising for crying, or for fucking up, or for lying. "I need to call him. He didn't actually tell me I'm fired. But I mean . . ."

"It wasn't your fault," Aid said. Except it was, and it was so stupid. If I'd only been wearing my hearing aids.

"I know, but—"

"It's okay, don't worry." He pulled in close, hugging me as we negotiated our drinks. I wasn't expecting him to be so relaxed about it, what with the money. Something in me still flinched sometimes, anticipating reactions like Simon's—the flare of his nostrils, the gait of his walk, the senseless derision.

"I was thinking maybe I could set something up on my own."

Something smaller. Something manageable. Something I could hear myself in.

"On your own?"

"It's what I've always wanted to do."

"How would you pay for it?"

"I could get some backing. Get a loan. Maybe use some of the money from your next—"

"Oh, Lil, I'm still waiting on the Margate development. Things aren't shifting. And we've got bills to pay now."

"What about Chloe? I could borrow some off her?"

"Get in bed with your sister . . . ? Come on, you're better than that."
He hugged into me again. He smelt of lime zest. "Don't worry. It'll be all
right. We'll figure it out."

"Promise?"

"Promise." He leant in and kissed me on the neck.

4

The sun dropped from the sky like a pebble, and the night turned black. Days get swallowed up so quickly in Belize. I spent the rest of the party with a bottle I pilfered from the bar. Everyone was so drunk they didn't notice, or maybe I was so drunk I didn't notice them noticing me. Slumped with the rum, I picked at the label by the firepit Erian had set up on the beach. My phone pinged. A text from Tris:

Kitchen sucks without you x

I swiped it away, dropping my phone to the sand.

The music inside was picking up, the thumping finale of "Sweet Dreams" accompanied by happy laughter, rum, and drunken sadness, the warm air already tinged with regrets. Every now and again, the children, darting like fireflies—quick shadows under terrace lights—chased one another in and out, lacing themselves between the raucousness, the adults oblivious. Two separate worlds.

Mounia appeared on the terrace, her voice honeying through the breeze. I couldn't work out if she and Dad were together; she seemed too content a woman. No drama. No messy emotion. No oyster shell to crack.

Cheers rang out as the music bumpily segmented into "Come on Eileen," its bittersweet fiddle intro. I couldn't help but snap back to Cornwall. My audiologist had told me hearing loss can affect long-term memory. Short term, too. *Cognitive decline.* Most of my memories now were hazy recollections, muted face-missing snapshots of my mother, and I couldn't re-create recipes like I used to; but I remembered that night like I could taste it.

I always told people it was just a thing that came on one morning, the lines I'd sketched up over the years were almost solid now; the half-truths I'd told myself almost real memories. When Si said he'd never touch me again, I believed him. We never spoke about that night ever, and I still hadn't, to anyone. Not even the locum GP. I told her the ringing started when I'd bumped my head putting up shelves. The audiologist told me it would have happened anyway; it often starts during times of stress.

I looked down to my hand, lit amber by the firepit light. I waited six months to change the tattoo, at least on my skin. In my head, I changed it over and over and over again on the car ride home back from Padstow. I'd imagined the needle, shiny like a gift, digging into my skin and injecting its painful relief—rewriting my past, offering me a present. Soft black ink puncturing and feathering, spelling out my story, letter by letter, organised into a neat curling line. Where my ring finger once read a soft, easy *Si*, it now screamed *Silence*, like a command begging me to listen.

"Lil?" A voice shouted out from the terrace. I looked up to see Chloe. "We're going to do the speeches soon. Will you please come and join in?" As quickly as she appeared, she was gone. "Come on Eileen" faded into a crescendo of whoops and cheers.

Dropping the bottle to the sand, I stumbled up, my head spinning. I straightened my dress. Blinking towards the terrace lights, I readied myself to venture indoors, to be looked at, questioned. If anyone asked, I'd say I felt sick, needed fresh air; that wasn't a lie.

When the music stopped, I noticed the figures at the water's edge. The voices broke through my tinnitus like a knife through cling film. Dad's voice, but I couldn't make out what he was saying. And someone else. Who was that? At first, I thought it was Mounia, but I hadn't seen her walk down onto the beach. If the speeches were starting soon, I should get Dad.

The shadow people collapsed into one. As I got closer, I could see them, two figures, hugging maybe, or grappling. Falling into each other, splashing in the shallows. The moon lit up the drifting line of the horizon, and I struggled to focus. The waves crashed little heartaches against the sand.

"No . . ." Dad's voice cracked.

"Ellis?" The other shouted.

"Aid?" I called.

"Lil . . . ? Help . . ."

"Aid? Is that you?" Salty bile leaked up into my throat.

"Laelia, fuck . . ." Aid's eyes shone, cerulean pebbles in the moonlight. "Help. Your dad's collapsed."

My head spun. "What?"

"He's collapsed. Get help!"

Pivoting on the sand to turn back up the beach, I lost my footing over mounds that felt like mountains. I thudded down onto the cold, black powder and promptly threw up.

Ellis

Mangrove River Village, Stann Creek District, Belize
6th March 1986

The smell of it. The scents of living death; the vegetable reek of hot vines and wood flesh, decay always there, hanging in the air. Things lurking just beyond. Within moments of being here, Ellis knew they'd made the right decision: for him to come on his own, for Helena to stay behind.

She would hate it. The heat alone would fry her senses, explode her nerves. The unpredictable sounds of the jungle: its caws, its trills, its croaks. It would all be too startling, all be too much for her, especially at night. In the daytime, she could have told herself the jungle is beautiful, lush—romantic even: stockpiled stories to tell her friends about. At night, though, through damp and feverish tangled sleep, the power of the darkness would be unbearable for her. And for Ellis, who knows she cannot help but think, and she thinks too much as it is.

It is beyond beautiful. The forest is heaven on earth. An abundance of flora and fauna. Bromeliads and medicinal plants abound. The orchids shudder before his eyes. He's seen crocodiles and howler monkeys and turtles. Iguanas perch in trees like leaves; "bamboo chicken," the locals call them. The Caribbean Sea is always so flat, so calm. His host, Polo, has told him there are dolphins and whale sharks and manatees out there. He's falling in love with it all.

His new home is a small but adequate hut with bay leaf palm for its roof. The desk is large, and the light is good. It is a village of just over thirty they tell him, though there is only a handful of people ever around.

There are more dogs and chickens and pigs, the odd lightbulb and plastic chair. Across the narrow river the jungle looks even more verdant, bursting with life. Polo says he'll take him over in his boat soon and show him the old run-down lodge, and when it rains, the logwood tree planted there that drips its red dye like blood.

Ellis has constructed the skeleton of a routine now—two weeks in, though his body is still adjusting to the heat that is sticky and stuck, to the isolation and the disorientation, the vastness of beyond. He has taken onboard plenty of new things: remembering to shake his shoes free of scorpions before his feet find them, to watch for the bees in the citrus groves, to reroot the plants *away* from the leaf-cutter ants, to tag on the way up and collect on the way down (orchids being heavier than they look), and to trek on to the sparser forest at the top to find where the bromeliads bloom unrivalled in sheer abundance. He is getting to grips with the machete ("Mr. Ellis, follow behind, and don't cut off your leg"), though he is still adjusting to coffee with powdered milk; he might never become accustomed to that.

The locals are not bothered by him; he is an unremarkable arrival. Polo and his wife, Cualli, have introduced him around the village, the pale and naive foreigner.

As if from nowhere, unmarked gifts arrive daily at his door: cloth-wrapped parcels of still-warm bread, sweet potatoes and tattered yams, eggs that tap together in baskets laden with technicolour fruit like he's never seen before: mangosteens, lychees, citruses—majestic treats that keep on coming. Though, of course, he needs to start growing things, start cooking properly for himself; this gifting will not go on forever. He knows he will have to work on his repertoire; go back to Helena with something beyond a rubber omelette and stuck burned rice.

God, he misses her laughter. Though he's missed that for a while, long before this fieldwork project was even a sapling of an idea.

They did talk about it; Helena coming, bringing the girls. They thought it would be an adventure, something to spin stories from, sow smiles. A way to be, together. But that was all just playwriting, something to talk about; they both knew she would never come. She joked she didn't want to be so far away from a washing machine, or from her mother; said she didn't want to give up on *Dynasty*—wanted to find out what happened to Alexis, and she wasn't joking about that. It's better she stays in Oxford. Near Watkins. And she's got Penny and Adam nearby. Besides, he'll be away for only six months. It's not like he's never been away before. He'll be back by autumn to see the leaves turn and the fireworks burst. Then he will enjoy the cold.

His sketchbook is already crammed with notes—on the orchids, of course, but also on the way of life here. The light. He's been reflecting on the national motto "Sub umbra floreo," scrawling it like a mantra:

Sub umbra floreo
Under the shade, I flourish
Floreo
Flourish
Shade
I flourish

It refers to his favourite, *Swietenia macrophilla*, mahogany labelled "red gold" and raped to depletion by British corporations in the nineteenth century. It's there, writ large in strong letters nestled under the coat of arms. Few flags have humans depicted: Montserrat, the Virgin Islands, French Polynesia, but none so prominent as Belize. Mostly Ellis loves its olive leaves, fifty for 1950, the way they neatly stitch the perimeter, framing it all. A flowing wreath, bursting with life. So much history, moving and breathing, woven into one flag. He has painted it over and over again with the watercolour set Chloe saved up and gave him for his birthday. Though he cheats and uses pen and ink for the details of the men.

He's picked up some Belizean rum, his usual nightcap now. He prefers the Don Omario to the 5 Barrel everyone else seems to drink. It's oaky, well rounded. He works each night like this, with his tipple, under the throw of candlelight, before the framed photo of Helena—the one of her twirling in front of the beach huts at West Wittering, the flimsy cotton of a red dress floating above her long, pale legs. *Such gorgeous legs.* Her face blooms pure joy. Or it did. Then.

That was the day they walked the path to Itchenor, but the sun burnt so hot and their throats rasped so dry, they had to abandon their ambitious eleven-mile plans to seek out some shade. They ended up at the Ship Inn, drinking cold shandies and stealing warm kisses, before hitching a lift back to the beach with that old boy who was smoking a pipe of St. Bruno. Not long after, Ellis purchased his own churchwarden. He likes the feel of the longer stem, prefers to look clearly at the bowl while lighting.

Helena would have been pregnant with Chloe then, of course, although they wouldn't know it for weeks. How their lives would change so completely they wouldn't know for months—years. Even now Ellis cannot make sense of it all, the consequences of things.

He turns the page in his notebook:

$$6CO_2 + 6H_2O \; (+ \; chlorophyll + sunlight) = C_6H_{12}O_6 + 6O_2$$

He has been teaching Polo about photosynthesis, telling him it's the most important process on earth. He picks up a pencil and sketches out a skeletal orchid, then another and another, filling the page, decorating their formula. He scribbles:

Kept in the dark, a plant will grow tall and spindling, stretching itself while searching for the light: etiolation. When all it sees is gloom, it will wilt, becoming leggy and weak until it withers then dies.

Draining his rum, Ellis gets to thinking; Helena would always have been seeking out the light here. Searching for it, craving it.

Though maybe she wouldn't have looked for it at all.

Looking would never be enough anyway; the magnificence of this world cannot simply be seen, nor can it be heard.

5

Laelia

Karl Heusner Memorial Hospital, Belize City
14th? January 2023

It had been four days . . . I thought. Each night I'd counted stars like pin-pricks when the skies curtained black, and each morning I traced aero-plane trails in sunbeams through smeared hospital glass (something to do), but it was hard to be sure for how many days, for how many broken, shattered nights. I would snatch brief moments of respite in the furthest loo at the furthest end of the furthest corridor, sometimes on another floor—simply for the walk, away from the bleeps and the clipboards and the tubes. Each time I stared into a toilet mirror, strange eyes glared back, desperate for real sleep. Muscle fibres throbbed and shifted, begging me to notice them, attend to them, but there was no time. Or it was not the time. Time was playing tricks on us. It lagged so slow. Yet it seemed sheer minutes since Dad was dragged like a jellyfish from the water, his linen shorts clinging, sodden, his shirt translucent under blinding helicopter beams and busying head torches. I kept reliving it all; the "no response" authoritative voices had thrown out so firmly, the ebbing crowd being pushed back then pushed back again, Chloe's histrionic screams. And Dad's final words whispered to me as he lay on the sand. "Lavender feels," whatever that meant, if I'd heard it right in the confusion of it all, the tinnitus-enraging cacophony of the night.

"Intracerebral stroke," the doctor said. Like that. Announcing it like a new guest at a party. *Meet Intracerebral Stroke.* She said other words too: *Aneurysm. Blood clot. Severity. IV. AVM. MRI. CT. EKG.* So many letters with such important work to do. And words that made even less sense: *lucky*. How was this lucky? A stroke of luck? Chloe grilled her on all the details, the nuances; she hoovered up the information we would need. *Suffered uncontrolled bleeding*. I dissolved at that point. I couldn't keep up. *Minimal activity*. I gazed at Dad, his mottled arms, his greying lips, the way the blanket skimmed over him as he lay so still, so lifeless. *Swelling on the brain*.

"We clipped the aneurysm," the doctor told us with her plinky Spanish accent. "He cannot hear you but keep touching him."

As Dad lay on his back as if in a coffin, a net of support swooped into action, almost unseen, furtive around the sides of our days, the edges of our nights: scooping up children, bringing clothes and toothbrushes and whatnot, parcels of pies and stews and curries—none of which we ate. The nauseating smell of food lingered long, so I started giving away foil tins at nurses' stations and ditching half-eaten cartons in heaving car park bins.

Aid was amazing with the kids, keeping them occupied. He moved them to Tom's hotel to be with their cousins, to make everything more manageable. Despite some feeble mumbled protestations from Tom, Chloe said she would pay, not to worry; it was better the children were altogether, that Aid had Tom. I didn't have the energy to object, or to think about whether I should. Chloe booked Mounia into their hotel, too, to help.

I managed to get back to Caye Caulker for a couple of nights' sleep, though I didn't really sleep. The children had come to visit once, to see their Grandpa, to hold his hand, but then we decided to try to make things as normal as possible—keep them away until we knew what was what. It was just me, and Chloe, and Mounia at the hospital most of the time, trying to make sense of things that made no sense at all, like why Aid had been out on his own with Dad when he collapsed. What could they possibly have had to talk about? I'd barely seen him to ask.

"You should think about a plan," the doctor said. Her white coat seemed tired, greyed even, or maybe it was the flat light whipping shadows.

"A plan?" I asked, digging my fingers along my temple.

"Your father is very ill." The cursive embroidery on her pocket stitched her out as Dr. Victoria Guevarra. Wide curious eyes.

"Haven't you been listening, Laelia?" Chloe asked, raising her eyebrows at me.

"I just . . . It's a lot to take in."

"He's out of danger, but he is still very ill." Guevarra scritched a biro across her clipboard. "You can check his insurance, if you want to try and get him to England. If it's an option."

"He might have insurance documents at his place?" Chloe said.

Mounia shook her head. "I don't know."

"Back to the UK?" I asked. It felt like I'd missed a conversation.

"It would be better for him there," Chloe said. "Near us."

"But Belize is his home now. This is where he wanted to be . . ."

Guevarra slipped the clipboard back at the end of the bed with a gripped smile, before leaving the room. Mounia sat staring at the floor in awkward silence.

Chloe knew I was still waiting for an explanation. "I don't think when he mapped out his retirement, Dad was imagining spending his time lying in a coma in a . . . an under-resourced hospital here," she spat. I pierced my eyes back at her. "I'm sorry, Laelia, but it's true. This place is always in those Most Dangerous Capitals lists. It's not safe."

"Chloe, he's lying in a hospital bed, not roaming the streets, and the care here is incredible."

"We need to get back for work," she insisted. My stomach buckled with the thought of going back to life as it was, the mundanity of before, but now with a sick father and no job. How could we leave, get back to normal? There was no normal now.

"Dad should come before work," I said.

"Lil, they're not going to reschedule the *Regenerata* case for me. If we get him back to the UK, we can get on with our lives."

"Wow, so Florence Nightingale."

"Someone needs to be practical."

"But—"

"Girls, you are both exhausted." Mounia smiled, pushing her glasses back onto her nose. "Why don't we get out of here? Have a break?"

Chloe looked up. "You two go. I'm fine here." She dropped Dad's limp hand out of hers. "I've got some calls to make."

Mounia led me through the thronging streets along the creek to the Hungry Lizard. We sat on stools overlooking the boats, a stench of fish infusing the hot breeze. Reggae beat all around. Carnival bunting flick-ered across the rafters, with stickers and beer advertisements for Belikin and Landshark graffitiing the bar. It was trying to look like a party but seemed more like a hangover.

"This gyal needs feeding up, Gila," Mounia called to a stout woman bustling from table to table.

"Well, we got the best comfort food in Belize City." She grinned, handing us some laminated sticky menus decorated with hand-drawn lizards.

"Thank the Lord Aidrian was there when it happened," Mounia said once we'd got our food. I played with the label on my beer bottle but didn't say anything. "You know, your father is proud of you." I tasted the shrimp ceviche; it was beautifully acidic, with the right amount of lime. "He talks about you a lot. You especially."

"Really?" Slightly too much coriander. "I can't think there's much to say. Chloe's always been the one worth talking about. She's the lawyer with the perfect life . . . and she makes sure everyone knows it." I necked the end of my beer and signalled for another. "Tom's boring as fuck, but he ticks all her boxes . . . and Dad's."

"Yes, well . . ." Mounia smiled. "No-one tells you when their own but-termilk is sour." A soft silence nestled between us. "Aidrian is so great with your kids, supporting you through all this. Your father told me how good he'd been for you, after the divorce."

"What else did he say about me?" I asked, adding more salt.

Mounia's eyes sparkled. "You're an incredible chef, an amazing mother. That you are kind, honest. Headstrong and confident, or you used to be . . ."

Tears nestled in my eyes. "He's never told me those things."

"Your father is a complicated creature."

I laughed. "He is. So, are you two, like . . . together?"

"Me and your dad?" She dropped down her rum and Coke. "Lord, no," she cackled. "Every pot has a cover, but love him like I do, he's not for me, nor me him. He's like a brother."

"Oh, sorry. I just . . ." I pushed my plate away. *Like a brother.* I some-how thought of my dysfunctional, predictable ex-husband; desperately sugar-glazed, but still just vanilla. Simon was nice and dutiful and stable enough, what I'd thought I needed, or maybe what the world thought I deserved, but I was hardly confident back then; I was young and naive, and fooled by attentiveness, the lure of security and solidity, a seemingly together older man.

"He's helped me a lot." Mounia smiled. "I run a co-operative back in the village, teaching women the traditional skills—embroidery, pottery, cooking. Your father helps sponsor girls' education, provides scholarships."

"Wow, I didn't know . . ." I took a sip of beer. "What did he mean? That I used to be headstrong?"

"That you lost yourself a little." My eyes welled up as Mounia stared across the port.

My throat was a lump. "Do you know what 'lavender feels' means?"

"Lavender feels?"

"It's the last thing Dad said to me, I think, when he was lying in the water. I don't know what it means."

"Sorry, no." She shook her head. "He's always said you would love it here."

"Here?" I managed.

"Well, not *here*. Stann Creek. He thought you would love the jungle. The wildlife, the peace. Though it is not for everyone." She beckoned Gila over and ordered another couple of drinks.

I handed over my empty plate. "The limes you use . . . I've never tasted anything like them. They're so . . ."

Gila smiled. "Sweet *and* sour, right?"

"They're really good." I took out a pouch of tobacco I'd pinched off Aid and began rolling up a Rizla. I hadn't smoked for years, but my body was craving any kind of relief.

"I don't think your father would want to go back to England." Mounia's face crumpled.

"No shit . . ." I laughed until it quickly dissolved. "But Chloe's right. He should be with us. We're the only family he's got."

My iPhone double chimed, lighting up on the table. Text message from Tris:

Sorry to hear the news. Call me. Soz didn't pick up ur vmail. Was on that pastry course. no service. Sending love xoxo

And an older text from him I hadn't noticed before:

Blade & Stone have appointed Abigail D new Head Chef. Shit, u would have been good for that x

I would have been. In a world where I could understand what was going on around me in a clattering kitchen, where I could hear myself think, where I could breathe, I would have been good for that.

While Mounia chatted to Gila I called Aktar. A last-ditch attempt to claw back my career. My heart hammered.

"I'm so sorry," I said. "It shouldn't have happened."

"It's so unlike you. Frances clearly told you there was an allergy. We all heard it."

"I know . . . I'm sorry."

Aktar asked me about Dad, and I told him. "Is there . . . a job for me still? When I come back? I can't . . . I need to stay out here a bit longer, but . . . when I'm back?"

"Look, you messed up. You're a fucking good chef, but with all this . . . I can't hang on for you . . . I'm sorry, Laelia."

Back at the hospital the air had shifted, though it swallowed us straight back in. Latex and disinfectant hung sweet and tarry. Corridors struck nauseating and bright, stretching endless; longer than we had left them. Doctors and nurses and porters weaved themselves along with unknown but critical purpose. Machines hummed ceaselessly, perpetually on. A fatigue of noise.

Chloe sat crumpled, alone in a waiting room of abandoned chairs and strewn magazines, a place we'd not sat for days.

"Where's Dad?"

She looked up, her eyes bloodshot and wet. "They're giving him a bed bath." Distant machines bleeped, incessant. I turned my hearing aids down to lose the background noise.

"Then what is it?" I slid onto a chair.

"I just . . . I know   can't stay in Belize. We can't   with him."

"But we can't leave him. We'll work it out," I said. "We'll fly him back." I turned my aids back up. A filing cabinet scraped its metal open somewhere, shrieked itself closed again.

"They're saying he won't improve enough. It could be weeks." A determined tear streamed down her face, which she promptly swiped away. "I can't stay, Laelia."

"I know." She collapsed into me, and I hugged her. Our rare real embraces were tight.

"I've got to get back to work." She stood and started pacing, clearing her throat. "Sorry, I know you do, too." I hooked my hair, lacklustre, back behind my ears and sighed. Chloe glared at me. "Laelia? What is it?"

She knew me too well, and I'd hesitated too long, let my guard down.

"Nothing." My knee-jerk reaction was not to tell her. I never shared much with her.

"Lil, come on. Something's up. Tell me."

I couldn't bear the criticism, but I didn't have the energy to fight it. I was so tired. So I told her. Not the whole truth; not about the shellfish, or the frantic phone calls, or the shattered glass. And definitely not about the hearing aids, about being too embarrassed to wear them with my hair up. I couldn't handle her harsh hurtled words, her "fucking stupid"s. It was best to be sparing with details, so I spluttered out some vague words about cashflow and Brexit and Aktar cutting costs.

"Oh, Laelia," Chloe offered. "What are you going to do?"

The sounds along the corridor bleeped louder, higher, longer, streaming into my ears, merging with the tinnitus in my skull, pulsating and shrieking into a cacophony, so I no longer knew what was real and what was not.

I forced a smile at Chloe. "I've been thinking, maybe I could stay here with Dad?"

"What?"

"I've got nothing to go back to . . . and you're right, we can't leave him."

"What about the kids? And Aid?"

"I'll talk to him, work out a plan."

After Chloe left, I went back in to see Dad. His skin was pallid, crepey. The tubes on his face made him look like something from outer space.

I grasped his hand. *Can you feel me? Hear me?*

"I'm going to stay here with you, Dad," I said at last. The words sounded lost. "In Belize."

Are you there?

"I'm going to Stann Creek to get everything ready for you. I'm going to check on your place, take care of it. We're going to get you home."

6

What's the plan then?" Aid asked a couple of nights later, tearing into a bread roll. Chloe wasn't listening, engrossed in the wine list. She'd insisted upon the sauvignon blanc, exorbitantly priced, but she was paying and therefore choosing.

"I think I'll have the coconut curried lobster," I said. Aid was tucking into the wine, making the most of the fact Chloe was picking up the tab. I scowled at him, but his head was back in the plastic menu scrolling through the sea of Comic Sans.

"Stupid name, isn't it? The UnBelizeable Café?" Tom laughed, pointing at the logo on the paper napkin dispenser.

"So, what is the plan?" Aid asked after we ordered. "With your dad?"

"The girls have been looking into things, haven't you, love?" Tom's question was directed solely at Chloe because questions were always directed solely at Chloe.

"I spoke to the doctors," she said, already pouring from the second bottle. "We can keep him here until he's ready to be moved down south."

"We need to think about how much it's—" Tom started.

"I can fly back over and help . . ." Chloe interrupted. I grabbed my wineglass. "And I've said I'll pay whatever it takes . . . as long as he needs."

"And how long do you th—" Tom started.

"Laelia's said she can stay with him," Chloe went on.

They all looked at me. I lifted my wineglass, put it back down again. My breathing shallowed. "I said I'd stay," I said to Aid.

He dropped his glass to the table. "What?"

"It makes sense. I'm not working, and it's easy enough to take the kids out of school a bit longer. They'll get compassionate leave . . . I've not got anything to rush back for."

Aid shot me an urgent look. "But Lil, I can't . . . I can't leave Elijah in the shit; I've got to get back."

"I can go to Stann Creek with the kids, sort out Dad's things, check on his place, and then we can move him to a hospital there, like we said."

Aid shifted in his seat, glared at me. "We haven't talked about this."

"You should be fine with the visas," Chloe went on. "And we can change the plane tickets."

"Dad's *ill*," I said to Aid. "He needs someone to stay, and I can stay. You go home, sort the property stuff."

"The jungle? Really?" Tom asked. "Would you be okay down there?"

I smiled. "I guess." But I didn't know.

"I can come back soon," Chloe said. "I need my case to progress a bit. I need—"

"It's fine, honestly," I said.

"There's the rent," Aid said under his breath, leaning over the candle so close I thought it might singe his chin. "We've still got to make rent."

"I always thought there was big money in property?" Tom smiled. Aid glared at him, then at me. Everyone knew the market had been flat for months.

"I don't mind helping," Chloe said. "If Laelia's staying out here, I can chip in."

Tom stared at her, widening his eyes.

"No, Chlo. You're all right. We can handle it." Aid leaned back in his chair, rolling a cigarette in the half-light, squinting. "I can stay. I'll sort it with Elijah."

"Okay then," Chloe said. "Sounds like we have a plan."

I took a hefty swig of wine. Aid kept glaring at me, his blue eyes piercing through the dark.

"So where did you live out here?" Tom asked Aid after we'd ordered our food.

"The Cayo District . . . a few hours inland from Ellis's place."

"What's out there?" Chloe asked.

"Oh, it's beautiful. Big waterfalls, Mayan temples . . . jungle to die for."

"It's pretty remote then, where you were?" Chloe went on.

"There are rural parts, but you've also got Belmopan."

"I've read it's pretty dangerous there. Were you in Belmopan?"

"San Ignacio."

Chloe's questions kept coming. "What were you doing there?"

"Oh, you know, enjoying a different pace of life."

"He worked at the Botanic Gardens," I said.

"Really?" Chloe tore at her bread. "Wow. So you're used to remote Belize."

"It sounds so *raw*," Tom smirked.

"Belize *is* raw." Aid downed the last of his glass. "You find out who you are here, and there's no getting away from yourself, especially in the jungle."

"Are you going to be okay there, Laelia?" Chloe asked. "I mean, really?"

"I'll be fine," I said, getting up to go to the loo.

"She'll love it," I heard Aid say behind me. "Don't underestimate your sister."

"I wouldn't dare," Chloe replied under her breath. "She does that enough herself."

They were on to the third bottle before the curries even arrived; I was still nursing my second glass. The conversation moved on to cashless societies, then Aid waxing lyrical about the pervasiveness of violence in the media. "Creeping normality, they call it. Slow, gradual changes. Death by a thousand cuts. It's the whole lobster in hot water thing . . ." He pointed at the curried chunks on his plate. "Throw them into boiling water and they scream, but heat them up slowly from cold and they don't even notice."

"Poor bastards haven't got a clue," Tom said, laughing like a stooge.

I played with the stem of my glass. "Actually, it's not screaming."

"What?" Aid sniffed.

"It's not screaming," I said again. "They can't scream."

They all stopped with their forks and looked up, cutlery pausing mid-air.

"You can hear them." Aid leaned back in his chair. "If you listen, they definitely scream. I saw it on YouTube." He took a large gulp of wine.

"Lobsters don't have vocal cords," I said. "Or lungs. It's the sound of the air trapped under their shells rushing out of their bodies as they're heated up."

Aid dropped his fork down with a clatter. He finished chewing his mouthful, jaw clenched, breathing heavily through his nose, staring at his plate. Chloe moved her glass to her mouth and sipped, her eyes clocking Tom's before they fell to the side. She pushed her cutlery together. We sat in hot silence as Tom and Aid both did the same.

"Well . . ." Tom coughed. "You learn something every day. It's good we have a chef in our midst who knows about this kind of thing." He strained a smile at me before dropping his eyes to his plate.

"Yeah . . ." Aid said, tapping his fingers on the tabletop before he drained his glass and pushed his food away.

Chloe's eyes caught mine. "Right, well . . ."

We were all exhausted, stressed. Aid was worried about the money, and me dropping us in it. I'd overstepped, fucked up what had been a tolerable evening.

"Anyone for dessert?" Tom asked. Chloe widened her eyes and shook her head at him. "No . . . ? No . . ." He trailed off.

"We should probably get back." Chloe stood, gathering her bag. "Mounia will be climbing the walls with all the children."

So we left, strolling back to our hotel rooms in faux conversation. The walk felt stagnantly long, a blur of sand and sea punctuated by palm trees, the streetlamped colours heavier than I remembered them.

After I checked on the kids in the connecting room, I closed our door and turned the lock. Aid and I fell asleep at polar edges of the bed without a word. Without a word.

We'd never let things stew too long. We'd either fight it out or put on some Dua Lipa or *Maxinquaye* and fuck it all away until nothing seemed to matter anymore. Sex was our currency—easy and liquid—and we were indebted to each other with a running tab, but we hadn't touched at all that night and the gulfweed in my stomach was a tangle that would not wash away. I wasn't sure if he felt it, too, this tension, or if it was me imagining it.

He brought me coffee and a banana muffin; woke me stamping kisses over my arms. Collapsing back into the sheets, he nestled into my neck, smoothing my hair.

"You didn't ask me"—he smelt of sea salt and chewing gum—"before you volunteered us to go down to your dad's."

"Someone needs to stay."

"I know, but . . . we could have talked about it."

"Chloe was pissing me off, making all the decisions." We sat up against the headboard, bolstered back the pillows. I pulled back the paper case from my muffin. "Besides, Chloe doesn't think I can handle it. So I have to . . . I'm sorry. I should have asked you."

"It's okay. She was pissing me off, too." He kissed my lips and stuffed cake crumbs into my mouth with lingering fingers. They tasted like candy.

I visited Dad in hospital every day. There was no change. The air still hung stale. The sounds still jarred. His breaths were still not wholly his. And all the while, his words echoed through my head: *lavender feels.* What was that?

7

The day they were flying back to London, I couldn't sleep. In the early hours, I crept outside. Chloe found me on the beach. She couldn't sleep either. She asked if I wanted to go for a walk, and for a cigarette. I'd never seen Chloe smoke.

We strolled barefoot through the waves talking about Dad until the sun came up. I didn't want her to leave. There was something reassuring about her presence in this fucked-up situation, something solid in her matter-of-factness I was going to miss when she was gone.

"Chloe, do you know what 'lavender feels' means?"

"'Lavender feels'?"

"Dad said it. I don't know what it means."

"No, no idea." She pulled a bottle of water out from her bag and took a swig. "We'll have to bring the kids back another time, have a proper holiday. Tom wanted to go diving. You went, didn't you?"

"Hmm?"

"When we were here before? You dived the Blue Hole, didn't you?"

I nodded. "Yeah, yeah, I did." It was easier to keep up with the lie now than try to undo it. After I first met Aid at the beach bar that night, we'd hidden ourselves away from the world. I hadn't wanted Chloe's interrogations, so we'd fabricated the dive trip to the Blue Hole to spend more time together. Chloe had no interest in that. It was only a little white lie. She was still ill after those dodgy oysters, and she had to catch up on emails anyway, so it worked perfectly. I even told her I'd booked a separate cheap hotel room for the night before, so as not to wake her. I was thoughtful like that.

"Will you be all right?" Chloe asked. "At Dad's?"

Snapping my eyes back from the blue, I smiled. "Yes, of course. I'll be fine." I was always fine.

"But you will be careful?"

"Chloe, it's going to be way less exciting than you think it is. I'm just looking forward to having some time relaxing with the kids."

"It's hardly going to be relaxing, though, is it? In the jungle." She stifled a laugh. "Mounia will be back down there soon though, so that's good. Are there pharmacies? Will you be able to get your medication okay?"

"Of course there are pharmacies." *Are there pharmacies?*

"Will there be somewhere to charge your hearing aids?"

"I guess . . ." though I didn't know. Was there electricity down there? I was starting to realise how little I'd thought through.

"And you will come back up and visit Dad often, until we can move him?"

"Of course."

"Get a taxi if you need to." Chloe took another swig of water. "And what about Aid?"

"What about Aid?"

"What's going on with him?"

"He'll stay as long as he can, and then he might—"

"I meant, is everything okay . . . ?" She turned to look at me. "He seems distracted. It's not like him." She stopped walking now. "I'm at the end of the phone if you need me. I've got this case to—"

"It's fine. Don't worry."

"I *do* worry about you, Laelia."

"Please don't."

Kicking at the sand, she asked, "Do you still think about her?"

I stopped. We hadn't talked about Mum in years. "All the time."

"What do you remember? You were so little."

"The scent of her . . ." I replied. "Her perfume." I would creep back into their bedroom once she and Dad had gone out, to smell that smell of her. I longed for traces of her, even then. The violet-wood scent of LouLou lingering.

"Can you remember? Can you picture her face?"

Mum was fuzzy felt pieces that didn't fit together anymore.

I shook my head. "Not really."

I knew her lips, her eyes that were "kind" (everyone said they were kind), a warm halo of hair. I remembered ballooning ball gowns and fancy cocktail dresses—fairy tales come to life. Magentas and crimsons and lemon sorbets floating out the door, off to greet important men, to sip chardonnay with their wives, to dance until dawn. That's what I'd imagined.

"She was so pretty," Chloe said.

The memories were like butterflies I couldn't quite touch. We would watch her getting ready to go out, studying everything, as she made up her face with a myriad of colours, painting on fresh contentment. Lipstick smiles bruising her lips; each flick of eyeliner, each brush of blusher, transforming her into some made-up creature I didn't recognise, but always beautiful. Images of my mother whirled through my mind like a zoetrope. "Striking" was the word adults would use, labelling her like lightning, then when she was dead, she was just that "poor, poor woman"; she wasn't striking anymore.

"She looked like you." Chloe's face beamed. "Do you remember, she used to say, 'I love you wildly.' Always 'wildly.'"

I smiled. I didn't remember much. "Sometimes it hurts less to forget . . . What happened?"

Chloe stopped. "What do you mean?"

"Why did she do it? I never really knew." Or maybe I forgot. "Dad would never talk about it, so I could never ask. I just imagined."

Chloe flicked her hair out of her eyes, and a gust of wind caught my breath. "She'd been ill for so long."

"Yes, I know," I muttered.

Though I didn't know. Not enough.

"We never really talked about it," Chloe said before we hugged goodbye.

"I know," I said. We never really talked about anything.

I awoke in the early-morning hours sweating, seawater lapping behind the tinnitus, my gut heavy with something rotten I could not dislodge. I sat in the breeze on the balcony, staring over the sea before the others woke up. No-one ever told me why she did it; I was so young. I ached to know what happened—what really happened. To her. To Dad. To us. I wanted to ask him so many questions—adult to adult, to beg him to tell me the stories he'd never shared, the secrets I was sure he'd carried to the jungle, the ones I was worried I may never now know.

As girls, Dad always told us: "If you put your faith in nature, it will never fail you," though I didn't believe it. I didn't believe any of this; that my dad—my energetic, charismatic, larger-than-life dad—had skimmed so close to death, was communing with it still.

PART TWO

Leaves

Ceiba petandra. Ceiba (Spanish), *katn chree* (Kriol), kapok, cotton tree. A deciduous tree native to Central America. With its pagoda-shaped crown it towers over other plants, reaching almost seventy metres in height. Its bark decoction can be used as a diuretic, or as an aphrodisiac. Revered by the ancient Maya as the Sacred Tree of Life, connecting the gods of the underworld (Xibalba) with those above, it is believed to be the hiding place of the mythical X'tabai, a deceptive but bewitching forest spirit who lures unfaithful men to their death.

8

Laelia

Stann Creek District, Belize
22nd January 2023

Diving deep through warm water, the reef screamed vivid hues. Schools of fish darted by, this way, that way, this way. I couldn't keep up. Nature-sequinned creatures—neon-bright like rock candy, electric cyans, and unnatural laser limes. It was a palace of excitement, a safe wonderland, where the muted sunlight enveloped us all, gently warming up the party; a riot of colour backdropped with muffled sound. And where my tinnitus should be, it was gone. It was gone.

I gasped, grappling for air, but there was nothing but liquid—dark water and straggled seaweeds right up in my face. Then just black, rasping. My head jolted forward. I managed a sharp, sudden intake of breath.

Light hit my retinas. We were braking.

The static screeching was back. The seat belt tightened across my chest. I wiped dribble from my chin. For moments, I couldn't settle on where I was, in place or in time. Outside, patchworks of trees swooshed by, the truck soupy with heat, my body thick with exhaustion.

We passed a person walking along the roadside, a cart laden with dairy, a signpost to a jungle reserve, a community centre, a Mayan healer. Fleet Foxes' "Mykonos" thrummed from the speakers. Aid was driving, the passenger area stuffed with luggage and a box crammed with supermarket packets—cartooned tigers and rainbowed leprechauns. The kids were squished in the back next to me, cocooned by backpacks, wedged in like Tetris. Dylan, fast asleep on his bunched-up hoodie against the window. Ella reading *Rebecca*, the scars on her forearms dancing in sun-beams as she turned the pages. We came to a halt and sat watching a chicken crossing the road. There was no punch line.

"Hey," Aid said, meeting my eyes in the rearview mirror. "Had a good sleep?" He was clutching a can of beer.

"Where are we?" I asked.

"It's not far," he said, nestling the beer between his legs.

"How long?"

"About a half hour. How d'you like the Frontier?" He steered with one hand while grappling for his tobacco pouch off the dashboard. For a moment I thought he was talking about this place, this unknown land.

"It's nice." I grabbed a bottle of water from the seat netting.

"Nice?"

"I love it," Ella said, wide-eyed, dropping the book into her lap. "It's so American." She had somehow retained a childlike sense of the good ole' US of A, a distant dreamland sponsored by Disney, all pancakes and Hershey bars and slumber parties.

Aid heard from Elijah a few days ago. The Quays development had finally gone through, so he bought the pickup from a guy in Belize City. "He was this old hippy dude, desperate to do a deal," Aid had explained—buzzing with pride at his forward-thinking entrepreneurialism. He got it for a great price—down from thirty-five thousand Belize dollars to twenty-eight, and we'd be able to resell it for more. He'd surprised me with it in the hospital car park the day before. "D'you like the blue?" he'd asked.

"Sure," I nodded, unable to get too excited about an old truck in a peeling electric cyan.

"We said we'd spend ten thousand sterling, but we'll need something reliable." He danced around the bonnet, grinning from ear to ear. "It could do with a paint job but—"

"It's great," I replied, kicking at the tyres because I'd seen someone do that once. "I love it."

"It drives like a dream," he told me.

We'd said eight thousand.

Mounia had given me a bag filled with Dad's iPhone, wallet, keys. She thought it was better I looked after them than they get lost into the hospital abyss. I clutched it in my lap. She'd scrawled out a Tolkien map with pencilled scribblings depicting thick jungle. Sharper lines signified roads, with labels for "Jaguar Point," "Coco Lookout" and "Falicia's." Neat, pointed arrows showed our route. I gripped the paper like it was the Holy Grail.

"Can we swim in the river?" Ella asked.

"I guess," I said. "We'll need to watch for currents." My mind filled with an imaginary phone call back home to Chloe: my fumbled explanations, her judgmental silence; the confession of my failure to prevent the inevitable drowning of my own children; the devastated sob; then, an inexorable sigh, "Oh, Lil. I did warn you . . ."

"Will there be waves, like in the sea?" Dyl asked, biting his thumbnail.

"No, it shouldn't be wavy." I rested my hand on his leg. "But you still need to be careful." I took my hand away and afterwards realised he was of an age where he wouldn't let me do that many more times. I breathed in the moment, trying to superglue the feeling into my memory.

"How long?" Ella asked, snapping her book shut.

"Not long," said Aid, his eyes bright in the mirror.

"How long in Belize?" Ella pleaded. "When do we go home?"

I turned in my seat and was confronted by her pressed lips and furrowed brow. "Only until Paw-Paw gets better," I said. Ella turned and looked out the window. I was surprised she'd asked about home. I thought more time off school would come as a relief after everything.

The truck jolted, shoving us forward and back, our seat belts straining. Lights on the dashboard starting pinging and flashing. We lurched again, and the engine chugged.

"What the . . . ?" Aid wiggled at the gearstick, trying to get some traction, but we shook violently, losing momentum. He steered to the side of the road, where we juddered to a standstill. "Shit," Aid said, hitting the steering wheel. Turning the key, the engine spluttered over and over but wouldn't fire back up.

"It smells like burning," Ella said.

"Has it died?" I asked.

"Of course it's fucking died." Aid hit the wheel again, making me jump. "Shit, shit, SHIT!" He collapsed his forehead into the wheel, banging it again and again.

I took a deep breath. "How much fuel's left?"

He turned to face us, his temple cut with fresh blood, "For fuck's sake, Laelia. It's got fuel!"

"Okay. Sorry, I just . . ."

"That Grand Rapids asshole."

"Is it going to catch on fire?" Dylan asked.

"No, it's not going to catch on fire," I said, not completely sure it wasn't going to catch on fire.

There was a tapping on the glass. A young woman, late twenties, with dyed cherry-red hair and loops of gold and silver necklaces, was bending down peering in at us. "Weh di gaan an?"

"We're good," Aid looked out his window but didn't unwind it. "Thanks," he added loudly so she would definitely hear him. She blew a pink bubble of gum.

"She might know where a garage is?" I said, but Aid didn't answer. I took off my seat belt and ushered the kids from the car. We unpretzeled ourselves from the back seat, spilling out onto the road and smacking straight into the heat of the afternoon. The woman and a boy of about Dylan's age stood clutching shopping bags, staring at us. She smiled permanent dimples.

"Sorry about him." I gestured towards Aid, who was still sat in the truck, playing with switches and staring at the dashboard. "He'll calm down in a bit."

"You da vacation?" The woman asked, revealing an adorable gap between her teeth as she chewed her gum. She had a gorgeous lilt to her voice.

"We're . . . sort of. Mum, are we still on holiday?" Ella asked.

I smiled. "I guess. An extended holiday. We're staying on a bit longer to sort some things."

Aid finally got out of the truck, smiling briefly at the woman before moving around to lift the bonnet.

"You folks are not having much luck," the woman said, switching easily into an American English. She placed her shopping on the ground so she could rummage through her shoulder bag. "I can call a mechanic."

"Thank you." I smiled. Pulling out her mobile, she turned away, ushering the boy to relieve himself of his shopping bag. He dropped it, and several limes rolled out onto the dirt. We shared a smirk while I helped him pick them up.

"I think it's the gasket," shouted Aid. "But it's the transmission, too."

The kids heaped themselves onto the ground, and Ella concertinaed open her book. The boy introduced himself as Gabriel and gave Dylan his fidget spinner.

I put my hand on Aid's back as he leant over the bonnet. "I'm sorry the truck died. You couldn't have known. It's an old truck. They break down sometimes. I'm sure it'll—"

Aid shut his eyes and inhaled. "The cooling system is fucked."

"It doesn't matter. We can sort—"

"Of course it matters. We need something reliable down here. We don't have money to burn."

The woman stared. I brushed Aid's bicep. His eyes caught mine. With the pad of my thumb, I smeared the blood away from his eyebrow.

He finally smiled, his eyes ruckling into submission. "I'm sorry." The stench of engine oil burned through the air.

Mangrove River Village, Stann Creek District, Belize
10th March 1986

The sounds are a marvel. He's heard the shrieks of parakeets and the peeps of kingfishers, the buzz of hummingbirds and the warbles of parrots, and—he's sure—the three-syllable delivery of the kiskadee. He's spotted vampire bats and fruit bats and Lord-knows-what bats, and several painted tree frogs, the Jesus Christ lizard that walks on water (no, runs!), and a *Sphaerodactylus glaucus* gecko, the smallest of its kind. When the girls are older, he will bring them here, show them the majesty of this place so they can not only see it and hear it, but *feel* it, this achingly beautiful land.

He quickly sweeps the pictures from his mind, so the guilt does not creep in.

The days saunter on. Cualli has found him an extra hefty mahogany table, crafted by a Mennonite from Indian Creek. Polo has helped him knock up a shelf to house his treasures: his Olympus OM-2, his binoculars, the plankton and insect nets, plus the few books he managed to fit into his luggage: *Ancient Maya Civilization*, Peterson's *Field Guide to Mexican Birds*, and the copy of *Zen and the Art of Motorcycle Maintenance* Helena gave him for his birthday, which he has still never read. He didn't bother bringing any other material; he'd studied the extracurricular protists and organisms of Belize before he even booked his flights.

He's collected many samples now, photographed and annotated them, sketched a dozen notebooks over four dozen rums. And finally, he's started recording ideas for his next paper, to be titled something along the lines of "The Effects of Plant Size, Floral Display, and Habitat on the Reproduction of the *Brassavola nodosa.*"

He spends the morning out on the lagoon with Polo, where the mangroves kiss the sea. They've spotted manatees, and crocodiles, and iguanas. A boa constrictor in the trees. They're finding orchids everywhere, attached to twisted trunks of the buttonwoods (*Conocarpus erectus*) brimming with secrets, basking in the sun. Photo-documenting species, sketching flower parts, sampling leaves. He is smitten.

At lunchtime, when it reaches thirty, they retreat to the beach at Placencia to sit under the palms. Polo leads them past the dories to a salt-bitten metal food shack and its magnetic collection of men: Creoles, Garifuna, Mestizos, and an unfortunate loud American effervescing about the economy of Belize ("Sugar growers damn turned to marijuana to make a better buck.") They demolish bowls of rice and beans, washing them down with glasses of limeade.

"You married?" Polo asks him. "She's a patient woman, you here so long."

Ellis stares out at the sea. "Academia is such a selfish sport," Helena declared once early on, at a dinner party (to their nonacademic friends). He didn't speak up to disagree. He knows he's pushing his luck here, staying out for so long, pulling on the threads of his dreams. She has always punished him for feeding passions she cannot muster. He shakes his head, waving a fly from his food.

He doesn't know why he says it, but he does. "I'm not married." Maybe to keep things simpler for himself, out here. To separate his life in England, to not get distracted, to try not to think about her. He takes another spoonful of food.

"Cualli's been worrying herself making you cashew wine and guava jelly. She thinks you must miss your wife."

Ellis's ears tune in to the American still waxing lyrical. "I won't ever go back; I love the pace here. The sunsets. The fishing . . . The *women.*" The men around him laugh along.

"Maybe you'll find a good Belizean woman," Polo says.

Ellis forces a smile. He does not want to think about Helena; her erratic phone calls and turbulent letters, the words he picked up from Dangriga yesterday that burn in his pocket today:

We have to stop punishing each other, only caring about ourselves.

And you, your orchids.

I wonder if you still love me.

It's unfair of her to do this, so soon into his trip. She is overemotional again. Of course he still loves her; not giddily, not like in the beginning, but that's normal; not feverishly, like he loves his profession, which—he recognises—is not. But he loves her. Of course he loves her. He cannot contain his excitement to publish; that much is true. He's riding a wave of momentum: the anticipation in the field electric, this project so well championed at Oxford, the work so highly sought after, so widely regarded, seminal to the development of a fuller checklist for the region. Of course he cares about his orchids, but they are not everything; they're just what makes his heart pound and his brain surge.

She promised to keep the home fires burning and her head on. She said she would be fine, she wanted him to do this, he must. Besides, it's not selfish to pursue your dreams if they're everyone's, Ellis thinks, dropping his empty bottle to the sand.

9

Laelia

It was the sound of it. The heat, and the sound. Both were relentless. Chirping verses of crickets, frogs, and birds. Maestros pulsing beyond the tree line. The heat was something else. Intense like I'd never felt before, a throbbing, all-encompassing heat slick with humidity. There was no breeze like at Caye Caulker. No respite, no relief; nowhere to go.

The woman—Esther—led me and the children off the main road while Aid waited with the truck and their shopping bags for the mechanic. As we walked, she taught us Kriol phrases as she popped her bubblegum ("How yuh di do?," "Evrything aarite," and Dylan's favourite, "Mi love Bileez!").

"It's a beautiful language." I smiled. "I need to learn more."

"We're nearly there," Esther said. A dirt track finally sank us into a verdant sea of trees. My heart raced, pumping with anticipation. I was finally so close, so near to knowing this place that had captured my father's heart. I'd seen photographs, of course, but they had no real context: Dad with his arm around this local or that foreigner or this dog or that cat, keen close-ups of bromeliads and lithophytic ferns, butterflies and beetles, and toasted sunsets you knew would be something else entirely if you could see them in real life. No photo could ever translate the bursting beauty, the cacophony, the scents. Here, more than anywhere, everything felt alive. Though I could not forget—since I'd been told so many times—in the jungle there are an infinite number of ways to die.

"You have to look for tygas," Gabriel said, spinning on his feet as though he was ringmastering a circus.

"They're not out this time of day," Esther said with her infectious smile.

"We *are*," Gabriel giggled.

"Our name is Balam," Esther explained. "It means tyga . . . Jaguar." I thought of big, muscular cats ripping flesh from ravaged bone. She turned to me. "You have to be careful, especially at night. My neighbour hit one once with his car."

"What?" Dylan asked, eyes wide. "Can they kill you?"

"Tygas? If you're not watching the road." She laughed. "No . . . they don't attack humans. They're just big cats. You can smell when they're near."

"Are there snakes?" Ella asked, dragging her trainers through the dirt.

"Fu tru, you have to watch for them. In the jungle, you have to stay alert. Tommy Goff, he's the worst. Keep your legs covered. Chew and spit tobacco. They say the fer-de-lance, they hate tobacco." I made a mental note to ask Aid to give me a stash, then realised maybe Esther was joking, messing with me.

"Shit, Mum," Ella muttered.

"Ella! Language."

"Sorry, but, like, can't we stay in a hotel?"

"What else?" Dylan asked as we turned, following Esther up a drive-way.

"Snakes only attack when they feel threatened. If you're careful and respect the jungle, it will respect you. And don't be afraid. Creatures can sense fear."

"What if they bite?" Dylan stared at me, wide-eyed. "Do you DIE?"

"You see this?" Esther grabbed at some long, patterned leaves along the edge of a fence line. "Snakeplant. We call it mother-in-law's tongue. Once it takes hold, you can't get rid of it." She winked at me. "Your papá's got lots. This is the edge of his property. You know, it was an old jungle lodge? Back in the 1980s." *So this is his place.* He walked these paths, planted these begonias, touched this soil with his hands.

Esther showed us the leaf in her palm. "If a snake bites, eat this or rub it onto your skin. You still got to get to hospital, but it will lower your heart, buy you some time. It's good to carry in the forest."

"What else is there?" Dylan asked again. "What other animals?"

"Tapirs, and toucans, and you'll see . . ." Esther smiled. "There's so much to see in the Jewel."

We heard the wind chime before we got near, and Esther announced, "We done deh reach." She and Gabriel left us as soon as we saw the sign: WITTERING LODGE. The house stood alone in a clearing; a series of individual huts, some concrete, some wood, little boxes with thatched roofs, all edged by thick jungle. The buildings were decrepit, vines eating through windows, cracks in flaking walls. A slatted veranda spilled out from the largest structure, its ceiling dripping festoon lighting, and a slack hammock. There was electricity, at least. I would be able to hear. Chickens *buk buk buk-gawked* somewhere.

Mounia had given me two keys: one for the main living area and one for Dad's study. The doors weren't often secured. No need, Mounia had told me. She wasn't even sure Dad would have bothered to lock up before travelling north.

But he had. I tried the first key and needed to wiggle it around in the lock before I finally managed to turn it. There was a knack I didn't yet know. There was so much I didn't yet know.

The kids ran in, dumping their bags and hurtling through the room towards the back, where they found just one other door. A bedroom. One double bed.

"Where will we sleep?" Dylan asked. I hadn't even thought about it; hadn't considered that of course Dad wouldn't have extra spare beds. He was a single man in his seventies whose children and grandchildren lived oceans away. I couldn't imagine he had many visitors, certainly not ones who would stay overnight, and any who did would probably just slump drunk in the armchair until dawn.

"Aid and I will be fine out here." I glanced around the living space, eyeing up unstable cliffs of books and pipe tray graveyards before spotting a sofa in the corner. "You guys take Paw-Paw's bed." We'd sort something longer term.

"I'm not sharing with him!" Ella protested, glaring at Dylan, but I ignored her, hoping she'd realise this was probably her best option right now.

It was all so much dingier, messier than I'd imagined it. I made my way to the kitchen area, a utilitarian space with a two stove Campingaz, a makeshift sink, and a draining board scattered with coffee grains. A bucket sat on the side with some sort of filtering contraption attached. The fridge was stuffed with beer bottles in its door but bereft on its shelves, a plate of butter and three shrivelled green peppers the only food. A tray on the counter held a clutter of cutlery and a couple of blunt paring knives. I grabbed a notebook from the fruit bowl that contained no fruit and scribbled:

> Knives
> Hammer & nails
> Sheets & blankets

The children rushed back out to investigate the other buildings, so I followed. Nearest to the living hut was a small separate loo. It was basic and dirty. A tap outside dripped slowly into a faded washing-up bowl, the sole washing station. Mounia had warned me there was no proper bathroom, no shower. The plumbing in the lodge bedrooms had given up decades ago. I couldn't imagine Dad living without a shower; he used to take so much pride in his appearance, though it was these contradictions, these eccentricities that made him. Aid had said we could hook something up, but not for a while. I hadn't yet broken this news to the kids, and I didn't plan to tell them about the cockroaches I'd seen either. Dylan would think they were cool. Ella, though, would not. A restaurant inspector told me once, he could always smell them before he ever saw them: musty and oily and sweet. This whole place needed airing.

"Mum, look at this," Dylan shouted from the furthest building. The kids were on tiptoes peering in, shielding their eyes up against the window. The glass was so coated with grime it was hard to see much of anything.

The door ricocheted open to reveal a shell-shocked room. The smell hit first: tobacco and mildew and stale coffee grounds, the faded scent of him. A piano stood in the corner. When we were little, Dad played by ear, anything and everything; but I hadn't known him to play in years. A Silver-Reed typewriter sat surrounded by a stormy sea of papers, notebooks, and pencil shavings. Forgotten glasses and corpsed apple cores, and tree-high towers of books blocking out the light—the room a cave even in the middle of the day. Cobwebs, dust, and dead rum bottles. Everything abandoned midthought. This life he chose.

The scene didn't fit in my mind; I always remembered Dad being so neat. But I hadn't lived with him in years, hadn't spoken to him in months. Maybe it was hard to be clean and tidy in the middle of the jungle, a man on his own. A man all alone.

Shelves and shelves of books lined the walls: *A History of Botany*, *Palace of Palms*, and his own *Orchidology in the Rainforests of Central and South America* by Dr. Ellis C. Wylde. Boxes of sun-bleached vinyl: The Wailers, Marlena Shaw, Zappa. Eclectic taste, my dad. The kids had already lost interest, rushing out as fast as they'd run in, on to find the next time capsule. I took Joni Mitchell out of her sleeve, but she had buckled in the heat. I dropped the needle on Regina Spektor, who was already lying, dusty but unwarped, on the record player sat atop a metal safe.

The intro of "Up the Mountain" thundered as I shuffled through Dad's desk: consortium notes, botanic paper leaves, a couple of grocery receipts. I removed the lid from the ceramic tobacco jar, and in one deep breath, years of bewildering love diffused out. He didn't smoke as much as he used to, at least I didn't think he did, but when I was a child, his pipe was as much a part of him as his nose.

I opened the top drawer: fountain ink, stamps, staples, pencils sharpened to ridiculous points, a used tea bag growing mould. The music propelled me. Swaying, I collapsed into dance. Twisting the volume up loud, I fell back out into the clearing. Dylan and Ella were threading the hem of the forest, laughing and giddy. Now we were here they seemed to love it, this strange foreign place. It was a relief to see them enjoying themselves, embracing the weirdness of this whole situation with childlike curiosity. They showed more resilience than I could ever muster.

I pulled out my hearing aids. Instantly the music softened, as though

Regina had dived underwater. I could still hear the bass notes clearly, but the highest tones were gone, and the tinnitus screeched on. Tears were in my eyes, on my cheeks, as if from nowhere.

I closed my eyes. A pause. For a moment.

I could no longer hear birdsong, and I lost the ends of people's words. I missed what else I missed. Even with my hearing aids in, I often couldn't understand what was being said, couldn't find the answers, especially in crowded places, busy bars, and restaurants with crap acoustics—which, it turns out, is most of them. And kitchens. The idea of a new bustling London workplace filled me with dread. I relied more and more on the movement of mouths, the look of lips, and—when he was there—Aid filling in the blanks. He was patient with me. He knew when I gave him a vacant look or took too long to answer a stranger's question I was struggling to hear, and he'd give me subtle clues or little cues, so I didn't look quite so useless, or so rude. I always worried I seemed rude.

"I've never talked about myself this much," I'd told him that night when we first met. He'd smiled and stared into his daiquiri, then at me. "Maybe you've just never had someone really listen." And then we chatted and chatted together deep into the night.

A whisper startled in my ear, "Wakey-wakey." I opened my eyes. Aid was standing next to me. I brushed the tears from my cheeks and put my aids back in.

"Mum?" Ella shouted somewhere in the distance. "Mum? Can we go and find the river now?"

Hacking our way through the jungle, Aid led the way with a machete he'd found propped up against some boots by the door in a still life, as though Dad was about to pick it up and take a walk himself.

There was a sort of path, overgrowing but still walkable, down to the river. We trailed through a riot of greens—tangled vines and palms and lichens, mighty tree trunks waved with veins, and hanging lianas—everything moving, as if growing before our eyes.

The air was melodic with scuttling and buzzing and shrieking. I turned up my hearing aids to take in as much of the birdsong as I could, the trills ecstatic.

"Is that an orchid?" Ella asked, pointing up at a cedar tree.

"Yes," I said. "I think it's a *Cattleya*. You can tell because of the ruffled edges and the thin pseudobulbs—you see these bits . . . ? Maybe Paw-Paw put it here. Can you see the twine used to fix it to the trunk?"

"Why hasn't it got a flower?" Dylan asked.

"They only bloom once a year. Sometimes twice."

"What colour will it be?"

I smiled. "We'll have to wait and see."

At the riverbank we found Dad's boat and heard the exhilarating wails and cries of kids on the other side of the water.

"This is sooo cool," Dylan yelled as he paddled his way to the vessel. "Can we take it?" Ella pulled off her trainers and hitched up her trousers to wade in.

Aid was already inside starting up the engine, smiling like a kid. "Come on, Lil." They whooped excitedly as the boat chugged into life and I hopped aboard.

When we reached the other side, a clamour of children enveloped us in animated greetings. A young boy offered us his melting chocolate. A girl told us where to tie up the boat. Ella and Dylan peeled away, beaming, to check out a couple of turtles resting on a log. It was the happiest I'd seen them in weeks.

Aid and I barely slept that first night on the sofa, just held each other tight and restless. Exhausted from the journey and the afternoon at the river, we were both too wired for sleep. As beautiful as the daytime was here, at night it felt so remote; the darkness was so black it had no edges. The jungle raged all around us, rustling and cawing, the deafening buzz of cicadas a continual wall of sound. Even without my hearing aids in, I could hear them. Or most of them, I guessed. Hoots and shrieks and cries.

I woke early with the light and gazed at Dad's clutter—things I hadn't noticed the previous day: the vintage *Playboys* I'd have to hide, a weary rubber plant that had long seen better days, and the angry springs striking up through the sofa. I'd have to add a proper mattress to the list.

Something bit hard at my ankle. Inhaling sharply, I somehow managed to quell an instinctive and overwhelming need to scream, glancing down just fast enough to see the blur of a cockroach scuttling under the cupboard into an ocean of grime, and realising in that blink of a moment, as if I had been ignoring it before, this definitely wasn't a holiday anymore.

10

There is a bewitching comfort that comes from stirring, watching a spoon turning through a changing texture, building, and transforming ingredients like alchemy; elements bursting together as sauces thicken, warmth dispersing around and around. Time slows. The cacao silkened in the crackled enamel saucepan, one of only two I'd been able to find in Dad's attempt at a kitchen. I ached for my utensils sat in their jar next to the stove in Forest Hill, the wooden spoon my mother had gifted me not long before she died. Wrapped in crinkling tissue paper, tied with a velvet green bow, I loved beauty in simplicity, even then. Whenever I held that spoon I felt close to her, knowing she had poured her love into choosing it, and that she'd once touched it, too; she had noticed me—she had *known* me. I watched its beech age over the years, bowing and darkening gradually— just as she might have eased older and wiser if only she could have stayed.

A rogue finger came from behind me and plunged into the bowl.

"Shit. You scared me."

"Ow! It's hot!" Aid said, his finger coated in chocolate. I slapped the back of his errant hand. He smelt of stale beer.

"Of course it's hot!" I laughed but when I turned to look, he stood like stone. He wasn't laughing. "It wasn't meant to be hard. I'm sorry."

I turned back to the mixture and stirred.

"Are the pancakes ready?" Dylan called from the rug, where he was surfing a sea of paper and coloured pencils.

"Won't be long," I said, shutting off the gas and grabbing the foiled plate I'd set aside. Aid stood over me, still staring.

Ella lay the table and lit the candles. I insisted on us sitting down properly now, eating together. I was determined to make memories here, happy ones to punctuate the underlying sadness, the weirdness of all of this, the fatigue.

It had been long days of hard grind fighting the heat and the rainforest. Together we'd attacked overgrown vegetable patches, cleared back wanton weeds. Dylan had found another machete behind the storage hut door, and I had been working on my technique. Aid made it clear he didn't think my technique was the right one, but we were slowly pushing back the jungle, and I hadn't yet cut off a limb. The weeds were relentless. You'd strip them back, tear them down to nothing, then the very next day they would be back as before, like a joke.

This place had so much untapped potential, such incredible bones. I fantasised over its possibilities; a tourist lodge again—white and natural wood, the outside in, the inside out, jungle palms and orchids spilling all around. A restaurant under a timber gazebo, an outdoor kitchen in the breeze. Lionfish ceviche, bowls of limes, and fresh chilli jam. The sounds of nature and tranquillity and remoteness all around.

But for now, it felt like everything was laughing at us. A war against nature for which we were not prepared. The storage hut was falling to pieces—termites had eaten through the structure, and damp was mulching the wood; the study roof needed rethatching before heavier rains seeped in; when we opened cupboard doors, roaches shot away like fireworks, scorpions bedded down in our shoes, and after long, arduous days, when we finally lay on our pillows at night, we dreamt only of ravenous jaguars and snakes of strangling vines. We were all losing weight, shedding calories we couldn't top up fast enough, even with stacks upon stacks of chocolate pancakes. It was exhausting. How had Dad managed all this on his own? No wonder he'd never got to clearing the lodge rooms out, fixing the windows, painting it all. I missed him so much. I saw him everywhere: in all the unfinished business, the orchids, the bookshelves, the jobs somewhat half done.

There were small wins: From the hillside we'd harvested relays of sweet potatoes and squat bananas bundled into T-shirts, Ella and Dylan had found a new shortcut to a tyre swing over the river, which attracted kids like flies, and I had finally gotten my head around the bucket filtering system—had deduced it was only the tiny, magic flecks of silver embedded in ceramic keeping us all from impending stomach sickness and diarrhoea. Small wins.

We headed down to the river village-side with a small picnic and our swimming gear. The kids ran off immediately with Gabriel and a cluster of newfound friends.

Aid and I threw down a blanket and, after a dip, lay sprawled, dozing together in the shade. I couldn't stop thinking about Dad, about his lying so still in that hospital bed. I'd struggled to find any service to call Mounia. I'd managed to text her a few times, but there was no update, no more news.

When I woke up, Aid was reading. His eyes were bloodshot, swollen.

He felt me stirring and stroked at the curve of my neck. "Hey, sleepy." I rolled over, propping myself up on my elbows. He placed his book down, splayed to keep the page: a tattered copy of *The Mosquito Coast*.

"You had that with you when we first met . . . On Caye Caulker." That exact copy. The same murky cover, the same curvy flute-playing woman in the shadows, a snake coiled around her neck, another jolting out at her from the trees. It was the only book I'd ever seen him with. "Do you remember?"

He sat up, gazing at me intently. "What else do *you* remember?"

I smiled. "Oh, I don't know. Your chat-up lines."

He smiled back and wiped his brow. "Coffee?" He started pouring from the flask. "It's funny to think of your dad here."

"It's strange being here without him. It's like he has this whole other life I don't know about. I mean, I always imagined it, but . . ."

"How long do you think it'll be?" Aid asked, passing me a cup.

"Aid," Dylan shouted from the river. "Will you come back in with us?"

"What do you mean?" I sipped at the coffee, acrid and bitter.

"I mean . . ." He shifted on the rug. "Tom was asking me before. He was getting antsy about the money . . . He didn't say anything, but—"

"What? You mean how much Dad is costing?"

Aid shrugged. "I don't know."

"Please, Aid," Dylan shouted again.

Tom was always fretting about money. Ridiculous when they had so much. Where Chloe was generous, Tom was controlling, cautious.

"My God, he needs to shut the fuck up . . ." I said under my breath. I flashed back again to that night: the helicopter, the paramedics, the vomit in my throat.

"Give me a minute," Aid called, and Dylan nodded, diving back into the water.

"What were you and Dad talking about?" I asked. "At the party. When he collapsed? What were you saying?"

"You asked me about this already."

"When did I?"

"The morning after."

"I don't remember."

Aid stared off into the distance, shook his head a little. "He was telling me about the boats. About how much he loves Caye Caulker." He stood up and pulled off his shirt. He was so brown now, his skin chronicled in tattoos, lines, and scars.

"Do you know what 'lavender feels' means?"

He looked blank and shook his head, then ran down into the river with a splash. Dylan monkeyed himself around his shoulders until he sank beneath the surface. Aid embraced this chance at fatherhood, something he'd barely had himself; his own dad so absent, and then gone so young.

When Aid's head reemerged, the children laughed and pushed him straight back down under the water.

The nearest supermart, the only supermart, was a short drive away on the main road. I could have walked there in a few hours probably, but not in the heat and not when it would get dark so quickly. Aid stayed on with the kids at the river so I could take the truck.

Outside, the shop was colourful and bright, its walls painted turquoise and green. Inside, despite the overbearing striplights and the garish supersized packets bursting from the shelves, it was insipid and dusty. I stared at my list, but I couldn't focus on the words. Nights of catching thin sleep on the sofa were beginning to take their toll.

Knives
Hammer & nails
Sheets & blankets

"Aftanoon," chimed a throaty singsong voice. A woman in carmine stared out across the counter. She looked about my age, but her hair was already greying like bleached coral. "Need some help?"

"Do you sell hammers?" I smiled.

The laughter sent back told me all I needed to know. "Placencia over the water. There's hardware shops there. They got hammers, nails, paint, varnish—whatever you need." She looked me up and down. "You Ellis's daughter?"

I widened my eyes. "Er . . . yes."

She nodded. "Laelia!" My name tripped off her tongue. "You know, your papá told me about you . . . He told everybody about you."

"Really?" I walked towards the kiosk, disturbing a sand and white dog curled up next to shelves of Coca-Cola. Lifting its head, it looked around and then fell back to sleep with a huff.

"How is he?" the woman asked.

"You know he's in hospital?"

"I heard." She smiled softly. "Life moves slow round here, but word moves fast."

"He's okay. He's stable."

"Mounia's been texting, keeping us updated."

"You know Mounia?"

"She's my husband's tía."

"It's kind of her," I said, ". . . to stay with Dad."

"Well, they have a special bond. And she's got family in Belize City, so I guess she's able to see them when she's not at the hospital." She beamed that smile again, so warm it felt like a hug. It devastated me. "You all right, gyal?"

She'd caught me welling up.

"I'm sorry . . . I'm so tired." She moved around the counter and, before I knew it, engulfed me in a wide embrace. I didn't flinch. I softened against her. I wanted her to hold me like that, for a moment. A woman's warmth.

She began gently prising me away. "You know, everything's gonna be aarite." I nodded, moulding my lips together. "I mean it . . . But it's aarite to cry. Soft as petals, Mounia says."

I smiled softly.

"I'm Falicia . . . And you'll be wanting Ursula—"

"Ursula?"

The dog pricked up its ears.

"She'll be wanting to go back home."

"Back home?"

"I told your papá I'd look after her when he was in Caye Caulker. Been looking after his chickens, too . . . I'm his nearest neighbour this side of the river. His only neighbour really. She's been a good girl, but I'm going to my aunty Cece's tomorrow, and if there's one thing Aunty Cece cannot stand, it's a bug-ridden dog."

"Right, it's . . . I—"

She began thrusting packets of dog food into my arms. "Ursula don't need much."

"Okay, it's just—"

"Don't you worry, honey. She hasn't actually got bugs! Cece thinks all dogs are flea cushions."

I smiled. "No, of course. It's fine."

"You know, the boss won't mind if I shut up shop," Falicia said, handing me a tatty rope lead. "Because I'm the boss." She laughed. "Why don't we go next door? Get a little rum?" I looked up at the clock above a rack of potato chips. It was half past three. "It'll keep us going." She gave a conspiratorial wink.

"It's . . . I've left my family at the riverbank in the village. They don't kn—"

"They'll be fine. They won't be worrying about you."

"And I need to call the hospital, check in on my dad."

"The Jaguar Lodge, they've got good phone coverage. And Wi-Fi. A quick drink won't hurt."

I smiled. "One quick rum."

"Well, maybe two." Falicia winked again.

"Two daiquiris. Extra rum. Extra lime." The bartender, Francisco, presented the glasses like trophies. I managed half my glass in minutes, the icy sweetness quenching my exhaustion as well as my thirst. "Next door" had turned out to be a twenty-minute walk through thick jungle, and by the time we got there my T-shirt was dripping with sweat. I was desperate for a drink, the humidity stifling.

Falicia was like a tonic. She buzzed with a vitality I was sure I used to know, but I couldn't remember. She'd spent a few years living with her husband in California when he moved to run a conservation project at a zoo there. When their elderly relatives got sick, they moved back to Belize. Her mother, Cualli, died of pancreatic cancer, and her father was now very frail. Her husband's late uncle had owned the supermart, then Falicia took it on.

She asked about my family. So I told her: about kindhearted Dylan, his love of climbing trees and anime and ancient history; about Ella, her vulnerabilities, her insecurities, her intensity—how when she'd come home from the school bus that last time, mascara vandalising her cheeks, ragged words clogging her throat, it was Aid who finally got through to her, recalibrated things. I was just a sponge, there to hug the hugs and soak up the emotions, pull perforated tissues from their box. Aid was the one she listened to, the one she heard.

"Do you have kids?" I asked, after downloading the snippets of my life.

Falicia adjusted herself in her chair and looked past me out towards the jungle. "No. No . . . Henry, he wants kids. But we've not been blessed."

"I'm sorry," I said.

"His momma has been making me see the medicine man." She laughed, stroking Ursula under the table.

"The medicine man?"

"In the rainforest. Superstitious folks think a few herbs and old prayers can halt a miscarriage." She downed the rest of her drink.

"I'm sorry," I said again.

"Four times." Her eyes welled up. "I'm tired of trying, but Henry . . . he cannot let it go. He's close with his nephew. Realises how much he wants a child of his own . . ."

"I didn't mean to upset you."

She smiled. "It's okay, gyal, we must accept things as they are . . . The gifts in the darkness shine brighter than the ones in the light. I'm sure there's a plan for me . . ." She pushed her empty glass away. "Now, shall we get that second drink?"

While Falicia was at the bar, my phone rang.

"Yo bitch, how you doin'?" Tris's warmth was a relief. "How's your dad?"

"He's okay. He's stable."

"I got your text. You're staying out there? For real?"

"I'm trying to move him down south. I need to look after his place."

"Aktar's still pissed. He's barely talking to me, or anyone really. What did Aid say?"

"He's worried about the money."

"That Blade and Stone job is still going. Abigail Danes was supposed to take it, but bitch got a CDC role in Paris. Some Michelin joint in the fifth."

"Oh" was all I could muster.

"You should go for it."

"Tris, I can't. I don't know what's happening with Dad, and—"

"How long are you staying out there?"

"I'm not sure."

"You always said Blade's was the dream."

"I can't, Tris." *I can't hear enough to work in a kitchen like Blade's.*

"Promise me you'll think about it." I promised him I would, knowing that I wouldn't, and we air-kissed and hung up.

After what had happened at Aktar's, I couldn't imagine working in a city kitchen again. My hearing had deteriorated so much over the past few years. I'd noticed it slowly, too late, like sunburn. When the jarringly cheery audiologist had told me that overall, it was nothing to worry about, but "regretfully" the sound at the highest pitches was "falling faster than we would like at your age," I tried not to feel alarmed, or patronised. I tried not to feel anything at all. I wondered if it shouldn't have been "regrettably," made a joke about his loud purple socks, and carried on, because that was all I could do. I couldn't stretch to anything like the four and a half grand for the more advanced aids. I'd had to stick the pair

I did get on a 0 per cent card I worked hard to ignore, though the cartoon logo'ed envelope still clattered through the letterbox each month like an insult.

An hour and two daiquiris later, Ursula and I said goodbye to Falicia and found our way back. Aid and the kids wandered home from the river wearing damp towels and fresh smiles. Home. Miles away from London and from everything I knew, but—Dad was right—I was beginning to like it here. The dark beauty of the forest, its long days and lulling nights, its calm. Its beautiful cacophony and lack of city sounds.

The sun was still low but doggedly hot when the kids and I visited Esther and Gabriel on the sixth or seventh morning (days disappearing into themselves). They lived across the river at the edge of the village in a sea-fronted, green-painted home on stilts, brimming with hibiscus flowers, washing, and love. They had uninterrupted views of the ocean, of the sweeping ecstatic sky.

Gabriel and Dylan played hide-and-seek, threading themselves between the trees and houses while we basked in the shade of the porch and the salt of ocean breeze. Ella sat on the wooden boards, her skirt sprawled around her, picking the paint on her toenails. She inhabited an in-between world now, too knowing to play with the boys but not knowing enough to chat wholeheartedly with Esther and me. We tried to bring her into the conversation, but she floated, lost at the edges, navigating an unmapped universe of her own thoughts.

Esther poured orange and ginger juice from a mighty jug. "Gabriel loves playing with Dylan. We can invite him here more. I can teach him more Spanish and Kriol."

"He'd love that . . ." I said, gazing over at the boys who were crouched, inspecting a butterfly on the ground. "To spend more time with you. As long as he's not swimming on his own." I flashed back again to Dylan floating, distorted, in the water. A wave of grief. What might have been.

"He'll be okay." Esther smiled her tooth-gapped grin. "I'll make sure he is."

I took a sip of juice, shaking the image from my mind.

Across a little walkway an older boy, about fifteen or sixteen, came out and sat on his steps with a book. Ella's eyes flitted towards him. He smiled a warm, open smile at us, saying "Gud maahnin."

"Maahnin, Jonas," Esther called back. "You studying?" The boy nodded, held up his book. His cotton shirt was unbuttoned, revealing his lithe torso, taut and brown. Ella was looking back to her toenails, but her eyes couldn't help but drift back towards him. "He wants to follow in his grandfather's footsteps," Esther said quietly. "He's a local healer."

"A healer?" Ella asked.

Esther nodded. "Using the herbs and plants of the jungle. Nature's medicine." She began pouring another juice. "Here . . ." She gave Ella the glass. "Go give this to Jonas. Ask him about Kantun's work. He speaks good English." Ella took the glass but looked unsure, checking with me. I smiled encouragement until she slipped on her flip-flops and sauntered over, Dylan and Gabriel rushing past her making helicopter sounds. Esther and I pretended not to watch as Jonas invited Ella to sit with him. They huddled together on the steps of his home; Jonas showing her his book, Ella showing him her dimples.

"He's a good boy." Esther passed me another glass. "She'll like him."

Placencia Village, the nearest tourist centre, thrived, a motorboat ride away, past the mangroves, an hour or so across the peninsula. We went across one morning to check out the handful of market stalls and ice-cream bars and art galleries, to gather homeschooling supplies.

As we thrummed across the water, crystal azures patterned past. Mounia had told us the water dances with manatees and dolphins and sharks. The children wanted to see it all.

"Have you spotted any?" Dylan shouted over the engine so I could only just hear. Aid said something I couldn't make out. He anchored a hug into Dylan, who looked up at him like he was the world.

"Look." Ella pointed. "There's something . . . There." The boat slowed, and the engine softened. A flash of grey slipping by, then another. A small pod of dolphins teasing through the water, chasing nearer, glinting in the sunlight.

"Oh, sik." Dylan's face was a plate of delight.

Aid broke into a smile. "They're awesome." He'd seen dolphins before, of course, though he made it seem like he hadn't, for the kids. Maybe for himself.

"I love it here," Ella said, hugging into me.

"I do, too," I replied, clocking Aid unveiling a beer from his rucksack. I spotted another four or five tucked inside.

"Want one?" he asked, holding it up.

I shook my head. "It's not even ten o'clock."

He muttered something under his breath, snapping open his can. It hissed like a snake.

11

Karl Heusner Memorial Hospital, Belize City
11th February 2023

The hospital was anaesthetising. It numbed me every time I visited, which I did every few days, trekking back up north in the Frontier, or by bus, sometimes meeting Mounia for lunch. She was spending most of her time in Belize City now. Close. In case.

As I turned the corner, a woman came out of Dad's room at the end of the corridor. She was tall and slim, her skin a mellow brown. About my age, draped in a green dress and shades. Not a nurse. Not a doctor.

"Hello?" I called. She turned and looked, raising strong lustrous eyebrows, but then dropped her head and kept walking away, picking up pace. And then she was gone like a ghost. I tried asking at the nurses' station, but no-one knew who she was or had even seen her.

Dad lay in his bed, the same. The same. I pulled up a chair. It scraped across the vinyl floor and across my ears.

Tubes, pumps, needles. Everything sterilised to within an inch of its life. Cannulae, fluids, masks. Everywhere you looked, there was sickness. It was the machines that jarred the most. I could never get used to them, despite the fact they were always on, always sounding their incessant, continual bleeps. Like tinnitus, they never let up.

"I love you," I sighed, grasping Dad's hand. "Please come back." *Come back and teach me about the jungle, about the orchids, about Mum. Tell me.*

Dad wasn't religious; he didn't believe in gods or spirits or other fantastic worlds. He believed in this one. He believed in nature—its full force. That was his secret, his magic; knowing we are all ants—so small, so forgettable, so ordinary, but living enormously anyway in a big fuck you. He was a giant, filling every day with infinite questions, and though he had no time for make-believe, he lived like an endless boy—exploring the world in all its wonder and its mystery with a mighty, open heart. Interested in others, intrigued by everyone, fascinated by everything. A scientist with a painter's mind, my grandmother used to say, perceptive in so many different ways. *Tell me everything. Everything you've never taught me, never told me. I need to know.*

I could still hear the words from the shoreline echoing in my head. *Lavender feels.* It haunted me: if that's what Dad had said, if I'd heard it right. I grabbed my phone and googled "lavender feels" again. A body scrub. An essential oil. A song with few lyrics. Nothing relevant. Nothing I could find. Nothing that meant anything to me.

The tinnitus surged on, tapping and whooshing. My body screaming to tell me things I couldn't understand.

Dad's hand felt heavy. I pinched his skin again. I must have pinched it a thousand times. He didn't move. No change. No change.

We bought a dead pig off the back of a truck at the side of the Southern Highway, a money-meat exchange under a pregnant cloak of darkness, everything hush-hush. Aid joked it felt more illicit than buying coke in Peckham. It certainly felt more difficult. The farmer must have been avoiding disclosing his income, trying to skirt the tax. We'd been instructed to only text his mobile asking to "meet for a beer" before we had to drive to the side of the roadway, find the right spot next to the almond trees by the "Jaguar Xing" sign beyond the tamales shack, and wait. And wait.

I hoped the meat would be worth it, what with the time it took, the arguments over exactly which almond trees were *the* almond trees, and the price. We handed this stranger so many notes. But we needed some proper protein—Aid insisted upon it, as well as a weekend off together with no work and no weeding. Just rest. The days had been so tiring—chopping, hauling, harvesting—and we needed a break. And a feast. I couldn't wait to get my hands onto the pork flesh, tear my knives into it, butcher it to bits. I seasoned it with salt and cracked black pepper, coated it in a pineapple glaze. As it cooked, the juice trickled over the meat, forming a dark, caramelised crust like a shield. I would garnish it with coriander and lime, and it would last for days.

While I shuffled plates and tossed a yam and mango salad, Aid opened another beer. He'd already finished the first case. I lay out an embroidered cloth Ella found stuffed at the back of a cupboard, furnished it with some tea lights and a bottle of red from Dad's collection.

"He's *not* my boyfriend," Ella protested, half-heartedly. The kids were prodding the pig over the firepit, Dylan teasing Ella about Jonas.

"He so is. You LOVE him."

Ursula watched on. The children were smitten by this four-legged distraction. With my shifts at the restaurant, they'd never been able to have a pet. Ursula had already made her way into their bedroom at night, had sussed out the comfortable bed (the *only* bed) and where to get the most attention. Maybe she usually slept in there with Dad. Maybe I would be able to ask him soon. I hoped so. God, I hoped so.

Dylan revelled in lighting each coil with an overabundance of matches until the air hung thick with citronella. The mosquitoes barely bothered with Aid, but the children and I were covered in furious bites. I found gentle pleasure in tracking the welts across my body, curating these strange jungle souvenirs.

"Did you know, it's only the females that bite?" Ella asked, seeing me scratching again at my neck. "They need the blood to grow their eggs."

"Sounds about right." Aid swigged at his bottle. "The female of the species is more deadly than the male."

"Hey . . ." I intervened, grinning at Ella, but she was already smirking.

"The males aren't evolved enough to grow piercing proboscises yet," Ella said, twirling the tortilla chip in her hand. "I read that the other day."

"See?" Aid raised his eyebrows at Dylan. "Deadly."

Ella was grasping at adulthood. She could go head-to-head with Aid now, spar with him and give as good as she got. Her confidence was reassuring but disconcerting, too. There was so much she did not know, that I had yet to teach her. I knew I wouldn't be able to shield her for much longer, not from her fears or her pain or her shame, or from the hidden truths she didn't even know to be wary of—might not ever need to be. It was those what-if's that haunted me more than anything, those unknowns she should never need to know.

"Your neck," Aid said, pointing with his cigarette before flicking the butt into the fire. "It's bleeding." I wiped the back of my head, then inspected my finger smeared in angry red. "Let's eat soon. Before it gets dark."

I nodded, distracted by the blood. Aid yanked the pig down from its spike while it spat hot fat at us.

Over dinner I fielded questions about Falicia, the kids excited to learn more about my new friend.

"So, Paw-Paw knows her?"

"He left Ursula with her, so . . ."

"Did you   he   a dog?" asked Ella.

I turned up my hearing aids. "What?"

"She said, 'Did you even know he had a dog . . . ?'" Aid was drunk, but there was an edge to his voice. Or did I imagine it? Mishear his tone?

I squeezed my eyes shut before turning back to Ella. "No, darling. But Paw-Paw has never been great about staying in touch." I knew so little about his life in Belize. "I've invited Falicia and her husband over for dinner tomorrow. They're bringing their nephew. He's Dylan's age."

"Who's Falicia?" Aid asked.

"We've just been talking about her. Falicia. The woman I met at the shop. And her husband, Henry, works at the Jaguar reserve."

"Oh." Aid looked down at his plate, then took a sip of wine. He was so distracted. Since Dad's stroke. Drinking more. Arguing more. Anyone would think it was *his* father in the hospital.

"Falicia was asking me how we met," I went on. "It's strange remembering Caye Caulker the first time around. It feels so long ago."

"I thought you met in Brighton?" Dylan pushed his empty plate away. He'd done well, eaten two massive servings.

"We started dating when I moved to Brighton, but we met in Belize. I was on holiday on Caye Caulker and Aid was, too."

"When you were there with Aunt Chloe?" Ella asked, picking at her crackling.

"That's right, after your father and I split up."

"So it wasn't an affair?" Dylan asked. I didn't know he knew that word.

I dropped down my fork. "No, of course it wasn't an affair."

"But Dad had an affair," Dylan retorted.

Several actually.

"Did he tell you that?" I asked casually, before taking a sip of wine. I was surprised Simon had been so honest with them. With himself.

Dylan looked up to the sky. "I don't remember. I guess so."

"I'm glad you found out about it," Ella said, flinging a last remnant of crackling onto her plate.

I furrowed my eyebrows.

"I *am*. Dad showed his true colours, and without finding out, you wouldn't have been in Belize, and you wouldn't have found Aid, so I'm glad you did. I'm happy you got divorced."

"Me, too." Aid wrapped his arm around my shoulder, pulling me close. He smelt of bergamot and Belikin. I flashed to an image of Simon, the contrast of him, his narrow hips and angular jaw, the pervasive smell of Head and Shoulders.

"Well, your dad was in a really unhappy place," I said, flashing in my mind to the unravelling final months together. "He didn't know how a husband is supposed to act, how a man is supposed to be . . ."

Ella leaned back in her chair. "Did you love him?"

I stared at my tattooed ring finger: *Silence.*

She'd never asked me that before. The children never talked about him. Glancing at Aid, I took a glug of wine.

"I'll make coffee," he said, staggering up to take the plates then bumping into one of the chairs. How much had he drunk?

I picked a final rogue piece of mango from the bowl.

"So? Did you?" Ella asked.

"Of course I did, but we were young. Or I was. It's better we didn't stay together. I'm sorry he didn't want to be a part of your lives anymore or get to see how amazing you're growing up to be."

"He's so selfish," Ella said. "He's never even replied to my emails."

"I know, hon."

"Why? Why doesn't he want to spend time with us?" Dylan asked.

"Because he's a narcissist." Ella was playing with her knife and fork, tapping them for distraction.

"What's a narcissus?" Dylan asked.

"Narcis*sist*, dummy. It means he can only think about himself."

I took another long sip of wine. "I'm sorry. I know it sucks."

"It's okay, Mum. We've got Aid." Dylan smiled so wide I wanted to bask in it. "He's way better at football than Dad was."

"And surfing," Ella said. "And making eggy bread."

The kids had fallen instantly for Aid's zest for life: the way he would rock up at the school gates to take them away for the weekend camping or to hang out in a friend's recording studio playing with the mixing tables; how he would be there to watch every match, every meet, every moment they wanted him there. He showed them attention back then when they needed it, when I needed it for them, too; caught us when we were falling.

"You guys are incredible. You know that, right?" I asked.

They nodded, before both got up from the table, choosing to clear the dishes rather than listen to more of my mothering schmaltz.

I hadn't realised Dylan knew so much; he'd seen Simon only a couple of times after we split. I didn't know how much was said or not said, how much they'd soaked up, or just knew, they were so young.

Ella and Dylan cleared the final plates, taking them into Aid in the kitchen. The mosquitoes buzzed around the lightbulbs. They were better off without their father. I got to thinking about Cornwall again, where it all started to unravel.

Sometimes I wondered, what if we'd RSVP'd to say we couldn't go? How would it have ended? Because it was always going to end somehow. I hadn't wanted to go to the wedding. It was Si's cousin Pete's, and I didn't know that side of the family at all. He didn't really, either. It was only through obligation, and the lure of a couple of nights away from the kids, that we were even there.

No-one knew Si had pushed me to the ground, like a rag doll. He didn't actually hit me, and maybe if I'd been sober and not wearing those crazy three-inch heels, maybe I wouldn't have fallen back—maybe I would have punched him. I should have punched him. Blood seeping out of my skull, my palm dabbing away at the back of my head, I was calm. I wasn't scared of Si, not by then; he was pathetic. I knew it was his last desperate attempt at something, a final act of passion. And honestly, it excited me. I *liked* it when he pushed me. Not the drama of it—thank fuck no-one saw; all the wedding dregs were still inside, necking their final champagnes before the buses came—no, the fervency he finally mustered for me, for us. Some actual passion after all that time. All that time, roaming a landscape of marital boredom.

When he said he'd never do it again, I knew he wouldn't. He was a coward. He proved that later when, after a couple of Pizza Express nights and a cinema trip, he didn't even bother trying to see Ella and Dylan anymore. He'd already checked out.

We didn't go back inside to the wedding. We got a taxi together, in silence, back to that funny little B&B near Constantine his aunt Andrea had booked for us. When we left the next day, we drove back in a demanding silence. The whole way—five fucking hours. It wasn't until we got to Chloe's to pick up the kids we feigned being ourselves, whoever they were. I slugged a handful of paracetamols at the services outside Salisbury and managed to put my hair up in a ponytail to cover the worst of the blood. Chloe didn't even notice.

Maybe I *had* got too close to Pete's best man. Maybe I *was* asking for it. But it was time. Later I found out Si had been sleeping around for months by that point. Then I found out about him shagging Penelope, and Shauna, and that temp receptionist with the pink hair. I should have seen the signs, of course. But we never do—not really—when we're in love, or some warped iteration of it.

I felt a sudden firm grip on my shoulder that made me jump.

Ella was standing over me, holding a mug of steaming hot coffee that was spilling over its sides. "Ow," she cried.

"Sorry," I said. "I was miles away." She placed the cup down in front of me, then headed back inside, flicking the liquid off her hand.

I never needed a man, I just dared to want one. After Si, I was a husk, empty and done. I was not looking for Aid. I was not looking for anything at all, just a break, a breath. Then in breezed this man with these ridiculous eyes, this wild intrigue, so spontaneous and unafraid. He listened to me, really *listened*. And he took the kids under his wing immediately, loving and generous and kind. He hung out with them and was there for them, more than Simon ever was. They'd become reliant on him, too.

"How did you, like, know?" Ella asked, grabbing a tea towel.

"Know what?"

"That you were in love? With Aid? How did you know?" Maybe she was getting closer to Jonas than I'd realised. Falling for him.

I plunged my gloved hands back into the suds. I smiled, trying to remember. "He lifted me up, made me feel light . . . Life somehow tasted sweet like it never had before."

"Does he still make you feel like that?"

"Yeah . . . I mean, relationships shift and change. But yes, I love him."

"He seems different here. Less chilled."

"Well, it's a lot with Paw-Paw, and he's had to take time away from work, so—"

"Is that how you know you're happy? When you don't feel heavy anymore?"

She was thinking too much again.

I peeled off the gloves, throwing them onto the counter. I didn't want her to get down like this. "You know, we don't have to stay here long. Only until—"

"I like it here." She clattered the forks down. "I don't want to go back." The kids had made friends at the river, spending their days as kids should. The past few mornings I'd watched Ella wolf down Lucky Charms, too impatient to wait for me to mix up an omelette or toast her some bread, so desperate was she to get down to the water to see if Jonas was there. "I don't want to go back. Ever." Tears formed in the corners of her eyes. I tried to pull her in close but instantly regretted it. She balked. "It's okay, Mum," she sobbed, wiping the side of her nose. "I'm okay." She dropped the tea towel and slunk off to the bedroom, pushing the door closed. I didn't want her hiding things from me. That's what mothers and daughters do, isn't it? Hide things from each other.

"I get it," Aid had told Ella—or something like it—the last time she came home from school in tears. He'd given her a talk on resilience and fearlessness and the ability to not give a fuck. "When people reject you, they're not judging you, not really. They can't deal with who you are. And that's their problem. Not yours."

"But they hate me," Ella spurted, twisting ragged tissues in her hands.

"Screw their hate," Aid spat. "Act like you couldn't give a shit. Just be you."

"Everyone else is taken?" Ella joked back, half crying.

"I'm serious; don't you ever worry what other people think . . ." He began rolling up a Rizla. "You know something, Ella? The biggest trap in life isn't money or popularity or success; it's self-rejection. It's those voices in your head telling you you're unlovable or worthless or not good enough." Aid fired his cigarette alight and inhaled a long, deep drag. He had slain his voices long ago.

I thought she'd seemed better after that, had seemed okay. But standing there then, as I shoved my hands back into the scolding water, thousands of miles from London—from that school, from those boys—I wondered if she really was. The lesions on her arms had healed, but maybe the ones on her heart had not. And my palms burned.

Ellis

Mangrove River Village, Stann Creek District, Belize
17th March 1986

It's a warm and hazy day, not too hot. After a bit of asking around, Polo found Ellis a smart secondhand Honda H100S from a fellow out in Hopkins. It's 99c, two-stroke, but light and easy enough to handle—reliable for getting around.

Ellis has been catching the chicken bus to Dangriga every now and again, but today he rides his new machine to collect his post, have a beer, pick up some hot sauce to flavour his food (his cooking has not improved). It's a soulful, friendly town about an hour and a half away by bike, full of Garifuna galleries, musicians, and shops—an injection of life outside the jungle.

He uses a pay phone to call home. When she picks up, he can tell Helena is distracted; there's an artificial happiness to her voice, or perhaps he's not used to hearing her sound so upbeat, he's not sure.

"Pen's here," she says. "She's dropped by with the kids to say goodbye before she heads off on her tour." The children prattle on in the background. "I can't speak for long. Can you call later?"

Ellis can hear the television, that awful *Grange Hill* theme tune.

"Don't let them watch that."

"Michael wants it on . . . This line is very bad. I've got to go."

"It's not suitable for Laelia . . . Is Chloe there?"

"I'll get her . . ." She hesitates, then says quietly, "We miss you."

He says, "I love you," but there's a pause, as though she's dropped the phone to hang by its cord, and then she's hollering for Chloe.

"Daddy?!" At least Chloe sounds happy to hear from him. "How are you?"

"I'm well, my darling. And how are you? Are you looking after your sister?"

"Mum's put my Lolo ball somewhere and I can't find it."

"Oh, well. I'm sure it will turn up . . . Do you want to know something exciting?"

"Mmm?"

"Indiana Jones is here. In Belize."

Young Michael's voice starts up in the background. "Chloe, come on before it gets dark."

"What?" Chloe says.

"He's shooting a new film here up on one of the islands . . ."

"Wow. Will you meet him?"

"I don't think so."

"What's the film called?"

"*The Mosquito Coast.* It's based on a book."

She doesn't say anything, distracted.

"We've found your pogo stick," he hears Michael say.

"Can I speak to Mummy?" Ellis asks.

There's a hubbub as Chloe steps away from the phone, and then comes back again. "She's talking to Uncle Adam."

"Oh."

Uncle Adam.

"She says to say goodbye." A crackle on the line.

"Oh, okay. Well, I love you, sweetie."

"Love you, Daddy."

The line cuts off.

After buying the most up-to-date copy of the *New York Times* he can find, he picks up his mail consignment then heads to his bar of choice, Tipsy Breeze, which plays good reggae and punta rock, and not too loud. He sits in the shade to scan the week-old headlines: French TV crewmen abducted in West Beirut; radon contaminating homes in New York; and navy divers have found the remains of the *Challenger* astronauts. Poor bastards. He would like some better news.

He has a swig of Belikin and opens the envelope. The paper is stained in black ink smudges and brown cup circles, littered with crossing outs and unfathomable doodles: the silhouette of a cat? a tree maybe? *Are those supposed to be stars?* There's no salutation, though it's dated:

5th March 1986

Watkins says I have a storm inside of me. It feels like it aches through my soul. He says it will pass with the newer temazepam, as though it's a weather pattern. Brighter days will come. Normal service will resume. I do think that. It is going to get better. We are going to be better. I'm not sure I feel it yet, still.

I've been taking the girls to the park with Pen and her boys. Chloe and Michael love the swings, Laelia and William like feeding the ducks. Penny's ~~been~~ is amazing, a kind and trusted friend. She understands what it is to have an academic for a husband—how it ~~ov~~ commandeers one's life so, though of course Adam ~~doesn't need to be~~ isn't away as much as you. They have both been so kind. She's heading off herself soon on her book tour. It's only a month, but I will miss our walks, our chats.

Ellis cannot take his eyes off the wild loops of handwriting, in a thicker blue ink towards the end:

You have your orchids. And me, I have our girls. So don't worry. This is not my "Edge." You have been patient with me. And I am feeling brighter. Better days will come.

And you say you still love me.

Helena x

Ellis folds up the paper, pushing it into his pocket. He takes a thoughtful sip of beer. He's at an endless loss, her mood swings ungovernable pendulums he's given up trying to interpret. He no longer knows what to feel: sympathetic, or pitiful, or just plain afraid.

They had discussed it, agreed it all together; he would come out here, get the fieldwork done as quickly as he can. She would stay there, look after the girls. It was the only way to make it work, and Christ, they still have to pay the mortgage, and Watkins's bills, and Ellis is doing the best he can.

12

Laelia

Ginger and coconut wafted through the air, everything bubbling.

Falicia was dressed in a gorgeous, patterned dress—teak like her eyes—laden with a giant basket of papayas, mangos, and sapodillas, all bursting to be opened. I dreamt up instant dishes in my mind: Keralan papaya curry, spicy Mexican salad, sweet velvety ice cream. Henry was heaped with tortilla chips and wine. And their nephew, Christopher, carried a huge bunch of heliconias. He was the spit of his uncle.

I ushered them onto the veranda, hoping the mosquitoes would leave us alone. "Do you kids want to light the coils?" I asked. They were already grabbing the matches.

Aid strolled back after securing the chickens. "Falicia . . . Good to meet you." They greeted each other and he piled on the compliments and the charisma. "Thanks for looking after Laelia, welcoming her so warmly here."

Falicia smiled wide. "Well, as my ma always said, kindness is a gift everyone can afford to give."

"I like the sound of your ma," Aid replied.

Ursula bounded over, showering our new arrivals with attention.

"Gyal." Falicia stroked her old housemate.

"They're stunning," I said lifting the flowers to admire the bright lobster bracts. "Thank you."

Henry beamed. "To bring you great returns." He was older than Falicia, rugged and craggy, with forty years or so of laughter lines. After more formalities, handshakes, and embraces, he asked, "Wit   odge. Why is   alled that?" I hit the volume up behind my ear.

Aid caught me looking blank and saved me. "Why did your dad call it Wittering Lodge?"

"Oh," I nodded, turning back to Henry.

He smiled. "It used to be called the Mangrove Lodge, back when it was a hotel."

"Dad named it after the beach we used to go to." Halcyon days sharing spades, and 99 Flakes, and sea salt cuddles.

"It would make a great lodge again," he said. "There's nothing this side. Not for miles. All the tourists I see at the reserve, they come from far away. We need something here . . . I was sorry to hear about your father, Laelia." Henry's eyes exuded a warm kindness, gentle like Falicia's.

"Thank you." I felt awkward, silly for thanking him when I didn't want his sorrys. I didn't want to have to have them.

"How do you like Belize?" he asked, shifting the tone.

Aid cracked a beer bottle, letting the cap tumble to the floor.

"We really like it." I pulled the cork on the red, started pouring. "I can see what Dad fell in love with. The flowers, the creatures. The people . . ." Falicia beamed back at me as I handed her a glass. "Though I don't think I'll ever get used to the jungle at night. It's so loud."

"It's so *dark*," Ella piped up.

Falicia gazed up to the sky. "It's a super new moon soon."

"Really?" Dylan asked, enraptured.

"It'll be at the closest point to Earth."

"It's beautiful tonight," said Henry. "The animals come alive after dark."

"You know to stay out of there at night, right?" Falicia asked the kids.

"Or X'tabai will get you!" Christopher laughed, wide-eyed.

Falicia raised her eyebrows. "Christopher Hernandez!"

"What's X'tabai?" Dylan asked, staring urgently at me.

"She's a spirit who lives in the forest," Henry continued.

Falicia rested her hand on Dylan's arm. "It's just folklore."

"There's a book on the Mayan legends on Paw-Paw's bookshelf," Ella told him.

"Christopher, would you show Dylan and Ella how to play Bul?" Falicia handed him a cloth bag. Ella looked like she was about to roll her eyes but thought better of it, tailing the boys and their lemonades inside.

"What's X'tabai?" Aid asked, once the kids were out of earshot.

"Folks say X'tabai roams the forest in search of lonely men," said Falicia. "Lures them with her beauty and her long, dark hair. She attracts them, makes love to them, and when they cannot satisfy her desires—which of course they cannot . . ." We stifled our laughter, before Falicia went on. "She poisons them, or chokes them, to seek revenge for the lies told to her by her husband and her lover."

"Seems fair enough," I quipped.

Falicia finished a sip of her wine. "There was a man from Big Creek claimed he followed her one night and made love to her . . . Days later he caught a fever. Got sicker and sicker. A week later he died."

Aid smirked behind his beer bottle. "Superstitious bull."

"There's lots in this world that cannot be explained," Henry said. "It is a wise man who chooses not to question too much . . . just in case." Aid laughed.

I topped up Falicia's glass, before heading inside to finish off the rice.

"Four spaces," Christopher was telling Dylan. They were deep into their board game, enacting great warfare upon each other; Ella was back in her usual curled-up position under the lamp, book in her lap.

"Have you played Scrabble before?" asked Dylan.

"No," said Christopher. "What's that?"

"You make different words out of seven letters. I play it all the time with my dad." *With my dad? Aid. Aid's who Dylan plays Scrabble with.* He was calling him Dad? I guessed that was good, that he felt so close to him, that he felt like he could.

When I returned outside carrying the food, the others were sat around the table, deep in conversation. Henry's voice was steady, self-assured. "Oh, man, back then, with our mosquitos, and our tarantulas, and our deadly fevers; self-righteous Americans, Europeans—they all got to thinking of Belize like a tropical Wild West . . . the only way they knew how to get through was hunting . . . drinking . . . raping."

Aid started tucking into the rum, neat, by himself. "Want some?" Aid asked when he saw Henry staring.

Henry shook his head, pulling out a cigarillo. "The old Kill Devil? Nah London, you're good man. I don't drink much."

"What's the main export of Belize?" I asked.

Henry threw a dying match into the ashtray. "For years it was mahogany. Then sugarcane. Now seafood, bananas . . . limes."

"And drug trafficking," joked Aid, downing his glass. I shot him a look.

Henry stamped his beer bottle back down on the table. "Well, Belize has always been a land of opportunity, a magnet for the British and Americans searching for quick bucks. Loggers, poachers. Drug dealers. Here, when you got money, it gets you a long way . . ." He drew on his cigarillo. "Which is why you need to be careful . . . I love this country. Damn proud of it. But gringos need to watch they don't get chanced, you don't become shark bait."

I manoeuvred the rice bowl into the centre of the table, gave each dish a serving spoon.

"You'll be alright." Falicia said. "Your papá, he's known here. He has time for everyone . . ." I smiled, thinking of Dad here, sitting in these seats, drinking from these glasses, chatting with these people. "It used to be a fishing community around here. Lobster. Conch. My granny used to fish with the menfolk, saltdry the marine. Now it's tourism that brings the money. That Microsoft Gates man owns an island. Francis Ford Coppola, too. And Leonardo . . . from *Titanic*."

"DiCaprio," said Aid, flicking his ash. I grabbed the bottle and poured fresh glasses, then called the kids for dinner.

"Last great tax haven on earth," said Henry. "Hicks, you heard of him . . . ? It's crazy who we've welcomed in."

"What about police?" Aid asked, drawing on his cigarette.

Henry laughed. "What about them? They ignore what they want, what they're told to. These parts, we look out for one another . . ." The children appeared on the veranda and Henry lowered his voice. "Blood falla vein."

"Anyway . . ." I said, hoping the others would catch on to the change in tone now the kids were back at the table. I served up the curry, and Aid poured himself another glass of rum.

"Have you ever met a healer?" Dylan asked over dessert. I worried what the children had been talking about inside, whether they'd found that book Ella had mentioned.

"There's this woman in Maya Centre," chimed Christopher. I clocked Aid swaying in his seat, his eyelids drooping. "She talks to the spirits. Everywhere she goes she carries a sack full of tarantulas and scorpions . . . and dead crow's feet."

Ella laughed uncertainly. "That's not true!"

"Could you pass   plea ?" Falicia asked me.

I hesitated. "Sorry, pass what?"

Aid turned to me. "She said, 'Can you *passss* the wine?'" He said it slowly. His tongue lingered drunk around every word. Maybe an edge to his voice, if I'd heard it right.

Falicia redirected the conversation back to Ella as I passed the bottle. "There's a lot of old wives' tales; charlatans and people playing with the spirit world. But there are real healers, too, and some of them are a lifeline for desperate people."

"Hey, we need some music," Henry announced, after we finished up our fruit. "You got a record player?"

"We can do better than that," said Aid. "Laelia's Dad has a piano."

"Do you play?" Falicia asked me, picking at the papaya on her plate.

I started to say no, but Aid got in before me. "I play," he announced, staggering to his feet and draining the last of his drink.

The men wheeled the rickety piano from the study up towards the veranda, Falicia following with the mould-smattered stool. Aid sat, the centrepiece, slurring through a down-tempo rendition of "Come on Eileen," his singing a deep, sugary lilt I hadn't even known he possessed. They all gathered around, arm in arm, swaying to and fro, singing along where they knew the words. The song took me back now, not only to the wedding with Si, but also to that night with Dad, by the water. It chilled me to the bones. I didn't want to listen again, but it was mesmerising. Something kept me there—frozen to the spot—some misplaced fascination with this unexpected moment.

Fragmented memories from Cornwall came flooding again. The

ivy-covered wall light. The push of Simon's hand. That feeling in my skull. The morning after there were rusty smears over the pillowcase, embroidered lilacs caked with angry blood. I'd given the B&B owner a desperate £40 in furling notes at breakfast, to pay for it, to say sorry. She took it and didn't ask me about my head. Simon and I barely spoke over the breakfast table, just essential niceties that weren't really essential. "Can you pass the pepper?" Through gritted teeth, and with bloated eyes. I couldn't eat, just sipped on under-steeped Earl Grey, the teacup trembling in my hands—unsure if that was from the hangover or the shock. The china had felt so thin, too dainty in my fingers while the tinnitus—my new companion—felt all too loud. My head had pounded then. The vodka and cocaine had worn off, and my skull finally felt. Fuck, it felt.

A howler monkey roared in the distance, then another, as if joining in. Rain started bulleting, showering our clothes to our skin in seconds, bouncing off newly forming lakes on top of the piano, splishing rum back up out of our glasses. Everything reverberated. Everyone kept singing, the music weaving its magic. Aid was so at ease, rhythmically swaying his shoulders. Si never danced—would never do it—and he reflected his self-consciousness back at me so I wouldn't, too. But Aid moved like he owned himself, possessing his body so completely, until I wanted to own mine, too.

"I didn't know you played piano," Ella shouted through the raindrops as she wrapped her arm around me. Aid broke into a wide smile; his whole being soaking up the attention. I slicked back the hair from my face, water dripping off my nose in fast rivers to the ground—the mud now sloppy glue beneath my feet.

I didn't know. I didn't know either.

I awoke to a groaning sound, beastly low. Aid was writhing next to me, tangled in the sheet, moaning. It was still the middle of the night.

"Aid?" I whispered. "Aid? Are you all right?"

He normally slept so deeply. He shook his head, flickering himself awake. The blue of his eyes stunned me in the half-light. "It's nothing. A dream."

I hugged into him, and he held me, until we drifted back off to sleep.

In the morning, he was already awake, clearing up the kids' things from breakfast, cooking up his own.

I took a seat, poured a coffee. "You okay?"

He nodded, piling up the plates.

"I heard Dylan talking to Christopher last night. He called you Dad. Did you know . . . ? That he calls you Dad?"

Aid smiled. "He's called me that for a while."

"Really? You didn't tell me."

"We talked about it."

"Did we?" I took a sip of coffee. I would have remembered, surely. The audiologist had told me, had warned me, "Hearing loss is known to lead to cognitive impairment, mental decline." It can affect your memory. Was this that, already? Or perimenopause? So early. Or something. Shit.

Aid passed me a pancake. "I mean, it's nice he wants to, right? Are you okay with it?"

"I guess so . . . Yeah. I mean, yes. Of course. If he wants to."

"He's such a great kid."

"I'm worried about Ella," I said, playing with my fork.

"What's up with Ella? Is she cutting again?"

"No, she's not cutting. It's just . . . she's not herself. She's—"

"She's a teenager, Lil."

"I know, but . . . I think she's scared to go back to school, and I don't think we should make her. Not there anyway."

"Well, she's got to go somewhere . . . I thought Dr. Finch said she was better?"

"She did. Better than she was anyway. I don't know . . . do you ever really get over that kind of bullying?"

It had been a sludge of a school year, clambering together through weekly land mines of fresh drama, nightly blasts of new emotions. Ella would mull in a fug for days, and then out of nowhere blow up over nothing. Eventually, I got her talking. Older boys were hassling her, calling her "a frigid slut." She was gaining attention she wasn't ready for but wasn't sure she didn't want. Girls turned. Friends were no longer friends. They accused her of "dick teasing" and betrayal, and awful, horrid things; things she swore she hadn't done, things I argued with Mrs. Tomkins about meeting after meeting, email after email, phone call after phone call. Until the cutting started, and everything else seemed to stop.

"Do you want me to talk to her?" Aid asked, pouring me another coffee.

"I don't know. Maybe."

"I could take her hiking."

"She'd love that . . . I was thinking I might take her snorkelling, a girls' trip. Falicia's brother owns a dive school. He can take us out."

"How much is that gonna cost?"

"Nothing," I said. "We can piggyback on a tourist trip."

"'Cos we can't afford to be spending anything extra."

"Maybe we can go together another time? Actually dive the Blue Hole after all?" I laughed.

"Seriously?" He cleared his throat. "I don't know that's a good idea, Lil . . . I don't have time. I've got to hook up with some old contacts. This guy I know thinks he can get me some work."

"Yeah?"

"Says he knows this dude who's always looking for people."

"What does he do?"

"I don't know, but it's good money."

"Well, I still think we should go diving together. It would be nice to make the most of being here. Take the pressure off."

"I don't think so," he said, stealing a bite of my pancake.

Ellis

He usually enjoys his weekly ride along to Dangriga, skimming the most recent foreign papers he can find, collecting covert little packages (indulging in the newfound perks of Central American field projects), sorting his post consignment over a beer—but as his eyes flick between the date on the *New York Times* and the recognisable messy handwriting on today's package, his heart does nothing but sink: *16th March.*

He bloody forgot.

The reality is confirmed when he opens up the parcel: an antique tobacco jar enclosed in bubble wrap. Inside, an envelope.

His guilt is assuaged when he opens up the letter. Ellis reads it twice before he calls her, before she wails at him down the phone.

"Just friends," she promises. Penny was away, she says, and they were both lonely, and she's admitting it, she's telling him. She's not hiding a thing. But nothing happened. It was just a conversation, a shoulder to cry on. That is all it was.

Then why say anything?

Helena tells Ellis she loves him, that she is happily married; that Cairns is, too, and that he would never leave his wife. This should make Ellis feel better.

It does not.

Adam fucking Cairns.

Helena has treated him like they're a card game, and she holds all the cards. However much he's been tempted (and God, he's been tempted), he's never cheated. Never.

Adam fucking Cairns. The whole faculty will be talking about it; he'll know soon enough if there's something.

"Everything is in tatters," she says, with him there in Belize. She misses him so terribly, how they were, how it used to be. "When will you be back?"

Ellis used to think of Helena much like an orchid; his *Phalaenopsis*, impressive and resilient and hardy. It's what he fell in love with, what others saw in her, too, her allure so mesmerising, so addictive. Now, though, she is wilting; she no longer knows how to bloom.

He knows she's not in love with Cairns. Of course she's not. But what a mess she has created. It can't be nothing if she's raised it; mentioned how good he is, how supportive, how close they have become. He's *there*, that's all, when Ellis cannot be.

He tells her he will be back soon; he may cut short his trip.

Helena begs with him to do so, tells him she is struggling with the girls at mealtimes and radio news reports when Laelia wakes up in the night. She had always been so good, their little Snoozy Bug, though schedules always get upended, Helena tells him, when fathers are away. As though it's his fault. *All his fault.*

Ellis hangs up the phone as she's saying, "I love you." He just says, "Goodbye."

He won't have her blackmail him into leaving, that would not be fair. He cannot abandon this project, give up on the grant. Though, he could return temporarily to Oxford, if he must.

It would be a wrench to leave the jungle now. The bromeliads are beyond description and his orchidology book is edging along. He can think here. Be himself. Breathe. Plus, the rum is medicinally good.

He's reached out again to Watkins, and he's assured him, *she is fine.* They still have the alternative benzodiazepines to try, no need for the antipsychotics. She's anxious, of course, but that's normal—overwrought—but nothing too much to worry about. No more delusions. No hallucinations. He will adapt her prescription and promises to keep in touch.

Another week or two, considering the side effects of his choices, the side effects of hers, then Ellis will have to make the call, change his flight, if he must.

Polo has shown him across the river now, guided him around the old tourist lodge. The jungle there is swallowing up the buildings, though the wildness of it all is beautiful—ridiculously so: a sprawl of decrepit guest bedrooms and a large living hut, forest all around. The loamy soil is fertile and thick. Santa Marias, cedars, and cohune palms abound. And the most gorgeous black orchid Ellis has ever seen, a purple diamond amongst the greenery. The lagoon. The beach. And an engulfing silence. Not a sound apart from the animals. Peace and tranquillity and calm. Life feeding death, death feeding life. A botanist's utopia. Polo tells him is it up for sale soon, that it shouldn't go for much, that it's a bargain. A wedge of sweet paradise.

Life moves differently in Belize. The stars shine differently, the Milky Way so clear. Ellis feels like himself here: alive. He doesn't want to leave.

Adam fucking Cairns.

Maybe he had it wrong all along. Perhaps Helena is a *Habenaria*, beautiful but fragile, unable to thrive without due care and attention, and he has left her in the dark.

13

Laelia

Karl Heusner Memorial Hospital, Belize City
18th February 2023

When I got to Dad's room, I found him as he always was now. Faded. Still. Next to him on the bedside table was a potted orchid. A beautiful *Brassavola nodosa*, a lady of the night that smelled of citrus and gardenia, memories and hope. I picked up the pot and read the card clipped to a plastic peg: *Que te mejores pronto. C xx.*

I rearranged the sheet, tucking it neatly around his chest. "Hi, Dad." I would always pause. Wait for him to respond. In case he did. He didn't. Of course, he didn't. "Who's C?"

No reply.

"So . . . I've started organising things at yours." His breathing was slow and even, the tubes rising and falling in automatic pulses. "It's such a beautiful place. It could *be* such a beautiful place . . ."

Nothing. Just the *beepbeepbeepbeepbeep* of the machine.

"I'm going to fix the bedrooms, paint them up. Get them ready for when you come out . . . I thought me and Aid and the kids could move into them. Stay and look after you . . . Would you like that, Dad?"

Beepbeepbeepbeep. Nothing.

After I told him about my plans, about the children and their home-schooling, about Aid and his piano playing, I tried reading *Rebecca*—dipped into Manderlay, slipped out again. I scrolled my phone. Skimmed my emails. Sipped coffee. Read the UK news: a cabinet split over pay disputes; two children critically injured during a drive-by shooting; a

Cornish family's leasehold nightmare, the unaffordable sums. Read the Belizean news: an inquiry into a fire sale of government assets; a new traffic light system in Belmopan; police still on the hunt for that Zabaneh guy. Played Wordle. Got it in six. ("Phew.") Found a tabulated list on Wikipedia of "people who awoke from a coma after a significant period of time." Quite a few. A firefighter. A police officer. A railroad worker. And Annie Shapiro after twenty-nine years. *Twenty-nine years.*

"Don't be so long," I said. "Please. Not like this."

Nothing.

I breathed in the disinfected air, touching at a necklace Aid had given me. A gold moonstone pendant from the local cooperative. Tears welled in my eyes. "Aid's drinking more," I told Dad. "And I don't know why . . . Something's bothering him. He's not himself."

That morning, I'd found bottles lining the veranda like bad ornaments, beer caps scattered on the floor. The other night, after dinner, I suggested maybe he slow down. He snapped back in a heartbeat: "But the rum's so good here." He leaned in to kiss my cheek, unsteady on his feet, and told me, "You're drinking more, too." I could only half smile as he poured us both another. I was drinking more. But he was opening bottles at breakfast and drinking rum alone, deep into the night. Or sometimes out with the men he'd met here, some guy called Benny he used to work with in Belmopan. And staying away. Not coming back until morning, or sometimes midafternoon.

I held the cloud-white flowers close to Dad's nose. "*Brassavola nodosa . . .* but you know that." I wondered if he could sense that they were there, that I was there. That anything was there. He'd told me once that flowers are actually listening—for the buzz of a passing bee or the whoosh of a flying insect; then when they hear a pollinator passing by, they produce more of their sweet nectar to attract them. But the scientists don't understand it all. Nature has too many deeply held secrets.

I kissed him on the forehead, stroking the orchid petals gently, then harder, until they crushed in my hand.

The jungle spilled in all directions. I still hadn't got a handle on where the boundaries ended, or where the neighbours' plots began. Mounia had told me Dad owned eighteen or so hectares, but none of us had found their ends. Scale was so different here. Through the humidity and the overgrowth, it took minutes to cover mere metres trudging thick forest. I walked along what must have been the western side, hacking with my machete, careful to tread purposefully and willing any Tommy Goffs away with the power of my mind.

Every so often I stopped, pulled out my mobile, and checked the screen. Nothing. No signal. I didn't have a clue how to get back. Sunlight sliced through the cloud green canopy, the heat pulsing all around. I held the phone over my head, waving it at arm's length, willing the little grey bars to fill with black. Still nothing.

I hadn't heard from Chloe for days—weeks even—but the service was so sporadic it was likely I hadn't got her messages yet. I was starting to worry, nonetheless, which was ridiculous. It should be her worrying about me.

I hadn't meant to be out in the morning heat so long, though it was good to get some air, be away from Aid for a bit. I hadn't meant to get this far. I was just trying to find a signal. Kept inching a bit further to try again, and before I knew it, I was deep in the throb of the forest, my T-shirt damp through.

Still nothing.

The heat beat violently onto my skin, the sun nearing its peak. So short-sighted to set out without even a flask. I'd picked up some leaves from the mother-in-law's tongue Esther had shown us; had the foresight to grab some of that as soon as I saw it, the threat of snakes always in the back of my mind. I felt the leaves in my pocket, rubbed to check they were still there.

A flock of rainbow-beaked toucans squawked, flustering away through the trees. They flew off beyond a heaving fence line, swallowed up by vines. Something to follow, a way back. I edged along the boundary, hacking my machete into thick leaves, pushing my way through as best I could, every lift of metal heavier than the one before. My throat burned dry. Such an idiot not to bring any water. Dad would have been horrified by my stupidity. Aid would, too. He'd be wondering where I'd got to. I slipped out before breakfast, while they were all still asleep. *Would they come to look for me?* Minutes felt so much longer in the jungle. I pulled my phone from my pocket again: 12:09.

No signal.

A bead of sweat slipped onto my lips, the saltiness dissolving on my tongue making me thirstier. My muscles ached from tearing at vines. I considered a quick rest before a final push, sinking to the ground. Propping myself up against a mahogany, I scanned for snakes and tarantulas and biting stinging creatures I had yet to meet. I took deep breaths to steady myself, to calm the buzzing—the tinnitus always so much angrier when I was tired, screaming electric volts. But here in Belize, stripping out the unwanted sounds of the city, of people, it was less. I turned up my aids to listen to the sounds I could hear: the buzz of an insect, the scuttle of something under a log, the indelible chorus of birdsong.

A glint of turquoise caught my eye, teasing through the hem of trees and a crisscrossed metal fence. I steadied myself against the trunk to get a better look, my head spinning. Sharp blue against slick white, lapping pool water shone like a sapphire. Every bit of me wanted to rip through that metal and plunge straight in. Beyond, sleek walls brimmed with hibiscus-nudged glass angles and colonial impositions. An architect's wet dream. CCTV cameras anchored high corners. A parasol shaded a woman bikinied into tiny triangles reading *Time*. Amplified breasts— definitely fake—and legs for days, her mouth smacked with bright pink lipstick. From this distance it was hard to tell; she was maybe twenty, but she could have been midforties. Hard to tell from any distance. A cat slept at her ankles. Sunglasses. And a gun, its hard blackness emboldened by the brightness of her hypercolour towel.

Her tanned arm lifted a can of Coke to her lips, but I couldn't take my eyes off the gun. I swallowed dry. It was all so incongruous, this massive compound sitting here as though it had fallen from the sky into the jungle from LA. Maybe I was hallucinating. Perhaps it was a mirage. My dream of lush water. I so wanted a drink.

"Serena?" A heavy voice boomed. The woman dropped the magazine and scooped up the cat. "Se-re-na?" Closer now. Angrier.

Grabbing the gun, the woman bunched it into the towel with everything else then darted across the patio towards a pool house. The sauna door swung open, and a long-haired, fiftysomething white guy stood naked, clutching a bong, edging towards the pool. He blew out a plume of smoke. The woman's finger made an urgent silencing sign across her lips before her hand pushed his chest back into the sauna. They eased the door shut behind them.

"Serena?! Where the fuck are you?!" Closer still.

Sweat inched down my forehead. Scrunching my eyes, I blinked away the stinging saltwater. A thick-set white man with a shaved head came storming around the corner. He came to a halt over the empty sun loungers. Bare-chested, he was clad in army boots and camouflage combats, cartoon tattoos, and a crazed moustache.

"Serena?! What the fuck?" His words spat bricks across the patio. My heart thrashed against my rib cage, and I could hardly breathe. If he looked over, he might be able to see me. I urged a shallow breath. He kicked at the pairs of flip-flops the couple had left behind, then in a swoop he picked up a sun lounger and launched it into the pool. Splashing water swallowed it up, fat bubbles exploding at the surface.

My back pocket buzzed, loud. *Now* I get fucking signal?! The man turned to look in my direction. I fumbled at my pocket, grabbing my phone to see Chloe's name. I flicked it to silent, but he was already ambling towards me, lifting his chin, his head scanning left and right, glaring urgently between the trees. Thrusting the phone back into my pocket, I began walking then jogging as fast as I could. I raced back through the space I'd just torn down, scrambling through the undergrowth, vines hitting my face, vegetation thrashing at my calves.

Finding a clearing deep in the forest, I stopped for breath, grabbing my phone. One bar. I was about to try to call Aid, but it buzzed in my palm. Chloe.

"Hey, I've been try—"

"Chloe, I'm—"

"... get hold of you for days. How's everything?" There was a delay on the line, and the signal was terrible. "How's Dad?"

"He's okay." My heart pounded. "No change."

"How are you? In the jungle?"

"I'm fine, but—" She couldn't hear me properly.

"I think we need to talk about organising some things in case he doesn't get better."

"In case he doesn't get better?"

"He's got a filing cabinet there, right? See if you can find any power of attorney documents, anything to do with his estate, any financials . . . gather up everything you can. You might need to scan it to me or fax it or use whatever they've got out there."

"Okay, I'll see what I can find."

"Chlo?" Tom said in the background.

"I'll have a look, but—"

"Thanks, sis. Sorry, we're at Scarlett's ballet recital. Got to go. Call me soon." She hung up before I got a chance to say goodbye, or ask her to post my kitchen stuff, or tell her I was dying in the heat.

I stared at my phone again. No signal. Nothing. Somewhere behind me, I heard the shuffle of leaves, the crack of a twig. I turned and looked up. Him.

He stood legs astride. His shirtless chest sprouted tufting strands. Eyes that could puncture concrete. He looked like a hairless dog. Smelt like one, too. Oil-smudged fat fingers grabbed towards me, snatching for the phone.

"What you doin'?" he drawled as he eyed me up and down.

"I was just . . . I'm lost. I can't find my way—"

"Ain't nothin' round here for you, sugar." A gravelly southern accent, but I couldn't place the state. He scrolled through the screen.

"I'm . . . I was—"

"Stupid hot for a hike." He flicked through my latest photos: a shot of Dylan hugging Ursula; Ella feeding the chickens; a sea bass curry.

"I got lost. It was only supposed to—"

"You travellin'? A tourist?" he asked as he threw the phone back to me. I missed, and it thudded to the floor of dead leaves.

"I'm staying at my father's." I bent to the ground, keeping my eyes on him as I picked up the phone. "Better be getting back." I turned, desperate to leave.

"Here . . ." he rasped. I glanced over my shoulder, unsure of what he could be wanting now, what he might say. His outstretched arm was holding a military-style water canteen. "Looks like y'all could use this, sugar."

I forced a smile. He grinned back, too wide. As I reached to take the bottle, his fingers trapped over my hand like a cage. His gold signet ring pushed into my skin. It lasted only a second, but it felt too long, too blanketing, like a dark, sleepless night.

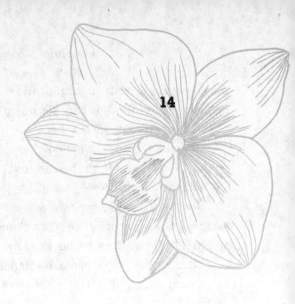

14

Lil . . . ? Hey, Laelia?"

A gentle rocking lulled me awake. I blinked and rubbed my eyes. The light had shifted. My head ached.

Aid hung over me, pushing at my arm. He wore his beard so scraggly now. "Hey . . . Where did you go? What   you up to?"

Mountains of Dad's clothes surrounded us, lay under us. When I'd come in from the heat, I'd opened the wardrobe door, desperate to inhale the last scents of him. Grabbing a handful of his clothes, I'd yanked them down on their hangers, breathing him in urgently—his gentleness, his warmth. Piling up the mounds of cotton and linen, I collapsed onto the bed. I must have fallen asleep.

"I wanted to call Chloe. I was trying to find a signal, but I got lost . . ." My head pounded.

"You've cut your legs," he said, running his hand over my calves. "And what's all this?"

I lifted my head to see. At my ankles blood had blotted onto some of the shirts.

"I just wanted to—" I stopped. I felt ridiculous.

"Are   sorting out his clothes already? Maybe   t's good idea."

"What do you mean?" I asked. I tried to turn up my aids, but they'd run out of battery. I focused on Aid's lips.

"Chloe said he's not getting better . . . that he's not going to get better."

I flicked him a hard stare. "What? What does Chloe know? She's not even here."

"She's been   touch with the doctors. They've said we need   make plans."

"Make plans?"

"If we need to turn off the machines."

They'd been talking without me. Aid had been talking to Chloe. All this time when I couldn't get hold of her, they'd been speaking. My legs were thrumming now.

"Turn off the machines? But he's going to be okay. The doctor said he would be okay."

"Lil, you're tired . . . You should rest." He smiled gently. "We can talk about   later when you're feeling better . . . When you can think straight, you crazy bitch."

My stomach lurched. *Did he just say that?*

"I can think straight now!" I threw my legs over the bed and sat up. Instantly, the room started spinning, everything kaleidoscoping.

He can't have done; I must have misheard. He's too calm, too composed.

He grabbed my shoulder, propping me up. "You're not fine. Come on, you're exhausted." He tugged my feet up off the floor and rotated me back into bed. My head eased onto the pillow. "You need to rest."

"But the kids . . . I should make them some food."

"Laelia, they're fine. You need to sleep."

My head was thudding. "Okay, okay."

"And promise me you won't go venturing out into the jungle alone like that again?"

I gazed up at him.

"Promise?"

Crazy bitch. It's what my father would call my mother. Before he knew . . . before anyone did. Of course Aid didn't say that, he wouldn't have.

"Promise," I said.

He pulled the blinds. Closed the door behind him.

I drifted in and out of sleep for two days, sometimes hearing the distant sound of a howler monkey, or the dreamy lull of a guitar. My body was exhausted; my mind was, too.

When I finally got up and migrated to the living room, it was like the world had carried on without me. I was the anomaly. Everything was clean and organised into its place. The thick smell of vegetables steamed from the stove. Aid was outside chopping wood and shooing chickens. Jonas was curled next to Ella under the lamp, leaning together reading *The Healing Power of Medicinal Plants* with an intensity that made me proud. Dylan was biting his nails, churning through another manga next to Ursula. He came hurtling over to give me a hug. "Mum! Are you better?" I nodded tentatively, and he carried on excitedly, "Dad let us help him and Henry building a new playground at the community centre." Ella smiled at me but stayed nestled where she was.

"That's great, Dyl."

"Hey . . ." Aid said, wiping his forehead with the shirt in his hands. He was often bare-chested now, the mosquitoes not bothering with him at all. "How you feeling?"

I leaned on the table to sit down, trying not to upset the stubborn thumping inside my head. "Yeah, okay."

"I made you some soup."

I nodded. "Mmmm, thanks."

Aid ladled thick broth into a bowl for me, flicked the cap off a bottle of beer for himself. "We've already eaten." He passed me the bread. "What do you think it was?"

"Too much sun. A migraine or sunstroke or something."

"Lucky you didn't get eaten by a jaguar, going out like that on your own." He swigged his bottle. I couldn't tell if he was joking or not.

Ella started playing an acoustic guitar, strumming chords. It sounded like the beginning to "The Man Who Sold the World."

"Henry gave it to her," Aid said.

"Oh. That's kind of him." I ripped apart my bread. "I bumped into this weird guy. When I was in the forest. I thought I was hallucinating."

"Maybe you were."

Crazy bitch.

"He took my phone, started looking through my photos."

"Why would he do that?"

"I guess he thought I was trespassing." I didn't want to tell Aid about the woman I saw, about the gun; I didn't want to in front of the kids, but I didn't want to anyway. Maybe I'd imagined it, but if I hadn't, it felt like a secret I needed to keep, for protection—mine and hers.

"Were you?" Aid asked, the blues of his eyes stabbing through the dusky light.

"What?"

"Trespassing?"

"No, God no. I was still on Dad's land. *He* was trespassing."

"Yeah, well, maybe it's not a good idea to go venturing out like that on your own."

I slurped at my spoon and the soup burnt hot on my tongue.

15

Days bled into nights bled into days. While everything was not the same, nothing had changed. At least, not enough. Dad was still unconscious in a hospital bed. "No change" was the only information I could glean. The doctors had said those words more than any others. Maybe Aid was right; maybe it was time to start making plans.

I couldn't get hold of Chloe. She was deep in her case, pulling all-nighters, and Tom didn't know anything more about Dad's condition other than some unfounded snippets about the cost. I tried Dr. Guevarra several more times, but she didn't return my calls. She was off sick, and the hospital was run off its feet. The doctors wouldn't speak to Mounia—she wasn't blood, but she reassured me Dad was fine. Or at least, there was no change. I asked Mounia over the phone about "C," if Dad had a girlfriend here. She fumbled a little, her pitch rising. "No, no, Laelia. He doesn't have a girlfriend." An effervescent receptionist told me someone would call me soon. Someone never did. Not that my phone ever had much signal. I planned to drive up to the hospital to find out what was going on, but Aid needed the truck for another day or so. He'd put the feelers out for work to make some extra cash, and Benny had introduced him to some people. He'd landed a job shifting plants for some Floridian guy called Hector. He couldn't let him down. The money was too good.

The nights were long here. We turned in earlier than we ever did in Forest Hill. With no real screens to light up the evenings (the internet a distant memory), and a darkness that descended before dinnertime, sleep had become an activity again; something to do, to seek out and discover—an actual pastime we all seemed to embrace. More so since Aid and I now had a mosquito-netted slumber area furnished with a mattress Falicia had found us from a friend. It was lumpy but comfortable enough if you avoided the sloping middle—or vowed to stay lodged within it all night.

Yet I couldn't sleep. Worry kept me awake, souring my tongue and undulating my stomach. Aid snored beside me; his breath sugared with rum. Beyond my tinnitus, the usual nighttime symphony of crickets, frogs, and owls competed, the occasional howler monkey whooping over the chorus. I came to love these sounds that masked the electrics in my head, but they weren't able to sing me back to sleep.

Wrapped in a cardigan and armed with a lantern, I crept out under an edgy sky to Dad's study. Pouring myself a neat rum in his honour, I eyed the piles of paper and jettisoned notebooks. A lifetime of ideas he'd tended like flowers. It felt impossible there could be no more, that this might be it, his legacy. How fragile our thoughts are; how ephemeral really—just chickweed.

Rifling through drawers and files, I found nothing more than some weary bank statements and old mortgage documents from the house in Oxford, a couple of faded car hire contracts, some handwritten receipts. It took me two guesses to crack the combination for his safe, his birthday too obvious. But 1409 flicked up the green "proceed" light in a flash. Of course. *Virgo. Creative and stubborn. Prone to overthinking. May sometimes exhibit a spontaneous nature.* Chloe used to say I'd inherited mum's spontaneity. I always took her word for it; I couldn't remember my mother's characteristics. I'd filled in the blanks with photographs and zodiac charts, and it had always been easier to accept whatever Chloe told me to be true.

I rotated the handle, but the door wouldn't open. He'd used the secondary lock. A rum-fuelled search through the depths of the desk turned up nothing until I found a dusty picture frame wedged face down under a stack of papers. My mother, radiant, whirling in a pinup red dress at West Wittering, ramshackle pastel huts blurred in the background. It hit me like a sucker punch, the grief I carried in my gut for a woman I'd barely known.

Dad never talked about her. Yet he kept her like this, a souvenir stashed in the darkness of a drawer. I liked to think she was hidden like this somewhere in his heart, too, but he never said.

Still, I could not find the key. I could not find the rest of his secrets. So I drained the last of my rum—his rum—sprinted through the slicing rain, and sloped back to bed. The tinnitus screamed.

16

I could get a full phone signal on the inside tables at the Jaguar Lodge. It wasn't the worst situation to know I would have to buy a drink every time I wanted to call someone. I flicked through the emails on my screen while waiting to order a beer: Mrs. Tomkins on her high horse about overzealous interpretations of school uniform; Tris forwarding something about coma research from the *HSJ*, which I would read later; a hearing centre reminder informing me I'd missed my last appointment.

"Hey, Chlo?" I said, placing my beer bottle back on its mat.

"Laelia! Thank goodness. Tom said you'd called. I've been trying to get hold of you. Have you not found Dad's insurance documents yet? His power of attorney?"

"There's nothing," I said. "Just academic work. There's no filing cabinet . . . There is a safe. I've figured out the code, but there's a secondary lock and I can't find the key."

"Seriously? Where have you looked?"

"Everywhere. I don't know where else to look."

"Shit. Okay, let me think. Leave it with me."

"Chlo?" I asked.

"Yeah?"

"Have you been speaking to Aid? About Dad?"

"What?"

"He mentioned you'd been talking to the doctors . . . that they'd mentioned about . . ." My voice trembled. "Switching off the machines?"

"What?"

"Have you been speaking to Dr. Guevarra? She hasn't said anything like that to me. And I can't get hold of her now. I—"

"I haven't spoken to anyone, Laelia. I haven't had time."

"You haven't called Aid?"

"I haven't spoken to him for ages . . . What are you talking about? I thought Dad was stable?"

"He is, he is," I said. "Sorry. Something's got lost in translation. Ignore me."

Aid and I escaped for a night alone without the kids. Dinner at Maya Beach along the peninsula, a thirteen-mile boat ride across the dark lagoon. We could have driven around. It was over an hour by road, but faster and more special by boat, the edges skimmed with mangroves and pretty orchids, beauty amongst the mud.

I waited until we were alone to ask—waited until we were a bottle and a half in, until we were both more relaxed. Maybe I was thinking I could catch him off guard, I don't know. "Why did you tell me they want to switch off the machines?"

Aid looked up from his braised lamb, from smudging rum jus across his plate. "What?"

"You told me they want to switch off the machines . . . but I spoke to Chloe, and she didn't know anything about it."

"What are you talking about?" His eyes pierced so blue. He finished his glass, and we both watched as he placed it back down on the bright white cloth. The waves lapped like silk beyond our table, though the tinnitus raged so much I could barely hear them.

I leaned in. "The other night, after I'd come back from the forest . . . you said . . . you told me Chloe—"

"Laelia, you were out of it. You were so confused; you could barely talk."

"What are . . . Are you telling me I'm wrong?" *Crazy bitch.*

He began pouring us both another glass, finishing up the bottle. "Of course not. I'm saying you're misremembering. You forget shit sometimes. You weren't well. I said we should start thinking about *if* we need to make plans. You know—if they talk about switching off the machines."

That wasn't what we said. That wasn't it.

"But you said Chloe had told you—"

"Lil, come on, you're stressed out. I thought taking you out like this would relax you a bit. Come on, let's not spoil the—"

"No."

"What?"

"No, that's not right. Chloe told me she didn't say that to you."

He snuffed, then took a large glug of fizz. "Well, maybe Chloe's lying."

"Why would she do that?"

"I don't know. She's batshit crazy, you know that. Maybe she wants this all to be over . . . I mean, it's a lot." It was a lot. It was too much.

"But she's never lied to me before . . ."

"It's understandable. I mean, she's a long way away. She's not in control of anything. Maybe it's her way of having a handle on things . . . Having a say? And you know, if we're honest—and I know you don't want to hear this, Laelia, of course you don't—but he is really ill. Maybe it is worth at least thinking about options. Maybe she's not wrong."

"No," I said. And that was enough.

"Okay." He sniffed again and reached for my hand across the table. "I'm sorry." I pulled away. I wasn't sure I believed him. Though I wasn't sure I believed Chloe either. In this oppressive heat nothing made sense. Everything felt confused. Maybe I was. Maybe he was. I couldn't understand why he would lie. If he would lie. But in that moment, I realised he might be capable of it. We all are, after all, when we need to be.

"Let's get some more champagne," he said, his tattooed hand flagging down the waiter. "How's the pig tail?"

"It's nice," I said. It worked well with the split peas and pimento peppers, could handle a bit more garlic. "Maybe we should curb it now? We need to get back for the kids. Get back to the boat." Aid had been drinking nonstop; I was only on my third glass.

"Chill. I've got it sorted." He was playing with his food, shredding the meat with his knife but not really eating.

"We can't afford a taxi on top of the meal."

"I said I've sorted it."

"Okay, okay . . ." I glanced around at the tables in the half-light. All couples. A resort restaurant a million miles away from our jungle lodge, and even further from our budget. Especially with the champagne, which was near impossible to get in Belize. Possible, for a price. I tried to lighten the conversation back again. "This is such a great spot . . . The gazpacho was good."

"The beach is stunning here, right?" He pushed his plate away, leaning back to spark up a cigarette. He'd hardly touched his lamb. Left most of his starter, too. "I thought we could get some more drinks, and then I've got a surprise for you."

"A surprise?"

"I booked a room."

"What . . . ? What about the kids?" Ella was old enough now to look after Dylan, but I wasn't sure about leaving them alone in the jungle, so isolated, the trees always seeming more alive in the throbbing black—a darkness that felt anything but asleep, with unknown creatures shrieking, scuttling, yelping to be known.

"Falicia and Christopher are going to stay over with them. They're bringing popcorn and playing Monopoly." He was edgy, jogging his knee up and down. "I thought you'd be happy."

"How are we affording all this?" I asked, smushing the coconut rice around my plate.

"I've been getting well paid for this work I've been doing." He leaned in and spoke in a low voice. "Like *really* well paid."

"That's great. I mean, it's good you're making some money." The champagne was starting to make sense. "Don't you need a work permit?"

"It's fine, Laelia. Hector's sorting it."

I placed my knife and fork together as the waiter came to pick up our plates. Aid leaned in even closer, as if to say something, but paused while we were asked if we wanted dessert. "Yes, please," I said. The waiter nodded before turning away.

Aid frowned. "Really? You're still hungry?"

"The souffle looks amazing." I gazed over to the next table, where the couple were feeding each other spoons across the flickering candlelight.

Aid looked over at them, too. He was still leaning in close, his cigarette smoking into my eyes. "I thought we could head off and . . ." Under the side of the table, he opened his palm. A wrap of coke.

That again.

"I'm fine . . ." I said. It had been years since we'd done anything more than weed. We'd only ever done little lines of coke—socially—for a week or two when we first got together, at Aid's friends' eclectic dinner parties or in their music studios. It was exciting, at that point, after the hum-drum marriage I was getting out of, but I thought we'd moved on from all that. I thought he had. "I don't really want any. Where did you get it?" This Hector guy must have been paying him really well.

"Oh, you know, asked around." He smirked. "It's so good here. It would be rude not to, right? Come on . . . It's one time." I stifled a yawn, but his eyes were dancing. Maybe a small line would help clear my head.

And it did. We tumbled into a seven-hundred-fifty-dollar-a-night suite dripping with soft cottons, which we basked in until the cleaners tried to turf us out, until Aid thrust high-dollar bills into their hands, un-til their smiles grew super-king wide. The early-morning hours slipped by like satin over skin. Two more bottles of Laurent-Perrier, one wrap of cocaine, barely any sleep. The tinnitus raged. But for the first time in a long time, I didn't feel tired. I felt utterly alive.

Ellis

He wants to die. In this moment now, he wants to die. Or to dare to think about it, like she has done a thousand times.

He dips his toe into the water. It is cool and silky. This part of the river is flat and still.

Drowning would be relatively quick and comparatively painless. It would be peaceful and calm. When he inhaled—which he would have to eventually—it would shock but not completely overwhelm. The water would flood his lungs, then rush deep through his bloodstream, causing his cells to swell and to burst, like raspberries making jam.

He could do it to spite her.

How often does she think about it? Is it always somewhere in her mind? That beautiful, overthinking mind. It feels so utterly self-indulgent, so completely selfish. Leave him, yes. But the girls, how could she ever leave the girls?

He would be unconscious by the time his heart stopped. It would be like a light switching off, flicking away to nothing. Everything blacking out.

How could she think like this? She is ill, of course. But also, manipulative. She knows what she is doing, trying to punish him. As if she hasn't punished him enough.

Ellis tosses his towel onto a fallen kapok, imagining whoever found him would use it to dry off his bloated body, or maybe themselves, though it would also alert them to his being here, of course. It would be better, if he did do it, if he was left undiscovered, left to drift like a leaf downriver, to rot in the heat and disappear, to disintegrate, to leave nothing but bare bones. He wouldn't want to be found, wouldn't want to give Helena the satisfaction or the closure.

He could punish her, too.

He was honest with her from the beginning, how committed he had to be. She knew his orchids—his "bollockworts," she always calls them—were everything before he met her, and nearly everything still.

They'd mapped it all out on their honeymoon in the Balearics, over ice creams on clifftops, and with after-dinner cigarettes at Sausalito's. House purchase arrangements were set. Holidays mapped out. Babies preimagined. A decade-long forecast of work objectives (for her as well as for him), financial expectations, and child-rearing proposals. It was all negotiated out. Better to have a plan and to deviate from it, they told each other, than to have never planned anything at all. They were nothing if not methodical: *"Wylde and practical!"* They would prioritise his work, and she would give him the gift of that. A marriage made in heaven or, at least, in Ibiza Town.

The water shimmers.

Virginia Woolf drowned; William Arnold, too, while collecting orchids along the Orinoco; and Frank Meyer, off a steamboat in the Yangtze, who never got to know the full fruits of his labour. The honey-floral lemons he'd found in Fengtai weren't named after him until decades later. "I will be famous," he'd promised his family—and himself—years before his death. "Just wait a century or two."

Poor bastard was found floating in the water still wearing his yellow shoes.

Ellis stares down at his toes. He hasn't discovered *his* citruses yet. There are sure to be so many unclaimed orchids, plentiful obscure bromeliads not yet spotted by human eyes, more waiting out there, here, for him. Or someone like him. And they would wait. Someone else would find them, eventually.

Helena has been patient with him, of course. She has given up so much, he knows, though he had always been frank it would need to be so. She would be the secret of his success, and he of hers. Through PhD to postdoc to faculty appointment; all the long, tedious hours of research, teaching, writing, he had always been candid about that. And she understood it. They were in it together; suffering the problems, celebrating the successes, jointly. It was as much her as it was him.

Until the nights away became weeks became months, all of which the work demanded. The rhythm of academic life.

The symposia and the conferences were one thing; travelling to far-flung outposts quite another—for Helena, at least. But it's all a part of the job. The life. The choices they have made. *Together.* The first year was the hardest; her not understanding what to expect. And if he's honest, maybe this last one. Where she gets it all too much.

He is not a selfish man. He may have done selfish things, but he is not a selfish man. No more than he needs to be, at least. No more than she is.

He moves slowly down the bank. A stretching squawk sounds above. A lone scarlet macaw, its rainbow plumage clashing against the verdant trees.

"Hello," Ellis says without thinking. *First sign of madness.* The parrot caws back.

Ellis eases himself into the river, water sleeking over his hot skin. Lifting his feet, he pushes himself backwards to lie buoyant, to let go. *Oh, Helena.* The sky is a mighty canvas, clear and bright. He breathes it all in and shuts his eyes.

Paddling back upright, the weight of his body drags him down below the surface. Exhaling, he lets himself sink. Hitting the riverbed, he splits his eyes open, blinking through the cool water.

He could wait for nighttime, for its gentle shroud of secrecy, its comfort and forgiveness. Come back without his towel. He wouldn't want the girls to know, to believe he was a coward. He is anything but.

His toes nestle into the silt. It's not that deep. His lungs hold still. Ellis wonders if they would ever forgive him if he did it. He cannot forgive Helena. For making him look like a fool, for all the times she has tried and half tried, for everything she has put them through. He knows she is ill, but she basks in not wanting to get better.

Everything is peaceful and calm.

His heart throbs like a featherless bird.

A splash disrupts the water above him. An immersion of new kicking legs swirl around and around, catching themselves in a pluming dress, billowing. Milk in water. Ellis can hold his chest no more. Pushing his feet against the riverbed, he propels himself upwards. His lungs sting. He breaks through the surface, heaving for oxygen.

He wipes at his face and opens his eyes, treading water. Back into the day. Back into the tethering sunlight.

Like a vision, a trick of the light scintillating before him, a beauty in white cotton, she floats. A water lily.

"Buenos días," she says, as she swims towards him.

"Buenos días," he says, a smile taking him over.

"Cómo estás?" She's maybe twenty-eight, twenty-nine. Her face is heart-shaped, inquisitive, her skin iridescent.

"I'm fine," he replies in Spanish. He pushes back his dripping hair, catching his breath as water drops onto his lip. "I think I'm going to be fine."

"Curiosity will keep you fine," she says. She sings waves of laughter. "I'm Agapita."

Ellis hasn't discovered his citruses yet. Curiosity will keep him fine.

17

Laelia

The stream of fresh dollars ebbed and flowed into our hut like a rising river. Aid was buoyant—buzzing, throwing himself into life so deeply. And drinking more and more. He made friends here with everyone; knew all the locals like old acquaintances and weaved his stories into their lives, as I guess Dad must have done, too. Aid had been helping Henry and the men at the community centre with building projects, and in the borders of our days he was still getting things done around the lodge; we'd rethatched the study roof together—mastered the unwieldy cohune fronds; threaded elaborate rope swings and hammocks through carefully selected trees; and replaced the kitchen table with a vast run of reclaimed timber, "the Feast Beast," Dylan had named it. One day, Aid came home with Henry, both laden with copper pipes, nuts and washers, and a silver snaking hose. We finally had our solar shower. And water flowed like money.

Freshly caught lobsters appeared at the end of days like flower bouquets, juicier and sweeter than any I'd ever sourced in London. We had a new bed Aid had trucked down from Mexico, cloudy pillows, and soft, fresh linen. Cast-iron pots and pans. Don Omario every night—for him, not me. We'd sometimes share a joint before bedtime, but I left him to the rum and the whisky. He would sleep until early afternoon most days, but he was keeping busy; and things seemed less complicated when Aid was busy.

"What did he do then, before? Hector?" I asked one day as we ate tamales watching the children diving in the lagoon. "How did he make his money?"

"He sold a tech business in California. DX transformation or something. Made an absolute bomb, lost a bit, made it back again . . . then he moved to Florida and got into orchids. He fucking loves them. He grows these unusual ones. Crazy beautiful. Collects them like stamps. Sells them, too. You'll have to see them one day . . . meet him."

"Sure," I said.

"He's stupidly loaded, swimming in dollars he doesn't know what to do with . . . and he likes me." Aid liked to be liked. He'd always kept his job separate, but orchids—or working with Hector—animated him in a way the wheeling and dealing of the property world never had. I'd come to understand it was really Elijah who managed their business in London, decreed the dividends, kept the wolf outside the door. Aid was just an old friend who'd been there at the right place, right time—invited on board to coordinate the contractors, pay the invoices, do the day-to-day lifting. It was Elijah who found the finance, wore the fancy suits, asked the asks. Aid had always seemed a bit uncomfortable—out of his depth even—with all that. That was just money, or the promise of money. This was something else.

18

We spent hazy Belizean days together, basking in each other's company. The children loved exploring our surroundings, every day an adventure; bats in forgotten caves and bilimbi fruit for pickling, eggs and cheese off Mennonite carts and bananas from the handlebars of roadside bicycles, searing sunrises and technicolour sunsets, toucans and howler monkeys and piam-piams, we took it all in.

"What does your tattoo mean?" Falicia asked one afternoon, as we sat on the beach eating pineapple, watching the kids digging holes with Aid and Henry in the sand.

I stroked at my wrist, its interlinking black feathers. "Nothing really . . . I guess it's me and Aid. I got it when we first started dating."

"It's beautiful . . . When did you   ?"

With the sound of the waves, the background noise of the others, the tinnitus, all competing, I couldn't hear properly. I flicked up my aids. "Sorry?"

"When did you and   ?"

The words were still lost to me. I couldn't bear it. There are only so many times you can ask someone to repeat themselves. If Aid was sat with me, he would have helped me untangle the situation, guide me through it.

I took a guess at what Falicia might have said, threw myself in to an answer, hoping it didn't sound weird. "A few years ago. On Caye Caulker.

It was kind of a holiday romance." She nodded. My answer must have been about right. I looked over at Aid who was throwing sand at Dylan.

"Kind of?"

I still couldn't hear properly so kept talking. "That's all we thought it was. But then he found me again, in Brighton, when he moved back to England."

"Soulmates. Meant to   . He's been so helpful at the community centre. He's been   ." I gazed down at Aid spading the sand, his muscles taut and bronzed, his L.F. tattoo flexing on his bicep as he worked. I couldn't bear it anymore, hiding the shame, struggling on trying to understand. "The old folks," Falicia went on. "They love him, no? He's always   and—"

"I'm sorry. I can't hear so well . . ." I took a breath then pulled my hair back to show her. "I wear hearing aids." The first person I'd told, beyond family.

"Why didn't you tell me?"

"It's . . . I . . . It must be annoying, having to repeat stuff for me." *Plus, they look ridiculous. So cumbersome and ugly.*

"You don't ever worry. Not with me. Ever. How long have you had them?"

"A couple of years . . . but it took me a while to get them. I was in denial . . . I thought people might not want to spend time with me, make the effort. It's so much extra energy to communicate, for them and for me . . . It is easier, though, here. In London it's always so crowded. Crazy loud bars, and restaurants with bad acoustics. Noise everywhere. I found excuses not to go out, or to leave things early. It was exhausting."

"How was it, working?"

"Difficult. Really." And then I told her. About what happened with the fish sauce, my fuckup, Aktar sacking me. And she listened. She didn't judge. She didn't pity me. She didn't make me feel ashamed. "Please, don't tell Aid," I said. She stared at me, confused. "He thinks my colleague did it."

"What do you mean?"

"I couldn't tell him it was me . . . I panicked. He was so stressed about money."

Aid was wandering back up the sand, so we were quiet.

He collapsed onto the rug. "I'm knackered . . ." he said. "Those kids don't stop."

"Henry . . . ?" Falicia called. "We should go home." She pushed herself up and headed down to the shoreline.

I leaned into Aid, brushed at his hair. "I love you," I whispered.

"Not now, Laelia." He pushed my hand away and lay himself down. He would withhold himself like this sometimes now, so distant and exhausted. I collapsed down next to him.

Stretching out in the final throes of the day's sunshine, I welcomed lapping drowsiness. Aid sat up again and pulled *The Mosquito Coast* out of his bag. I drifted in and out of dreamy end-of-day sleep, rekindling memories.

When I saw him with that book for the first time, in that bar on Caye Caulker, without his even looking up I knew it was him; sensed him before I saw him, heard him. I could feel his heat, smell the essence of him—heavy rum and sandalwood and salt like ocean wind—rushing to find the blood in my veins.

"'Tell me why you're here,'" he'd read in an accent over my shoulder—*East Coast*, I'd thought, but I couldn't really tell—his words buzzing through my aids, flitting into blue morphos in my stomach.

I grinned and read on from *The Beach* out loud. "'The horror.'"

"'What horror?'" he read back, teasingly.

"'*The* horror!'"

"'*What* horror?'" He pointed at my daiquiri resting on the bamboo bar. His smile was expansive, offering me the world. "Can I get you another?"

"Sure," I said. His eyes were lagoons, the lines around them sharp and crinkled, like water reeds. I'd snatched glances at him—with him—in the days before: dripping in seawater snatching towels from the sand, over syrupy pancakes at breakfasts, on balconies after dark. And then, again— eyes catching eyes—in the pink light of sunset across the beach bar.

He was staring at the envelope I used as a bookmark, its cursive watercolour font. "Laelia," he said, my name dancing off his tongue, wrapping around him like sunlight. "It's so unusual . . . like a lily flower?"

I smiled. "It's after the orchid."

"Beautifully strange?"

"The most unflowerlike flower of them all."

"You're funny." He eased a smile, touched the cover of my book. "And like me, you're reading a tropical horror story."

"I felt like something beachy while in paradise. You?"

He pulled a tattered paperback from his pocket: *The Mosquito Coast.*

"That's a horror?" I asked.

"It doesn't start out like that. But, you know, paranoia and disillusionment always take hold eventually . . ." His laughter was intense. Water reed crinkles again. I could drink his smile. "What brings you to Caye Caulker, Laelia?"

"Divorce. Exhaustion," I offered. He wanted more. "My sister. She's whisked me as far away from London as possible for sunshine and seafood. Mexico and Belize. Two weeks."

"She sounds like a great sister."

"You haven't met her."

Soft laughter. "I have a feeling I will." He sipped his drink.

Those eyes. The way he looked at me.

"Are you here by yourself?" I asked, wiping icy drips from my glass.

"I'm with old friends on vacation." He nodded towards the crowd, the throng of bodies and distant sparks of laughter. "But they're getting wasted and ripping on each other, and if she would like to, I'd rather spend my time drinking daiquiris with a literary-loving English orchid." He stared into the depths of me. Such blue eyes.

"So they won't mind you being here?" I asked. "With me?"

"They won't even notice I'm gone . . . And your sister?"

I felt a rub on my arm.

"She won't even notice I'm gone."

"Laelia?" A voice said. "We should go now . . ."

I blinked my eyes open a little. "Hmm?"

Aid was a shadow leaning over me, a chorus of birds singing behind him. "You fell asleep . . . We should get back. Get the kids some dinner."

I smiled, heaved in a gentle breath.

Such blue eyes.

Ellis

Mangrove Lodge, Stann Creek District, Belize
31st May 1986

She is intrigued by him, he's sure—interested in his orchids, and his papers, and his dreams. He's at ease like he hasn't been for years. She nurtures a warm curiosity in everything he shares with her. She is calm and intelligent, with an open heart and a tantalising laugh.

They've spent long days like this in each other's company, delighting in fresh friendship in the jungle and down by the lagoon; Ellis has shown her bromeliads and seedpods and flower pressings, Agapita has shown him tortillas and kohlrabi and corn coffee. He's been teaching her Latin names of plants; she's been teaching him Kriol (and more Spanish). She breathes life back into him, sharing simple pleasures and a passion for the earth. Nature binds them together like touch-me-nots.

He's met her older sisters, Dacey and Aapo, and her mother, Itzel. Her father passed not long ago. The mother is formidable, a hive of productivity and support. She involves her girls in everything—facilitating church workshops, counselling local drop-ins, selling bread and coconut oil—and herself in the details of their lives. They've started making jams and washing laundry for incapable expats across the lagoon, swapping scented sheets and smiles for US dollars. Ellis continues to scrub his own underwear. Itzel has invited him to their home to eat tamales, once and then not again. There's a tension between Agapita and her mother Ellis cannot fathom. An abrasive look here. A sorry glance there. He senses he is in the eye of an unsettling storm, though Agapita tells him not to worry, it's all just in his head. But Itzel is a force of nature, a mobiliser and advocate for local women, most especially her youngest daughter.

Once Ellis has shown Agapita some of the lodge rooms and all of the outbuildings, they bound back out into the clearing.

"So what do you think?" he asks, his skin flushing.

Agapita looks at him quizzically and gazes around. "You actually bought it?" A howler monkey barks somewhere.

"Have I lost my mind? It's such a slice of paradise. The mahoganies, the palms, the orchids. The river. The sea just beyond. There are bromeliads on the doorstep I've spent my whole career dreaming about . . . I can bring field teams back out here; the ethnobotanists will love it." Adams and Cribb wrote a paper on it last year; detailed how unexplored Belize is, taxonomically speaking. "The Chiquibul Forest is fairly well mapped, but they never made it down here and they're everywhere—there are orchids that haven't been classified yet, others that haven't even been discovered. I can be right at the centre of things. Imagine the species we might find . . . Besides, this place was a bargain." He looks around. "Maybe it *is* crazy . . ."

"It's not totally crazy."

"My impulses overtook my judgement . . . They do that sometimes."

She laughs, touches her throat. "I like a man who follows his instincts."

"I'm gabbling on. Sorry," he says. "It's the orchids . . . they're not like any other species on earth. They're mysterious and alluring, and well . . ."

"Addictive?"

"Yes. Addictive." He smiles. "Listen, I want to show you something."

Ellis leads her from the edge of the lagoon back into the forest, deep past the mango tree, and the gumbo limbos, and all the trailing climbers. On the way, he points out the leaf of the *Clidemia septuplinervia*, the buttressed roots of a kaway tree, the spikes of the *Cryosophila stauracantha*.

"The jungle seems so different through your eyes," she tells him as they walk.

He cleaves a piece of water vine with his machete, and they steer its magical liquid into each other's mouth. Agapita pulls cohune plants from the ground, and they pass each other its nutty insides. Eventually, they reach the mahogany.

Ellis points up to his crowning jewel: the most magnificent black orchid either of them has ever seen, its upside-down flowers perfect shell-like lips, the twists of their pale green sepals dancing midair.

"*Prosthechea cochleata.*"

Agapita gazes up. "Our national flower. Does it feed from the tree?" She brims with wonder.

"Epiphytic orchids like this, attached to a tree, they aren't parasites. They've adapted to take their water and nutrients from the air around . . . away from the threat of animal species or the competition of other plants on the ground." Ellis strokes at the petals, inhaling their gentle peppery fragrance. "Over the years, orchids have come to represent many things: power, violence, love . . ." He smiles at her. "The black orchid is full of mystery. They say it symbolises strength and determination. Rebirth."

Agapita leans in a little closer and strokes at the petals, too. "It's beautiful."

He breathes the scent of her: coconut and honey. She rotates towards him and kisses him on the cheek, and he turns, stumbles, and kisses her back on the mouth. It is even sweeter than he imagined it would be.

19

Laelia

Maybe we should stay?" I suggested one evening while the two of us were swaying together in the hammock.

Aid turned his head towards me. "What?" I'd been dreaming about the lodge, experimenting with ingredients, new dishes. I felt so inspired here, finally, again. "Really?"

"I mean, it's ridiculous to be paying London rent when we're not even there . . . maybe we should let the flat go? Not renew the rent? At least until we know what's happening with Dad." It was a half-formed idea, but there was something in it. I didn't want to go back to London, to its frenzy or its sounds. I didn't want to go back to working in cacophonous, pressure-cooker kitchens I couldn't hear in. "Maybe it's stupid," I said then.

"Maybe." He took a drag on his cigarette. "Are you sure?"

"Yeah, I mean . . . why not?"

He smoked, lost in thought. "I suppose I'm making good money here, and the kids are happier . . ." Ella seemed more relaxed, thinking less about the things that happened at school.

"If we stayed, what would we do with our stuff?" I asked. "In the flat?" But really, I was thinking about starting up my restaurant, the fact it would have to remain even longer in my head.

"We can organise someone to pack it all up, put it into storage. Better to pay to keep our shit in a warehouse in Essex than an empty flat in Forest Hill." Aid's tattooed arm wrapped around me, his hand warm over my breast. "The visas need renewing each month, but it's easy enough . . . But only if you're sure. A lot's gone on here, you know?" He was staring at me, his blue eyes piercing.

"I know. But I want to be with Dad."

Our half-abandoned life in London was haemorrhaging money. We needed to make some decisions, settle the kids properly here or there, one way or another. It felt like we'd never have enough to buy a place in London. Not now. We would be able to make a life in Belize, one we could actually afford. It wasn't really a decision for me anyway, I needed to stay. Dr. Guevarra was clear Dad would need more time. I would not leave him, could not. But for Aid, for the children, I knew it was best to make the decision. Stop the limbo. Plant some roots, at least for a while. Chloe could help with grabbing our personal items, my keepsakes and things—or maybe Tris could. Chloe might revel a bit too much in rifling through the drawers.

Six months or so, at least. A fresh start.

"I'm sure," I said. "The kids'll need to carry on with the homeschooling, but they'll probably do better. Ella's reading more here than she ever did in London." She'd been devouring Dad's botany papers and his history books as fast as she was the novels Chloe had posted on. "Dylan, too. He loves learning about the animals." And the Mayan culture, the cooking, and the politics. He was lapping it up. The school of real life: no screens, no distractions. In many ways it felt easier than London; away from the wordless, stressful tube journeys; the social media; the pace. The slog of survival there had been relentless, and we were tired. In Belize, life felt more connected without even being online. We were a family again, unsubscribed from the circus.

Spending time together, without the boys, was reenergising for Ella and for me. Falicia's brother, Dominik, let us on his boat—*Feelin' Nauti*—with a bunch of tourists venturing out to the Silk Cayes.

"You ladies are gonna love it," he promised, eyes sparkling with excitement. "Relaxin' all day . . ."

We soaked up the turquoise: drinking mocktails and cocktails, laughing and chatting like old friends, snacking on an endless sea of watermelons, and posing for hypercolour bikini selfies—pineapples held aloft like spiky crowns. *Only ever bears one fruit each year. They're bromeliads*, Dad would have told me for the umpteenth time.

Falicia was so gracious, so generous of spirit, taking Ella and me under her wing, guiding us through the pristine underwater, eyes wide, pointing out the stingrays and the nurse sharks and the majestic turtles swimming below in a cartoon reel of beauty. This was it. This was what we were here for, what we would stay for. All of this.

"Really?" Ella's face lit up. "We can stay?" She stroked dripping hair back out of her face, her girl-pink nails scratty like graffiti.

"We can stay," I repeated. "If you want to."

She pulled the snorkel mask off her forehead and tossed it down on the deck. "Yes! Yes." She leaned in and gave me a wet hug. "Thanks, Mum." Falicia climbed up the ladder onto the boat. She winked at me, her face spreading with an understanding smile. I could see she was relieved. I was relieved, too.

"But if you don't want to, we don't have to . . . We don't have to stay."

"I want to," Ella insisted. "I love it here. Everyone's so kind." Most of her friendships in London had diluted away. When the bullying started, only a couple of girls stuck with her, but she never seemed to hang out with them outside of school. She had spent most of her evenings online, texting and chatting to strangers, and I was not sorry that had all stopped.

"And how about you?" Falicia asked once Ella had jumped back overboard.

"How about me?"

"How are you feeling about staying?"

"I'm glad we're putting some roots down. I do love it here. I feel closer to my dad."

"And Aid?"

"Hmm?"

"How are things with him?"

"Oh, you know. He's Aid. He seems happier now we've got some income, now we've got a plan."

When we dropped Falicia home, I offered to give Christopher some cooking lessons—show him how to make pavlova, then she asked if I'd like to go with her and Mounia to the food festival in San Pedro.

"I'd love that," I said. The idea of a few days away on the beach with the girls, surrounded by Belizean food, filled my heart and made my taste buds tingle. I could pick up some local recipe books, some more herbs.

I was thinking about my life here coming together—the friends, the food—when Ella and I pulled back into the driveway, our half-wet hair drying frizzy, salt crystals still tingling on our skin. When I shut off the ignition, the noise was immediately replaced with loud, uneven sounds snapping sharp off in the distance. *Whracck.*

"What's that?" Ella asked me, eyes startled.

A sound. There was definitely a sound.

"I'm not sure," I said. "Stay here." I dropped my bag to the ground, rushing towards the noise—*Whracck*—following the ricochets—louder—to the trees—*Whracck. Whracck*—the sounds reverberating off the tinnitus in my head.

At the edge of the forest, I saw half a dozen or so fat watermelons, doomed soldiers lined up along a fallen trunk. Aid appeared, bare-chested, sporting dark combats and aggressively honed biceps. The metal of unfamiliar shooting glasses reflected photoelectric in the dying sunlight, burning into my eyes. And then I saw it. An assault rifle. Black as a nightmare.

"Aid," I shouted. "What are you doing?" But he couldn't hear me, too focused on his targets.

Whracck. Whracck. Whracck. The melons blew wide apart into smithereens, a mess of flesh smattering outwards, flung in all directions into the trees, their urgent brightness oozing down the mahoganies. Soft sludgy tissue.

Insides out, exploded green carcasses lay obliterated on the ground. I saw Dylan then, under the trees watching from the shadows, his eyes saucer wide.

"Where did you get it?" I asked once the kids had gone to bed.

"Borrowed it," Aid said dismissively.

"Who from?"

"Does it matter?"

"Yes, it matters. Of course it matters . . ." I poured myself a large glass of red, filling it fast to near the brim before taking a giant mouthful. Aid turned his back to me, made a faux-charade of starting the drying up. I tried again, slamming the bottle back down on the countertop. "Dylan's eight! What were you thinking?"

"I didn't let him shoot it. He was only watching . . ."

Aid knew I hated guns. We'd spoken about it many times, too many times: how frightening the States felt now; how tormented; how we would never move there. Each time shaky cell phone footage overtook the airwaves—flooded social media—parading too many sirens, too many flashing lights; each time another trigger-happy shooter decided to let rip, spattering his angst all over a previously forgettable small town that would never be forgotten again; another one. Again. And again. And again. I thought he hated them, too.

"God, Lil, you sound crazy."

"Did you let him hold it?" I asked, my heart still cantering.

"I got it for hunting . . . I was trying it out." He seemed more American than British to me then; more like his father—an unknown man I'd sketched in my mind through ragged threads. Aid barely ever talked about him.

"Did. You. Let. Him. Hold. It?"

Silence. Aid just stared.

"Get rid of it," I spat. "Why do you even need it?"

"Shit, Lil, you're overreacting. We're in Belize. Everyone here's got a gun. We might need it, scare off people like that trespa—"

"Get rid of it!" I shot him a look. Everyone here did not have a gun. Henry had told me how hard it was to get a licence here. Not like in America, thank God.

Aid tossed down the tea towel and flung his palms up, fixing his eyes on the floor. "Okay, okay. I'm sorry. I will."

I downed the rest of my wine. We both knew he would not.

Nr. Mangrove River Village, Stann Creek District, Belize
23rd September 1986

An ink-filled night, Cualli leads them like shadows, edging the blackened jungle where the jaguars roam, to Kantun's isolated hut. By day, they tell Ellis, Kantun practises medicinal healing, all herbs and roots and leaves. By night—it is said—he is magical beyond belief. At least, that's what they say.

Ellis grasps Agapita's hand tightly—trying to offset her pain with a pathetic show of strength. She is struggling to walk, stopping every few steps to search for breath against the hard support of a mahogany or a Santa Maria, or to lean farther into his chest, as they stumble together through the undergrowth.

The forest smells stronger in the darkness. Soil and decay; the pungent smell of life. Powerful sounds of night birds, and crickets, and unknown hidden creatures. He can feel his heart beating strong, pounding like gunfire, pumping a river of blood around his veins, flickering kinetic. And it isn't just the cocaine, although that helps. Everything feels more alive in the dead of night.

Cualli hacks through the forest ahead, clearing a sort of path as best she can in the trying light of their kerosene lamps. The vines grow fast here, as if before your eyes. She says there was a route through this way days ago. Though you wouldn't know it. All the while Ellis is wary of all the things he cannot see. "At night, there's always a Tommy Goff close," Cualli had warned them before they set out. "If you get bitten, we'll kill the snake. The poison travels slow." Then she told them not to worry; they were on their way to the medicine man anyway, and snakebites are rare. But Ellis is not convinced. He has heard stories of men—athletic, robust men—stricken down by a single zap from the fer-de-lance, their flesh stripped away to reveal hard bones and soft tendons, pulsing muscles and shredded nerves. In the middle of the night the jungle is not for man, and definitely not for a fucked-up Englishman. He is still adapting to this land in the daytime; still learning its secrets, its mysteries, its dangers. He is not ready for its nighttime surprises, the ones he cannot stop pondering about.

Agapita, though, is concerned with other things. She told him an old Mayan woman warned her once; evil things are set into being on a Tuesday.

She had screamed like a howler monkey. In the early hours of the night, after Monday had closed its eyes and slipped away, a jolting pain in her stomach piercing her awake. At first, he thought she must have eaten something bad, some rotten meat or mouldy fruit, but they had shared the same meals. In the shadowed light of the hut, her forehead grew thick with sweat, patterned into rivulets and heavy creases.

"I'll fetch your mother," Ellis had told her.

"No," Agapita shook her head.

"Your sisters?"

"No, please. Please, not them."

"But they know you're here."

She shakes her head again.

Ellis instead ran to Polo's but he was away visiting his brother, so Ellis woke Cualli. It needed a local's eye, a woman's touch.

Together they sat over Agapita in the shadows, assessing the gravity of the moment. She whimpered, writhing like an animal, unable to find comfort. They could do little to ease her pain, cold washcloths and lemon balm tea laughable in their inadequacies.

When they noticed the sheet, bespeckled with bright red blots, Cualli—covering over the scene so as not to alert Agapita—insisted, pleading with her eyes: We need to get her to Kantun. Now.

"Not long now," Cualli cries out. She pauses, catching her breath.

Agapita leans back against a tree. A chance for Ellis to take a little extra bump from his pocket. Good to keep alert. It is always laboured progress macheting through the jungle—even in daylight, but under the cover of darkness, it is torturously slow.

When, finally, they emerge into a clearing and arrive at the hut, Cualli knocks at the door. Inside it is darker even than the moonlit-soaked outside. Their lamps illuminate a serene scene. There are no candles, no rum and puros, no dead crow's feet. Everything is settled and still, the room no larger than Ellis's bathroom in England. Wooden chopping blocks are piled high in the corner next to sacks stuffed with leaves and corn; dried herbs hang from the low ceiling over a clay hearth. Agapita moans and collapses into him, and he helps her slide down into a chair.

A man appears, all crinkled skin and bony edges. He scuttles through from a side room holding a thick candle.

"Cualli?" He blinkers his eyes.

"Si. Kantun, por favor ayuda. My friend Agapita, she woke with belly pain. I told her you can fix her." Cualli's voice breaks.

Kantun looks over towards the white man in the shadows. "Who is this?" he asks in Kriol.

"My name is Ellis. I live outside the village."

"How long have you been in Belize?"

He doesn't want to think too much about how little time he has left. "Five or six months. I am studying the flora."

Kantun looks unimpressed.

"I am from Oxford University," Ellis adds.

Kantun looks even more unimpressed. "Bring her here." He signals towards the room he has come from.

Ellis gathers Agapita into his arms, carrying her through onto a low bed. When Kantun asks, Ellis nods, saying he is a believer in all that he is, all that he does. As cynical as he is about everything otherworldly, in this land he is yet to fully apprehend, caution tells him to leave a little room for the unexplainable. Just in case.

The old man waves his hand, ushering them to leave. Ellis and Cualli shuffle back into the entry room where a wizened woman appears, plump and wrapped in a rebozo shawl, her gentle eyes brightening the darkness. She squeezes lime into squat glasses and laces them with sugar. They sit in soft silence on tree-hard stools, sipping sweet juice in the half-light, waiting, waiting, blinking sleepiness away.

Ellis lets the cocaine wear off, lets night dissolve into day.

When the old man finally emerges, the morning is bursting slivers of light through the cracks in the door.

His eyes dart back and forth between them. "How long has she been with child?"

"With child?" Ellis asks, his voice breaking reluctantly into the day.

"She is pregnant. Two or three months, I think."

And just like that, the world seems to stop

. . . to forget how to breathe.

20

Laelia

Nr. Mangrove River Village, Stann Creek District, Belize
16th March 2023

T he babies bled away to nothing. She'd told me, even with the endless tonics of hibiscus flowers, ginger, and white China root, the miscarriages had continued anyway; showed no constraint. So Falicia was as sceptical now as I was about the medicine man—his spells and herbs and potions, and probably scared to get pregnant again, but Henry had pleaded for her to go back. "Well, his mother really. He's been begging me for her," Falicia said. "She's desperate for a grandchild. But I'm not so young, not so fertile anymore. I cannot carry on trying forever."

Falicia wanted me to go with her. She had done so much for me, I wanted to help her in any small way I could. So we packed up our daypacks and macheted our way through the forest, snaking to find trails I'd never seen before. I'd spotted other signs for herbal healers—Mayan clinics and the like—along the roadways, in easily accessible buildings in concrete, with actual driveways you could park in. I couldn't understand why we didn't visit any one of them. We could have driven. "There are lots of medicinal folk around here," Falicia explained. "But this man, he's the oldest and the best."

It took a couple of hours to reach a clearing, a tiring slog through choking trees. The hut stood immersed in greenery, thick with foliage, as if it had been born from the soil itself. Knocking, Falicia pushed the door wide open.

The waiting area was a low-ceilinged room, its colours muted like an old oil painting. Dried herbs hung over a hearth laden with sacks, plump with mystery, that rested against a solitary chair. Falicia told me this hut had been here since before her mother was born. I imagined all the people who must have sat here waiting over the years, the decades. The hurt these walls must have witnessed. The desperation, the hope, the pain.

The only internal door opened, and an elderly man shuffled in across the timber floor. A wide smile made his face seem younger, sparked his eyes into life.

"Weh di go aan?" He waved his hand towards the next room, and we followed him inside. The walls were lined with shelves upon shelves of concoctions: dried leaves, tubs and tinctures. He handed us each a small clay cup brimming with warm, cinnamon liquid. "Atole. Corn drink."

Falicia smiled at me. "Kantun, this is my friend. Laelia."

He looked me up and down. "Laelia? Like the orchids."

I took a quick sip, which comforted milky-sweet on my tongue. "My father was a botanist, and my mother didn't have much say."

"Mothers often don't," he said, fixing his eyes on Falicia, his subject. He beckoned her onto a low-slung bed, and she lay still, expectantly.

Chloe told me my mother had wanted to name me Valerie—strong and brave and fierce. My father, though, had not. He wanted something floral again after Chloe, a tribute to nature—wild and free.

"You take the hogweed?" Kantun asked.

"I drink it as you said."

"Boiling the branches, starting nine days before your bleed?"

"Every day."

Kantun gathered up Falicia's shirt, felt at her stomach. "You will be more fertile."

Falicia sighed. "Really? Because I'm getting pretty tired of all this." Tears were welling up in her eyes. "My body doesn't want to be pregnant."

"Maybe it doesn't . . ." he said. "And maybe you don't."

"What do you mean?" she asked, sitting upright.

Kantun stopped, turned to face her with his whole being. "Not everything bad that happens to us is predetermined, or even happens to us at all . . . We often forget the power we have over ourselves."

"You think it's my fault?" Falicia asked, her voice breaking. She looked at me, searchingly, and started to get up from the bed as if we were about to leave.

"Look, she's desperate," I started. Kantun ignored me, selecting glass pots to take down from a shelf. "She's come here looking for help, begging for answers, and you're—"

"It's not your fault, mija," he said calmly. "You don't know what you want."

She stopped, sat back down on the couch, then stared back at him. "I don't . . . I don't know what I want."

"Your body doesn't know either," he said. Falicia nodded then looked at me. Kantun placed some roots and herbs into a paper bag. "We must be honest with ourselves and listen to our hearts . . . There's no shame in fear. Healing is born from acceptance."

He turned to me, opened up my hand, and placed the bag into my palm. It was only then I realised he'd been talking to me.

I organised a dive trip to the Blue Hole with Dominik. I'd been asking Aid about it for ages, but he didn't seem like he wanted to go, always brushing me off when I suggested it, so I went ahead and booked us up. I wondered if he was worried about the money, or was hoping for a freebie, but in the event, he revelled in peeling out notes to Dominik at breakfast. Money didn't seem to be an object now; Aid enjoyed throwing it around.

I'd wanted to do this, spend time together without the kids, live out the lie and make it real; do what we were already supposed to have done. Except then Aid invited his workmates along with us. They carried the extra beer.

Benny was rugged, North American—early fifties, maybe, rocked up to the dive school wearing a filthy shirt that used to be cream, possibly. I recognised him but couldn't place him. His pot belly hung over his trunks. With his shaggy, long hair and defined, angular looks, he was probably quite handsome once.

Nico was French; "French Nico" they called him with self-satisfied originality, and I'm sure I saw him wince. He was younger with gentle eyes, softly spoken. He bought everyone coffee, even the Canadians we'd all just met, before we got onto the boat.

The plankton burst below us like dotted stars, like space. Deep, deep space. It was darker than I imagined it would be, colder. Emptier. The sea has a way of making you feel so small—alone—and I had to keep reminding myself Aid was right there, bobbing along next to me there, just there. Metres away. Still there.

OK?

OK.

In the photos—the aerial ones on the glossy guidebook covers, and on the posters plastered over tourist shop boards all over the cayes, the Blue Hole always looked so blue; but it was almost black.

I was always nervous on a dive; always felt the butterflies flitting like krill in my stomach. I felt them swarm heavier today. Even with the other divers so close, the moment of descent felt instantly isolating. And quiet. The muting of the senses—the cut of speech, the lack of sound—so sudden. But the tinnitus still there, always there, hissing like an oxygen leak.

OK?

OK.

I'd never dived this depth before. I hadn't dived any depth for years, not since the last time I was on holiday with Chloe. Although of course I didn't actually dive the Blue Hole then, despite what I'd told her. I'd been too busy fucking Aid—being irresponsible and slutty—because I'd never been that before.

OK? Dominik signalled.

OK, Aid signed.

OK, I copied. *Okay.*

Floating through the inky abyss, I wondered what it was like for everybody else, everyone who didn't have voltage hurtling through their heads. Was the silence ever really silent? Calm? I couldn't remember.

There was nothing much to see; the rough coral wall to our left and darkness all around, ghost-like plankton shooting in front of my mask. Everything endless.

There was a clang. I looked up, across. Dominik banging on his tank. He pointed. Down there. Deep to our right, a dark silhouette—a shark piloting through the water, circling in the void. And another, and another. Suddenly there were a dozen. More. Reef sharks and nurse sharks and black tips everywhere. Such strong, majestic shapes. It was incredible to see them so close, to be immersed so entirely in their eerie quiet world, which was most definitely theirs.

OK?

OK.

It was over so quickly, Dominik signalling to start our ascent. No faster than thirty feet per minute. Slowly. Slowly. Stop there. Safety stop, fifteen feet under or thereabouts. That bit always felt so long. Floating about vertical in solid blue space, watching the bubbles dance, waiting, waiting, waiting, thinking about the secrets the ocean held down there.

We sat together on the beach over lunch: Aid and Benny, Nico and me. Dominik was busy entertaining the other four guys, the Canadians, and checking the equipment before our second dive.

"Are you okay?" Aid asked me again, twisting the watch on his wrist. "Was it okay?"

I nodded. "It was beautiful."

"It's not weirding you out or anything?"

I shook my head. "Why would it weird me out?" Sharks didn't make me nervous. Not in their world, safe like a womb. I'd always loved the magic of the ocean, the privilege of seeing close up how everything teemed with the mystery of life, the curious beauty of it all.

"It's the Aquarium next, no?" Nico asked, forking at the snapper on his plate. Dominik had briefed us about it this morning. The Blue Hole first, lunch, then a longer dive on the western side of the Lighthouse Reef Atoll.

"It's awesome. I dived it when I first moved here," said Benny, leaning back on his elbow on the blanket next to Aid. "Tons of parrotfish and sea urchins and shit." I really felt like I knew him from somewhere.

"I dived it before," Aid said, turning to Benny.

I dropped my fork. "You've dived here before?"

Aid paused and swigged his beer. "When we first met . . ." he said, rubbing his eyebrow. "After you'd flown home, me and some of the guys went out." His college buddies he was there with, the ones I never got to meet.

"You never told me that."

Did Aid just roll his eyes at me?

"The Aquarium dive, it's beautiful . . ." Nico beamed.

No-one said anything, so I smiled back. Benny and Aid carried on talking about poisonous animals—which were the most lethal, the most likely to kill—and I tucked back into my plate. The fish fell apart.

Nico leaned in closer. "Do you dive often, Laelia?" My name melted like butterscotch around his soft French accent.

"Not really. Dad and I were supposed to dive here together when I came to Caye Caulker before, but we ran out of time. He did the Blue Hole without me."

Nico rubbed at the label on his beer bottle. "It's a shame. Aid said your dad is in the hospital?"

I laid my plate down on the sand and gazed over at Aid, who was busy laughing with Benny. And finally, I realised where I knew him from. He was the man who was naked that day, hiding in the sauna with that woman at the mansion.

"He had a stroke."

"I'm sorry," Nico said, looking deep into my eyes. "That must be hard for you." He spoke with so much conviction, such kindness. I wanted to smile, but the muscles around my mouth rallied against me. I couldn't counteract the tears. I couldn't hide them, and Nico saw. He reached across and squeezed my shoulder. Over a swig of beer, Aid's eyes met mine, his smile dissolving.

"Guys enjoyin' your snapper?" Dominik shouted, pounding back up the beach. "When you finish, stick it in the trash there and we'll get back on the boat. Head for the Aquarium, yeah?"

Only then did Aid break my gaze. "Yeah," he said, standing, picking up the empty beer bottles and launching them towards the bin. "Thanks, Dom."

I knew the Aquarium dive would feel easier, safer. It would be shallower and brighter, full of picture-perfect fish. I was looking forward to it—now I was into the swing of things and had reminded myself how everything worked.

"*Feelin' Nauti*?! Fucking funny, that. Did you come up with that, Dom?" Benny asked, flicking his cigarette ash over the side of the boat.

"Nah. I bought her like that," Dominik shouted above the *put-put-put* of the engine, which was slowing to a halt. "She was already naughty." Benny and the Canadians all laughed. I pulled the bikini straps off my shoulders and massaged more lotion over my skin. Benny and Nico were watching me, Aid watching them.

The ignition switched off, leaving only the sound of the ocean—which I couldn't really hear, and the tinnitus pulsing through my head—which I really could. There were a few seconds of calm before everyone started bustling, the Canadians suddenly animated, grabbing fins and belts and jackets. I started looking for my wetsuit.

"Can you pass that mask?" Benny asked, as we shuffled awkwardly around each other, squeezed in at the back of the boat. I bent over to pick it up, and as I did, Nico brushed up against me. I felt his hand on my coccyx as he tried to steady himself. The boat, bobbing up, bobbing down, threw him back towards me and we collapsed into each other on the seat.

"Careful, man," Benny said, and I'm sure I saw him winking. Prat.

"I'm sorry," Nico said quickly, rebalancing himself. He held out his hand to help me back up. A show of apology. Aid was watching, an earnestness overtaking his face I'd never seen before.

I smiled at Nico. "No worries. Just an accident." Aid's face hadn't changed. "It's so choppy," I added, but Aid's face stayed cemented.

"Dude, what you doin'?" he said loudly. Everything cut to silence. I stared at the deck. I couldn't look up.

"It was an accident," Nico said. "I slipped."

I glanced at the Canadians. They'd all stopped fussing over equipment, their hands halted midair—weight belts held out to one another—exchanging concerned looks. They were all staring at Aid, at Nico, at whatever was about to go down.

Aid was right up in Nico's face.

"Aid," I said calmly, but he didn't flinch. "Aid . . . ?"

"I said it was an accident," Nico said again.

Dominik stepped towards them. "Guys, what's going on?"

"Nothing," said Aid. "A misunderstanding." He finally broke his iron gaze. "Nothing." He forced an exaggerated smile, came over to stand next to me, everyone still watching. He helped me into my wetsuit as the eyes finally left us and everyone carried on, the quiet deafening still.

Dominik distributed the cylinders, breaking the silence with an overly cheery tone. "Same buddies as before, okay?" People nodded, organising themselves along the edge of the boat, readying to roll backwards.

Neoprened up again, I went through the protocol in my head: buoyancy aid, weights, releases, air, check the gauges and double-check again. I turned to Aid to buddy check with him.

He grabbed my regulator and took a couple of deep breaths through it. "Okay?"

I narrowed my eyes, scowling, but he barely noticed. "Okay," I said, but I was far from okay.

"Is this too much for you?" he asked. I couldn't bear to answer, couldn't look at him.

There was a part of me that felt it—sensed it—before I thought it: *Tamper with the equipment, turn the valve off on the air cylinder. So easy. No-one would even know.* I wasn't sure where the idea came from, the image of twisting the cylinder valve like that. If I'd imagined it before, maybe. If it was a dream.

As quickly as I'd seen it in my mind, before I'd even finished thinking it, I knew it was ludicrous, one of those insane fantasies everyone has sometimes—like overturning the steering wheel to send you to the other side to hurtle into oncoming traffic, before you've even had time to think. Everyone has those kinds of thoughts from time to time, don't they? Don't they? When you've thought the thought—actually thought it through— you think in slow motion, you rationalise it steadily; I would never do it. I couldn't actually do it. I'm not a crazy bitch.

"What the fuck was that?" I asked as soon as Benny and Nico had jumped out of the truck.

"What was what?" Aid asked, eyes on the road.

"You know what. On the boat. With Nico. What the fuck, Aid?"

"It was a joke."

"It wasn't funny. It was so unlike you. Benny's . . . well, he's something.

But Nico, he's actually nice. Why would you do that? It was an accident, and—"

"It was a joke, Lil," he said again. "I'm sorry. You're right. It wasn't funny."

No kidding. It wasn't funny at all.

I awoke in the early hours, Aid restless in his sleep. I thought I'd heard him shouting out my name, groaning, but when I opened my eyes he was silent, frowning softly in the half-light, peaceful. Maybe I'd dreamt it. Maybe it wasn't my name.

I couldn't get back off again, taunted by a relentless thrum of crickets and cicadas, the whoops of howler monkeys and distant creatures I couldn't quite place. I stared at Aid's face—disturbed but still sleeping, and—where he'd wrestle-kicked the sheet down—his broad chest, his arms, his hips. The body art seemed to dance, alive in the moonlight, the slates and blacks and greys whirling magic over his skin. "Bodies are blank pages left to be filled with the ink of our souls," he'd told me before he kissed me in some graffitied alley in Brighton, after we'd gone together to stamp love on our skin. I'd gotten my two tiny feathers, entwined forever, on the inside of my wrist. Aid had sketched out a swirling font, "no apologies" (all lowercase) to add to his collection, which he got inked into a gap on his spine.

The full-throttled whistling of some bird or other pierced through the chorus, and I turned again on the pillow. Aid sighed in his sleep, let out a turbulent snore. With my finger I traced over my wrist, making out the greying edges in the moonlight. It was quiet, the artwork with its soft feather shapes, but it played off the silence I'd already edited before. I remembered; later Aid had told me another thing: "Tattoos are there to document your regrets."

Sleep ran away from me. Restless, I got up and wandered out with my torch. I was spending more and more time in Dad's study, especially at night. When everyone else was asleep, it was just me and the jungle. And Dad. Then everything felt more alive. Sensing the same senses he must have sensed, right there, I felt near to him, close to his essence.

Picking up a well-thumbed copy of one of Dad's books, *The Orchid*

Hunters, I flicked through the pages. A biro'ed heart in the margin sign-posted a passage he'd double underlined: ". . . when a man falls in love with orchids, he'll do anything to possess the one he wants. It's like chasing a green-eyed woman or taking cocaine . . . it's a sort of madness . . ." Amen. Dad had always had a passion for orchids, beyond anything else. I picked up on it, what people said, especially after Mum died. The orchids came first. They always would.

Drinking his rum, filling his ashtray, listening to his records; it felt like gentle communion—with him, with myself. Leafing through books under candlelight, I thought I might find something worth finding; I didn't know what. Dad was a prolific writer. Scribbled over everything: textbooks, novels, scrappy bits of errant paper. I couldn't believe he wouldn't have kept a journal. His life was constantly writing, observing. Surely, he would have written diaries. In this cacophony of a room though, it was hard to find anything, including the key to his safe. I knew it would be somewhere obvious once I'd found it. Somewhere purposeful. Somewhere meaningful. Somewhere close.

Mangrove Lodge, Stann Creek District, Belize
15th October 1986

Ellis removes his latest pressed cutting, a fine example of *Epidendrum ibaguense* he has collected from the highest reaches of the Mountain Pine Ridge Reserve, so common in so much of Central America, though rare in Belize. He sketches into his notebook, letting his mind wander as he adds the orange watercolour wash.

Agapita is outside the window, hanging sheets up on the line. She's spending more time here at the lodge now, much to her mother's distaste.

Each morning he awakes feeling happy, full of longing, until he remembers what he has done, and his heart sinks from his chest down into his stomach, and he feels nauseous with deceit. He has told no-one.

Agapita is blooming, bursting with life like a water lily. Whereas Helena had been like a yeasty loaf of bread, both times. She said it herself: "Twice risen." She said she felt encumbered, barrelled up like Plath's cow in calf. No longer herself.

It was not long into the second trimester with Chloe when the fainting spells started, the anxiety, the sleepless nights. Watkins had said it was common; normal to feel unable to cope with all the changes, none of it unexpected. After Chloe came, it felt like things were getting better, like Helena was getting better. Walks in the woods, trips to the beach, bubbles at bath time. They were a proper little family, for a time. But then from nowhere, even the littlest thing would suddenly overwhelm her. A nappy change might reduce her to tears. She would find no joy pushing swings or feeding pigeons in the park. A baby's cry could push her over the edge she was always teetering on. Breastfeeding hurt. Worry stuck tight to her like a friendless friend. She was terrified of falling pregnant again. And when she did, Watkins prescribed new pills of magic salvation; *bottled sunshine*, she called it, and she was able to smile real smiles once more.

Helena coped. She was coping. And she had been so much better since. Until he came out here, and things started unravelling.

He's sure she must be self-medicating again.

He can feed the pain no longer, this much he knows. She is not the woman he married; she is not the Helena he knew. Where they are submerged—trying not to drown—with Agapita, he floats. He stares out the window at her now as she pegs a shirt up on the line.

The truth cannot survive in the shade. It searches out the light it needs, forges itself a way. As much as Ellis knows it will rip through Helena's soul—and he knows it will—he must tell her. He owes her that much, at least. It will set them both free.

He watches Agapita, her dress billowing over her bump in the breeze. Who will this child be? What will they become? Will they have his nose? Her sea green eyes? Her smile?

He places the herbarium sheet flat and closes his sketchbook.

He will bike to the pay phone tomorrow to call Helena.

21

Laelia

Is Aid back for dinner?" Ella asked, pulling a tangle of knives and forks from the drawer. The silvered scars on her forearms shone like lenticels on a birch.

"No, I don't think so, hon," I said, blowing steam across the spoon before sampling my stew chicken. More salt, another couple of minutes. If Aid wasn't back by suppertime, he'd likely be out until the early hours at least. It happened a couple of times a week, and he would never let me know in advance. Even if he was able to call, my phone reception was so crap I barely bothered to turn it on now. The work Aid was doing seemed ad hoc, whatever Hector asked them to do each day: lugging plants, building new greenhouses, taking old ones apart. That was all local. Sometimes Aid would come home for lunch. Sometimes he wouldn't go to work at all. Sometimes he'd take a trip into Placencia or up to Belmopan with Benny to scout for materials, or to the Jaguar Lodge "for a change of scene," to cool down with a beer or three. Hector was obsessed with his flowers, he'd barely ever leave them unattended, so they'd take it in turns—the men who worked for him—to watch over them. Twenty-four / seven. Aid said it was the easiest money he'd ever made.

The door flung open. Dylan stood, Ursula barking behind him, silhouetted by the fading sun. "Mum, there's a truck coming up the drive-way." We weren't expecting anyone. We watched from the veranda as a battered pickup propelled its way towards us, its engine roaring. It was going far too fast. "Who is it?"

"I'm not sure," I said, though I could see Aid clearly in the passenger seat clinging to the grab handle. There was the driver—was that Benny?—and someone else in the back, all three being tossed about by the bumps, laughing. Drunk; I could tell before Aid had even fallen out the door.

"They were caning it." Ella smirked.

"Yes, they were." *In more ways than one.*

I heard Aid calling after me, "Laeeeeeeeeelia." Definitely drunk. I lit a cigarette, took a long drag.

"Hey, guys," Benny said, jumping out the truck clutching a near-empty bottle of whisky and a smouldering cigar.

Nico walked around from the other side, dressed in a sculpting grey T-shirt and cargos, a single metal chain hanging from his neck. He grinned widely. "Hi, Laelia." Definitely all drunk, though he seemed more composed than the other two.

I forced a smile and said, "Hi." They palmed their hands up at me, and Benny flicked his dead cigar butt into the trees.

Though he was swaying from side to side, Aid's feet stayed locked on the ground, as if waiting for permission to come up onto the decking, as if knowing I was less than impressed. "We're staaaarving, Lil . . ."

I didn't react.

"There's nothing at Hector'sss but nachos." Aid was keeling side to side, his head flopping to his shoulder. "Can we . . . get sssomething?"

I took a deep breath.

"Are you *deaf*, Laelia?" he barked. "I said, can we get sssomething to eat . . . ? I was telling them whaatt . . . whaatt a great chef you are. Said you'd make something for usss."

"Is that okay?" Nico asked, shuffling his heavy booted feet. He seemed embarrassed by his complicity in this presumptuous plan. "It was Hec-tor's anniversary, so we were celebrating, but he passed out . . . But we can go, I can take them if—"

"Sure." I nodded, taking a drag of my cigarette. "Come in," I said, as if I had a choice. "We were about to sit down."

There was barely enough for all of us. The kids had a big lunch and weren't that hungry, so I gave them smaller portions first. They were so distracted by the novelty of these strange visitors they didn't notice. Aid was so pissed he didn't notice either. He got the smallest dollop, dumped on his plate like an afterthought. With my back turned, I helped myself to a massive spoonful. And an extra-large glass of wine. The good one, the one we'd been saving to have together. After the kids finished up, I sent them off to bed. I didn't want them around Aid any longer.

"Laelia, this is incredible," Nico said. The men slopped the stew into their faces with urgent attention. Benny let sauce dribble down his chin. Spat while he ate. Spoke while he spat. I could tell he was a man who had known things, seen things, done things. His hands were unapologetic. Hardened with dirt, his skin was callused and sagging, his nails thick and ridged. He tongued at his lips, wet and repulsive, in between desperate shovels of food. Every now and again he would hold a scrap of tortilla under the table, offering it to Ursula then snatching it back away, then forward, then back, until she barked, until he laughed and threw it across the room. Aid was deep into his food, too pissed to notice.

Nico was looking at me, gauging my reaction. "Don't do that," he told Benny with urgent eyes.

"He likes it," Benny answered, dropping his fork to the plate.

"She," I said.

"She does not like it," Nico insisted. "Have some respect."

Benny gave Ursula a final piece of flatbread, dropping it straight into her mouth. He pushed his plate away, pulling a cigar from his breast pocket. Producing a straight cutter from his jeans, with a theatrical push, he guillotined it across the cap of his cigar. It crunched to a snap. He picked up his beer and headed outside.

"Sorry," Nico said, just to me.

I shook my head gently. "It's okay."

"He's drunk. But it's no excuse. She's a dog."

"It's okay. Really."

Aid was leaning back in his chair, his eyes drooping, half asleep.

"You wear aids for your hearing?" Nico asked, pointing at my ears. He was the only person who'd ever noticed.

I rubbed the back of my neck, realising I'd left my hair up in a bun. "I . . . I'm losing the highest pitches."

He smiled. "They suit you well."

The men ate, and smoke, and drank—and God knows what—deep into the night. I sloped off, nestling together with the kids in Dad's room, Dylan letting me cuddle into him without a fuss. I lay wondering what I'd done bringing them here, whether I shouldn't have kept them in school in London, found a way to make it work, juggle seeing Dad with staying in England; I considered a thousand alternative scenarios, but everything always came back to the impossibility of motherhood.

Taking out my aids, my hearing dampened, but not enough. I could still hear the heavy laughter, the stale singing the other side of the door.

Anyone who's had a few drinks thinks they know what it is to be out of control. Most don't, though, not really. But Aid did. He had seen it—felt it—up close. He didn't talk about him much—other than to say he was a waste of life that had wasted his life and drained it out of everyone else around him—he didn't have to. I could read between the lines. The only thing Aid was terrified of was becoming like his father.

I pushed my earplugs into my ears, listening to my tinnitus until my heart stopped racing and I fell raggedly to sleep.

At sunrise, the howler monkeys barking and the cockerel crowing, I slid out of bed, trying not to wake the kids. I pulled my hearing aids from their case, but they had no charge. Drained of battery, the switch was turned off at the wall. But I was sure I'd turned them on the night before. I flashed to what I had to do that day, who I would have to talk to, what I might misunderstand.

I sloped into the living space reluctantly, girding myself for the aftermath: the sea of empty beer bottles, cigarette butts, and dirty plates. But there was nothing. It was spotless. Gleamingly clean, someone had cleared up. Everything. And I could have kissed him.

But it was near-silent, and Aid and the others had already left.

When I came home midafternoon from the supermart, I found Aid chopping wood. "Okay?"

I nodded. "You . . . ?"

"I'm good. I fixed the sink."

"You were really drunk."

"Leave it out, Lil. It was Hector's birthday."

"You embarrassed me."

He froze, his axe midair. "I didn't mean to. I'm sorry."

"You called me 'deaf.'"

"Did I?" He flung the axe to the ground, wiped the sweat from his forehead with his bandanna. "Like I said, I'm sorry." He picked up the few pieces of wood he'd chopped, started assembling them in his arms. "It was only meant as a joke. Can you help?"

I picked up a couple of pieces, stacked them onto the pile. He suggested we meet the kids in the village, go for a swim before dinner.

Aid walked in front of me through the forest, carrying his machete. He hacked at vines every now and again, but he didn't really need to, the track being so well walked by us all. I trailed him, his back slick with sweat, his tattoos dancing in the verdant sunlight.

"Aid?"

"Yeah?"

"You're not still doing coke, are you? It's just drinking, right?"

He turned to look at me as I jumped the gnarling buttress of a mahogany. "What?"

"I know it's been stressful, coming here, but I don't want you doing that around the kids."

"I'm not. We were having a good time. I—"

"I know, I get it. It's just, you've never spoken to me like that before. Like you did last night."

He stopped. Shot me a look. "I was drunk. I'm sorry. Can you stop?"

"I know you're doing this for me. You're here for me, but—"

"I was trying to switch off a bit. Forget about things."

"By drinking . . . ? You drank quite a lot." *You're drinking quite a lot.*

I felt a sudden jolt. I skidded across the soil, found myself plummeting forward, the duff of leaves enlarging before my eyes. I thudded, sprawling to the earth. I managed to shove my elbow to the ground just quickly enough to shield my face from a broken branch. Shards of splintering wood narrowly missed my eye.

The pain struck instantly. I looked up and Aid was standing over me, his silhouette blocking out the tree-speckled sun. For a split second, I could have sworn he looked like Simon. Almost a grimace.

"Did you push me?" I asked without thinking, dabbing at the urgent red of my elbow.

Aid looked confused. "What? No . . . Of course not." *Crazy bitch.* He reached out his hand, grabbed at mine to help. "Are you okay?"

I staggered up, nodding, brushing the debris off my clothes. "I think so." My flesh stung red raw.

"You took a tumble. Here . . ." He untied his bandanna, pressing it upon my elbow, gently, before he kissed into my hair. "It's not too bad. I think you tripped on that root."

I glanced over but I couldn't see it. I must have lost my footing. I took over holding the cloth.

After dinner, once he'd put away the chickens, Aid found me in the bedroom changing the plaster on my arm. He slunk in next to me, kissed at my neck and down my shoulder. He kissed at my elbow, stroking round the scabbing blood.

"Does it still hurt?" he whispered.

I shook my head.

"You've got to be more careful."

I nodded, tears in my eyes. He placed the new plaster over the cut, then kissed me again. We made love—soft and steady and fierce, our breath like ocean waves. Then we held each other tightly until we fell to hungry sleep.

22

The festival was incredible; an abundance of gourmet and street food to a soundtrack of soca, punta, and Latin beats. Tonic for the stomach and for the soul.

Mounia spun her miniature wooden spoon through her fingers. "It's tickling my taste buds." She laughed, licking the ice cream. "Soooo good."

I delved into my cardboard tub—felt the sweet cold, the honeycomb popping on my tongue. "Hokeypokey," Chloe had told me Mum used to call it. I remembered having it as child, how strong the flavour was. At catering school, we were told a child has ten thousand taste buds. Babies are more attuned to sweetness; it makes them more receptive to their mother's milk. Then, as we grow older, our taste buds shrink and things don't taste as sweet anymore. We need to surprise them in new ways.

"It's delicious." Falicia stirred at her tub. "But I'm stuffed so full. Gotta leave room for a little rum still, no?" She giggled.

Mounia elbowed me. "See she's always leading me astray?"

"There's always room for rum!" Falcia said, looping her arm through mine. The three of us weaved our way together towards the bar.

"Your hair is beautiful worn up," Mounia told me as we walked. I was wearing my hair in a bun more and more, comfortable enough to show my ears now, to not feel so self-conscious with these women who didn't care for vanity and found strength in vulnerability. "What kin of things do you   ?"

We settled at the table with our drinks. I could barely hear, pressing the volume up on my aids, but it distorted everything, the volume of the music so loud.

"What?" I hollered, making an extra effort to focus on Mounia's lips.

"What do you cook?" she shouted. "What food?"

"Oh, my restaurant was classic French-European . . . But now I'm mostly cooking for the kids!"

"She's famous in London," Falicia grinned, turning to me. "I googled."

I dropped my chin. "Yeah, well, the restaurant is quite well known. Not me so much."

"Do you   ?" Mounia asked.

"What?!" I shouted.

"Do you *miss* it?"

"Not really. The London food scene isn't for the fainthearted." The band finished up, and there was a welcome hiatus as they shuffled off the stage. "I don't want to go back to a city job. It got too much . . . I had this crazy idea I could start a restaurant here, do something for myself."

"Why can't you?" Falicia asked. "You are so talented."

I was relieved to finally be able to hear the conversation properly. "I don't have any money to set it up."

"Can you get a loan?"

"Aid doesn't want me to." Aid didn't want me to do much. When I'd asked him about going to the festival, he'd balked at the idea. *Why would you want to do that?* he asked dismissively, more interested in his beer than an actual conversation.

"*It would be good to get some ideas, make some contacts with Belizean chefs.*"

"*Why?*"

"*If I want to set something up here. I need to get to know the local suppliers.*"

"*It's just with Mounia and Falicia, yeah?*" he checked, reconciling it all in his mind.

"*Yes,*" I insisted. I didn't know who else he was expecting, what paranoia was seeding in his mind. And then he said he'd look after the children, let me go.

Falicia played with the lime in her daiquiri. "There's Marley's ice-cream parlour. It's sitting empty."

"That's a great spot," agreed Mounia.

"It's too far. I couldn't get there every day . . . I want to save up to install a kitchen at Dad's lodge. Maybe start a restaurant there."

"Well, that would be great, too," said Mounia. "Apart from the Jaguar, there's nothing that side of the lagoon, not for miles."

"And if I refurbished, it could be a lodge again, too." I took another sip of daiquiri. "I'd need to save up the money."

Falicia dredged the last of her cocktail. "Why don't you cook something for River Day? You could earn quite a bit."

"What's River Day?"

Mounia smiled. "Oh, my. The kids will love it. Everyone goes to the river, and there are canoe races, and music, and rum. It's next month. Big excuse for a party."

Falicia joined in. "Everyone in Mangrove River gets involved. Teams from all over come to practice for La Ruta Maya next year."

"They'll be looking for food stalls." Mounia winked. "You could start earning for your restaurant. We can help. I'm a great pot washer." She cackled.

I searched their faces. Both of them were staring at me, wide-eyed.

"Will you do it?" Falicia asked as the next band started up.

"What?" I shouted, buying time.

"*Will you do it?*"

"Erm . . . I guess so . . . but can we keep it to ourselves for now? About the restaurant plans. I'll need to work on Aid." I sipped at my drink and thought how exciting it would be to chef again, here, in an outdoor kitchen in the breeze, where I could hear everyone, everything, where I wouldn't make any more mistakes. Where I could breathe.

The Eurythmics play out from the record player, "Sweet Dreams" pulling him into the night. Ellis pours a rum. Lights up his pipe. He's stopped with the cocaine (an increasingly expensive routine he can no longer afford).

He holds the orchid in his hand, his latest find. *Encyclia porrecta*. Pseudobulbs clustered, pyriform, three-leaved. He strokes at its petals, as soft as a woman's skin. The rarity of what he is holding. The price.

A trial separation. It sounds so formal. They've agreed it's for the best, better for the girls. Helena can keep the house, for the time being at least. He'll push for a divorce eventually, but right now, she'll not be able to handle any more news; he must bide his time while he speaks with his lawyer, while she adapts to this new situation. He is staying in Belize; that much is clear. And Helena understands. She always knew. He needs to be near these orchids, needs to build on Adams and Cribb's taxonomy for Kew. The university is enthralled, excited by developments and the prospect of his new grant, and his book is coming along. There is so much more to do here—a country so rich in flora, yet so poorly mapped and documented, so untagged and unexplored.

He puts his pipe down in the ashtray, closes Helena's tobacco jar. He will visit the girls as often as he can, every few months or so. That won't be so different for them. He's always been off on field trips, at symposia, attending conferences around the world. He's started gathering gifts for his return—Mayan baskets and necklaces, Belizean stamps and chocolate. He will make it special, a final Christmas with them, for now.

Opening the top drawer of his desk, he scavenges through his notebooks, grocery receipts, ink, stamps, bank statements, and mortgage documents. Then he finds it, the cover his favourite yet: three alluring ghost orchids, in their subtropical Floridian scene of palms and turtles, an alligator in the foreground, a tree frog near the spine. He picks up the brochure: *Proceedings of the 11th World Orchid Conference 1984.*

Helena is worried about money, of course. *He* is worried about money. Though he's told her he will support her, look after the girls. He hasn't told her he bought the lodge—that she doesn't need to know. He hasn't told her about Agapita either, not yet, or about the baby she is carrying. She is radiant, beautiful, though sometimes, when he catches sight of her, he cannot help the thought arising that he's gotten in too deep. But while guilt is a heavy burden to carry, it does not strip you of your dignity, like despair, and he's glad to be rid of that.

He flicks through the catalogue and finds what he is looking for—there in the margin on page 14. The scribble of a Florida telephone number, and his name; the collector he got talking to that night, Montgomery Addison, five whiskys in at the bar. *"If you ever want to sell anything, anything at all, gimme a call."*

He grabs a biro and scribbles down a few quick calculations. If he sold a caseload of the rarest—not *the* rarest, not the black orchids or the *Lycaste aromaticas*, which he loves so much, and not the *Sobralia macrantha*, which don't transplant so well, but maybe some *Epidendrum nocturnums*, some *Myrmecophila tibicinis*. He tots up his sums. Forty. Fifty. Maybe fifty-five thousand dollars. Enough to establish a buffer, buy him some time, support Agapita and this new life they have made.

He downs the last of his Don Omario. Betrayal being the only truth he knows will endure; he vows to keep this one a secret. After all, deceit against the wild, against his beloved orchids, may be the worst deceit of all.

23

Laelia

Karl Heusner Memorial Hospital, Belize City
19th March 2023

Hospitals are sick, sick hosts. I sat in the solitary chair, again, curled up over Dad, staring at the polyvinyl tube breathing for him, the same machines still *bleep-bleep-bleeping* through the tinnitus in my head. *What are you thinking? Remembering?*

Pulling out a copy of *Orchidology in the Rainforests of Central and South America* by Ellis C. Wylde, I began reading him his own words, hoping to break the spell with a jolt of memories. "Orchids on a tree, with few exceptions, will benefit from copious light. Most *Cattleyas*, *Vandas*, and *Laelias* require near full exposure to the sun in order to flower to their full capability."

I pinched the crepey skin on the back of his hand once more. *Is your life flashing before you?* Nothing. No response.

After a day building a pizza oven together out of dead wine bottles, we took the kids to Dangriga for a change of scene. It was easier to get them to open their textbooks at night when it was cooler, and all the practical jobs of the day had been done.

"Dangriga is from the Garifuna meaning 'sweet water,'" Ella read from the guidebook as we drove. "Birthplace of punta rock."

We found a beachfront grill on the other side of town for burgers and hot wings, cocktails and ice cream. We sat helping Dylan learn fractions, then after dessert we played pinball, sheltering from the rain.

Aid said we needed to head back into Dangriga town. "I need to meet someone."

"What? Now?"

"I told you before I need to meet someone tonight."

"What?" *Did he?*

"You never hear shit. I told you yesterday."

"It's getting dark." I played with my cocktail umbrella. "We've got a long drive ba—"

"It's ten minutes, Lil . . . It's work."

So that was that. We dragged the kids away from the arcade machine and walked the darkening streets through spitting rain to find Hector's someone. As we wandered, Aid told me about a party Hector was planning, about wanting me to meet him. "He's such a character—eccentric for sure. Hey, I think this is the street." Aid flicked his cigarette butt with his finger. It javelined a couple of metres before disappearing into a fluorescent puddle. "It's here," he said, pointing at the sign overhead: LA CABAN. COCKTAILS. DANCING. GIRLS. The final "a" in "cabana" had died.

Heavy bass pulsed from inside with an overlay of shatteringly bad nineties karaoke. A couple of men spilled out, swaying, regurgitated into the near darkness. A woman in a purple minidress stood leaning, one heel propped up against the cracking wall, cigarette in hand, her whole being multiplied in wavy neon puddles. She watched us intently, this strange ensemble family.

"We can't take the kids in th—" but Aid had already turned away from me, starting towards the door. "Aid?" But he couldn't hear me. Or pretended not to.

I grabbed Dylan by the hand and Ella by the shoulder.

"Mum?" Her face lit up in strobing pink. "What are we doing?" She stopped and tugged my wrist.

"It won't . . . Aid won't be long . . ." I said. He was already near the door.

"But—"

"Weh yuh gwein?" The purple dress hollered. "This no place for kids."

"Ella, take him in there . . ." I pointed at a restaurant a few doors down. "I'll tell Aid where we'll be."

Ella took Dylan by the hand to walk towards the neon-signed "Grill."

"Ganigi!" The woman shouted towards the door. "Clientes."

A man appeared, his neck craning back inside, speaking to someone behind the wooden screen. "Mañana, no. Viernes." He turned back to us and smiled, "Weh gaan ahn?" A big, fake white and silver smile. Too many crowding teeth.

"Hi," Aid said. "We want a drink. At the bar."

The man shook his head, wide, side to side. "Nah, man." He had a squint, and deep-set puffy eyes.

"What do you mean, 'nah, man'?" Aid mimicked.

"No can do."

"Aid—" I tried.

"No can do? We just want a drink."

The woman in the purple dress coughed and took her heel down from the wall. She started clacking towards us, splishing up the puddles. "Hey! Fu chroo?"

"Sorry?" Aid turned towards her, his accent leaning now into the British. "We just want a drink."

"Nah, man." Ganigi widened his stance, his hat seeming to take up the whole entrance.

Aid shifted his feet. "I'm meeting someone. I'll only be five minutes."

"Who you meeting?" The woman asked. I squeezed out a smile at her. Ganigi began scrolling his phone.

"Please. I'll be quick . . . She'll stay out here." Aid nodded towards me.

"Aid," I tried again but he brushed me away with his hand.

Ganigi looked up. "You're not going in."

"Man, come on. Help me out here."

"You're . . . not . . . go-ing . . . in."

"Look, can I just—" Aid rifled around in his back pocket.

"No."

"This will help . . ." Aid pulled out a note. I couldn't see how much it was. The man smirked, went back to scrolling.

"White folks always thinking they can buy their way into things," the woman said, lighting another cigarette. "Or outta things." She laughed, a deep hearty cackle.

"I'm really sorry," I said, unsure if I was talking to the bouncer or the woman. Or maybe myself.

"Lil, we're not sorry." Aid turned to me. "We just want a fucking drink."

"Go home, bwoi." Ganigi smiled, flashing metallic teeth again. "Get your kids to bed."

"Can you just find a guy called Dion and tell him I—"

Ganigi looked up, straightening off his stool. "Dion? You looking for Mr. Dion?" He smiled another flash of silver. "Why didn't you say so? You a friend of his?"

"Yes. Can I come in now?"

While Aid went in, I caught up with the kids at the grill down the street. I got them some Cokes to try to normalise this situation, to try to keep them awake. But Dylan fell asleep on a banquette of cushions. Ella huffed and rolled her eyes at me, playing with a stray kitten.

It was over an hour until Aid found us.

I asked him, of course, but he wouldn't tell me what was so urgent, what he needed to see that guy about. I knew not to think about it too much, ask too many questions; I didn't want to know the answers anyway.

Jungle days and nights snaked by. Aid was working away a lot. I started clearing and cleaning the old lodge rooms on my own, picking paint colours and testing samples.

The children went to stay at Falicia and Henry's so Aid and I could have a break. As soon as we dropped them off and hugged goodbye, we made the most of every moment—each minute unfurling like a leaf. Aid made us dinner, spent ages lining up candles, picking out wine, and cooking up a chimichurri feast. Si never spoilt me—he barely even cooked.

Smudging on lip gloss, I realised it was the first time I'd worn makeup in weeks, months even. My foundation, caking from the heat, was too pale now for my skin. I would need to ask Chloe to bring me some a couple of shades darker; she was talking about coming back out soon. I started a list in my head: Marmite, magazines, that Cédric Grolet book I'd lent Tris.

Aid came in from his shower and pressed up against me, teasing damp hair away from my face. I inhaled the warmth of him, tobacco and blood orange. He breathed kisses into the nape of my neck, and it overpowered me, all of it, his scent intoxicating. His need. Mine. He pawed my breast, his fingers teasing the fabric away.

"That dress . . . it's killing me." His whispers melted into my ear.

I sank towards him, dropping the lip gloss to the floor. He edged down my body, pushed aside my knickers. I felt a pull stronger than gravity, fiercer than love; I could almost hear it. In the jungle, everything felt hyperreal. There was no hiding from anything—not from each other, not from ourselves.

We fucked twice before we left for the party. And then he told me not to wear that dress.

24

It took less than one song to get there. Aid's iPhone thundered out an old Jay-Z/Ye track through the speakers—full volume—to surge us along through the dark. It pounded at my ears, the sound like a jungle. Silhouettes rushed by either side, the forest dancing in the wake of our headlights as we wound along the narrow tracks.

The house—mansion really—was so much closer than I realised it would be. *Did Aid really need to take the truck each day to get here?* It was a hidden compound—jarring in this area amongst Mayan villages of wood and fronds and metal. A fuck-off big monstrosity that should stick out like a sore thumb, except it was sympathetically disguised, set back in abundance, its walls gagged in leaves. In the daytime, without these pulsating anthems and streaming lights, you would never even know it was there. The forest keeps its secrets close. Now, though, it was a lodestone with a heartbeat. The music strobing like sugar candy. I hadn't danced in so long, and the beats were magnetic—pulling us closer, activating something inside I hadn't felt for what seemed like forever. The depths of me enlivened, injected with energy, I remembered what it was to feel high with happiness—from the sound. I was grateful for this night already, for this invitation. Hector was known to throw the most elaborate parties—"off the scale"—and Aid was top of the list, and Hector liked him, apparently.

Driving into a gap between high walls, wrought iron gates stopped us dead. We were forced to remain as spectators (auditors), teetering on the edge of the night that was awakening like a jaguar in its cage. CCTV surveilled us from on high. Two men stood either side of the truck brandishing assault rifles fiercer than the night.

Aid flicked a smile as he lowered the window. "Hey, Adnan." *He knows this guy, this guy with a gun.*

"Hey, man."

"See you inside?" Aid asked, so casual.

"Maybe late-late," Adnan replied. "We're out here all night . . . Gotta keep the riffriff away." They laughed and the gates opened up.

I was probably uptight for worrying about the guns—a little at least. They were only a precaution. Protection. For us. In the middle of nowhere, in the jungle, in Central America. That was only normal, natural—right? Chloe would have a fit if she could see us now. But honestly, that exhilarated me more. It was like how things used to be with Aid and me in the beginning—dancing at the edge of excitement, never knowing what was going to happen next, not wanting to know anyway. Living in the moment, like you didn't give a shit, like I'd never been able to do before I met Aid because I'd never been given the chance—had never given myself the chance—to just live.

Windows slit up and down the mansion, scarring it with cool modernity, the whole thing uplit by expensive, fulfilled dreams. Hector had made it and wanted everyone to know. I didn't like the guy and I'd never even met him, but I was excited to be at his party, so I'd like him for tonight.

Aid parked the truck, and we hotfooted it towards the sound. Double doors at the entrance opened up like a chocolate box:

buzzing laughter flashing lights casting shadows flashing dark dollar bills diesely stench flashing thong-clad women hyped-up men gyrating flashing sweat rampant beats cigarette smoke bikini breasts bad karaoke flashing no air no air

Bodies against bodies against bodies moving into each other, in for the night. Secrets shared into strangers' ears; truths into might-be lovers'. Half-truths and little lies; all such make believe. A party without a price tag: Moët & Chandon waterfalls gushing straight into eager mouths—flooding down overflowing bikinis, lime segments falling to the floor like sorry smiles, metal caps and cardboard roaches floating discarded—flotsam and jetsam on rivers of forgotten spillage, white lines laid out—bright little promises—gone. It was a trash bin of a party; the dregs of the night forming already before our eyes.

Aid pulled me in close, shouting into my ear. "This is unreal!" His irises bluer than the sea, even in the dark. I nodded and smiled, though I wasn't so sure. There was a definite undertow, unease crackling somewhere beneath the surface. I needed a drink. We found our way to the bar and downed a couple of quick tequilas each. I didn't know anyone, didn't recognise a single face.

"Are Benny and Nico here?" I asked into Aid's ear.

"Somewhere maybe." He downed another tequila without me. "Not   if Nico's coming." It was hard to hear him, the words lost in the noise. Aid started pulsing back and forth then leaned into me. "I don't like him!" His shouting made my hearing aid ring. I could barely breathe. The house was swimming in undercurrents; locals, and expats, and nowhere-ats mixing it up like the cocktails they were all accessorising, an entourage of sixty or so: bar guys and bar girls, prostitutes and farmers, fishermen and everymen, entrepreneurs and right-hand fixers—at least, that's what I imagined them to be.

I found somewhere to dump our jackets, down the corridor, checking out the eclectic artwork, ocelot skulls, and jaguar skin hangings as I went. The contemporary pieces reminded me of the Dan Baldwins Si had picked out for his fortieth, their technicolour shambles. I'd always found them too obvious and try-hard, too modern art for modern art's sake.

Easing my way back, I made out Aid through the surging crowd, his shoulders draped in a hot-panted woman. He was laughing along with her. My stomach lurched. He'd always got attention, but he never responded to it. At least, not that I'd seen.

"Aid!" a voice hollered as I got closer. Benny, cigar poking up above the sea of heads, was surfing his way towards us.

"Dude," Aid shouted back, smiling to acknowledge me, too. Hot Pants slid away down the bar with her bottle of rum.

The men grabbed at forearms, pulling each other in for a bullish back-slapping hug before Benny turned to give me an awkward embrace. "Hi, Laelia." He reeked of funking wood. He said something into my ear, but over the noise I couldn't make it out. I smiled and nodded as though I understood. I was adept at pretending like this, to ease the discomfort. We downed more drinks before Benny ushered us through the sea of people, towards the side, through a run of open glass. The cool air hit me, and I could finally breathe.

We fell out onto a hibiscus-brimmed patio surrounding a lit-up pool. *That* pool. *The* pool. Fuck. I hadn't recognised this place from the front. So stupid. It was his house. Him. The cock with the military boots and the fat fingers.

"Hector!" Benny called over to a gazebo in the corner, and sure enough, there he lay like Rylance's Rooster, slouching on a lounger clutching a bong, dressed in the same down-at-heel getup he'd worn when I'd met him before. Flocked by women. Girls—they were girls. None more than twenty; one looked barely sixteen. Barely dressed. Of course, it was his house. There couldn't be many—*any*—other sprawling mansions around here. We followed Benny over to the group.

Hector's eyes clocked mine. He didn't take them off me as he said, "Aid! Y'all got a drink?"

A woman passed with a mirrored tray. Aid took a beer, and I lifted a daiquiri. The men shook hands, and still Hector's eyes didn't leave me. "This must be your sweet sugar," he snarled, metal glinting inside his mouth. "Lie-lee-a, ain't it?" My name tangled like bindweed on his tongue.

"Lay-lee-a" was all I could manage, my voice brittle as bone.

"Su-gar," came a retort from behind me. A yellow-headed parrot perched on the gazebo, silent and still, as if it had never said a thing.

"Y'all need to watch her," Hector told Aid, crumbling weed into the bowl of his bong with his puffed-up fingers and thumbs.

"Su-gar," the bird cawed again.

"Watch her?" Aid asked. He frowned, his eyes scanning mine then shifting back and forth between us.

"She's curious." Hector smiled. "Ain't ya, Lie-lee-a?"

How abruptly a moment can turn dangerous and keep turning, swept up in its own momentum. I felt the intensity of eyes upon me. Everyone staring, waiting for my reaction, and I didn't know what to say. Aid was searching my face, then Hector's.

Finally, I managed to speak. "Well, you need to keep your wits about you . . . in the jungle."

"Jungle. Jungle," the parrot mimicked.

"Sure do, Lie-lee-a. Sure do." Hector lit the bong, focusing in on the bubbles. Exhaling the smoke, he inhaled a smug grin under his thick moustache. "Why is it, whenever y'all build a boundary, put up a wall—or a fence line—the next motherfucker who comes along has to know what's on the other side . . . ?" He laughed, and after a stilted second, everyone laughed along with him. Aid laughed awkwardly, too.

Hector got up, handed the bong to the nearest hanger-on, and staggered towards me. "You know . . . knowledge is a kinda madness." *Crazy bitch.*

"Madness. Madness," recited the bird.

I sipped my daiquiri, the lime sharp on my tongue. Hector moved in, his face close to mine, his aftershave sickly sweet. Heliotrope and cinnamon lodged in my nose, my eyes, my throat. I felt sick. He thrust a ham hock hand under my chin before forcing it upwards, trying to get my eye contact. "Sometimes it's best y'all don't see things, hey sugar?" His words fugged like curry and stale tobacco. "Or better . . . not go lookin' for 'em at all." The pressure of his fingers pushed up into my jaw, my teeth grinding together.

"Life's easier with your eyes closed, huh?" Benny drawled, trying to lighten the tension. Aid let out an uncertain laugh that clattered like bones. The girls shuffled on their heels, sipped at their drinks.

Hector leaned in even closer, whispering through my hair so I could feel his spittle, smell his dank breath. "Easier with your ears closed, too, hey sugar?" His proximity made my hearing aid screech angry feedback. I could hardly breathe. Fat fingers began massaging at my ear like it was his plaything, the gold of his signet ring flashing in the corner of my eye before he tugged my lobe taut. He licked at it, bristling wet. I felt the damp warmth of him, so close. With his tongue and his teeth, he flicked the device off the back of my ear, then dropped it out of his mouth. It plopped into the slush of my daiquiri, and I watched it sink to the bottom. Everyone was glaring. No-one said a word.

Hector stepped back. He clamped his palm over his mouth like a circus clown. "Oops."

I stared down at the glass, unsure where to look, who or what to focus on. I did not want to look at him, did not want to give him the satisfaction. The hearing aid lay drowning in my daiquiri.

"Hey . . . mate . . ." Aid urged but Hector remained unfazed, laughing. I felt like I was going to be sick. *Mate?*

Hector carried on entertaining his crowd. "D'ya reckon I'm stupid, Lie-lee-a?" My whole body tensed. I couldn't speak. "Y'know, I love this country . . . It fuckin' loves Americans." He laughed. "It's put up with years of your British slavery, all this interferin' foreign ownership, all our gringo guns and our lusts and our Jesus . . . But you know somethin' . . . ?" He was swaying on his feet. "They still love me, like I'm the fuckin' king round here. God bless Belize . . ." He wandered back towards his harem. "Serena . . . ? Where's Serena?"

From the back of the gaggle of girls, Serena emerged, blinding in a bronze sequinned jumpsuit and gold kitten heels. She seemed smaller than when I'd seen her through the fence. "Why don't y'all take Laelia so Aid and me can have a little talk?"

I stood, frozen. Serena grabbed my daiquiri and downed it in one, sticking out her tongue to present the hearing aid. "Here . . . you'd better have this." She secured it into my palm, wrapping my fingers gently back over it, her manicured nails picket fence spikes.

"Have this, have this." Even though its face barely moved, I was sure the parrot was smirking at me; they all were. Serena tugged my wrist and led me away. With my other hand I managed to hook the device, dripping and ice cold, back over my ear—relieved to hear the shuffling of my hair again as I adjusted the volume.

As we walked, I glanced over my shoulder. Hector was slumped back on the lounger glued to his bong; his girls gathered around him like flies on shit. Aid was still staring right at me, speechless, his silence deafening.

Serena kicked off her heels, left them stranded somewhere off the path in the dark.

"Are you going to leave them?"

"What?"

"Your shoes. They're gorgeous. Don't leave them . . ." But she ran on. I followed her glittery outfit deep into the garden. The tequila and rum had gone to my head, and I was still buzzing with adrenaline, but moving farther away from the party—from those people—I felt lighter.

"I'm sorry he did that," Serena said when we were far enough away. I wasn't sure if she was talking about Hector or Aid. "He goes too far, doesn't know to stop."

I still felt nauseous, couldn't find any words so tried to smile. "Where are we going?" I eventually asked.

She skipped on ahead. "You'll see . . ."

We came to the front of a huge building at the black seam of rainforest. Endless wood and glass for days. Serena made me hold her phone, shining its torch while she played with a glinting brass padlock. Close up in the moonlight, I could see her skin was pitted with scars, though she hid a strong, natural beauty. She was probably only midtwenties—hard fought for sure, but she didn't need to hide behind the cemented makeup, the sparkling barbed eyelashes, the plush tattooed lips.

"Thank you," she said, turning to me.

"What for?"

"For saying nothing . . . I know you saw us. Me and Benny. By the pool." I eased a gentle smile. "Hector sleeps with all the women in the world . . ." She flicked the lock and pushed the door open. "I fuck one guy, and I have to hide it."

"Why don't you leave him?" I asked, realising as soon as the words tumbled out of my mouth I'd had too much to drink. "Sorry, it's none of my business."

She stared into nothing, towards the darkness beyond. "I guess . . . he has a kind of hold on me." She flung the door wide and fumbled for a switch. Artificial white lights flashed a surreal scene into view: a thousand orchids, beyond beautiful, cascading with a million invincible colours I'd never seen before—bubblegum pinks, tie-dye magentas, ecstatic oranges, more. The scent was overwhelming, waves of butterscotch, citrus, cinnamon.

"Hector's addicted to them," Serena said, twirling on her toes. "He's trying to collect all of them, every species on earth . . ."

"Oh," I said, still surveying the shock of flowers tiered amongst the foliage. Orchids that looked like monkey faces, onions, jellyfish.

"He'll never do it, of course. It's impossible, there's too many. People make them in labs now. Genetically engineer them. Though he won't stop." She cusped at ruffled petals, inhaling their scent. "It's like a fever." She danced along in front of me, stopping every now and again to point out a flower or stroke at a leaf. "He says I'm like an epiphyte." Orchids that looked like spiders, goats' heads, birds in flight.

"Hmm?"

She started playing with a clamshell-shaped flower. "You asked why I can't leave him . . . He loves me like an orchid—"

"My queer little freaks," belted a voice from behind us. "Sexy little things . . . How d'ya like 'em, Lie-lee-a?" Hector picked up a gold atomiser and began misting.

"They're—"

"Monstrously beautiful, I reckon. My boy Aidrian tells me your old man knows somethin' about orchids?"

I strained, reluctant to reply. "He studied them. In the wild."

"Some of 'em are pretty ugly when they're not flowerin'. And some of 'em are fuckin' ugly when they are. But most of 'em . . . when they burst into life, when they finally bloom . . . their beauty is so alien. Like nothin' else. It's like they're singin' a dozen languages all at once. Y'all can actually hear 'em." He plucked a pair of ornate scissors from his pocket. The small blades looked ridiculous in his meat cleaver hand. He laughed, tapping at his ear. "Oh, maybe you can't."

He started clipping at a plant, edging even closer towards me. My breathing shallowed. "Folks think orchids are fragile . . . but they'll outlive us all."

Raising the scissors in front of my face, he held them for a lingering moment, then snipped them, sharp. "They're fuckin' tough."

I flinched.

He smirked at Serena, and his mouth curled. "Deceptive, too." Serena forced a smile back at him, her eyes flitting between us both. "They mimic the scents of insects and push out their sexy pheromones until they trick the poor little bees into fuckin' 'em."

He cut a lime-coloured flower, rolled its stem between his fat fingers. "They burn the forests for farmland here, raze them to the ground, not even thinkin' twice about the orchids." He lifted the flower to his nose.

"Half these babies would have been ravaged to ashes if I hadn't saved 'em." He moved towards me again, pawing my hair back behind my ear, sliding the orchid there. My hearing aid rustled. I could hardly breathe. "I would never let 'em burn away to nothin'. They're the most precious things in the world. I love 'em so much. Guess it's like a sickness . . . Passion is a strong and barely controllable emotion. You get that, don't ya, Lie-lee-a? Being Dr. Ellis Wylde's daughter 'n' all." I balked at the mention of Dad.

I nodded. It was all I could do.

Nico caught me like a net when he saw me coming back into the party. He let me hang out with him, forget my embarrassment, bury my shame. We were pushed into a corner, wedged on a sofa far from the bar. It felt safe near him, hidden.

"Will you not stay for one more drink?" he asked, having to lean right in close to shout into my ear. He smelled of Black Orchid; I could almost taste the bergamot and blackcurrant.

"I've got to get home . . ." I said, leaning back into him, holding his shoulder. "I need to be there for the kids in the morning."

"Come on . . . let your hair down." It was said with a smile. He didn't mean it unkindly, but it irked me a little—reminded me of how I used to be, how life was back then, Si begging me to stay up for "one more"; as if an extra G&T on the sofa was throwing caution to the wind, like we could drink ourselves out of banality and spice up our life with another shot of Jodhpur gin.

"Aid's going to have . . ." Nico snickered, muttering to himself. "Comment dit-on la gueule de bois . . . ? He's lucky to have you." I looked down at the rum in my glass I wasn't drinking. The music shifted, changed to a slower, quieter tune. Nico brought his lips back to my ear. The scent of him again, so close. "I don't think he appreciates you . . ." He took a sip of his beer. "My ex, back in France, she was cheating on me. Took me months to find out. But I knew deep down, I knew . . . You always know—"

"I'm sorry . . ."

"I was embarrassed in the beginning. Everybody knew. But shame, it eat you up if you let it."

"I'm sorry, Nico . . . I've got to get back."

"A hangover . . ." he said, remembering. "Aid's going to have a hang-over." He downed the rest of his drink. "Go carefully, Laelia . . . Look after yourself."

We kissed cheek-cheek-cheek because he's French, then I took the truck. The storm of emotions flooding my veins sobered me up enough to drive. No-one would be out on the twisted tracks at this time anyway, and I'd hardly drunk much.

My arms shook on the wheel as the Frontier growled, negotiating snaking turns. I started fumbling with the radio, scanning for stations until it hit some reggae . . . a weather forecast . . . some punta. As I lifted my eyes back to the road, I saw it, frozen in the headlights. I slammed my foot on the brake.

He didn't move, his luscious tawny pelt spotted with black rosettes. His cat eyes strobed back at me, through me, into me, with a majesty and strength I'd never felt before. He powered off silently into thick leaves, the jungle taking him back again as quickly as it had choked him out.

25

My head pounded. I felt the sun pulsing through the window before I opened my eyes; felt the pit in my stomach, too. There was a wild, furnacing heat. I was still seething, and I'd barely slept; worried sick what Aid had gotten into with this Hector guy, whether we could get out of it.

I brewed a pot of coffee and found *The Mosquito Coast* in Aid's drawer. I eased myself back into bed under the netting, and Ursula curled up around me. I tried reading, but my mind kept drifting back to the night before, to Hector and the parroting retorts; and all those eyes—all those pupils staring at me, daring me, willing me to do something, to say something. But I hadn't; I couldn't.

Placing the book back, I started to push the drawer closed when I spotted something bright white wedged in the back corner: three small plastic bags, soft powder bulging inside. I pulled them out, glared at them in my palm. Cocaine promises. He'd said it was only one time. This was so much more than that. What was he doing? I tore through his clothes then, found dead origami in pockets, tiny plastic baggies smeared in chalky white.

A rapid and overwhelming urge came over me to get rid of them. I wanted Aid to be done with this little habit—obviously becoming a bigger habit—that was seeping its way more and more into our lives. There would be more where this came from, of course, but maybe I could stem the flow for a while, buy some time.

Aid had asked me to hide his coke from him before, at his flat in Brighton at the beginning, when we both knew he was doing too much, though I'd tried to block out that memory. All I would have to do was chuck it down the loo and flush it away. Done and dusted. But frightened of the ramifications, I didn't even have the guts. I placed it all back into the drawer, hid it away again.

I strolled down to think and feed the chickens, Ursula trailing like a shadow. She barely bothered with them, or they with her, so I let her follow. The wire along one side of the coop was coming away from its frame, and the plumpest chicken, Ditsy, had got herself caught in the hole. Pulling her free, I let the birds roam while I put my mind to fixing the fencing. The metal was rusting in places, the wood rotting in others.

Rummaging through the storage hut, I found some spare batons and a vicious roll of wire, jagged along the edges where someone had cut away at it once before. Malleting the posts back and forth in the bullying heat, I tried willing them out of the ground so I could attack the frame. *What was Aid thinking?* I managed to pull the wood free from the soil, my T-shirt dampening fast. *Was he even thinking?* Ursula lay watching from the shade, gazing at me like I was a madwoman. Still simmering with fury, I *was* a madwoman. *Crazy bitch.*

I flashed back to the shouts echoing through the house, travelling up the stairs like ghosts: *You're hysterical, woman.* I'd run into Chloe's room, seeking reassurance "everything's okay," which Chloe would say but didn't really know, and we'd dive together into the world under her duvet while they fought like animals, until the doors stopped slamming and the screams died down to slaughtered silence. Then Dad would leave. Maybe it was days, though it felt like long weeks. He wouldn't be there, but the madwoman wouldn't be there either—at least not the same madwoman; not the loud, fiery one who'd been there before, in our faces and out of her mind.

Screw him for making me feel like this.

As soon as he stumbled back up the track, close to midday, I was on him. Didn't even let him say hello, as I staggered upright from hammering a nail down low. "That's who you're working for?"

He looked like shit. He didn't say anything at first, breathing shallow as he looked up to the sky searching for words. "I hear you were cosying up to Nico again last night . . ." He forced a smile, and I couldn't tell if he was joking.

"What . . . ?" I dropped the hammer to the ground with a thud.

"Whispering sweet nothings into each other's ears in the corner?"

"My God, Aid," I spat. "Give it up." I turned to walk back to the hut. I couldn't bear to be around him.

"Hector told me what happened . . ." Aid called after me. "Spying on him through the fence . . . What the hell were you thinking?" I turned to face him.

"I was lost!" I shouted.

He was right there in front of me, much closer than I was expecting. He looked at me like I was the blood from his veins. "Why didn't you tell me you'd met him before? You made me look like a prick."

"And we can't have that, can we?" I retorted, without thinking.

Aid glared at me, eyes cold and flinty, face reddening. "After everything, everything we've been through? Everything I've done for you . . . we need to stick together. Not go behind each other's backs, risking shit."

I felt awful, sick to my stomach. "I didn't mean anything, I promise." I felt so utterly stupid. He'd treated me so well, been so patient with me. And I'd triggered him, even if I hadn't meant to. "I'm sorry, Aid. I'm sorry."

He rubbed the back of his neck, shaking his head. "Don't you dare humiliate me like that again," he sniped, then grabbed his bag and took the truck.

Aid didn't come home that night. Or the next night. I tried to call him, from the Jaguar Lodge, but he never picked up, never replied to my texts.

After supper, the children played chess by candlelight while I weaved a macramé hammock through a mist of swear words. Working from a tattered printout Mounia had given me, it was hard to read the typeface. I couldn't stop the cords getting all tangled up. Each glass of red helped me ease out the knots a little more or maybe meant I cared about them a little less. Once Dylan had thrashed Ella into toppling her king, they sloped off to bed, Ursula trailing behind.

I gave up on the macramé and sat giving total attention to my wine, the last glass from the last bottle of imported Cabernet. I was so upset at Aid still, though the wine was diluting my fury, sip by sip. Three quarters of the bottle in, my thinking slipped, relaxed.

I thought of the depths of him, so strong. His laughter. His anger. His eyes. The deepest blue that ever got me. The only one who'd ever got me. The one who showed me how to find my way back to myself again.

"I don't know how to forget you," I'd told him after that lust-filled one-night stand together.

"Then don't," he'd told me.

When we saw each other, not for the first time, across that beach bar—crowded and buzzing, it was like the world spun around us, carried on, but we were fixed and fixated, entranced. Seconds felt like minutes. His friends were so drunk, holiday happy on all-day beers and rum. They were there together, the twelve of them from New England. A mixed group, some couples, but mainly friends, sunbathing and partying together on the caye. I'd seen them over the days before; everyone had. They'd made themselves known—lounging around the pool, throwing pastries at each other over the breakfast buffet, playing beach ball in the waves.

It was only supposed to have been one drink. I thought about it often; that feeling as he sat down next to me. The anticipation. The excitement. It wasn't love at first sight, but it was a lust like I had never known, heavy and intoxicating. "'Tell me why you're here,'" he'd read from the text on my page. And then we riffed together.

And then he bought me that drink.

I awoke to a crashing sound, right there, outside the door. My breath seized, my rib cage still. I must have fallen asleep on the sofa.

There. A clattering.

Grabbing the largest chef's knife and gripping it tightly, I edged towards the door. I breathed out, and in again, as quietly as I could.

There was something there, right there, the other side of the wood. Inches away. My breathing, though soft, felt so loud.

It was probably an ocelot. Maybe a stray dog.

The door started shifting within its makeshift frame. Something, someone, was pushing against it, trying to open it. The planks so flimsy. The handle turned. I slammed my hand over my mouth, my nose, to grab my breaths, stall my sounds.

Bang bang bang.

"Lil?!" A gravelly voice urged. "Laelia. Open the door."

"Is that you, Aid?"

"Yes. Open the door . . ."

I dropped the knife and exhaled a long breath.

"Please . . . Let me in. Let's talk."

I stood, my head resting against the wood of the door. *Please let him be calm.* I slid the bolt locks across and moved to the side of the hut. Aid stumbled in, chucking his backpack to the floor. His hair was ruffled, his face flushed.

"I'm sorry," he said. The door drifted half shut again, banging on its hinges. I looked up at him, speechless, for a moment. "I'm sorry," he said again.

"You were such a dick."

"I know. I'm sorry." He was unsteady on his feet.

"You scared me."

"I'm sorry, it's dark out. I knocked some stuff off the table."

"Not now. Before. You scared me before. I didn't know what you were going to do."

"I love you." He was drunk again, slurring his words—only a little, but enough. "I love you so much. I'm sorry. Do you hate me?"

"No, I don't hate you . . . Why did you just stand there, at the party? Let Hector humiliate me like that?"

"I didn't know what was going on. I was drunk. We were all drunk. I didn't know . . . and you hadn't told me you'd met him already."

"You have to stop drinking . . . doing so much coke."

"I know. I'm . . . It's this place, you know. It brings it all back." *His father's alcoholism, his absence.*

"And Hector. I think you should find something else, some other work."

He looked blank. "But the money—"

"Screw the money. It's not enough . . ." It would never be enough. Not for this. "The way he is . . . It's scary, Aid."

"Okay . . . I'm sorry. I missed you." He smiled, reaching towards me, pulling me in. "It was good for me to get away, though, Lil . . . be by my-self." Or maybe he said, "be myself." He smelt of rum. "I'm sorry I acted like that. It's just, I love you so much . . . Are Ella and Dylan okay?"

"They're fine; they've missed you . . . Where did you go?"

"Dangriga. Got a shitty hotel on the beach. Swam a bit, drank a bit." His eyes tracked over me. Fucking eyes. Such beautiful fucking eyes. He lifted his hand up, stroked my face, my cheek. "I'm sorry," he whispered, kissing my lips.

I relented, kissed him back. He touched my collarbone, tracing the skin near the edge of my dress strap while he teased it away.

"We can't . . ." I started. "The kids." But they would be asleep. His breath whispered over my skin. "Aid . . ."

He wasn't listening. He didn't need to. He'd mapped out my emo-tions, drawn an atlas of my vulnerabilities, years ago. He unhooked my bra, his lips pressing into my neck. His finger, so light it felt like a part of me, lingered over my nipple. I lifted off his T-shirt, unveiling his tat-toos, those stories of him. My fingers tracked across the faded greys and muted blacks.

His tongue, gliding sweet with rum, searched into me. An owl trilled outside, a staccato *gogogogogogogo*. My tongue, tentative, kissed back, quietly urging him to explore me more. More. The intensity of how he looked at me, then, like I was everything. Kissing in the amber glow of candlelight, we drowned into each other like this; like that. Seconds felt like minutes felt like seconds.

I felt him harden through his shorts, teasing back and forth against me. His fingers slid down under my knickers as his breath traced my skin and he pushed me back, hard, against the hut wall. I arched as his fin-gers slid inside, my body yielding, our lusts adrift.

Rum breaths skimmed my neck, my breasts, as he pulled down his shorts, peeled off my thong. I pushed his head gently down. His tongue inside me, I arched again. He lifted me, pushed me up, urgently, holding me, as my legs wrapped tight around his waist. He pushed inside, deep, slowing as, breathless, I brayed into him. Seconds, quick seconds. I felt the magnitude of him, of us, together.

"I'm sorry," he whispered.

"I love you," breathed out of me.

Seconds felt like minutes.

Gogogogogo the bird called, closer now, the jungle alive outside. I felt the rhythm of us, sensed our shapes. He was so hard in me, against me; so hard, my body gripping and pulsing. His tongue licked and locked onto me, the alcohol on his breath nauseating now. He gripped at the sides of my neck, massaging his thumb and fingers around me, pushing, squeezing, stroking.

"Aid . . ." My voice croaked as he tightened his hold, then softened his grip round the front of my throat. Lightheaded, I felt the room whirl around us. He whispered in my ear.

You crazy bitch.

Did he say that? Or did I just think it?

He came hard, deep into me, as his hand released from my neck and I dragged quick inhalations. I ached, moaned relief, into him. He groaned, deep, deep into himself. My throat burned.

"I love you," he whispered until it echoed in my head.

Collapsing onto the thinly sheeted mattress, away from each other, we searched for breaths in the sleek darkness. My toes touched against his, and our legs wrapped back in together. Entwined like vines we lay, slick with sweat, welcoming lapping waves of sleep.

My fingers traced the curvature of his spine, sweeping over his tattoos in the half-light: the moon—inverted, Renaissance planets, stars, a dove, "no apologies," angels and religious nods (although he's not religious), scorpions with their quest for truth, the dragonfly at the centre of his back (change and rebirth); moths curving over the soft ridges of his shoulders (light in the dark, faith, determination); the dogwood blossom for his mother; five more across his arms; starlings murmuring over his collarbone (for letting go of the old); a fox under stars (resourceful/playful); the ambigram of love/pain; then the Gothic cursive "L.F." over his bicep, threaded through the centre of a thick black heart. He'd told me once it stood for "Live Forever" because that's what he wanted to do.

The jungle sounds screamed louder, an enlivened chorus, as though the wild creatures were talking only to us. I lay listening to the screech owl, its ghostly drilling still punctuating the night. *Gogogogogogogo.*

Dad told me once: Strength needs to grow in the dark before it can

ever push you towards the light. We are all just seeds waiting to germi-
nate, searching for the sun.

"Aid?" I said.

But he had fallen asleep.

The sense of someone gone is somehow stronger than the sense of
someone there. I awoke in the half-light knowing he wasn't next to me.
Reaching out, I felt the blank emptiness of the sheet and the mosquito
net puddled where he should have been. My throat raged in pain. He'd
never been so physical before, not like that. Not so it hurt. The hearing
aids ached in my ears, and the batteries started to beep, slowly dying.

Stumbling out onto the deck, the air hit fresh, metallic. Trees set
sharp ink silhouettes in the distance across a streaking, shifting canvas.
Purple-orange skies.

Thwock.

A discordant hum of bees backdropped the birth of the morning.
Intermittent chirps flickered in my chest as if before my ears had even
heard them: urgent calls of nameless birds, cascading and crescendoing;
hidden creatures I could not see but felt all around; others I could not
hear and would never hear, their pitch too high.

Thwock. Thwock.

I saw him by the study hut. Hacking back and forth, he levered a
heavy axe, splintering pieces of timber from the doomed woodpile, split-
ting wedges as easy as butter. *Thwock.*

He'd slung on his cargo pants, but no T-shirt, his muscles pulsing
thick and taut as he worked. Ursula pattered out and sprawled down
beside me on the decking. The metal ashtray lay upside down on the
floor, its contents spilled underneath like a dead volcano. I began clearing the detritus, the ashen mess smearing my fingers. *The Mosquito Coast*
sat on the table, the voluptuous, naked curves of the flute-playing cover
woman, soft and strong. I lit a Marlboro Light from the packet lying
next to it and sat watching.

Thwock.

I flicked through the dog-eared book absentmindedly. Something
flashing by on the title page caught my eye: a black web of handwritten

ink. It was hard to see properly in the dawn light, but opening the pages out and pulling it closer, I was able to study the beautifully embroidered lines: *Aid, Forever, L. 17th November 2019.*

An electric shock on the page, I could only stare. That solitary sloping letter: L. Looping back into itself, unto itself; it was so hauntingly self-assured, an intricate flowing script devouring the paper like it owned it. An L for someone else—someone I did not know; an L he had never spoken about that left me wondering on a tangle of reasons why not. The date: his birthday. We'd met soon after—that first week of January, when I'd flown to Caye Caulker with Chloe.

Thwock.

And "Forever." It was meant to be forever.

PART THREE
Acid

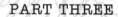

Citrus X aurantifolia. Lime, Adam's apple. Part of the Rutacae family, widely grown in tropical and subtropical areas, including Belize, known for its edible acidic fruit. An ever-bearing tree with glossy leaves, winged stalks, and creamy white or pink-tinged flowers. Pollen is released once the flower has opened. Fruit usually requires six months from flowering to harvest. Provided they have good drainage, limes can grow well even on relatively poor soil.

26

Laelia

"Why are you wearing my scarf?" Ella dumped her textbooks on the kitchen table, glaring at me.

I touched my hand to my neck, the skin bruised and tender. "I . . . had a sore throat . . . they say a scarf helps keep it warm."

She collapsed into a chair next to me. "Like it's not hot enough already?"

I darted my eyes away. "I'm heading to Falicia's to plan the stall for River Day." Ella nodded. "Come if you like?"

She unzipped her pencil case. "Jonas said he'd show us how to use man vine. We're meeting after I've finished my essay." She was still studying *The Scarlet Letter*.

"Man vine?"

"It's for headaches and anxiety."

"Anxiety?"

She rolled her eyes. "It's not for me, Mum . . . He's showing us lots of different remedies, for all kinds of things."

"Okay, honey." I poured us both a mango juice. "Are you still enjoying it here? In Belize?"

"It's so cool," she replied, picking up her biro. "I love it."

"You and Jonas seem to be getting on well."

She was doodling a flower in the margin. "The healing stuff he's showing us is so amazing . . . He's sweet. I like him." She curled a smile. "Like, really like him."

"That's good." I smiled back. "I like him, too."

As I took a sip of juice, I glanced over Ella's shoulder to read a section of her essay: "The Strength of Hester Prynne." Bubble writing burst from the page: "The original meaning of 'courage' derived from the Old French corage, meaning 'heart, innermost feelings, temper.'" She'd underlined the last word three times.

I touched my hand to the scarf again, the juice still burning in my throat.

"You're lost in thought," Falicia said, reaching over across her table.

"Sorry." I scooped up some more beans, helped her scatter them across the metate. A chorus of birds tweeted outside her window, welcoming the morning. We were engineering menus, noting down prices, making grocery lists. Lionfish crudo, plantain chips with coriander aioli, then red curry snapper if we could source enough fish.

"You were miles away . . . I said we should do a trial run, have a dinner here. Invite Mounia if she's around. Would Aid come?"

I nodded. "Sure. Good idea."

Falicia began grinding the cacao again, pushing back and forth across the stone, the beans smushing into pieces. It was a mesmerising process, the transformation of beans to paste. I'd tempered chocolate time and again in training and in restaurants, slicking it into shininess, flirting with the chemistry and magic of it until it snaps, flawless, but I'd never seen this, the origins of it all. "You want a try?"

I smiled, taking a teaspoon of the chocolate slurry. It tasted dense and earthy. Between us, we ground the pulp for longer, until Falicia scooped it into bowls with hot water, chili pepper, and globs of honey.

"You've dropped a bit," Falicia said. "On your scarf." I felt for the silk, noticed a blob of cacao near the knot. "Here, let me wash it for you." She went to help me untie it.

"No," I urged, grabbing at the material. I spoke too hard and it hurt my throat. I could still feel Aid's hand. "It's Ella's. She won't want me to mess with it."

"But we can clean it up—it won't take a moment soaked in cold water."

I flinched. "No. I'll wipe it. She can do what she wants to it later." I grabbed a damp cloth, began pressing at the stain, my neck still scream-ing. "She'd kill me if I made it worse."

"Okay, gyal, if you're sure."

I smiled. "I'm sure. Thanks."

"Let's go outside. Henry will be back soon . . . Kantun thinks I'm fer-tile now, so he's hanging around all the time like a bunch of bananas." She feigned a laugh, and I eased a smile.

We made our way out to the veranda, sat down in her rocking chairs. "What were you thinking about before? In the kitchen?"

I took a sip from my bowl, the chocolate sinking warm. "I was . . . I'm so happy here. I can't stop thinking about new recipes, new ideas, I feel alive. And the kids are doing so well. They've made friends, and they're learning so much more than they ever did in school. I get to spend more time with them, and Ella's opening up."

"So . . . ?"

"I'm worried about Aid. He's angry. Drinking. A lot . . . I think he's struggling here. It's hard."

"It is hard here . . . and you've gone through so much with your dad. It's hard on all of you, I'm sure."

"Since Dad's stroke, Aid's so distracted . . . Distant, you know?" My neck roared, but I had to get the words out, tell Falicia what I could. "He never used to be like that, not really. And I get it. I mean, it was me who pushed for us to be here, to be near my dad. To try something new. For the kids . . ." Maybe we shouldn't have stayed.

Falicia stirred at her bowl. "Laelia . . ." I took another sip of choco-late. "Does he hit you . . . ?"

I swallowed down the liquid, hot in my throat. "What?"

"Aid? Does he hit you?" It felt like Falicia had thrown a grenade at me.

"God. No . . ." My body tightened. "No. I mean, he gets angry some-times, but . . . He'd never do that."

"You're on your own here and—"

"I've asked him to stop working with that Hector guy. He's gone to-day to tell him."

Falicia went back to stirring her cacao. "That's not a bad thing. I don't know much about Hector Hicks, but folks around here don't like him. He's nothing but trouble."

"I'm worried about the money, though. At least Hector paid well. I'm not sure where we'll get that kind of income again. And Aid's spending so much. Living way beyond his means, and—"

There was a bang from inside.

Falicia unpursed her lips. "Champagne dreams wid lime juice money . . ."

I looked up. "Hmm?" But she was getting up to go back into the house.

"Back in a minute."

Champagne dreams with lime juice money. I felt like I'd heard that phrase before. It was so unusual. I couldn't think where . . . *reggae thumping, a flash of gold, daiquiris* . . . At a bar maybe. It felt like I'd heard it at a bar.

Falicia came back out onto the veranda, clutching the saucepan. "Henry . . . I told you he's always hanging around now." She poured more chocolate into my bowl. "He's off tonight to lead a tyga hike. You okay, honeybunch?"

I smiled weakly. "Yes, sorry . . . I'm fine." I was always fine.

Mangrove Lodge, Stann Creek District, Belize
16th March 1987

He needs to get rid of it, thinks about crushing it under a glass. It is the pitch-dark hours of Monday night, and the scraping sound above Ellis's bed has gathered him awake. It's the biggest scorpion yet, crawling inches from his nose.

Trapping the beast into the vessel, he shines the torch into its face. He flicks it outside across the veranda, before dozing back to sleep.

It is the early hours of Tuesday when Cualli appears at the door, the moon still teasing above as the sun finds its way back to life.

"Come quickly," she says, a look of abject uncertainty overtaking her.

Together, they boat across the river, running through spectacular mist. Itzel opens her door, nostrils flaring. She stares sternly at them, and then away.

Ellis catches a glance of Agapita in the background, her bump so large now, writhing on a cot surrounded by her sisters, an expression of panic on her face. Itzel shakes her head at Cualli, pushing the door firmly closed again. They are shrouded in his shame. They do not want him here, he is not welcome; "El hombre orquídia," the white man who has caused all of this, out of wedlock and out of mind.

"Kantun is coming," Ellis hears Itzel say in Kriol behind the door. "He will stop the pain."

He cannot. Kantun's uterine massage, hilie'ek, does not remedy away the hurt, not for Agapita and not for Ellis.

When she went into labour, they tell him, the low-lying placenta detached. She suffered massive uterine bleeding, severe foetal distress. "Perinatal complications," the doctors tell him, when he gets there, to the hospital he's insisted upon, that he will pay for.

When Itzel finds him in the corridor, distraught-eyed and weary, she cannot bear to look at him and cannot hide her rage. She curses him with a dozen epithets that strike like a thousand snakes.

27

Laelia

They sounded animalistic; the pained groans that gathered me awake. I was unsure if I'd even been asleep, if the dreams weren't mere reflections of the days, warped feelings pinching at me through the night. It was pitch-black, Aid still dead to the world.

At first, I thought it was a dog, something outside the hut, but I realised the muffled sounds were closer than that, calling for me, "Mum . . . ? Mum . . . ?!" *Dylan?*

Aid still hadn't moved. I nestled my hearing aids into my ears. They beeped low on battery. Hadn't I switched them on to charge? I stuck them in anyway. I needed the aids now to make out most conversations; everything was so dull, so deadened without them.

Pushing the bedroom door, I found Dyl sitting at the edge of the bed, half-asleep. Ella was a mound under the sheet lying still, Ursula stirring on the rug.

"Dylan?" I moved slowly towards him. "It's okay . . . It was a dream." I put my arm around his shoulder and held him tight, a damp patch visible on the fitted sheet. He hadn't wet the bed since he was three. "It's okay. You're okay."

He started shivering. "I'm sorry."

I shook my head. "Don't worry."

"I dreamt I was by the river, and this snake slid out of nowhere and I couldn't get away. It was slithering, it had big fangs, and then it ate itse—"

"It's okay. It wasn't real."

Rolling Ella back and forth I managed to strip and change the sheet without waking her. Once we'd swapped his pyjamas, Dylan settled back down. I stroked his forehead, like I used to night after night after night; it didn't take long for him to drift back to sleep.

Back in our bed, Aid hadn't shifted, totally passed out. I placed my aids back to charge and lay, achingly awake, listening to the sounds of my mind. I could close my eyes, but I could never close my ears. The static and whirrs and sirens and pulses and *hzzz* of it would not stop, would never go away—their stranglehold tightening.

I'd tried to confront Aid about the book inscription a couple of times, and again once the kids had gone to bed, once he'd had a few beers, but I'd left it too long. When I'd finished with the washing up, he was already asleep, blind drunk again. Henry had told Falicia Aid propped up the Jaguar Lodge now like a semipermanent fixture. He was there most afternoons. People taming.

Aid didn't want to be like his father. He promised he'd try to stop drinking so much but had not, and the only way I knew to try to rein him in was to drink with him. Tonight, he'd been relaxed and happy—we all had—and it was good to hang out like a family, not cause a scene or make a fuss. I wolfed a couple of glasses of rum, though it gave me restless sleep and I should have been easing up, too, especially as it made the ringing worse. I found something oddly comforting, though, in the constancy of the tinnitus—the rage of it, making it all feel less quiet when I was feeling more alone, fear crackling on in the dark.

Worries seem to feast on empty hours. What was I doing? I'd brought my kids to a jungle far from anything I knew, in which I felt helpless, my dreams stuck in the weeds. Aid away more, drinking more; me feeling emptier, less. This was not how it was supposed to be. I'd wanted to be here for Dad, but I also wanted to kindle something afresh in me, for the kids, and start anew. I wanted to prove I was in control, a success—or at least not a fuckup. How naive I'd been to think it would be any different here. I could not escape myself, wherever.

A sudden snap, whiplike, shot into my ears. And again. Ursula barked.

"Aid," I urged, pushing at his arm. Then louder, "Aid, did you hear that?"

"Ugggmmm." He rolled over. "Whaaat . . . ?" A drunken slur.

"Did you hear? Gunshots!" The fear of unknowns amplified in my gut.

He moaned. Another shot. Breathing out a heavy sigh, his eyes didn't even flicker. "It's poachers."

"But Aid—"

"Ssssh," he hugged into me. "Close your eyesss . . . go back to sleep." I shut them. Heaved a breath.

The tinnitus still hissed, wide awake.

The morning sunlight evaporated away the nighttime's worries like they were nothing. Like it was laughing at me, wryly. Like I was the joke. It was Saturday, and Aid would have a lie-in. He'd have a lie-in most days now.

The children sat on the floor of the veranda playing a game that involved slapping their thighs and pointing finger guns at each other. "Lock, load, shoot."

Ella had been graffiti'ing her hands in trailing henna-style tattoos.

"Do you have to keep doing that to your skin?"

She rolled her eyes. "It's only pen." I was about to reply, find something snappy and discussion-ending to say, but stopped myself.

After brewing a pot of thick coffee, I wandered to the coop to let the chickens out and gather up the eggs. It took me a moment to realise there was one missing. Only four chickens. Ditsy was gone. The door was closed, the fencing tight. I was sure she'd been there the night before. I'd put them in before supper. I counted again, as I watched them flapping about. Four. Definitely only four. Was this someone's idea of a funny stunt? Aid wouldn't have done this; he would have known I wouldn't have found it amusing.

I asked the kids over breakfast, but they looked blank. "What if someone's taken her?"

Aid dished out more eggs from the pan. "Don't be ridiculous. No-one around here needs to steal a chicken! Are you sure she was definitely there last night? Sure you're not imagining it? You were pretty tired."

"Of course I'm not imagining it! There were five."

"I'll bet it was a snake," Ella chimed in.

"What?!" Dylan dropped his fork onto his plate. "Snakes eat chickens?"

"But the fencing's tight," I said quietly to Aid at the sink, where the kids couldn't hear. "The chicken wire's too small for a snake to get through. What if someone took her?"

"Lil, you're overthinking it." Aid rubbed at his eyebrow. "Snakes can squeeze through chicken wire . . . We need to pick up some hardware cloth in town."

"But, what if some—" I stopped myself. *Crazy bitch.*

"Who's L?" I asked—finally, once the children had gone outside. The words came out playfully, coquettishly even. I wanted him to think I'd just had the thought, as if I hadn't been ruminating on it for hours and hours, days and days, playing crazy scenarios over and over in my head.

"Who's who?" Aid dropped his bowl into the sink and ran the tap.

I prodded at my fry jacks, trying to sound casual. "L . . . ? In your book . . . I picked it up the other day when I was cleaning. The inscription . . . ? From 'L'?"

"Are you joking?"

"What?"

"You've forgotten . . ." He kept his back to me.

"Forgotten what?"

He sighed. "You forget so much . . . We've talked about this." *Have we?* "It was from my mother."

"L?" I asked.

"Liz . . . Elizabeth."

"Not 'Mum'?"

He turned around. "We were never that close. I called her Liz the last few years."

"Oh," I replied, taking a sip of coffee. Elizabeth. Aid hardly ever talked about his parents other than his dad's alcoholism. All I knew was his mother died suddenly of cancer—pancreatic, I thought he'd said, early on. "Are you reading it again then?"

"I read it constantly . . . find new things every time."

"D'you remember, you had that with you when we first met?" I asked. "On Caye Caulker."

"I like sucking on its secrets like candy."

"What?"

"It's a quote. From the book."

"Oh." I drained my coffee, smeared the tiredness from my eyes. "Did you hear those gunshots last night?"

He started tidying up the rest of the plates from the table, taking them over to the sink. "Hmm?"

"Last night. There were shots. In the distance."

"Yeah. Just poachers. Surprised you could hear them without your hearing aids in." Gunshots I could hear. "You worry too much . . ."

"Shouldn't I be worried about poachers?!"

"Not here . . . You need to relax, stop trying to control things. Accept things work differently in the middle of nowhere in Belize."

"I don't like guns."

"I know. Me neither." *Then why did you shoot a rifle with my son?!* "I figure I'll head into town," Aid said, changing the subject as he stuffed his things into his daypack. "Get that cloth for the coop."

Ellis

Mangrove Lodge, Stann Creek District, Belize
17th March 1987

Itzel wants him gone. She cannot bear what has happened to her daughter, to their family, to their good name. The locals are starting to talk, and secrets skim the air. There are rumours he's married, though he has told no-one, and he's barely married anyway. Maybe Itzel needs some time to come to terms with this thing they have done. That *he* has done. But he knows it is all too much for her, now Agapita has almost died.

He's headed home from the hospital to think and freshen up, though he can barely think at all, exhausted and hungry as he is. He turns up the gas for coffee, is cutting the mould off the bread, when there is an emphatic knock at the door.

Polo early again. But surely he knows the news? Cualli would have told him that they've been at the hospital all night; that Agapita nearly lost her life; that he won't want to go out collecting today, certainly not to Chiquibul, not all that way.

But when he opens the door, it is not Polo. It is a uniformed British solider, standing firm.

"Dr. Wylde?" The soldier's eyes narrow, his eyebrows pull together. "Dr. Ellis Wylde?"

"Yes?"

"Lance-Corporal Mason. I've been sent by the High Commission."

Ellis stops buttering the bread roll he is still holding.

"Are you husband of Mrs. Helena Lauren Wylde? Of Pusey Road, Oxford?"

Ellis's chest tightens. "Yes?"

He coughs, this uninvited man from the government. "I'm sorry to inform you. She was found dead yesterday afternoon." Two sentences, not one. A gentle run-up, meandering—this is what Ellis focuses on in this moment: the intricacies of language, the shade and the shadows of it people hide behind.

Ellis stumbles, his heart pumping in his head. "She's . . . *dead?*"

"I'm sorry. Suicide, they're saying. An overdose."

She did it.

Ellis looks up from the swirling floor.

She really did it.

His stomach drops. "Who is with my girls?" His voice creaks. "My daughters."

"They are with a neighbour. A . . ."—the man pulls a piece of paper from his pocket and reads—"Mrs. Penny Cairns . . . The children have been asking for you. They've been told you're on your way. You'll need to pack for the next flight out in two days."

When he shuts the door behind the man, Ellis stares around the hut. This life here he was starting, paused in an instant. *You poor, poor woman.* The kettle whistles for attention, and he goes to switch off the gas. Guts lurching, he turns the mug back upside down on its towel, throws the bread into the bin. He thinks of the last time he saw his wife, felt her touch, the warmth of her embrace.

He collapses into a fit of tears. He cannot remember the last time he cried, if he even has since he was a child. Pulling his suitcase out from under the bed, he thinks of Agapita, who didn't want to die, and of Helena, who really did.

Yesterday afternoon. He scrolls through his latest notebook. Sixteenth March. Their wedding anniversary. *Oh, Helena.*

He just makes it outside before he throws up.

28

Laelia

Ella begged for Jonas to come next time we visited Dad. I kept thinking of that stoner kid who tagged along to the hospital with George Clooney and his family in *The Descendants*, then had to keep reminding myself, it was good Ella was making friends here. Jonas was a million miles away from those boys she hung around with in London. He was kind, and gentle, and smart. And they looked at each other like they were the world, working out its agonies and its ecstasies together. He could break her heart, but he would break it gently and then probably help her glue it back again.

"Thank you," Jonas said to me when Ella went to get a Sprite. "For letting me come." I smiled back, not knowing what else to say. *Don't hurt her. Don't ever hurt her.* "Will he get better?"

"I don't know" was all I could say.

Each time I visited now, it all still felt so unreal, an exhausted dream—vigilance meeting oblivion. The machines whirred and beeped and bleeped. The tinnitus pulsed on. Dad's skin was mottled and crepey. He was losing weight, his face so sallow. His fingernails were long. His hands were colder, more fragile. I thought of all the things they had done: held me as a newborn; rocked me to sleep nap after nap—when Mum was overtired, or exhausted, or had taken herself off for a break; pressed a thousand orchids (the reams of botanical papers he must have handled, scribbled notes upon), paragraphs he must have typed; the petals he must have touched.

I remembered planting my first seeds with him: marking my name onto lollipop sticks; volunteering for duty, and demolishing extra Mini Milks while I watched him preparing pots in the sun. The earthy smell of excitement. Sunflower kernels like rat droppings. Their promise of endless summer days. The magic of my hope; the certainty of his belief.

After the kids spent time with Dad asking tentative, brutal questions (*Does Paw-Paw know we're here? How does he go to the loo? Is he going to die?*), Mounia shuttled them off for ice cream before we planned to meet them at the Hungry Lizard. Dessert before dinner; everything the wrong way round because everything was upside down.

Dr. Guevarra wanted to have "a proper meeting" to discuss "Dad's case," like it was a bag he was carrying—heavy and cumbersome. The bureaucracy of grief.

Her office was stuffy and small, the striplights blindingly bright.

"I'm sorry, the air-con is broken." She battled with the blinds, then wrestled with a fan, helicoptering it into life. "Please, take a seat . . ." The chairs were hard and uncomfortable.

She stared at me across the desk, over a sea of papers, her eyes appropriately soft, her voice fittingly slow. "He remains very ill. The EEG shows good brain activity, but it is hard to say if he will make a full recovery, or what a recovery might look like if we can take him off life support." She let that sink in a little, before adding, "You need to be ready for all outcomes."

"Can he hear me yet?" I asked.

"Talk to him, touch him. We want to try a . . . espera . . . a . . . sedation hold soon, if we can. Take away the tubes to see how he responds."

"When will we be able to move him down to Stann Creek?" I asked.

She took a breath, her eyes flitting to Aid and then back to me. "He is stable, but he is too ill. We need to keep him here. Miss. Laelia, this really is the best medical facility for him." I nodded.

The fan whirred on.

"He may seem very different, if he comes around. Agitated, confused. And his memory may be affected."

"In what way?" Aid asked, shifting on his chair.

"With a big stroke like this, he may struggle to recall certain things."

Aid started bouncing one knee up and down. "What? He might not remember?"

Dr. Guevarra looked at me, then at Aid, before she answered. "Sí, long-term . . . If he is better, out of the coma, his rehabilitation will be critical. He lost muscle strength. His reflexes are slower. He will need help and support." She smiled at me, a comforting smile with no hint of pity. "Good you are here."

I nodded again, pursing my lips. I remembered when they bloomed—Dad's August shock of sunflowers, their faces bigger than my head.

"Have you started to think about what's next?" Aid asked as we walked towards the Hungry Lizard.

"Next for what?"

"To think about a pathway? To be prepared. In case we do need to turn off the machines?"

"What? What are you on about? Did you not hear what Dr. Guevarra said? He's getting better . . . Why would you say that?"

"I'm trying to stay realistic, you know. Think of all possibilities. Not get our hopes up." He stopped and kissed my cheek. "But you need to be prepared. I'm sorry. I know it's hard."

"It is so fucking hard. I hate it."

"I'm sorry," he hugged into me, breathed into my hair. "It's shit, I know . . . Look, you go on and I'll see you there. You need a drink."

"What?"

"I need to make a call . . ." He was already on his mobile.

As I turned the final corner before the bar, a mousy-blond, denim-shorted woman bumped her oversized tote bag into my arm.

"Oh. I'm sorry," she said in a delicious Californian accent.

I shook my head. "It's fine. No problem."

She stopped, dropping one shoulder and furrowing her brow. "Laelia? Are you Laelia?"

"Er . . . yeah. Do we—"

"Aid Lynch's girlfriend?"

I scrambled my brain to try to place her.

"Maia." She thrust out her skinny hand to shake at mine, then hugged into me. She smelt of coconut sunscreen. "How are you doing?"

I nodded slowly in vague recognition. "Yeah, good. Good."

"I'm married to Rich. We went to college with Aid . . . I recognise you from Instagram." Aid doesn't really post, but there was an old one on there from the day we got tattoos in Brighton. "Are you, like, on vacation?" she asked, checking her watch.

"No, well . . . sort of. My father lives here. We've been staying awhile."

"Aid always loved Belize." She looked into the distance. "Didn't think he'd come back, though."

"He'll be here soon. Do you want to join us for dinner? Is Rich here?"

She was a whirlwind now, flapping her hair back and forth. "Oh Lord, I'd love to. But I got to get the last ferry back to Ambergris. Rich is there . . . Where are you guys?"

"Stann Creek. Can you come down? Aid would love to see you both."

"We're heading to Tulum, but let me chat with Rich. He'd *love* to catch up with Aid."

Maia and I swapped details before I carried on to the bar. We were halfway through our drinks when Aid got there, Jonas dealing out a pack of cards.

"Hey, guess who I just met?" I asked Aid as he sat down.

"Er . . . no idea."

"Maia!"

"Maia?"

"Your friend from college."

"What . . . ? Where?"

"Outside on the street. She and Rich are staying on Ambergris Caye. She recognised me from your Instagram. I invited them down."

"What?"

"She thinks they can make it work."

"Okay. Sure . . . sounds good."

"You don't seem very excited? I thought you'd want to see them. Isn't Rich your friend?"

Aid took a long glug of beer. "Yeah, he is."

"I thought you'd want to see them."

"No . . . yeah, I do." He got up to go to the Men's.

"What's eating him?" Dylan asked, his freckles an explosion across his face now. He sounded so grown up.

"Where have you heard that expression?" I asked.

"Jonas thinks Aid's haunted by something," Ella announced. I shot her a look. "What . . . ?"

"Ella, stop it."

"It's true. You do, don't you, Jonas . . . ? He feels things like his grandfather does."

Jonas sat shuffling the pack. "Not now, Ella."

"But—"

"Not now." Jonas dealt out the rest of the cards in silence.

Ellis

Mangrove Lodge, Stann Creek District, Belize
18th March 1987

After packing his suitcase then unpacking it again, Ellis arrives back at the hospital around midday. He finds the waiting room oppressive with people, and heat, and worry. The attendant behind the desk is new, thick-brimmed spectacles hiding most of her face.

Ellis's heart pounds as he explains who he is, what he's here for, the urgency of his request. His voice cracks.

"You family?" she asks. He can barely hear her over the whirr of the fan.

"Can't you tell me anything . . . ? Please. I'm the father." It is the first time he has said that word out loud. This time around, at least.

The nurse looks him up and down, he thinks, though the large frames around her eyes conceal much of the judgement he still feels penetrate. "She's sleeping."

"Yes. You've said that. But I have to see her. Urgently."

"It's not up to me. The doctors say she cannot be disturbed."

"Then I'll wait." Ellis slumps into a plastic chair, holds his head in his hands.

A little later, Itzel rounds the corner with Dacey and Aapo looped through her arms. There's a slump in their shoulders, new dark circles under their eyes. Itzel stabilises herself when she sees him. "Mr. Ellis?"

"How is she?" he asks in Kriol.

Itzel tuts and shakes her head.

Aapo releases her arm from her mother. "Tired," she says. "But she'll be okay." Itzel and Dacey bend their heads and continue towards the door.

"And the baby?" Ellis asks.

Aapo urges a flat smile. "Agapita must stay here now until the birth."

Weeks, months even.

"Thank God," Ellis mutters under his breath, before his head falls back. "I need to see her."

She shakes her head. "No."

"But . . . There's something I need to tell her."

"I'm sorry."

"Is it your mother? Look, I cannot change what has happened . . . I really do need to speak with her."

Aapo turns away from him, muttering under her breath, "I'm sorry."

Ellis pleads with the surly attendant to lend him some paper and a pen. After she relents, with an irascible look through her spectacles, he hovers in the waiting room to scribble out a note.

At the start, he tells her he loves her. Then he tells her all of it. He tells her about Helena, the fact they are estranged, the news she has died (he can barely believe the words as he writes them), about Chloe and Laelia now alone and so afraid, how he didn't mean for any of this, he doesn't know what has happened, what to do, or how to make it right. He can't leave her, but he also can't not return to his girls. He has packed his bags and unpacked them and repacked them again. He will support her. He will be there for the baby whatever happens. He's been saving money. He's sorry. At the end, he again tells her he loves her.

He signs his name and folds the letter. The nurse promises to pass it on, then files it like a life raft on top of a stormy sea of papers.

The next day, Ellis goes back to the hospital. He is told he still cannot see her; they don't know if or when.

He goes home to the lodge and unpacks his bags again.

Ellis is woken in the early hours by a knocking. He weaves his way across the room over half-packed boxes and abandoned suitcases to open the door.

Aapo stands before him, eyes wide and with a wavering smile. She presents him with an envelope, his name scrawled in Agapita's hand.

"Man who shit da pass no remember, da who daab eena it," Aapo says, as she turns and leaves.

He tears the letter open.

Ellis,

I am so sorry to hear about Helena, about your daughters and their loss. I cannot imagine their pain.

Things took a turn. I miscarried the baby tonight. A full stop to our world.

Blood follows vein. You must go, be with your daughters. They need you. I have my family and my life here, and I will never leave Belize.

What feels like sacrifice is love. So do this final thing for me.

Agapita.

Ellis's breath hitches. He cannot think; his mind is racing. He reads the letter once more, then twice again, swallowing the words into his heart.

He squeezes shut his eyes, but he cannot stop the tears from falling. He rips the letter into pieces and throws them into the bin.

Grabbing the suitcases, he unzips them and packs them once again.

29

Laelia

I packed up the truck with our daypacks and took Ella and Dylan to San Ignacio to get away. We left before Aid woke up. I switched off my phone completely, threw it in the boot so I wouldn't even be tempted to speak to him. I needed not to have to answer to anyone, not to him, just for a day.

He was like the sea. It came in waves, pulsing gently then lashing like a storm, whipping and churning and beating against me—until, powerless, I thought I could take no more. Then suddenly, out of nowhere, and slowly as if at once, everything would calm back to nothing, near nothing—to breath, to beauty—the cataclysm unfathomable again. Like it had never even happened, a trick of the drink, an acidic fever dream. But I'd still wake up drowning, the sheets knotted slick with sweat.

Our world hinged on Aid's swings. He was drinking more, working more, absent more. He'd fixed the chicken coop, helped Ella rewire the dodgy reading lamp, would still read bedtime stories to Dylan, but he could never find the energy to machete back the forest now. That was too audacious an ask. Not that I would dare to ask him. He'd been leaving me to deal with the violence of nature while he was out running jobs, chasing leads, making money, and I couldn't say too much. He wasn't with Hector, and that was what I'd asked for—my dreams come true. Though, for Aid, that came at a price. He missed the free-flowing dollars, the cocaine around the edges, the hits and highs of it all; he missed the infamous Hector Hicks. And he kept talking about London, about wanting to leave. If Dad wasn't going to get better. But I knew I did not want to go. Not back to that cacophony. Not away from Belize.

We stopped off at a swimming hole for a dip halfway. We had it all to ourselves; just the three of us with the insects and the birds and the memories we were making, splashing, and diving and floating free. Dyl brought his goggles, and we took it in turns to swim down to find the underwater cave, breathless. We saw a yellow-chested gartered trogon and chased wee-wee ants over the rocks.

In San Ignacio we stopped for lunch at a dreamy outdoor bar festooned with plants and fairy lights. Baby ribs and shrimp pasta on the roadside. Leathery Malbec so good I ordered a second glass. Took a photo of the label for Chloe. The waitress was chatty and light, said she liked my shirt. The one-hundred-thirty-seven-dollar bill was a jolt, even in Belize dollars, but the kids downed two Cokes each and we all had dessert. I brought cash so Aid wouldn't see how much I spent.

The kids loved the wonder of Cahal Pech: climbing the steps, feeling the echoes of the burial chambers, whipping themselves into ecstasy with stone-cold tales and Mayan ghost stories; legends of twisted men turned mad, transparent women, and executed warriors, half dead in the half-light. Our tour guide showed us magical *mimosa pudica* hidden in the carpet of star grass beneath our feet, touch-me-nots that—when you touch them—retract like umbrellas on a sunny day. Dad told me once: Plants have feelings way beyond any scientific understanding. I wondered what these flowers felt—fear maybe, or anger. Mimosa pudica. I googled it later when we stopped for a drink: "Shy or shrinking; also called touch-me-not, sensitive plant, or shameplant. Its compound leaves fold inward when touched and reopen later."

I bought the children more Cokes and wangla bites, got myself a water. A woman with frost-blue eyes and burnt-orange hair got to talking from the pulpit of the next table, gathering speed with her otherworldly yarns. Her cousin had broken up with his girlfriend, finished things out of the blue. "She was so upset her grandfather placed a curse on him—my cousin—promise to strike him down like lightning."

One moon later, she told us, the boy started behaving apelike, climbing trees, convinced he was a howler monkey. He spent weeks walking, walking, walking around Belize, lacing the whole of the country until he could walk no more, his feet blistered and broken and bruised. He started riding his bike then—endlessly everywhere like a dervish—trying to pedal away the devil, cycle it into oblivion, but he was stuck in infinite circles, spinning and spinning and spinning until, sleepless one night, he drove himself into a ditch in the dark, flung himself over the handlebars. Mangled himself into a coffin.

"There's no such thing as good or evil, just power." At least, that's what she said, the fire-headed woman.

"Was that real?" Dylan asked as we jumped into the truck.

"I don't know, darling," I said. "What's real?"

Ella laughed. "There are more things in heaven and earth, Horatio, than are dreamt of in your philosophy."

"What?" Dylan asked, grabbing his manga book from the footwell.

"Shakespeare, dummy . . . It's like I told you with Jonas. He's in touch with the spirit world. He feels things. I wasn't joking when he said all that stuff about Aid—"

"Stop it now. You're scaring Dylan." I glared at her in the mirror.

"But Mum—"

"Now."

Both kids fell asleep on the journey back, and I got to dreaming again of my fantasy cantina; letting myself run wild choosing paint colours and oven models and menu ideas, picturing serving up dishes to a bustling lodge restaurant, customers queuing around the trees outside the door, Dad sitting at a table in the corner, smiling ear to ear, proud of his girl, of what she'd done. My mind ran away with possibilities. Something I could manage—an outdoor kitchen I could hear myself in, where I could finally be myself, where I could be free and find control.

The bats were skimming low when we got home. The cloying smell of cigar smoke. No lights on, I could see Aid wasn't there. He'd left a note under a stone on the outside table:

Don't even think about it.

As though he could read my thoughts, as though he knew I'd been daring to dream. But of course, he couldn't possibly have known about the restaurant idea. Falicia wouldn't have said anything. She'd promised.

The kids still spilling themselves out of the car, I managed to screw the paper up into my pocket before they saw it. *Don't even think about what . . . ? What was he on about?* Pissed off about something but not even bothering to confront me anymore. Maybe he was just pissed. Again.

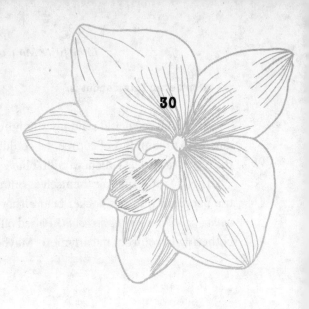

30

Untwisting from sleep, I took my morning coffee out onto the veranda, Ursula padding behind me. As I relaxed into my chair with a book, I spotted the new addition in front of our door. Fire ants. Reddish dots roving frenetic, threading into and under and onto and through themselves.

After scouring Dad's bookshelf I found *Native Growing Guide for Belize* and flicked through several pest remedies: hot pepper solution (I'd used all my habaneros for soup already, and this was best for mole crickets and chinch), garlic solution (best for aphids, slugs, and caterpillars), hot pepper and garlic solution (no actual instructions, but presumably a double whammy of kill power for someone with extra time on their hands, and Neem-x (I had no idea what this was). Finally, I found a specific recipe for fire ant killer: citrus oil (or citrus powder and car degreaser) and molasses. *Lime rinds contain d-limonene extract—toxic to fire ants.* Perfect. I got to zesting a pile of limes at the kitchen table, dumping their peels into water-filled Mason jars. The kids were still fast asleep.

"What you doing?" Aid asked, reemerging through the door, dropping his rucksack from the night before. He seemed light, not drunk. Not angry.

"Didn't you see? We've got fire ants. Right in front of the steps."

"Right . . ." He sounded exasperated. "And how is this going to help?" He came over and hooked his palm around my neck, kissed at my cheek. A stun of gentle alcohol.

"They hate citrus."

"Okay . . ." He grabbed a lime and a knife and started peeling, too. "Where were you yesterday?"

"I thought the kids could do with a day away from"—*don't say you*—"everything."

He stopped zesting, stared at me. "You took the truck."

I held my breath. "I couldn't get a taxi all the way to San Ignacio. I took the kids to look at Cahal Pech."

"But you didn't ask me . . . I had to bus to Benny's, get a lift with him."

"Sorry . . . I'm sorry." My breathing shallowed. That was pretty shitty of me. Benny lived miles away. I hadn't even thought Aid might have needed the Frontier.

"Don't do that again, okay?"

I nodded. Exhaled. Threw some more rinds into the jar.

"You need to tell me when you're going somewhere . . ." He scratched at his stubble. "I didn't know where you were." I nodded. "I mean it, Lil."

"I'm sorry . . ." I got up, started filling the kettle for another pot. "D'you want some coffee?"

"Thanks, yeah."

"Are you working with Benny again then?" I asked.

"I'm helping him with foundations at Maya Beach." He said it automatically, almost rehearsed. "Asked me to go in with him on it, on the project." He emptied his lime pile into a new jar.

"So I've been thinking . . ." Because he seemed calm, relatively, it felt like a good time to ask. "About setting up a restaurant here. A cantina for the tourists. Feeding back into the local economy. It's such a fantas—"

"Are you kidding?"

"No, I'm not kidding."

"That's a pretty permanent move."

"I thought we liked it here . . . ? I like it here. I want to—"

"We don't need the Labour Department sniffing around, Lil . . . all that form filling and box ticking. Drawing attention."

"What? Beca—" I started to ask what he meant, though I already knew he probably wasn't doing things aboveboard here. I wasn't so naive.

He interrupted anyway. "Chloe called yesterday. She couldn't get hold of you. She's in Belize City seeing your dad."

"What? Now?"

"She flew in on Sunday. She's talking about coming down in a couple of days. Said she emailed, but you never replied."

I grabbed another mug down from the shelf. "Is Dad okay? Did she say how he is?"

"The same," Aid replied. No change. Always no change.

"What was your note about, by the way?"

"What note?"

"The note you left out last night."

"I didn't leave a note out last night." Why did he have to be so pedantic?

"During the day then . . . what was it?"

"Lil, I don't know what you're talking about."

"The note! On the table."

"I didn't leave a note."

"What . . . ?" I left the kettle, rushed off behind the bedroom curtain to find the shorts I'd thrown off the night before. Rummaging in the pocket, I found the crumpled paper.

Aid appeared, reading over my shoulder. "What does that mean? 'Don't even think about it?'"

"I don't know. I thought it was from you!"

"It's not my writing," he said, his voice a whisper. I'd hardly ever seen his handwriting. Apart from his signature and the odd bit of homework help with Dylan, he barely ever wrote a thing.

He looked at me blankly, stiffening his posture. The kettle shrilled from the kitchen.

Don't even think about it. The words stung even more vicious now.

When we walked into the store, I couldn't help but think Falicia looked like she'd been crying, but her voice brightened when she saw us. "You guys look ready for a good day." She straightened her skirt. "You gonna help your mama?" Dylan nodded. I'd left Ella toiling over algebra at home, but Dylan was desperate to come.

"All okay?" I asked. Falicia tried a smile, and her eyes shot to Dylan. I told him to wait outside while we got the table out from the back room. "Is everything okay? Really?"

"It will be . . ." She sighed, searching for words. "The pregnancies are not taking, and you know, I can't keep doing this."

"I'm so sorry."

"Henry wants to give it another try. But . . . I don't think I can go through it again, and I don't want him to be angry."

"Oh, Falicia. You have to tell him. You can't keep hiding how you feel about it."

"I will. Anger is just misplaced fear. I understand he's scared. I'll talk to him. There's no shame if we shine a light on things . . . It's hard though, you know . . . ? Anyway, how are you?"

"I'm finalising things for River Day." We started moving the table across to the lay-by, Dylan tagging along. "I don't suppose you know where I can source some bulk fish?"

"Well, sure. There's Dominik at the shrimp farm. Or . . . why don't you speak to that friend of Aid's . . . ? The French one."

"Nico?"

"He's working for an aquaculture company in Placencia. He might know."

"But Nico works for Hector."

"I heard he left there . . ." We propped up our hand-painted signs: FISH CURRY WITH COCONUT AND TURMERIC $10. My new recipe, with extra ginger, less cayenne. "Right, you all set?"

I nodded. "Think so."

She smiled. "Good luck."

"Thanks . . . For everything."

"You're welcome, gyal. Now you go sell some curry . . ."

"Falicia," I said quietly as Dylan was pulling out the cartons of food. "Please don't say anything to Aid . . . about this, about the money. I'm not sure I want him to know yet. About the restaurant. About my plans."

She smiled a soft, reassuring smile. "Sisters' secret."

Dylan and I sat for hours drinking hibiscus juice and reading comics in the shade, exchanging servings and smiles for cash until we sold out.

"We did well, Mummy," Dylan said as we started to clear away, and I gave him ten dollars. "That was super fun."

We made one hundred eighty dollars. It wasn't a fortune, but it was something, and the next day we would go back again. At Dad's I stuffed the notes into the old tea tin I'd found, scribbling *TWL* over the faded label, smiling at my handiwork. I pushed it to the very back of the cupboard.

31

Chloe blew in with a prism of emotions, one smallish suitcase, and a tote bag stuffed with gifts. She arrived in a taxi she'd taken straight from the hospital, flipping a bounty of bills into the driver's hands.

"Laelia, how are you?" A big hug—longer than I was expecting—that caught me like home. Somehow, she still smelled of London; of petrol and perfume and glossy magazines. "You look exhausted." She looked knackered, too.

"How's Dad?" She'd cut her hair shorter, off the shoulders.

"Dr. Guevarra said they can't do the sedation hold yet. They want to wait a little longer. I've said not to rush things. I'll pay for as long as they need." She bit her lip and pushed her sunglasses onto her head. Her hair suited her, tousled like that. "How's Ella, and Dylan?" We dodged the citrusy remnants of the ant mound, Ursula following behind as we walked up the steps.

"They're with friends across the river . . . We weren't sure when you were coming."

"I told you in my email. Said I'd try to get here early afternoon." She stopped to stare out over the veranda.

"Sorry, I didn't see it. There's not much internet around here."

She gazed at the lodge buildings, breathing it all in, as if sketching pictures of him there in her mind. "So, thi i it . . . Dad ki   ."

"Hmm?"

"Dad's *kingdom*," she shouted at me.

"Yeah. It's pretty basic. But it's peaceful." After I'd said it, I realised what a strange word that was to choose. Life was beautiful here— mesmerising and alive and lush and wild and tricky and deep. But not peaceful. Not right now. I wheeled her case inside, and she followed. "How's Tom? And the kids?"

She stood in the doorway, eyes sweeping the room. "Edmund can't understand why I get two weeks off work, but he still has to go to school." Her face was a puzzle as she took everything in. "So this is where you're living . . . ?"

"You're here for a fortnight then?" I called, filling the kettle.

She ventured towards the sofa, peering around the bedroom curtain. "I'm flying back a week on Tuesday. I've got a lull in caseload." Tilting her head at the bookcase, she started dragging her fingers over spines. "He's got so many books."

"Ella's working her way through them." I lit the gas. "Have you eaten?"

"No, I'm starving. Mounia took me to this place by the port for breakfast. Have you tried those funny fry jack things?" She made a face. "So greasy. I couldn't eat them."

I used the last of the thundershaw mangoes for lunch, throwing them into a chicken and bell pepper salad. Lime, chilli, basil, mint. I loved collaging flavours together, the alchemy of it all.

"I've missed your food," Chloe said, chasing the leaves around her plate. When she spoke, the world curdled around her. "So why aren't you working? Running a kitchen in that touristy place across the lagoon or something? It's not far, is it?" Her voice honeyed barbed wire. "Stuck here all day, you must be going stir-fucking-crazy." I didn't tell her about the stall. Didn't want to tell her my plans, my dream of a restaurant. She'd think it was stupid, a waste of time and money, too risky to open a business in Belize. She'd focus on the red tape, the corruption, all the bad stuff she'd read about and overimagined in her head.

I flung down my fork. "Have you seen how much there is to do around here to keep it like this?"

"Christ, you sound like a fifties housewife! What happened to you? I thought you'd own your own restaurant by now. Out here, you could at least be cheffing somewhere."

"I can't," I said.

"Why not?"

"I'm homeschooling the kids, and we're refurbishing the lodge rooms. I've ruled it out."

Her eyes flicked like switchblades. "*You've* ruled it out? Or Aid has? Come on, Laelia. You need to do something for yourself."

"I can't. It's too much. And by the way, Placencia is, like, over an hour across the water. I couldn't do that every day."

"Well—"

"Chloe . . ." Aid breezed in through the door with peculiar relief. "How's things?" His shirt was vandalised with mud. He reeked of stale beer. Chloe got up to hug him, and they danced around each other loosely, negotiating her white shirt and his foul stench. "How's your dad?"

Chloe took the final glug of wine from her glass. "He's . . . he's okay." I stared at her, then at him. Their eyes stayed fixed on each other.

Aid grabbed a bottle of Belikin from the fridge. "Lil said they're going to bring him out of the coma soon."

"Hopefully."

"Is that a good idea?" Aid asked. "I mean, is he well enough?"

"Well, we're going with what the doctors say. They want to try, see how he responds. But we need to be prepared for anything." Chloe poured herself another glass of wine. "Did you ever find that power of attorney? His will? Anything?"

"No," I said. "Nothing."

She could see it was time to shift the subject. For now, at least. "So what plans have you got for Laelia's birthday?"

Aid swigged on his beer a little too long. "I thought we could get dinner out. Somewhere fancy."

Chloe said something I couldn't catch, then laughed. "Tomorrow? For her actual birthday?"

"Er . . . yeah. Or I was thinking maybe Friday. Make more of a night of it?"

"But it's her birthday tomorrow." Chloe glared at me.

"Honestly, it's fine. I really don't need—"

"I've got to see a guy in Tikal tomorrow." He moved in towards me, kissed my forehead.

"Okay," Chloe said. "I'll take her out tomorrow, then you guys can go for a meal or whatever on Friday, and I'll look after the kids."

"Thanks, Chlo," Aid shouted as he drifted out the door.

"He wasn't planning anything at all, was he?" Chloe said, clearing our plates. "What's up with him?"

"He's just stressed out." Tears were welling up in my eyes, and I couldn't stop them. With Chloe there like a bellwether, I could feel how much things had changed. Whenever Aid was at home, he was lashing out. Not physically, and never at the kids. He'd never hit me—he wasn't like Si—and he wasn't even really arguing; just spitting words like darts, confiding in tight-fisted silences, tearing little rips into my heart.

"Yeah, well, we're all stressed out." She caught me then, as she came back towards the table. "Oh, Lil. Fuck him . . . Don't worry, I'm booking you the best restaurant we can find, and we're going to drink cocktails faster than they can mix them."

Aid woke me up with banana pancakes—a solitary candle. They sang me "Happy Birthday" over breakfast and hibiscus juice, and the kids armed me with flowers and cards. After Aid left for Tikal, Chloe gave me a heavy little parcel of Marmite, so we devoured thick slabs of toast and fresh cups of tea.

I said I'd be fine with the Jaguar Lodge, but Chloe insisted on somewhere special, so Falicia organised a water taxi over the peninsula to a restaurant I'd read about in the guidebooks. Lionfish was a cosy, eclectic space overlooking the ball field in Placencia village—all fairy lights, timber, and vines. We sat up on the balcony, basking in the warmth of the night and the cool of our watermelon mojitos. We wore dresses and jewellery, and I made the effort to brush my hair. Falicia brought me flowers, and Mounia gave me a pair of lionfish earrings she'd made—black spots feathered on cream. "So you can remember this night always. They're sustainable. Lionfish have no natural predators, and they kill off tons of marine life, so . . ."

Chloe waved her menu. "Well, in that case, lionfish ceviche it is."

"Happy birthday!" Falicia declared as we cheersed our glasses together.

"Happy birthday!" Chloe winked at me. I couldn't remember the last time we'd gone out together, shared a joyful drink.

I squeezed the lime wedge into my glass. *Champagne dreams with lime juice money.* Where had I heard that? I tried to recall the images again, force them into a pattern. *Champagne dreams with lime juice money. Reggae thumping. A flash of gold. Daiquiris.* At a bar. Caye Caulker? Sunset?

"Chlo, have you heard the phrase 'Champagne dreams with lime juice money' before?"

She looked at me blankly, shaking her head. "What is it?"

"Just a phrase. I wondered if you'd heard it before. It reminded me of Caye Caulker maybe, and I don't know why."

"No, but I like it." She clinked her glass at mine. "Why are you always asking me about weird phrases?" She laughed. "Did you ever find out what that 'lavender feels' thing was?"

I shook my head. "No. I've got no idea."

We devoured the appetizers then tore into our steaks with sublime intention. They were delicious, though the salad could have handled more coriander, less onion.

I was hoovering up the last of my fries when I spotted Nico breeze in with another guy, perching themselves at the bar. Nico saw me seeing him. He left it a casual few minutes before he came over, once they'd ordered their drinks and his friend had slipped off to the Men's.

"Hi, Laelia." He smiled, his arms outstretched. We kissed all the cheeks.

"Nico, do you know Mounia and Falicia?" I asked. He shook their outstretched hands. "And this is my sister—"

"Chloe," she chimed, her face as sparkly as a jewellery box. Her eyes widened at me in a "wow."

"Nice to meet you, Chloe . . ." He pointed at the cards. "Is it somebody's birthday?"

"Laelia's," Falicia said.

"Well, happy birthday, Laelia. Sorry . . . I didn't know."

"That's okay. Why would you?"

"I haven't seen you since the party at Hector's. How are you . . . ? How is Aid?"

"He's been working with Benny in Maya Beach."

"I heard that. A massive property at the lagoon. Tell him to call me for a beer."

I nodded, knowing that I wouldn't. "Hey, do you reckon you can still source that lionfish and snapper for me for River Day? You said before about that guy you know?"

"Sure," he nodded. "Leave it with me." He started to turn back towards the bar. "Good to meet you, ladies." His words hung like peg rails.

"You, too," Chloe said, as if peeling off her clothes to hang them.

He turned back to look at me. "And happy birthday again, Laelia."

Chloe finally turned back to us, Mounia and Falicia both grinning.

"Stop it," I said.

Chloe raised her eyebrows. "What?"

I grabbed at the stem of my glass. "He's too young for you!"

"I can look, can't I?" She laughed. We all cackled like the best kind of witches, and then we ordered more drinks.

A full moon lit up the trees like ballerinas. Chloe clutched at me as we staggered our way along the path back from the water, lighting the way with our phones. "Your friends are nice . . ."

"Aren't they?" I smiled.

"You seem happy here . . . With them anyway."

"What does that mean?"

"I mean, what's going on with Aid?"

My breath lodged in my throat. I tried to sound casual, but my words were thick. "With Aid?"

"With you and Aid . . . ? There's so much tension at yours. It can't be great for the children. Are you sure you still want to be here?"

"They love it here. *I* love it here."

"Are you sure you want to be here . . . with him?" She stopped and stared at me, searching for an answer. I didn't say anything. I didn't know what to say. "Well, something's off . . . Are you sure he's not having an affair?"

"Stop it, Chloe. He's not having an affair."

"Well, I wouldn't put it past him. I mean—"

Whracck.

Her interlace tightened firm around my arm. "What was that—?"

Whracck. Whracck.

I never thought I'd feel relieved to hear gunshots.

"It's just poachers." I gently laughed, trying to lighten the fear, the same way Aid had tried to lighten mine when I'd heard those gunshots before.

"Just poachers? What the fuck? What are they poaching?"

"Parrots," I said, not having a clue what they were poaching or where or why or how.

Whracck.

"Are you serious?"

"Don't worry, they're miles away. It sounds closer than it is."

"Are there   out right now?"

"Hmm?"

"God, your hearing is getting so much worse . . . I said, are there jaguars out right now?" she shouted.

"No," I lied. "There aren't any around here."

"Are you sure?"

"Chloe, relax. We've been here for months, and I've never seen anything dangerous."

As we turned into Dad's, Chloe's grip around my arm finally seemed to settle, but then she asked, "Not even a snake?"

"Not even a snake."

The lamp was on in the study, so we went to let Aid know we were home, but, peering in through the window, we could see he was fast asleep, dozing in the hammock in a fug of marijuana. Aid had volunteered to stay in Dad's study, at least for the first couple of nights. That way no-one had to negotiate the springs of that hideous sofa. I'd wanted to ask Falicia if he could maybe stay with her and Henry for a bit, but Aid was still drinking so much and I didn't want him to embarrass himself, or me, so I didn't. Besides, Falicia had enough on her plate already.

Chloe turned to me, startled. "What's that noise?"

I couldn't hear anything. "What noise? God, Chloe, you're so paranoid."

"That . . . ?" She drunk-giggled, pointing into the air at nothing.

I laughed and rolled my eyes as we collapsed into each other in hysterics. "I can't hear anything." I'd lost the highest pitches forever, even with my hearing aids in and on loud.

"It's like a high-pitched *peep-peep*," she chuckled as we got nearer the hut. The faint smell of cigar smoke.

"I can kind of hear it now," I said, unlocking the door and turning on the light. "What is it?"

"In here." Chloe pointed, eyes wide. We flung back the bedroom curtain to find Ditsy squawking, caught up inside the mosquito net, the sheets smeared in chicken shit.

A scribbled note hung from a turquoise rope around her neck:

Pull in your hen and lock the coop.

Something woke me—the front door bursting open.

I flicked open my eyes. Moonlight wisped through the window. Chloe was somehow still asleep next to me in the kids' bed, her breath tainted with rum.

"Lil . . . ! Laelia . . . ?"

Aid?

It was Aid, panicked, his voice electric against Ursula's barking. Chloe murmured but sank back into heavy sleep. I shot up, stepping through the mess of Ella's floordrobe and rushed out to find the front door wide open, swinging on its hinges.

"Sssssshhh!" I grabbed Ursula's collar and flung back the bedroom curtain. Aid was standing at the foot of our empty bed, disoriented, staring blankly at the shit-slickened sheets, his eyes crisp with terror, sweat beads dripping from his face. "What is it?"

He stood rumpled frozen in a stupor, his eyes blue-wild and blood-shot.

"Aid?! What's the matter?"

He was glaring beyond me, through me, like I was a ghost. "I saw . . ."

"Saw what . . . ?" My breath caught, stuck.

I read his lips. "Under the cotton tree." He started fidgeting, shaking his hands erratically.

"What . . . ? What?"

He shook his head free of whatever he was thinking, imagining. "Nothing . . . no-one."

"Aid, what did you see?"

"Her hair . . . like crow's feathers."

"Whose hair? What are you on about?"

"What if . . . we're cursed?"

My heart slammed in my chest. "What . . . ? Why would we be cursed?"

"What if . . . ssshe's here? Following us?"

"Aid, you're scaring me . . . What are you on about?"

He snapped back to me, his eyes still crisp with terror. "Nothing . . . Nothing . . . A bad dream. That weed—"

"But if someone's down there—?"

"There's no-one there, Lil . . . It was nothing. I want to go back to sleep." Aid was adamant he wanted to sleep back in our bed with me, so I had to change the sheets covered in chicken shit. When we finally lay down, we clung to each other, his grip digging in, dragging at my arms, until eventually sleep swept him, then me, away.

With the stark light of morning, the resonances of the night continued to ripple, still disturbed. My ears shrieked metal on metal, the hangover clawing at me from within. I left Aid to sleep as I sloped out of bed and found Chloe hunting the cupboards for coffee.

"Let's go out for breakfast," I said, zipping up my shorts, throwing my bag over my shoulder. There must have been something in the way I said it because she knew not to ask questions, just changed into her clothes, and we left together in silence.

"Is Aid all right?" she asked after we'd closed the truck doors.

I fired up the engine. "I don't know. I don't know what's got into him. He freaked out in the night."

"I heard," she said. "What was he going on about? Was someone down there?"

"X'tabai," I said, under my breath.

"What?"

"Nothing."

"He needs to stop with the weed." She laughed. I shrugged off a half smile. I wanted to laugh; I really did, but I couldn't find it funny at all. "He's losing it . . . He keeps asking me weird questions about Dad."

"What do you mean?"

"I don't know," she said. "He keeps asking when they're going to bring him out of the coma."

"Why's that weird? He cares about Dad."

"He keeps going on about it. It's not his place."

Chloe knew not to push me too much, too quickly, but I knew it would be coming—a cascade of sisterliness. And sure enough, over pancakes at the Jaguar Lodge she made her move. "Lil, I don't think it feels safe here. That chicken on your bed . . . The gunshots. It's got a really dark vibe."

I heaved a sigh, sipped tentatively at my coffee. "Well, I like it. I love the weather, the people, the food. And I can hear myself think."

"But there are guns!"

"Not really. It's hard to get a licence here. It's only poachers."

"And what was with that note?"

"I told you before. It's probably a neighbour. Ditsy will have wandered off and they got annoyed they had to bring her back."

"You know, you could come home with me . . ." Here it was. "To London."

"I want to be here. Near Dad. For when he comes out . . . Besides, I like it. The kids are so happy. They're uncaged, learning about life hands-on, not stuck on screens all day."

"But, what's your long-term plan?" she asked. A rash flourished on her chest. Prickly heat.

"What do you mean?"

"How will you afford to rent somewhere in London when you're back?"

"I don't know, Chloe. Maybe I don't want to go back. I haven't thought that far. I'm literally trying to survive. Get through these weeks. Be here for Dad."

"What, because I'm not, you mean?"

"I didn't mean that."

"You know I can't be away from work too long. I'm trying my best, Laelia."

"I know. I'm sorry."

"Someone's got to pay the hospital bills." Raw red spots were blooming right up towards her neck. She finished her pancakes, pushed her plate away. "You know, Dad's outlook isn't good. I know it's shit . . . It's really shit, but maybe it's time to start thinking about what's best for him." She dabbed at her mouth with a manicured finger. "And for you."

I took another sip of coffee, but it made me feel even more sick.

Ellis

Pusey Road, Oxford
14th September 1990

He kisses Laelia on the cheek, tucking her in. "Don't be sad."

The wall above is postered with Bros, Neneh Cherry, and Transvision Vamp, the floor below a sea of *Twinkle* and *Smash Hits*. The girls sleep in the same room now, side by side in twin beds. They tried for a while with Laelia in her own room, but the long sad nights became too much, and she's never moved back.

It's been three years. He's tried to push them away, his memories of that time. The leaving. The loss. The grief. But today of all days the gates of his heart cannot stop the anguish flooding in. Their mother wouldn't want them to feel sad on her birthday.

"She would want you to be happy." He distracts them again with the story of their names, their origins and meanings; about the famous Laelias he knows, the famous Chloes.

"Tell us again about the orchids," Chloe pleads, her face a collapse of tears and smiles. He unfolds excitement about the hardiness of his favourite epiphytes, the beauty of their blooms, the invention of the Wardian case—its magical indoor jungle—the consignments of *Amherstia nobilis* shipped from India to England, Sir Joseph Dalton Hooker and his shipments to Kew. He talks about the uniqueness of the flowers, their extravagance and strangeness; the smell of them—the rotting flesh of *Satyrium pumilum*, the candy-like spice of *Cochleanthes amazonia*, roses, narcissus, verbena; the recently discovered Gold of Kinabalu, which fetches thousands of dollars for a single stem. They love hearing about the prices, the crazy market for these rarities, the delirium of addicted men.

"Tell us about Henry," Chloe beams.

"Again?"

"Again!" both girls chime.

"Henry Azadehdel was caught red-handed smuggling orchids into England. The police at the airport found his suitcase stuffed full of green shoots he'd plundered from—"

"What's plundered?" Laelia asks.

"Stolen!" says Chloe.

"From Peru and Ecuador." Ellis has pointed out these countries in the atlas before. "Henry sold a Rothschild's slipper from Borneo for nineteen thousand dollars!"

"Wow." The girls' faces light up.

"There's lots of money in orchids. Anyway, last summer, the judge sentenced Henry to a year in prison, and he had to pay a hefty fine for stealing plants from the rainforest."

"Do you ever sell them, Daddy?" Chloe asks.

As Ellis shakes his head, "No, poppet." His mind wanders to the locked safe he left in the jungle, to the orchids he'd betrayed, to the deeds he has done that he's also locked away; but he reassures his girls, or himself anyway. "Their beauty remains in the wild," and though he believes betrayal isn't always a choice—not really—Ellis has vowed never to look at that money again. Money meant for Helena, for Agapita, for another life. What might have been. What was.

"Will you read us a story?" Laelia asks him now.

"It's time to go to sleep."

"Please? A few pages?"

He smiles, wanting the distraction himself. *"The Lathe of Heaven?"*

He resettles on top of Laelia's bed, squished in against her My Little Pony and her slouchy bear, and opens the dog-eared book. They listen intently as he reads page after page after page.

He looks at each of his girls, both of whom have fallen fast asleep. He reads a final line for the night, to himself. "Love doesn't just sit there, like a stone, it has to be made, like bread; remade all the time, made new."

He loved Helena. He loved Agapita. Though sometimes, he knows, love isn't enough. The best kind of love isn't a feeling; it's a choice, one he now makes every day. That is the gift his wife left him.

32

Laelia

I was hungover, and neither of us had really slept, but Aid was determined to take me out the day after to celebrate my birthday, so I needed to let him. Chloe took the kids to a hotel she'd spotted across the peninsula for the night.

Aid tucked into the champagne he'd got Francisco to bring down from Belize City. Ordered a second bottle. After cocktails. He'd still wanted to go out for dinner, shrugging off the night terrors as though they were nothing. He'd laughed them off—with Chloe at least; then he told me he would be cutting down on the spliffs. "I drank some of that bay rum stuff Benny got hold of. Won't do that again . . . I was properly hallucinating."

"Who do you think the notes are from?" I asked, leaving most of my steak. I wasn't hungry, the hangover worse than it should have been, exacerbated by fatigue. "Who would do that?"

"It's someone dicking around . . . Like I said, dumb chicken probably just wandered off." He started rolling a cigarette.

"That's not what you said before . . . You said it was a snake."

He glared at me. "I don't know, Laelia. Maybe someone found her on their land and wasn't too happy about it, that's all."

"How did they get into the house? It was locked. Does that not worry you?"

"I probably left it open, and they threw her inside."

"But it was locked when Chloe and I got home."

"I would have locked it before I went down to the study." *No, he wouldn't. He wouldn't have done that.*

"What about the other note . . . ?"

"Maybe they got the wrong house. It wasn't meant for us."

"You don't seem worried about it." *Except he does. He does seem worried.*

"I'm not."

"Just ladies of the night that freak you out, huh?" I tried to say it lightly, as a joke, but it came out as vicious as a snake.

Aid got up from the table, slowly, purposefully, moving towards me, leaning into my ear, and then he whispered, "Don't be a bitch," until it crackled in my hearing aids.

When I couldn't take it anymore, I went to find him, to try to smooth things over. I found him in Dad's study drinking whisky, playing records.

"What are we doing?" I asked from the doorway.

He stamped his glass down on the desk before he turned to me. "I dunno. What *are* we doing . . . ? What are *you* doing?"

"What?"

"I'm scared, Laelia."

"What?"

"I'm fucking scared." He eyes pulsed with tears.

I wanted to say, *Of that thing you saw?* But I stopped myself and said, "What? What are you scared of?"

"Everything." He dragged his hands across his face, then jammed them into his armpits, rocking, taking deep breaths. "Don't even know . . . Of you saying shit. Of being out of control with all this . . . of being left."

"What?"

"The past, you know? It catches up with you. You know." *Was he talking about his dad again? Or his past in Belize?*

"Aid—"

"I love you so fucking much. I—" He stopped, looked out the window into the darkness. "Through it all. We've shared too much. If you ever leave me . . . I don't know what I'd do . . . I see how you are with Nico, and—"

"With Nico? What are you talking about?"

He threw his arms out in exasperation. "You're so at ease with him, and—"

"My God, Aid. Don't be ridiculous. There's nothing with Nico. Nothing."

"This, Laelia. You see, this . . ." His voice was raised now, surging with momentum. "This is what you do. Twisting shit. Treating me like shit. After everything I've done for you. You need to get a grip. Sort your head out." He tapped at his skull, grimacing a face at me. "I can't keep carrying all this." He reached behind him and grabbed a bottle from Dad's shelf of antique empties.

"Aid—?"

"Fuck, Laelia," he shouted, hurling the bottle across the room. A sudden shock of glass. I lost my breath in a spasm. "I can't lose you."

My voice cracked. "Then don't."

He moved in closer, daring me, begging me to forgive him. He pushed my hair behind my ear, his eyes stinging blue. He closed them and kissed me. "I'm sorry . . . I'm sorry I get so riled up. It's because I love you. I love you so fucking much."

"Ssssh," I said, kissing him back, my ears screaming. "It's okay. It's okay. I'm sorry."

Through my tears, I saw the broken smithereens glinting; little shards of danger on the floor.

33

I waited until Aid went out the next morning to clear up the mess. On my hands and knees, dragging sleep seeds from my eyes, I picked through the remnants of the night before. Like an animal. *What had he become? What had I? Jagged little edges tossed into the bin.*

"Mum?" Ella appeared in the doorway. "What are you doing?" I swept sharp pieces away.

"It was an accident." My voice croaked. "I dropped it last night."

She frowned. "Is Aid here? He promised me and Dyl a game of football."

"He's out."

"When's he back?"

"I don't know, hon. Shouldn't be too long . . . Did you have a nice time?"

"Can I go over to see Jonas then?"

"Of course . . . Will you be back before supper? And check whether Dylan wants to go." Ella was spending more and more time with Jonas, less and less time doing homeschool lessons, but I didn't mind. She was happy, and relaxed. And not cutting. Plus, Dylan loved the fact Ella visited Jonas so much. It meant she could take him over to see Gabriel. I didn't mind them going across the river as long as they were together, and Esther didn't mind keeping an eye on them over there. "So did you have fun with Chloe? What did you do?"

"It was good, yeah," Ella called, skipping back out the door. "The pool was sik . . ."

I looked back down at the debris. Picking up the final remains of the Don Omario bottle, the largest fragments still clinging to its sticky label and trying to hold themselves together, in the corner of the base, as I was about to fling it into the bin, something caught my eye. A tiny silver key.

Chloe was in the kitchen emptying a haul of bread and coffee and rice crackers out of a box. The key burned in my pocket.

"Where's Aid?" Chloe asked.

"Gone to work." I grabbed the basket of washing, starting back outside.

Chloe stood over me as I began pegging clothes up on the line. "Laelia . . ." I clipped up a pillowcase between us. She appeared from behind the floating cotton and moved in towards me, taking me by the wrists. She cradled my hands in hers, squeezing them tightly.

She looked me in the eyes, and I knew right then she knew more than I could ever tell her. "I've booked you and the children tickets—"

"What?"

"To come back with me, to have a break."

"I don't need a break."

"I think you need it, some time away."

"Please stop telling me what I need."

"Laelia, you need to get away from Aid for a bit. You can stay at mine and the kids can catch up with their friends . . . The flight's a week on Tuesday." She released my hands. Tears welled up in my eyes. I didn't know what to say. I couldn't say a thing. She'd tell me it was all my fault, that I put myself in this position. Put my children in it, too. I stopped myself. Parts of me instantly wanted to be boarding that aeroplane: the part uncertain what might happen next; the part that didn't want to feel afraid anymore; the part unsure of who we even were now, who I ever was. I wanted to go, wanted to feel safe, wanted to breathe again. But I didn't want to leave Dad, this place, the only place I felt close to him. Didn't want to let the kids down or say goodbye to this fresh beginning that hadn't quite begun.

"Okay" fell out of my mouth, a mask to my shame. "Let me think about it."

Dylan and I sat slouching over his textbook, maths formulas blurring across the page. I felt at the key in my pocket. I was waiting for a certain moment, when everyone was out, when I could use it, when I could open the safe without anyone prying, without anyone else knowing what was in it, or even that I had the key.

Dylan rolled his eyes. "You sai Ella an me cou   take the boa across to Ga   this morning. Can we? Please?"

"Hmm?"

"Can we ta   th   to Ga el's?"

"Darling, I haven't got my hearing aids in. Can you say it again?" *Gabriel's? Did he want to go to Gabriel's?*

Dylan groaned, running his fingers through his hair. "Mum. You ne   me prop ly." He looked exasperated. Sometimes, in brief moments, he displayed traces of Si, that foppish self-possession.

"Come on, honeybun," I said, pointing at the next question, trying to inject some enthusiasm into my voice and his learning. "Do this last section, then you can go."

Dylan huffed but regripped his pencil, ready to try the last calculation again. After I grabbed my aids, I sat with him, but I wasn't really there, my mind drifting to a fantasy. A life without Aid in it. Me and the kids. In Belize. With my restaurant. My outdoor cantina. Brimming with guests and bursting with warmth.

Though he'd know we were here. He could come back anytime. Trick me back to lust with scraps of love, compel my body to betray my mind, then I'd be in his hands again, at his mercy. Always at his mercy.

I imagined a flat, in London. Small but filled with love. Hot chocolate and snuggles, biscuits and a dog. We'd meet up with Chloe and their cousins. The kids would have to go back to school, though. I couldn't afford to homeschool them there. I'd be working in a new city restaurant. I'd have to be. Surrounded by a sea of noise. Drowning. Lost. But safe. We could be safe.

Would he follow us? Track me down? Seduce me back?

Or was I overreacting, to even think like this? After everything he'd done for me. More than Si ever did—forever in his vise, subjected to his whims, his impulses, his fancy. Maybe I was being over the top, blowing things all out of proportion.

"Can I go now?" Dylan asked, throwing down his pencil.

I glanced at the page, at his scribbles, and nodded. "But please be back for lunch."

"Do we have to?" he whined. "We've got packed lunches."

"Who made those?" I asked, expecting him to say Chloe or Ella.

"Dad."

Dad? Dad made them.

I left Chloe with the kids while I headed to Placencia. I took a boat across the water from the village after lunch, then met Nico by the pier. As we kissed cheeks, I told myself how okay that was. He's French. It's how he greets everyone. I couldn't help but scan over his shoulder though, check Aid hadn't dropped into town.

"You're sure?" He smiled, dragging his hand through his hair. "Lionfish and snapper?"

"Yeah, thanks."

"Because I can get you anything. Snook and tarpon from the estuary, or there's bonefish, or barracuda from the lagoon. Or—"

"Just the lionfish and snapper." I passed him a note with the quantities. "My mobile number's there . . . In case you need to check anything."

He put the paper in his pocket. "Ice cream?"

"Sure." We walked together back along the street.

"So is this the start of something?" he asked, turning towards me.

"Hmm?"

"Your event at River Day. Will you do more cooking?"

I smiled. "I'd love to open a restaurant . . . Somewhere that pulls people from far and wide. I could never imagine doing it in London. But here . . . here I can think. I can breathe, you know?"

"What about Aid?"

"What *about* Aid?"

"What does he think? About the restaurant?"

"He doesn't know about it."

Nico bit his lip. "Okay, I won't tell him."

We strolled to the shade of the ball field eating salted-caramel cones. We settled under a palm as a football match started up.

"They're called the Assassins," Nico told me. "I love watching them." He turned to me. "Can I tell you something . . . ?" I shrugged my shoulders. "You should never feel ashamed."

"What . . . ? I'm not ashamed." A player ran at the keeper, then scored a quick goal.

Nico rubbed a finger over his lips. "You're so shy with me."

I gently quelled an awkward laugh, twisting my cone to stop the ice cream from dripping. "I'm not shy."

He tilted his head. "With me, you're shy. You turn away from me, hide from me . . . Because you feel it . . ." I felt my cheeks flushing. "You turn away from him because he makes you feel ashamed."

I licked my ice cream and gazed at him. His gentle eyes. It was only when I was with Nico, I realised, that with Aid I was no longer myself.

"Sometimes we don't realise how bad things are," Nico went on. "When we're in it . . . It's like, how you say . . . a frog? In hot water. Or a lobster."

"Why did you leave Hector's?" I asked, trying to change the subject.

He looked out across at the pitch. "He got into some shit I don't like. I got out before he ask me to get involved . . . Hector does not like to be disappointed. He cannot deal with rejection." Nico crunched the top of his cone. "He's a man who likes . . . how do you say châtiment . . . ? Retribution?"

"Yeah, retribution . . . Revenge."

"It's good to be out of there."

"You know, I do love him," I said. "Aid."

Nico stared at me, as though he could taste it, too; the truth, fracturing on my tongue.

Chloe asked me again that evening while I was cooking chimole for the kids. They were putting the chickens away. Aid still wasn't home.

"So do you think you're going to come back?" She pulled the cork from the wine.

"Come back?"

"To London. With me. You and the kids."

"Oh, Chloe. I don't know." I went to stir the soup. Black liquid spat up into my face.

"Why not? It's paid for."

"I can't. I'm cheffing for the festival by the river, and—"

"Well, someone else can cook for that."

"Chlo, the kids are settled. Aid's here—"

"Exactly."

"Sorry?"

She grabbed my wrist, took the spoon out of my hand. "Please come," she said, turning me towards her with a gentle tug. "Please." *How much does she know?*

"I don't want to leave Dad."

"Dad's the same, Lil. He barely knows we're there. Have a break, at least. Please. He would want you to. Mounia's with him. She'll call us if there's any change, and we can get straight on a plane. We can be back within a day."

"But—"

"Laelia, come on. You need a break. From Aid. At least for a bit."

"What?"

"He's isolating you."

Shame was a box that surrounded me, that I had built into being. "But it was me who dragged him here. Made him stay."

"That's not what I meant . . . I'm worried about you. You're barely eating."

The truth rose up from within me, churning, until I spat it out like concrete. "I'm worried if I go, I won't come back."

"Is that such a bad thing?" Chloe muttered under her breath as the children walked in.

We left it there. Drank more wine. Ate our chimole.

She was right, of course. Not that I'd dare admit it to Chloe. A break would do us good; it might shock Aid back to not drinking, make him realise how close we'd come to an end, how potent I could be, that maybe I could be powerful, too.

If I did decide to go, I could pack light. Two small bags: one for me, one for the kids. Aid wouldn't need to know we were leaving until we were gone. If I told him at all.

His words hung in my mind: *If you ever leave me . . . I don't know what I'd do.*

What would he do?

I could have the bags packed, stored away, and tell him as we were going out the door. Or I could phone him when I got to London. That would be better, safer.

Perhaps I was overdramatising things.

Maybe I should have a conversation, tell him we needed a break. A little time apart. Would he lose it? Seek revenge? Wreck Dad's place?

He would freak out about me taking the kids, of course. But it would need be only a couple of weeks, a month maybe, tops. To recalibrate. A bit of distance. It wasn't like I would be abducting his children. *My* children. Aid wasn't their father.

34

I woke up with a pounding headache, my skin slick with sweat, my brain buzzing. Maybe I hadn't even got to sleep. I couldn't tell. Aid still hadn't come to bed. It was oppressively hot, no air, a storm surely brewing. I couldn't wait any longer.

I stole myself to the study hut, passing Aid collapsed on the sofa, and when I got there, stared inside the safe. A treasure trove of letters, jotters, photos, newspapers, files stuffed deep inside. Tomes of a life. The smell of him again, musk and mildew.

Shifting the candle closer, I pulled a couple of notebooks from the stack and opened the first until it creaked in my hands. I could make out only a few words. I was okay at listening but had always been terrible at reading and writing Spanish; I would need to ask Mounia if she wouldn't mind translating them. I flicked through the journals until I found one in English. Until I found him: Dad right there, alive on the page, his intricate writing unmistakably his, the ink flowing bold with intention, still wet-looking as though the sentences had just spilled out of him.

My eyes grazed at fragments as I turned the leaves: a page of Belizean flags, the formula for photosynthesis, intricate orchid sketches, *the peeling bark of the gumbo-limbo . . . Helena would have loved the sea here . . . the waves fold differently across the sand . . . girls might like a piano . . . terrible coffee . . . 1989 . . . an assortment of riches . . . the fer-de-lance poison . . . a generous tolerance of difference . . . took a walk out into the rainforest . . . Don Omario but no ice . . .*

There was a shuffling outside. I froze.

Closing the notebook, I slid it back inside the safe. Something caught my eye in the corner: bundles of thin banknotes, swirling greys and pastel greens, trapped in weary elastic bands.

A gentle whine, then Ursula glided inside. I pushed the safe door closed and slipped the key back into my pocket as Aid appeared in the doorway.

"Hey, what you doing?"

Raindrops started falling heavily on the roof, against the windows.

"I couldn't sleep." He'd fallen asleep on the couch, and Chloe had collapsed in with the kids over a book. "Didn't want to disturb you. I came down to have another look for that key."

"Find it?" He came closer.

I shook my head. "No." I flinched as he burrowed into my neck, hijacked my breath.

"Let's go back to bed."

I shuffled around some papers on the desk. "Okay," I said as I walked past him. I could feel him tracking me, his blue eyes glaring, searching for the lie.

He blew out the candle and followed me back inside through the pelting rain.

I waited until the next night to bury the money under the logwood tree, breathless, in the shadow of the moon; I waited until the night after that to start reading Dad's English journals, by candlelight, once everyone else was asleep.

The kids were sunbathing on the deck with Ursula: Ella on her tummy, picking at a plate of mango, nonchalant, legs flicking back towards her bum like a bored Lolita; Dylan in the hammock, his sketchpad saturated with the feathered ink of the Joker, lurid green hair and bruised purple eyes. His hands were covered in ink, his lips, too, with pencil shavings betraying a further crime scene all over the floor.

"Why isn't Aid ever here anymore?" Dylan asked. *Aid? He was calling him Aid again?*

"He's working, darling."

"He never plays with me anymore."

Ella flicked a piece of mango across her plate. She'd decorated her hands in elaborate black ink again, henna-styled in boredom. "He promised he'd take me out for curry last night. He didn't get back until after I'd gone to bed. He didn't even say sorry."

"Doesn't he like us anymore?" Dylan asked. Aid was so distracted. When he was home, he was drinking, or angry, or tired. Or drinking and angry and tired. Hiding from the truth of it, pulling me into the shade.

"Oh, darling, of course he likes you. He loves you."

"Yeah . . . like Dad loved us," said Ella.

That one hurt.

I didn't know what to say, how to protect them from the disappointment of would-be fathers making and breaking promises. I stumbled, feeling all the guilt of it, but deserving the brunt of it all. And I was failing them, again.

Words are not bruises, but they still hurt, and I warranted the pain.

I held on to my mother's letters as if they were the world, stashing them in my wash bag, where no-one would find them. During a moment of quiet, I snuck to the vegetable patch, lit a cigarette, and thumbed through the stash of sepia envelopes. One stood out from the rest. It was crumpled and worn, well handled, as if it had been read a thousand times:

16th March 1987.

Ellis,

The voices are back. Clawing at me. And you are not here. And you will never be here. You never really were.

Sometimes I scream to see if anyone can hear.

I cannot smell the scent of crushed orchids. Not like you. I cannot forgive you for not being here, and when you are here, not wanting to be. For falling in love with Agapita. For getting her pregnant.

I cannot go on. Not with the voices and not without your love. I feel like a fool. And a terrible mother. The pills blunt me but not enough.

We are all selfish in our own ways. I'm so, so sorry. You must stay now, in England. For the girls. You owe us that much, at least. They deserve the world, more than me.

Find me in the Wittering stars. I'll be shining like kisses. For you.

I loved you always. I'm sorry.

Helena. x

West Wittering Beach, West Sussex, England
14th September 1996

After days of pissing end-of-summer showers, the sky has finally cleared. Fighting a gentle breeze, the girls throw down the blanket, roll out their straw mats, prop up the parasol. They drop their beach bags, pulling off their sundresses and adjusting their swimsuits. Ellis notices the Marlboro Menthols poking out of Laelia's bag. She quickly shoves her towel back over, pushing them out of sight. He doesn't say anything, opts against it right now. He hasn't caught her in the act, and she would smell his pipe-smoking hypocrisy anyway. It's not worth falling out over, not today of all days.

Ellis flips open his deck chair, pulls it up next to their rug. Without a word, out of instinct, they have installed themselves by their favourite hut—the pink-and-white-striped one Chloe's always loved, where they always used to sit.

She's firmly into black now, edging on gothic (she likes The Cure), but it was always pink, for years and years and years. A tomboy at heart, Laelia's favourite was always green, and sometimes blue, but never pink. They both love this hut, though, its candy-cane sweetness and its recollections of childhood, its memories of their mother. The paint is flaking now, the salt corroding the colour. Someone has shoved a crisp packet down between the planks.

Ellis imagines Helena's here with them—sitting wrapped in a towel on the veranda, watching over the girls with their buckets and spades, smothering them in hats and sunscreen and kisses before settling into her Danielle Steel, opening a can of Cherry Coke fresh from the cool box, letting him massage her feet.

This is the first time he's come here with the girls since she died. He could not face the memories, not for years. They've finally worn him down, after begging him so many times: "She would want you to go today, on her birthday, to her favourite place." Ellis had found it macabre, their recognising the day she passed away. But the girls had always marked it, every 16th March. But he never would. He's relented today on her birthday, because the girls had pleaded so much. It is their last proper chance, after all; their final day together before the nest is unsettled again. Chloe drives off tomorrow, her grant and scholarship all set. She says she'll come back to visit often. Perhaps she will. But perhaps she will not. She deserves the freedom, and he must let her fly.

Ellis can see Helena as though she is here, spinning on the beach below the dunes, her skirt blooming out like crimson petals. The smile on her face is unimagined. It is real, this happiness she had here in this place, he is sure. He holds on to that, pushing down the bitterness she left him with. Though she gave him the gift of these girls, these girls he almost left behind.

"Do you remember when we found that old lady's dog?" Chloe asks from under her wide-brimmed hat. "Behind the toilet block?"

"That little Yorkie . . . ?" Laelia rubs lotion on her nose.

"She'd been looking for him all day. She gave us a one-pound note each to say thank you, then Mum took us to that toy shop in Chichester on the way home."

"I don't remember that," Laelia says.

"You bought fancy dress heels made of wood with plastic straps. They looked so uncomfortable. I got Crystal Barbie."

"I don't remember." Laelia opens up her *Just Seventeen*, shielding her face from the sun.

"Do you remember, Dad?" Chloe asks.

Ellis nods as he starts filling his pipe, pressing down the tobacco with the tamper. "Yes, a happy day." But he does not remember.

Over peanut butter sandwiches and ginger beer, the girls reminisce. Ellis is not hungry. He smokes in his deck chair, glancing over the *Telegraph* headlines, though his mind is wandering to other things, other times, other places. To Belize.

He thinks of Agapita often. What she did, where she went. Polo wrote and told him Agapita moved away soon after, with her family down to Toledo District. Itzel took them all to live with her brother. From time to time, Ellis thinks of finding Agapita, of what she must look like now, if he would recognise her, or her him.

Chloe keeps on. "The week after Mum died, do you remember how Aunty Penny bought us that new dollhouse? Tons of new Barbies and a Ken?"

Laelia jumps up, throwing her magazine down onto the sand. "Oh my God, Chloe. I don't remember." She starts down towards the sea. "I don't bloody remember."

Ellis exhales his smoke. He's never heard her swear before. It jars. She's fourteen but still his little girl.

"What?" Chloe asks. "What did I say?"

He shakes his head. "She was only little. What she does remember, she probably doesn't want to."

"What, you mean, like a coping mechanism?" Chloe picks up a handful of sand.

"If you forget the past," he tells her, "you can trick yourself into believing it never really happened . . ."

Down at the sea, Laelia dives under a small wave, submerging herself.

"Yeah, maybe," Chloe says, the sand sifting through her fingers. "But only for so long."

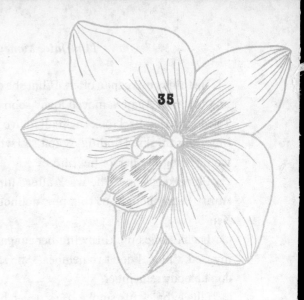

35

I stomped up the veranda steps, thrusting the paper at her. "Did you know?"

"Know what?" Chloe replied, closing her *Harper's Bazaar*, taking the letter.

"I found Dad's diaries. Mum's letters. Dad had an affair. Got a Mayan woman pregnant. Here, in Belize. But they lost it, the baby . . . Did you know?"

"No." She sat up from the hammock, moved into a more appropriate position for a conversation such as this. "I mean, not really."

"Not really? What does that mean . . . ? Did you know?"

She knew.

Chloe threw her magazine to the floor. "I mean . . . I knew he had a fling. Aunty Penny told me about it, but I didn't—"

"You knew?"

She nodded. "I think."

"And you never told me?"

"It was history, Laelia. They were always fighting like cats and dogs."

"Is that why she did it? Why Mum killed herself?"

"I don't know. I guess. But she was unwell for years. She probably would have done it at some point anyway. She needed help."

"And Dad didn't get it for her."

"Things were different then. It's not like now. It wasn't something people talked about."

"But she talked about it to Dad. He knew. He could have helped her."

"He did try. It was difficult for him. And he was away a lot."

"Exactly." I reached for the bottle of wine, poured myself some into Chloe's glass. "We never talked about it—about her death, not really. I didn't realise it was suicide, not for years. Why couldn't you have told me?" I didn't even know what I knew anymore. And she'd lied to me. My own sister. Or at least, withheld the truth. It was all such a tangled web, the memories a blur.

"You were so little," she said. "We were trying to protect you . . . And as you got older, we never talked about it. Dad never wanted to."

I took a swig of wine. "But we need to talk about it."

"I'm sorry," she said. "It never felt like the right time . . . I'm sorry. Hey, have you been talking to Aid about Dad?"

"What do you mean?"

"He keeps asking me about what's happening, pushing me to make a decision."

"What?"

"I guess he's sick of living in limbo. Wants to get back to London. Get back to—"

"I don't want to go back to London. Stop interfering in my life." I was near shouting.

"Lil, I'm not tr—"

"I can't believe you never told me," I said. "We need to remember her. Always. We need the kids to remember her. It's not okay to act like she never existed. To forget her . . . We need to tell them." Our family stories had been drawn in sand, not etched in stone. Rebuilt over and over like sandcastles, knocked down, recast, and then buried. "I can't believe you lied," I said, gulping the rest of the wine. I couldn't believe I'd almost confided in her. "Don't try to protect me ever again."

"Okay, okay," she said. "I won't."

When Aid came home that night, he brought me flowers.

"What's up with you?" He kissed at my neck as he placed the bouquet down on the table. A shock of dark crimson roses. "Where's Chloe?"

I touched at the necklace he'd given me and shook my head. "My dad had an affair." I rasped. "Here, in Belize."

"What?"

I burst into tears, and he brushed them away. We drank wine together, just a bottle, and I told him about Agapita, about the baby, and the stillbirth, and he listened like he used to. In gentle communion. "And I'm sure that's what led to my mum . . . to her decline. It must have been hell for her. And Chloe knew. She knew he'd had an affair. All these years, and she didn't tell me, ever."

"Where is Chloe?"

"She's gone back to check into the hotel. Give us both some space." I took a sip of wine. "Why wouldn't she tell me?"

"You know what she's like. She wants to be in control. Her and Tom have always treated you like a kid . . . She probably didn't think you needed to know."

I bit my lip. "I thought we were getting on so much better."

"Well, she's shown her true colours now. You know you can't trust her." Aid smiled a flat smile, taking the glass from my hand, placing it on the table. "Don't worry, she'll be gone soon." He grabbed me by the waist, turning me in the chair towards him, pulling me closer. "And then it'll just be us."

36

*G*₀ *go go.*

I dragged the bags out from under the bed and stared at their possibilities, their promise. The morning light streaked dreams through the
window. I could leave Aid, just for a couple of weeks; so he knew that I
could, so I knew that I could. To punish him, to show him, so he would
never treat me like this again. To have a break from each other, to have
a break from ourselves.

"Mum, can I have an orange juice?" Dylan yelled from the kitchen.

Yet when I thought about what Chloe had done, how she'd kept Dad's
secrets from me, I felt sick, like I could never trust her again. And I wasn't
sure I wanted to go with her. Those lies burned like acid, dissolving everything I knew to be real—the past disfiguring the present, sculpting
its clever tricks. Dad's lies, Chloe's lies; both designed to protect, to sac-
charin the past for me, but I wasn't a child anymore, and still she'd never
told me, never thought I needed to know. Any trust we'd had felt soured.

Stay stay stay.

"Mum?" Dylan shouted again.

I lugged the holdalls up on top of the mattress, unzipped them. "It's
in the fridge."

"When's Aid back from Tikal?" Ella asked, flinging back the curtain
before I had time to move. I could feel her standing behind me. "He said
he'd help with my woodwork."

I turned, trying to hold her gaze firm so she wouldn't see the bags. How could I derail them now? Disappoint them again. Leave them without a father figure once more. I couldn't tell the kids, not until I'd decided what to do. It wasn't fair to them. None of this was fair to them. "Not long . . . By this evening I think he said."

"Mum . . . ?" Dylan called again.

"Yes?"

"Where's the peanut butter?"

"Er . . ." If I shifted from where I was standing, Ella would see everything. She stared at me. "Bottom cupboard."

"I've looked there," Dylan shouted back.

Ella stood firm in the corner of the room. She tipped her chin, looked past me, then pointed with her felt-tipped hennaed hand. "What's that?"

"Hmm?"

"Why are you packing?"

Dylan joined her now, butter knife in hand. "It's not there." Ella stared at me, clenching her jaw. "What's going on?" Dylan asked, looking at Ella, then me, then Ella again.

"Mum?" Ella's voice was feeble now. "You're scaring me." I couldn't talk, couldn't think.

"Mum?" Dylan pleaded. "Where are we going?"

"Mum?" Ella begged at me, tears welling in her eyes, and then more desperately, "Mum?! Please don't make us go back to England. I don't want to leave."

I grabbed her, pulling her into me. "It's okay . . . it's okay. I'm sorting out your clothes." A beat settled between us. "Chloe's coming to pick you up. To take you back to the hotel. For a night or two."

Ella heaved a sigh, tears streaming down her face. "Promise we're not going back to London?" she whimpered.

"Promise."

37

Once Chloe had picked up the kids (with the usual busyness, and surface level pleasantries, and silent reference to our argument), Aid and I headed to the Jaguar Lodge to meet Rich and Maia. With their exhilarating stories and their menthol cigarettes, they were a breath of fresh air. After a few drinks, coasting on a sea of shared memories, inside jokes, and caricatures, Aid became buoyant again in their company: laughing and smiling with reclaimed ease. Rich was whip-smart and self-assured. He brought out the American in Aid, but he was funny and kind, and I liked him. Maia was quieter than she seemed when we first met. She was thoughtful. A dreamer. And beautiful. With sweeping mousy hair and burnt-hazel eyes, she was so extraordinarily ordinary, every movement so self-conscious and studied, so immaculately put together. A magnolia: soft and showy, yet powerfully plain.

Back at home for supper, I started prepping the chicken, adding the anchiote paste. As I brought out the plates to the veranda, I caught Aid and Maia huddled deep in conversation.

"You must miss her a ton," Maia was saying, pointing at the L.F. on his bicep. "It's beautiful . . . Like her." Aid smiled, then seeing me, dropped his head and lit his cigarette.

Live Forever. He'd always told me his tattoo meant 'live forever'. *Is it actually in tribute to his mother?*

"She would've loved it here." Maia smiled back. I didn't realise Maia would have known her; Aid told me his mum died a couple of years before he went to college. He moved from the UK to Boston then, to live with his aunt and uncle.

Why would he lie about such a thing?

Aid suddenly brightened, changing the tone. "Laelia's made an absolute feast . . ."

"It won't be long," I said, putting down a bowl of nachos. "Waiting on the rice. Are you sure you guys can't stay on longer? There's a festival down by the river on Friday. You should come."

Rich grabbed a handful of snacks. "Man . . . wish we could have, but we gotta get to Mexico. Only stayed on so we could see this guy." He smiled at Aid, organising nachos in his palm.

"Aww, dude," Aid joked, knuckling Rich's bicep. "How you getting there?"

Rich crunched, finished his mouthful. "Bussin' to San Ignacio tomorrow."

"I've gotta go to Tikal to meet a guy. I can give you a ride."

"For real?" Maia asked.

"Going anyway."

"Awesome . . . Will you come, too, Laelia?" Maia asked. "Save me from pep rally stories I already heard a hundred times?" Aid shot me a look.

"I'd love to."

"You won't have time," Aid said. "The kids'll be back in the afternoon."

I forced a tight smile. "Oh, of course." Chloe had said she might keep them longer, but it wasn't worth falling out about. I didn't need to go.

"Bummed we don't get to meet them," Rich said. "I'd love to see what a rambunctious mini-Aid looks like." *He's not his son.*

"He's perfect." Aid grinned.

"I don't doubt it."

Over dinner we tucked into beers and rum and more beers, and Aid seemed to relax into the night, riffing on stories from a lifetime ago: shoplifting kegs, pulling all-nighters, wrestling smirking street signs while high as kites, and the like. It was jazz—the way they weaved their fabled tales around each other, off each other, hitting cues, inviting refrains. The stuff of legends, half of which probably happened only in their minds, or never happened at all, at least, not in the way they rendered it. I could not get purchase on these shared symbols, this life before me.

"Dinner was, like, pretty good," Maia announced after we'd finished up my Yucatán chicken. All the plates were clean.

Aid laughed before getting up to go inside. "Well, she isss a chef," he said, slurring. Blind drunk.

"Maia never expects anything outside of France to be any good." Rich grinned. "She lived in Paris for ten years."

"Honestly, most of it isn't," Maia said, offering Rich's cigarettes around. I smiled and shook my head. I'd smoked too many bummed menthols as a fledgling teenager.

"That was wicked good." Rich smiled at me, draining the last of his Belikin.

"We've run out of beers," Aid reappeared on the veranda, eyes glossy and bloodshot. "Shall we head back to the Jaguar." It wasn't a question.

"You girls wanna come?" Rich asked.

"We'll stay. Finish the rum." Maia smiled at me, pointing towards the half-empty bottle with her cigarette.

"Sure?" Rich stroked her arm.

"I wanna get to know Laelia some more. But leave us some smokes . . . And maybe you drive the truck, yeah?" she said under her breath, referencing Aid, who was swaying in the doorway.

After they headed off, I brought out the key lime pie. We savoured lingering spoonfuls, zesty and light.

"Lord," Maia said. "The boys are missing out."

We talked about manatees and lingerie and the Canal Saint-Martin. She told me how she'd started learning qigong as well as yoga; about her teacher, who she swore was in her seventies but could still do the splits; about her love of Siamese cats, her obsession with cacti, and her sagacious views on Amber Heard—how she was such a cunning bitch.

Then finally, Maia moved on to what she was really bursting to talk about. "So you, like, met Aid in Brighton? That's on the coast, right?"

I shook my head. "No. No, I met him on holiday here in Belize . . ." She narrowed her eyes. "When you and all your college friends were on Caye Caulker"—I went on—"for that group holiday? I mean, I only met Aid but . . ." I took a drag of my cigarette.

"Really?" Her brows remained furrowed. "You met Aid then?"

"I saw you; I think. Your group. You were hard to miss. The guys were so loud."

"American guys are." She laughed. "You sure it was that vacation . . . ? When we were all there?"

"Yes, I'm certain. I mean—"

"I thought Aid met you in Brighton?"

Why was she pushing me on this?

"We met up again in Brighton a year or so later. Do you want more pie?"

"No. Thanks."

"Or there's fruit."

"No. I'm good. That was amazing . . . You should open a restaurant here. This spot is to die for." She smushed her cigarette butt dead into the ashtray, flicked her Vejas up onto the table, crossing her legs into an elongated X. "It's weird . . ." She lit another menthol. The crisp faux-mint smell hit sharp. Gazing off into the trees, it was like she was more there than here with me.

"What is?" I asked. The pause she left was a cavern. Two mosquitos buzzed, skimming around the festoon bulbs. Finally, she pointed nonchalantly with her cigarette towards my head. "Luisa wore her hair like that." Maia's lips twinkled, as if the stars had floated down from the sky and stuck to them. *Who?* I touched at my French braid, then took a giant mouthful of rum, too much. The liquid burned my lips, my tongue, my throat. The air stilled. The silence there again, teasing through the tinnitus. "Her hair was, like, so beautiful, so fucking lustrous. She was"— Maia searched for the word—"beguiling."

I coughed at the rum. "Luisa?" A mosquito zzzzzed by the side of my head.

Her eyes flicked like flashlights. "*Luisa,*" she said again, more forcefully, as though that alone could will me into knowledge. I shook my head, half shrugging my shoulders until I caught myself. "He's never talked to you about Luisa?" She leant forward, dropping her cigarette into the ashtray, abandoning it half gone. I shifted in my seat. The insect landed on my wrist, on my tattoo. Maia took a deep audible breath. She downed the last of her rum, started pouring us both fresh glasses. "I shouldn't have said anything."

"Just tell me," I said, surprised at how urgently the words spilled out. I slapped, hard, at the mosquito.

"They were such a great couple . . . She loved being his wife."

Wife?

I felt instantly sick.

"Has he never told you what happened? It wasn't long before you."

There would be reasons . . .

"They were so in love . . ."

Reasons why he'd never mentioned her.

I shook my head, trying to make sense of this.

Maia circled her finger around the rim of her glass. ". . . and then she, like, died."

38

Luisa. That was her name. Aid's wife. L-U-I-S-A. Maia literally spelled it out for me. I wasn't sure why. To honour her properly, perhaps, this friend of theirs who was taken too young, who was not remembered enough. At least, not by him.

"It was a diving accident," Maia said. "Off Caye Caulker." A disorienting wave of déjà-vu flooded over me. I knew Aid had travelled to Belize a lot beyond the six months or so he lived here. It must have happened years before, but hadn't she said they'd been together *not long before you?*

"When?" I asked, my eyes flicking between Maia's. She poured more rum, the liquid crashing into the glasses.

"Hmm?"

"When?" My voice quavered, high and awkward. "When did it happen?"

"He must have told you about it, surely . . ." *Have I forgotten? Had he? I would remember, wouldn't I? Him telling me something like that?* "He was crushed, of course . . ."

Why hadn't he told me? Maybe he had told me. Maybe I hadn't heard it.

My brain was addled. I had a thousand questions. I asked what felt like hundreds in my mind, and dozens to Maia, but she wouldn't tell me anything more, explained she'd already said too much. It wasn't her place; it wasn't her story. I'd have to ask Aid.

"She was so beautiful," she added, like a reflex, and then as a clumsy addendum, offered, "You know, he loves you." As though she knew me, as though that made up for the lie. *Was it a lie, if he'd just never told me? If I'd never even asked?* "He loves hard. I can see he's besotted with you," Maia said, her accent twisting around "besotted" like a weed. "He gets that way." She drifted up from the table, grabbing her phone to light the way to the loo.

I felt the acid churn in my stomach, rising past my lungs as I struggled for breath. I pushed back my chair, and leaned—fell almost, heaving, over the balustrade. My throat burned as vomit exploded into the darkness below. I collapsed back on the wall for support, my weight dragging me down as my knees buckled beneath me, crumpling down to the wood.

Hiding my face in my palms, I found breath. Ursula panted hard besides me. Had she been there all along? I couldn't think. There was an engine, somewhere in the distance. Gathering myself finally, I looked up, searching the sky for some sort of clarity. The stars mocked, majestic from their canvas.

The sky was purple, that first night when we met. I remembered the crash of gentle waves, the setting sun, the thrum of the beach bar pulsating around us.

"What happened?" Aid had asked me over lurid daiquiris and a backdrop of reggae. "With your ex? Why the divorce?"

"We grew apart," I replied. "And then he got volatile. Violent. He pushed me and . . . Have you ever been married?" I'd asked Aid then. I'd asked him. *Hadn't I?*

He'd shaken his head; I was sure he'd shaken his head. "No, I just got out of a relationship." Was that what he'd said? Something like it. *Hadn't he?*

I knew he'd had girlfriends—lots of them, strings of them. Countless. How could a guy like him not? He talked about some of them later, when we met again in Brighton, when we started things up properly. But not then. And not a wife. And I hadn't needed to know. It was only a one-night stand. A quick fling. A holiday fuck. That was all it was, all it was ever supposed to be.

A pair of headlights swooped into view from the driveway, an engine churning closer.

"You expecting a visitor?" Maia asked, coming back into sight.

"No." I shook my head. "I don't know." Maybe it was someone who'd got lost. I walked down from the veranda, headed towards the lights. The truck came to a standstill, and the driver's door opened.

"Hey, Laelia," a familiar voice called before I got near.

"Nico?"

He turned off the engine, kept the beams on. We would be silhouetted for Maia to see. "I wanted to bring you something . . . A gift."

"A gift?"

"For your birthday. I'm sorry I forgot."

"Honestly, Nico. You didn't need to—" My head was spinning.

"I know, but I wanted to . . ." He handed me a little canvas bag. "Are you okay?"

"Hmm?"

"You seem not yourself. Is everything okay?"

"I'm fine. I'm . . . just a bit drunk." I tried to smile. Maia was standing now, stretching her limbs up across the veranda, smoke flirting into the night. She would be able to hear us. I opened the present for something to do, something to focus on.

"It's a Mayan healing stone," Nico said. "Kantun told me it will bring you peace. And courage."

"Thank you . . . It's beautiful."

"I like your hair like that," he said. I touched at the plait; the *hair like hers*. Nico shuffled on his feet. "Anyway, you have guests, so . . ." Maia was leaning over the balustrade, gazing right at us, taking it all in.

"I'm sorry . . . and Aid's not here. He's at the Jaguar. You could catch him there?"

Nico smiled. "Sure. Goodnight, Laelia." He went to get back into his truck.

"Goodnight."

His truck purred away, and I ambled back to the hut.

"Who was that?" Maia asked, eyebrow raised, smoke swirling around her.

"One of Aid's friends. Nico."

"Why didn't you invite him for a drink?"

I pursed my lips. "I don't know him well."

"Well enough that he brings you a present." She smirked.

I hid the canvas pouch in my pocket.

Maia floated off to crash in the study, but I barely slept. I started rifling through Aid's drawers, his bag, trying to find *The Mosquito Coast* again, or anything, another clue to his past, something; but there was nothing. My mind raced.

Aid and Rich still weren't back. Drifting in and out of some kind of slumber, lying in the darkness, I couldn't stop thinking. Why had Aid never told me? He must have been devastated, of course. But to never say anything? Not refer to it, to her, ever? Not once? A wife? A wife. I was sure he'd never mentioned it. Maia said he'd wanted to forget, to move on with his life. And he'd sure done that. But to never mention it to me? Was that why his mood changed so much when we got to Belize? Why he said he didn't want to stay on Caye Caulker when we were planning Dad's birthday? Why he'd wanted to go down south onto the mainland, had lobbied so hard for that itinerary in our holiday plans? Maybe there were too many memories there on the island.

A diving accident. How awful. How shit for him—when I'd been there harping on about Dad's birthday, and Chloe's fucking organisation, and the sodding hors d'oeuvres, and all that time . . . That's why he'd been so distracted, why he froze with Dylan in the water, why he'd been so stressed out. And the dive trip we went on—not even wanting to go in the first place, then acting so weird, drinking so much, snorting so much. All this time, he'd been dealing with this deep, sweet hurt. The memories of her. Of a wife.

And I hadn't even known. He'd kept it to himself, harbouring a secret that must have been killing him inside. That's what they say, isn't it? Secrets are toxic, corrosive, they'll impact your health. And now I carried them, too.

I awoke to Aid sliding into the sheets next to me, his body warm and smooth, and I reached out, to show him I was there. I would look after him, protect him, be there for him as he had for me.

I put my hand on his shoulder and kissed at his skin.

Why didn't you tell me?

He smelt like amber, tasted like brine.

How do I tell you I know? What do I say? A wife? A wife.

He turned over, away from me, and I held him tightly until I somehow fell to sleep.

The morning was bright, buzzing with cicadas, bursting with birdsong. I went out onto the veranda, half expecting to find the three of them there, reminiscing again, caffeinating and nicotining themselves back to life. But the chairs were empty, the air was fresh. The sun was high, pounding like my head. It must have been late morning. Bottles and glasses from the night before stood empty, save for final dirty splashes of insurmountable rum. I could still taste the sugary dark nutmeg on my tongue, could still feel it fermenting in my stomach. I threw up again but made it, this time, to the sink.

After devouring a glass of water, I teased the plait out of my hair. The crimples would last for days, a persistent and mocking reminder. *She wore her hair like that.* Setting my hair band down on the bedside table, I caught the glint of Nico's healing stone. I picked it up, trying to take my mind off Aid, off his wife, off everything.

It fit perfectly into my palm, a sea of blue-green instant calm.

Opening the canvas sack, I pulled out a tiny piece of paper from inside: "Aquamarine is the stone of natural justice. It offers quiet courage and wisdom, enabling the bearer to articulate their own truth with clarity and conviction." There was another little notecard, handwritten in that luscious, ubiquitous French style:

Laelia, Happy birthday. I googled your name. Did you know it means "speaking well" ? Nico xx.

I wasn't sure if he meant "well spoken" or able to speak freely. He'd joked before about my cut-glass accent, even though my accent wasn't cut-glass at all; not like Chloe's affectation, studied and crisped and clipped. Maybe it got lost in translation.

He'd googled my name.

I used to tell people my name was Lily, used to biro it into my school clothes and rewrite it onto permission slips until eventually the teacher changed it on the register. It was easier that way, to fit in, to not have to elaborate or explain my parents' eccentric whims. I hadn't wanted to be any more different (a mother's suicide has an uncanny way of doing that all by itself). *Laelia, a tribute to nature; feminine and free.* Then, as I burst into my teens—fumbling for any point of distinction, a modicum of cool to cling to and portray—I learned how to grow to owning it, to wearing it, to liking it even; but only once Dad had spun elaborate tales of famous Laelias (most of whom were fanciful), festooned me with intricate stories of its meaning (most of which were made up), and sugared me with academic facts (all of which were real): *Laelias can grow fastened to tree trunks, but only if the tree does not cast deep shade.*

I folded up the little piece of paper and placed it back into the bag.

He'd googled my name.

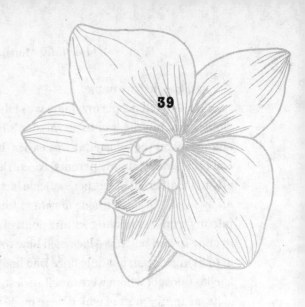

39

The rain started as a stutter but quickly gained confidence. By the time I reached the Jaguar Lodge, I was drenched, soaked from the slicing heavens but also from the roadside; the puddles were so big I couldn't jump them, and where I could, fast-streaming rivulets splashed up, just as astonishing. My T-shirt and shorts slicked against my skin, my socks were sopping, my bra sodden. Droplets gathered pear-shaped at the ends of my kinked hair, water streaming tears down my face.

"Hey," Francisco said, flicking a bar towel over his shoulder. "Weh di go aan?"

"Okay . . . yeah, okay. How are you?"

"Not bad, Miss Laelia. All is good. Beer?"

"Hot chocolate?" It was warm in the air, but wet weather always finds its way to the bones. He nodded, searching for a mug. I gathered the T-shirt at my belly to wring it out.

The bar was empty, save for a young family (North American tourists with baseball caps and overzealous whines) finishing up their lunch and a selection of birds tucking into pulpy pumpkin remains on the metal feeding ledge.

I kicked off my trainers, emptied them of rainwater and peeled off my socks, hanging them over the balcony. I hadn't charged my laptop in months, and it was dead. Remembering the Wi-Fi code (Treehouse123), as soon as the computer launched into life, I punched at the keys. I googled "diving accident Caye Caulker" and scrolled down the headlines . . . "Why You Have to Dive the Blue Hole Before You Die" . . . "Croc Attack on Caye Caulker" . . . "US Diver Dies in Night Dive Incident." I clicked in to read about a sixtysomething Californian woman who never resurfaced. I clicked out, scrolled further . . . "Female Tourist Dies While Scuba Diving Off Ambergris" . . . I tried that. "A female Brazilian tourist identified as Ana Santos died on Tuesday, 11th May 2007." Clicked out.

Francisco delivered my hot chocolate, steaming anticipation. "How's the hangover?"

"Yeah, not too bad."

"Aid didn't leave 'til after one." The Jaguar never stayed open after ten, eleven tops. "How's *his* hangover?" He laughed.

I shook my head. "I'm not sure. They left early this morning. He's driving his friends back to San Ignacio."

"He's a player, his friend." Francisco gathered up the salt and pepper.

"Hmm?"

"Aid's friend . . . Rich? Flirting with the bar staff all night."

"Really?"

"I had to throw them out. I couldn't stay, and I didn't want to leave Eva on her own with them." He wiped at the table, smearing away the remnants of salt crystals and pepper dust. "And he's already got a great woman . . . That was her at lunchtime, wasn't it? The blond one?"

I nodded.

"Good looking." Francisco smiled.

"Yes. Yes, she is."

"Anyway, they didn't settle their bill, so can I leave it with you . . . ? Aid's always so generous, buying the whole bar drinks." Francisco pulled out a scrappy receipt from his pocket. I stared down at the bill, the ink of the digits blurring across the paper. Three hundred and twenty dollars. "More than you were expecting?"

"Er . . . a bit."

"Champagne dreams."

"What's that?"

"They spent a lot. Bought a couple of—"

"No. I mean, that phrase? 'Champagne dreams'?"

"Champagne dreams wid lime juice money. It's from a song Eva keeps playing." *Champagne dreams wid lime juice money. Reggae thumping, a flash of gold, daiquiris, a bar, the sea, a beach bar.* Caye Caulker. "Soldiers of fortune."

Was it in Caye Caulker? Someone was there. A feeling, a sense of something, so strong. Emerald eyes.

"It's fine, Francisco. I'll, erm . . . pay for it all at the end." I took a sip of chocolate, and it scalded my tongue.

I blinked the half memory away, staring back at the screen. "Young Belizean American Woman Dies Following Incident at the Famous Blue Hole." I clicked in, crashing the mug back to its saucer until it spilled. The incongruous image at the top of the page: the most exquisite turquoise dappled sea.

Experienced diver Luisa Farrante, 28, holidaying on Caye Caulker from San Ignacio, died following a scuba diving accident on 12th January. By the time she was rushed back to Ambergris, she was pronounced dead.

The most scant and transactional of details. I scanned down the page.

The divers entered the water from the boat, The Kraken, in pairs. Farrante and her partner were at the back of the group.

"You having lunch?" Francisco asked, over my shoulder.

Fifteen minutes into the dive, Farrante was brought back to the vessel and

"No, no, thanks. I've got to get back for the kids."

both CPR and oxygen were administered onboard, but she was unresponsive. The crew then headed to San Pedro and took Farrante to the Ambergris Hope Clinic, where she was pronounced dead on arrival. A police investigation is underway. Farrante's body will be transported to Belize City for a full postmortem examination.

I stared at the image on the screen; its dazzling flat sea, sand like clouds lined with palms, the cobalt sky teasing infinity until it hit the edges of its frame. My eyes softened and the image pixelated fuzzy.

Paradise. Until it wasn't.

I spent over an hour in the bar, trawling websites and social media forums and local newspapers online. There was little more than a rehash of the same article from different outlets. No photos. No more names. No mention of Aid. Belizean newspapers only ever seem to cover the bare essentials, rehash scant information.

I searched "Luisa Farrante" across social media, but she had no digital presence. I found an "L. Farrante" linked to an address in Charlestown, Boston, USA, that could have been her, but nothing more. I searched through Aid's online profiles, backtracked through his posting history, but he'd never been showy about his endeavours, never bought into all that bullshit—too busy living his life to the extreme to worry about documenting it. I found Maia, then Rich, but no Luisa, no mention of her. It was like she'd barely existed at all, which made me want to know her even more.

I went back into Aid's Instagram. He hadn't added to it for ages. I scrolled down through the months and the years.

And then I saw it. Like I'd never seen it before: a close-up image of his bicep, the artwork blackfresh, blood radiating to the surface of his skin, sacrificial pain around an endless, snaking heart. "L.F."

"Live Forever," that's what he'd told me.

Except it didn't mean Live Forever anymore.

Aid still wasn't back by dinnertime. I guessed he'd got stuck longer in Tikal, hit traffic. Chloe dropped the kids back to me with barely a word. They sloped straight off to their room.

"I'll go back to the hotel, then," Chloe said, slouching. "Give you some more space."

"I'm not angry with you. I'm disappointed you never told me . . . It's like you've been lying to me, treating me like a kid."

She turned back, moving closer. "I didn't want to worry you."

I sighed. "It feels like a lie."

"I just never thought to tell you."

"Which is it?" My voice was raised now, crackling. "You wanted to protect me, or you never even thought about telling me? At least get your story straight."

"I don't know, Laelia. I'm sorry, okay? It was years ago." She looked over my shoulder, checking the kids were out of earshot. "Are you going to come back with me?"

"Oh, Chlo. I don't know—"

"Well, can you make your mind up? I need to know what to do with the tickets . . ."

"There's no need to get aggressive."

"It was you who was shouting at me. I just want you to make a decision. I've tried to help you. Given you options. I can't do any more than that." She started muttering through her teeth so I could barely hear her. "I don't think Aid's any more chilled . . . I'm sure he's having an af—"

"Oh my God, Chloe. Stop having a go at Aid—"

"Why shouldn't I speak up about Aid? There's definitely something not right there. He's taking you for a fool." She started back down the steps to her taxi. "He's a fucking alcoholic, Laelia, and you—"

I slammed the door shut behind her.

After dinner, I found Ella and Dylan in their room sprawling with plantain chips in front of one of Dad's old VHS movies.

Helen Mirren screamed, inconsolable.

"What are you watching?"

Ella glanced up at me. "*Mosquito Coast.*"

"Again," said Dylan, rolling his eyes. He got up to leave the room. "I'm hungry."

"You just ate," I called.

I stared at the TV, at the family in the boat. "I didn't know we had this."

Ella yawned. "It was in that stack of tapes in the cupboard . . . He's so horrible, the dad," she said, not taking her eyes off the screen. "He's so controlling." Harrison Ford sat clutching the tiller, towing his sons along the water. I hadn't watched this film in years.

I drew the curtains. "I don't remember."

As I turned to leave, River Phoenix started narrating a savage voice-over above the *put-put-put* of the engine, talking about his father, how he wanted to push a knife into him, murder him.

As I edged towards the door, out the corner of my eye, I clocked the inside of Ella's arm blackened in desperate thick ink. "Ella?" I grabbed at her wrist.

She tried to shake me off. "Leave me alone . . . ! Get off me."

"Ella, what's going on . . . ?" I dropped her arm; I'd gripped too tight. She pulled it back in towards her chest. "Are you cutting again? Is that why you've been henna-ing your hands? To cover it?" Her eyes were wet pink, her mouth crumbling. She couldn't speak. "I thought you were happy here . . . You seem so happy."

"Stop."

"Is it Jonas? Has he done something?"

"Oh my God, Mum. Stop!" She started crying. "I'm happy here. I *love* it here. I'm not cutting! I can't believe you'd even think that. It's *ink*." She thrust her arms at me, showing me the markings. Just pen. "I'm . . . I just . . . It's you." Her voice crumpled. "I can't bear watching you . . . how you are." She spat the words.

"What do you mean?"

"How you are with him. With Aid. It makes me feel sick."

My lips trembled. "What? I . . ." I couldn't speak.

"The way he treats you. The way he talks to you."

"Has he done something? To you? Or Dylan?"

Her face was aghast. "No, never . . . But I've heard how he is with you. How he talks to you. Why can't you stand up to him more . . . ? Why don't you?" I couldn't reply. "*Why don't you?*" she screamed again.

"Ella!" I shouted. "You stop . . . You stop. We love each other . . . I love him."

She stood up, pushed past me. Muttered something under her breath. "Maybe love isn't enough." I'm not sure if she said that, or if I made it up.

I lay on the bed, waiting for Aid to come home, thinking about the knotty entanglement of family, the agonising complexity of love.

I'd never understood them before—women who put up with violent men. How wild, to stay like that, to hang around for more—to take it— hounded like a dog to within the final throes of a whimper.

The reasons are not excuses. They are reasons. Aid had always loved me so strong, so fierce, like nothing I'd ever felt before. And he'd never hit me. He'd never hit me. The highs were so high. And the lows? Somehow, over time, I'd diminished those to nothing, diluted them somehow. But there were reasons; reasons, I knew now, why he'd behaved like that.

I was a mix of nervous excitement, knowing finally I could chat to him, confront him and our sleeping demons. We would be able to talk about it, speak about his past, his wife, his fears. I wanted to learn all about her, know her, console him. Then I could explain to Ella, make it all good with her. She would understand. I could help him. And then we could get back to being a family. It was going to be all right. We were going to be all right.

The kids were asleep, and I was drifting off when I heard the truck pull in. I drained the last of my wine, Dutch courage, and ran out to greet him.

"Hey," Aid called, falling out the Frontier.

"How are you?"

He started walking towards me, and then the passenger door opened. A figure stepped out into the darkness. "I picked up Henry on the way back. Can he stay for the night?"

My heart dropped. "Er . . . yeah. Yes, of course."

"He'll go in the study. Sure that's okay, Henry? We haven't got the lodge rooms ready yet."

"I'll be good. Hi, Laelia. How are you?"

"Fine. Thanks."

Aid walked past me, pecked my cheek. "I'm knackered . . . See you in the morning, yeah?"

I nodded. "Sure. Goodnight."

When I found Aid in bed, he was nearly asleep. I kissed at his shoulder, at his neck, but he pushed me away. "No, Laelia."

I couldn't drift off. I lay wide awake staring at his L.F. tattoo, feeling the flitters of the butterflies in my gut that were very much alive; blue morphos desperate to be set free.

40

Someone had brought me three giant sacks of limes, left them on the veranda. I eyed them up over my coffee cup in the murderous morning heat. Shit. Falicia had organised the ingredients, but they were supposed to have been delivered to Esther's the other side of the river. Reggae thumpered thick and heavy from the radio. I turned it down so as to not wake Aid. He was still dead to the world. It would be easier to slice the citrus wedges in advance, though, crate them, and take them over by boat in the morning. Get one job done, ticked off the list. I could mobilise the kids to help me chop.

I went through to the bedroom. Their bed was unmade, a note lying on top:

> Gone to meet Jonas. I'll drop Dylan to Gabriel's. Esther's said we
> can stay overnight. Come over and get us if not okay,
>   Ella

No kisses. She was still mad at me.

After clearing up their breakfast plates, I made another pot of coffee then headed outside to make a start. The bags were so heavy, I couldn't shift them. I'd have to prep the limes right there. I cleaned out a couple of storage bins I found in the shed and filled them with water, careful not to wake Henry, who was still fast asleep in the study hammock, then began slicing.

I caught the end of a radio news bulletin: ". . . searching for Dion Zabaneh. He was last seen in the Dangriga area on Friday, and the police say they are now closing in . . . The government of Belize has extended its—" The station flipped to gentle reggae.

I turned to see Aid in his PJs, bed-headed and scrunched with sleep, leaning over the radio. "Morning, sexy."

"Morning," I said, my palms starting to itch. I scratched at them, drawing red scores across my fingers. I wanted to talk to him so badly— ask him so much about what happened, about the accident, about his wife—but Henry could emerge, interrupt us, at any moment. I needed to find the right time.

"What are you doing?" Aid kept playing with the tuner, shifting stations until he found the haunting crackle of Tricky's "Hell Is Round the Corner."

"They're for River Day on Friday . . . Can you help?" The lime was burning my skin, my hands raw with citrus juice.

How could we go on, with a lie like this lurking between us? And it was a lie; it felt like a lie. It was a lie.

"I don't want to help." He came closer and grabbed me by the waist. "I want to do this." My hearing aids tore through my ears, the tinnitus metal. He started kissing at my neck then whispered into me, "I can't keep my hands off of you."

I gasped, dropping my knife. "We need to get to Falicia's."

He carried on, ignoring me. "We've got time."

"Henry's still here."

"I don't mind . . ." He tugged at my vest, pushed it up over my belly.

Seeing Henry emerging from the study, I shoved Aid off, rearranging my top. "Not now . . . Please."

Aid held up his hands in surrender, then leaned his head in towards mine. He pulled the aids from my ears as he whispered into my neck, "You're so uptight." Then he tossed them to the floor. As I scrambled down on my hands and knees to find them, Aid grinned and turned the radio up again.

$\mathbf{D}$o you think it needs more lime?" Falicia asked, going in for another mouthful. She passed me the spoon to try. The curry tasted good—rich and textured.

"A little," I mumbled, sprinkling more salt, grabbing the pepper mill from Mounia. Falicia smacked her lips. "Mmmm, it's good." She went for another spoonful. "It's a pity Chloe couldn't come."

"She's got so much work on," I said, forcing a gentle smile. I spooned another mouthful of curry. I hadn't even bothered to invite Chloe to Falicia's, still so annoyed at her.

Falicia smiled. "Shame she's not able to leave her work at work, be here with you."

"That's just Chloe," Aid chipped in. "No great surprise."

"She works too hard," said Henry. He and Aid were chopping coriander over beers in the corner. They wanted to help, although they were doing more drinking than prepping and were really only there for the lunch. "She coming to River Day?"

"Oh, I don't know," I said. "She's got so much on." I hadn't invited her to that either.

"So shall I order another couple of kilos of okra?" Falicia asked, tapping a biro at her lips.

I nodded. "That would be great, thanks."

"And your French friend is sourcing lionfish, right? Can he get enough?" She started scribbling notes.

"Yes, he can," I said abruptly. The steel of Aid's knife flashed in the light.

Mounia laughed, her eyes sparkling over her glasses. "Ahhhh. French Nico . . . Your sister took a shine to him."

"Didn't we all, no?" Falicia smirked.

Aid's knife stopped chopping. "Nico? When did Chloe meet Nico?"

"We all met him," Mounia said, before I could stop it. "At Laelia's birthday."

Aid dropped his knife down on the block. He took a swig of beer before looking over, wild-eyed. "Nico came to your birthday?" He was moving towards me now, Falicia and Mounia and Henry watching on like bit players to our drama.

"No. No, he didn't. He was just there. At the bar. We only said hello." I held my breath.

"So you didn't invite him?"

I shook my head. "Of course not."

Aid flicked his gaze around, glared at Falicia then at Henry. Something in their eyes halted him. His shoulders dropped. "Okay. Okay. Well . . . good." He moved back to his chopping board, to his beer, and took a swig, Henry's eyes still firmly on him. I could feel Mounia and Falicia staring at me. I couldn't look up.

I grabbed the spoon again, took another mouthful. "Mmm . . . I think it's ready." My voice cracked.

Aid knocked back beer after beer over the curry, then headed off early. Feeble excuses hung redundant in the air. The rest of us were left to clear up the dishes, and the mess. It was a stilted silence.

"Is everything okay with him?" Henry asked after he'd gone.

I lifted my shoulders, half smiled. "It's a lot, being here. Adjusting."

"But with Nico? What was that?" Mounia asked gently, pushing her fork and spoon together.

I shook my head, closed my eyes. "He doesn't like him . . . I don't know why."

My coconut flan had too much caramel. They seemed to devour it, but I barely touched mine. I made an effort at a couple of mouthfuls. Hid the rest under my napkin, took solace in my wine.

They wouldn't let me help with the washing up. Instead, they each hugged me tightly, urgently, and watched from the veranda as I set off home.

"Are you sure you don't want to stay, no?" Falicia asked, pushing her lips together with a half smile.

I shook my head. "No. Thank you. I should get back."

"Take care of yourself," she called as I turned. "Promise me."

I walked down the driveway thinking of my parents. The tension, the shouting, the stilted silences. The unravelling of a marriage. I'd seen my dad hit my mother once, fighting like animals, in a furious rage. A fist like a valve. Releasing the pressure. Calming her down. *Crazy bitch.* As though she was the centre of it all. *Because* she was the centre of it all, his world. I'd heard them fighting a thousand times, barbed and spiking. Though he never hit her again. Not that I knew. Still, being with your family can feel—simultaneously—like the safest, and the most dangerous, place to be.

I'd always thought love could conquer all. Turns out, maybe it can't. Turns out, if you're raised by animals, maybe you can't help but be seduced by wolves.

Wittering Lodge, Stann Creek District, Belize
17th July 2018

Fifty kmph. Ellis has missed this feeling. The speed. The danger. He's rebuilt the carburettor, changed the oil. The fuel stabiliser seems to have done its job well enough. He'll keep it topped up with the high-octane stuff, at least for the next few tanks, get her properly purring again. The freedom he feels to be here, to be back.

The lodge is overgrown beyond belief. Polo has tried to keep on top of things, but most of the buildings have been swallowed up by jungle. It hasn't changed much; the greens still so green, the flowers still bursting, the cicadas still trilling on. Ellis has changed its name, though—an attempt to lay claim to this new beginning, reclaim this old new home. He's knocked up a replacement sign to bury into the snake plant border on the track: WITTERING LODGE, an ode to past memories, to the little bit of England he's brought with him, to Helena, whom he left behind.

Nearing sixty kmph. He loves this straight bit of road, always has. If his students could see him now . . . half of them wouldn't believe it was him. *Professor Wylde, loose in the wild. Still got it.*

Hortense—older now, frailer—waves at him from the roadside and he warily waves back. Across in the village, a few faces still recognise him, most of them friendly. He has been welcomed back with warmth and curiosity, despite everything. Times have moved on. People have moved on. The past has been forgotten.

He still often thinks of Agapita—how she is, where she's gone. Polo's told him she's still in Toledo District, last he heard years ago. Her whole

family went down there, chickens and all. They've never been back. Ellis wonders if he might visit, if he could even find her if he did; what he
would say to her, what she would say to him. But then he dismisses the
idea as quickly as he thought it. Some things are best left unsaid, some
histories best laid to rest.

He's picked up a stray, a "potlicker," they call it, who followed him
and Mounia bar to bar last week in Dangriga, his second or third day
back. They asked around but couldn't find an owner, so he took her back
home on the bus. He's still not sure what to name her. He's been pondering on Ursula after Le Guin, another nod to the past, to the books he
read to the girls night after night when he returned back home with his
suitcase to them, alone without their mother.

This is home now. He's always known he would return, Belize a magnet for people who want to start again; where he left his life, his heart,
his orchids. Now a prestigious emeritus fellow, retired from teaching, he
can focus on his precious plants—collecting and writing and studying
until the day he dies. *Eighty kmph.* Oh, if his students could see him now.

He wanted to come over earlier, but Chloe and Laelia kept having babies. Chloe was against it, his packing up his life in England. Plus, he
couldn't shift the house in Oxford, couldn't get anyone to buy it, not for
years. Not until that German family fell in love with it. Their daughter—
carrying her slouchy bear wherever she went—reminded him of Laelia
at that age. Mummy's girl. Not that she could remember. Ellis asked her
about it recently, but she could not picture her mother's face, insisted she
had little to cling to, told him she did not recollect the memories he did—
the ones he now wonders about; if maybe they weren't accurate anyway.
Memory is like that, inventing more perfect worlds than ever really existed or refusing to re-create them at all.

Chloe's latest email worries him, though there's nothing he can
do. She says she has no evidence, but she's convinced Simon is sleeping
around. She hasn't said anything to Laelia, doesn't know how she would
react. He won't make too much of it. He isn't sure they want his advice
anyway. If they ever do, his irrepressible daughters.

The almond trees whoosh by. It was good to see the girls before he
left. Prior to a last goodbye dinner, he'd seen neither for months—both
so busy, though he would pop into Laelia's restaurant from time to time,

whenever he was in London. He loved watching her in her element, busying herself over sleek white plates and copper pans. Sometimes, if Aktar let her, Laelia would appear like a magician at his table; she might get a minute to give him a kiss, check on his food, top up his wine. And that would be enough, for him. He loved seeing her happy, where she was always meant to be. Cooking was her botany—the kitchen her forest—and she thrived in the heat of it; they weren't so different that way.

He rides past a trail of soil, something brown, discarded in the road. He sees another something ahead by the lay-by. He slows down. Another, and another. Pulling over, he jumps off his bike. Venturing onto the dirt, he picks one up.

He knew it. *Lycaste aromatica.*

Another. *Maxillaria hedwigiae.*

Another a bit farther along. *Barkeria spectabilis.*

Ellis gathers the plants into his rucksack before riding along to the supermart.

The black Ram 1500 on the curb catches his attention, mainly because the super shine of its paintwork is reflecting sunlight directly into his eyes, but also because he spots, poking out from the tarp on the open truck bed, a tell-tale sign: overspilling pillowcases. Ellis lifts the corner of the turquoise sheeting, peers in to see what else is underneath.

"Lookin' for somethin'?" an American voice thunders from behind.

"It's illegal, you know." Ellis turns.

The wide-built man standing over him is blocking out the sun. He's wearing an oil-smeared vest and combats, military boots. "Export is illegal. We're just gardenin'. What's it gotta do with you anyways?" He tosses a plastic bag of groceries into the truck.

"It's my job. Orchids."

The man laughs a deep drawl. "Yeah? Well, it's my life."

"They're damaged, half of them have broken roots . . . I should report you. Commercial collecting obliterates whole species."

"You're fulla shit."

"Trade has driven entire species extinct. *Paphiopedilum canhii* was all but wiped out within a year of its discovery . . . by people like you.

Many orchid species are at risk. If even five per cent of their population is harvested . . ." Ellis wipes his brow. "I don't know why I'm wasting my time . . . I should call the police."

"Ain't done nothin' illegal."

"Where are these orchids going? What are you planning to do with them?"

"Look, old man, why don't you mind your own business? Stop pokin' your interferin' nose into mine?" He walks away, opens his truck door. As Ellis is logging the numberplate, the man turns, trudges back again, a newfound smirk wide across his face. "'El hombre orquídia.' That's what they call you, ain't it? The locals round here. You're the lecturer . . ." Ellis tightens his shoulders. *Doctor, actually*, he thinks, though he doesn't say a word. "The academic . . . News travels fast. I heard about you."

"What have you heard?"

He moves in towards Ellis, broadens his chest. "Heard you're not whiter than white yourself . . ."

"I don't know what you mean."

"It's a small world, and this spell we're all under—this orchidelirium—people talk. Traders talk . . . I know shit."

"What could you possibly know?"

"I heard you sold plants before, years ago . . . Rare, beautiful motherfuckers."

Ellis bows his head, stares at his feet. "You don't know anything about me."

The man spits his words. "I know you're a hypocrite." He laughs. "You ain't that different. You should be thankin' me . . . Collectors put more legwork into findin' new species than academics ever do."

"C'mon, Hector," his long-haired associate calls, coming out of the store and nearing the truck.

The man laughs as he turns. "Y'all're as seduced by 'em as I am. They're as addictive as women. So fascinatin', we can't leave 'em alone . . ."

"C'mon, man . . ." his friend says again, lighting a cigar.

The men jump into their vehicle and drive away, kicking up dust. An orchid spills from the back of the truck bed and lands at Ellis's feet, the most sorry-looking *Cattleya* he has ever seen.

Ellis punches it in: 1409. Helena's birthday.

Chloe's voice echoes in his mind. *Virgo: the most complex woman of all the zodiac.* He would like to think that's all piffle, if only it wasn't so true. He's talked to Chloe recently about Helena, about her state of mind, about the things she did, the things he didn't, the mistakes they both made.

He turns the key, opening the safe and adding the new documentation: his passport, insurance documents, bank papers, and old photos. Staring at the pile of old journals and crumpled letters, he considers opening a page or two, rereading the past. Maybe he'll do it later with a drink, maybe next week. Maybe he'll never read it again.

As he closes the door, the flash of green catches his eye. He hitches for breath, paws at his hair. He can't even remember how much it was. *Forty thousand, was it? Fifty?* His chest tightens. He never could spend it. It wasn't even his to spend. It was for Agapita, and Helena and the girls. The baby that never was. He can't even bring himself to touch the money. It's the worst thing he's ever done, selling those orchids, the greatest betrayal of all—treachery against nature. And a shame that's shadowed him ever since.

Locking the safe, he grabs his glass and pours himself a final rum. Draining the last of the Don Omario, he drops the key into the empty bottle and places it back with the others on the shelf.

He realises he's not yet checked his mailbox. Polo gave up on emptying it long ago, so little ever now delivered.

Ursula trails him as he saunters up the overgrown pathway out front, past the mother-in-law's tongue and unruly bushes, down onto the track. Fighting back wild vegetation, he manages to locate the box. Inside he finds two snails and a dead beetle, an old *New Scientist*, and a ravaged clump of brochures, circulars, and flyers. Sieving through the dated detritus, he finds a fresher envelope postmarked four months ago, his name and address penned in a beautiful, flowing script.

Tearing open the letter, he reads about Agapita's illness, and then more shocking news. The secret she has kept.

He pauses, trying to steady his hands and shaky breaths.

He cannot help but think of the consequences of things, what was and what wasn't. What might have been.

Somehow, he gathers himself. He reads the update scrawled in a different hand, in a different pen, across the bottom:

Agapita died peacefully this morning surrounded by her family.

I know she would want you to have this letter she never got to send. She would have wanted you to know the truth, that she lied to you for the kindest of reasons.

I'm so sorry.

Yours faithfully,
Aapo.

Ellis rubs the heel of his palm against his chest. *Agapita.*

Beautiful Agapita. His water lily, his breath of fresh air. Gone. How could she be gone? And he never got to see her again.

He remembers, as his lips start to tremble and the tears start to fall, the last time he cried, over thirty years ago: the day he was told their baby was stillborn. The unfathomable pain of it. The helplessness. The grief.

Except she wasn't. She had survived. He knows now, his daughter had actually lived.

Locating a part-shaded cedar deep in the jungle, Ellis, still shaking, pulls the rescued *Cattleya aurantiaca* from his rucksack, aligning it on the south-facing limb. Wrapping the twine around the rhizome he secures the orchid in place, thinking of each of his girls, of the secrets he's kept from them, the ones they've kept from each other.

He strokes at the orchid's leaves, its pseudobulbs, its roots, wishing it the best.

Packing the yarn back into his bag, he wonders what Helena would say if she were here. *You can never live what might have been.* Or something like it. Picking up his machete, Ellis turns to trek back to the lodge, remembering her smile and something else she used to say: *I love you, Wylde, wildly.*

It never ceases to amaze him—the adaptability of these plants, their firm resilience, their grit, how this one survives and will still thrive despite all the odds. It should bloom again next year, he thinks—this beautiful *Cattleya.* He will take good care of it and see that it does; it's all he can do now, all he ever could have done.

PART FOUR

Dirt

Laelia rubescens. Pale Laelia. A neotropical species of perennial epi-phytic orchid native to Belize and other parts of Central America. Pre-fers a well-draining, loamy soil. In some areas, the orchid has been introduced intentionally as an ornamental plant and has subsequently be-come naturalised, appearing in the wild as an escapee from cultivation.

42

Laelia

The sky was clouding fast puffs of white. Christopher and Gabriel came to meet Dylan off our boat, and they ran away together to join the football game at the top of the bank.

"Your water bottle," I shouted. I was surprised when Dylan turned on his heels and came back for it. I went to kiss him, but he shook me off, knowing the other boys were watching. He was growing too fast.

The whole riverside was buzzing with fluster and flurry. Menfolk—and it was mainly men—were still constructing some of the craft stalls further along the bank. Our stand was set up already, complete with bunting, tables, and chairs. Pairs and pairs and pairs of hands helped us carry the boxes of limes and laundry bags of palm leaf plates, cutlery, and other paraphernalia from the boat to our stall. We'd made the curries at Falicia's. She and Henry brought the saucepans and refrigerated boxes across, including the seafood I'd ensured Nico drop to hers, not mine. The kitchen team were quick to start prepping the lionfish; we needed to heat up the curries.

"All set?" Falicia asked, hugging at my shoulders.

"All set." I smiled, pulling my hair into a bun. I relished this; cooking for people again, without the cacophony of a city kitchen, that stress of the unknown I could not hear. I began laying out pans, sharpening knives, organising the ceviche ingredients in Tupperware boxes.

"How's everything with you?" I asked. I wanted Falicia to ask me the same. I wanted to tell her, wanted to share what I'd found out, wanted to download it all. But I feared if I did, I might break somehow. And I had to stay strong, talk to Aid first. Keep his secret. See if we couldn't work everything out.

Falicia started spooning curry into a pan. "Oh, you know . . . We're okay."

"Really?" I asked gently. "You don't seem yourself."

She stopped stirring. "I'm all right." She dropped the spoon, turned towards me, her lips trembling. "I've decided to leave him." Her eyes welled up.

"What . . . ? Oh God, Falicia. I'm so sorry."

"It's the way of things."

"I've been so wrapped up in my own stuff, I didn't . . . I didn't know. I'm sorry."

"It's not your fault."

"But you seem so happy together."

"We are . . . We were. But there's a lot of tension, you know? Henry wants a child, and I cannot give that to him. I don't want to give that to him. He wants to keep trying, but I don't want to. I don't want a child. It's taken me a long time to say that out loud, but I'm not ashamed to admit it. God never gives you more than you can bear, but I cannot take it anymore."

I stood, stunned. I grabbed her and we tightened into a hug as I wiped the tears from her cheek.

"I've come to terms with it," she said. "The body has a way of knowing before the mind ever does. Something's not right—and deep down I've known it for a long time."

"I'm so sorry."

"I'm moving in with my cousin in the village in a couple of weeks. But we'll stay close. We're still friends."

I rubbed at her arm. "Well, it takes a lot of strength to leave."

Falicia pursed her lips. "It does, Laelia. It really does, and like you told me, I cannot keep hiding it . . . I'm sorry to bring the mood down on your big day." She leaned over to grab another spoon. "What's up with your hands?"

"Cutting lime in the sunshine. So stupid. I should have known . . . They're still so angry and sore."

"Youch. Kantun can mix you something. But you know what they say here? If your palms itch, you're gonna meet some money soon. It's a good omen." She looked up to the sky and chuckled. "Hortense over there says she thinks it's gonna rain today."

"Really?"

Falicia laughed. "She told me her ferns got damaged. Means it's gonna rain."

"Oh."

"Old wives' tale."

As I was firing up the gas burners, my phone pinged into life after days of no service. Seven text messages and four voicemails from Chloe. I scanned the first few texts:

Can we chat?

and

Lil, FFS. Please pick up. x

and

Please, Laelia. Pick up. x

I placed the phone into our makeshift till and ignored the rest.

43

Marimba melded through the gentle breeze, floating soft and cloudy. The canoes started streaming through around midday—traditional wooden vessels and hypermodern multicoloured machines, three paddlers apiece. Luminous vests, caps, and bandannas rushing past, surging through the water. Hundreds of people lined the river's edge, cheering and shouting and waving lively flags—tourists and locals from far-flung districts. I heard Americans and Mexicans and Belizeans. Placencia Village had laid on extra water taxis to ferry people back and forth, so there were tons of spectators from across the lagoon as well as those who'd driven from the main road. It was teeming with smiles and laughter, and the food was a great crowd pleaser.

"Best lionfish I ever tasted," one woman hummed, clutching at my arm with a handful of napkins, balancing her third helping of curry.

"How are we doing?" I asked.

Falicia was flicking through the dollars we'd taken so far. "Pretty good, gyal. Pretty good." Then she lowered her voice. "You're gonna get that restaurant started, don't you worry."

We dished up food to a fluctuating crowd, three people deep at its busiest. Francisco and Eva and their team helped prep at the back. Ella barely spoke to me, still indignant, though she helped with the ceviches until, through the throng, Jonas arrived shouting "Ella!" I loved watching her smile—unburdened—whenever he said her name. As soon as she saw him, she flung down her apron faster than I could stop her, then they ran off hand in hand. Aid and Henry were drifting stall to stall, helping run quick errands in between slow pitchers of rum.

The sun threw intervallic spears as the canoes paddled by, until eventually the muddy brewing skies unleashed an urgent, heavy shower. People bundled into our stall seeking shelter, chattering, pushing themselves up against the canvas, the tables, each other. I rushed around the front to make sure no-one touched the hot saucepans.

"If it's sunny while it's raining," I overhead Falicia telling someone, "the devil is having a fight with his wife."

"Sounds about right," said an accent behind me. I turned around. "Hi," he said, eyes bright. Little mirroring raindrops rolled down his face.

"Hi, Nico."

"How's it going? It smells amazing." He looked handsome. Always so handsome, warmth exuding through his words.

I pushed my hair out of my face. "Yeah, good, I think. Have you had some?"

He shook his head, flicked off the rainwater. "I'd love some."

Falicia passed him a plate of curry, and I went to grab him a wedge of lime. As I reached across to the bowl of citruses, Nico placed his hand on mine, tracing the raw, red rash with his fingers. They felt soft, reassuring. "What happened?"

"It's nothing. I"—I looked up at him—"Nico, I appreciated the gift. It was kind of you. But I'm not . . . I don't—"

Nico swung awkwardly around. Someone was pulling at him from behind; a rough hand grasping at his T-shirt, dragging it across his chest. He keeled a little, trying to regain his balance. I took a sharp intake of breath.

Aid's face was a storm, his body looming over us. He leaned back, threw a swift, hard punch towards Nico. Missed. They grappled into each other, wrestling. The crowd surged back and forth, people screaming, yelling; desperate hands trying to intervene and split them up.

"Aid!" I shouted. But he wasn't listening to me. "Aid, please . . . Stop!"

They tugged and they scrambled, and they pushed at each other until they fell apart, rebalanced, took a breath. Each man assessed himself.

Blood dripped from Aid's eyebrow, shimmered across Nico's lip. They stood staring at each other, matador to bull.

"Leave it, Aid. Please," I begged.

"Hey, London!" Someone shouted. Henry was jostling through the throng, edging towards the front. "What's going on?" He tried to sound upbeat, talk some sense into the senseless. "What you guys doing?" He made it to Aid, put a calming hand across his rapidly breathing chest. Aid pulled away, stroking his hand down his stubbled neck as he drew his eyes up to the sky, considering his next move.

"Let's go, man," Henry said to him firmly, taking hold of his shoulder. Nico stood, stunned, trying to catch his breath.

Aid turned away, went to walk off, end the show.

Nico wiped the red from his mouth, staring at his fingers, evaluating the damage. Aid spun around, a whirlwind, rushing back into the tent, charging towards Nico one more time. Nico shifted sideways, ducking out the way. Aid missed him, torpedoing straight into the tables. He fell, dragging at the cloths. Both tables lurched, then toppled over. The steaming pans smashed against one another, crashing to the ground.

Hot curry pooled across the dirt like rivers of shit. Someone screamed.

I screamed. It was me.

44

Aid was sat at Dad's desk, hunched over a glass of whisky like it distilled the meaning of life. The bottle next to him was nearly empty. My big day. In front of everyone. And now they all knew. What a mess we were, what a joke.

"What the fuck, Laelia?" He turned towards me, brewing like the wind. Eyes penetrating savage, his right eyebrow a shock of smeared blood. "Are you fucking him?"

"Oh, give it up, Aid. There's nothing—"

"He was touching your hand."

"I was literally telling him I'm not interested."

"Don't lie to me."

"Why won't you believe me?" I begged. "Why are you behaving like this?" Though we both knew why.

"And before, when you saw him on your birthday . . . you didn't tell me." Aid was seething with alcohol, teeming with the lies he was telling himself.

"I . . . I didn't know. It wasn't anything. I just forgot to tell you he w—"

"You forget a lot, don't you?" He collapsed his head into his hands, pulled his fingers back through his hair.

He was wrestling with the memories, the demons in his head, the secrets he harboured as deep as sunk submarines.

"I'm worried what you might say to him," Aid said into his palms. "I don't know what you might be sounding off about."

Howler monkeys barked outside.

"What do you mean?" My head was spinning. I edged closer and inhaled. "There's nothing going on with Nico."

"Why can't you face the fucking truth?"

The feedback screeched. He stood over me, his eyes pulsing dark. His hand pressed into my chest again, clutching at my breast, pushing as he whispered into my hearing aid.

The way he looked at me then.

"Aid, please—"

"I can't keep it up, this fucking facade." He glared, his eyes icy and wild, his nostrils flaring. "You're a joke . . . I carry all this guilt around. The scars. You carry on like nothing ever fucking happened." He was drunk, slurring. "And I protect you."

"What are you talking about?" I could hardly breathe. "It's you who's doing this. With your jealousy and your threats and the shit you make up in your head." I was screaming at him now.

"In *my* head?!" He laughed.

Crazy bitch.

"Why are you like this? Ever since you met Nico, since the Blue Hole that day, you've just spiralled . . . Why can't you stop?"

"You're so fucking stupid," he cried, throwing his eyes up to the ceiling. "Why do you like him so much anyway?"

"I don't know, Aid . . . Because he gives a shit . . . Because he's kind and he lets me be me . . . and he's not a complete alcoh—"

He slapped me. Hard, around the cheek, while the words were still stuck in my throat.

It stung instantly, the shock of it.

Then it burned, the pain of it.

I flashed to trailing ivy and the wedding disco cheers. Si's face then like Aid's face now.

I winced before my eyes widened. Aid's, too. We stood, staring at each other in defiance. Then, without even thinking, I spat. Right into his face. He roared, lurching to grab me, not quite close enough, but his fingers managed to seize me by the arm. He pushed, forcing me back onto the piano. My hip and elbow slammed, the notes plonking sombre dirges. I shifted, dragging myself over the keys, discordant, pulling myself away, but he followed, tracking me around the room.

"Get off!" I screamed. But he was there. On me. Urgent hands palmed at me, lingered, pulled my hair. "Get off!" His breath smelt toxic and pungent. He kissed whisky musk at me, necking me, tugging at my clothes. "Please, Aid, don't." How abruptly a moment can turn. His whim, his desire.

"I'm sorry." He gripped at my throat, squeezing, his thumb and fingers pressing hard. He pushed into me, at me, until I wheezed shallow air.

Until I couldn't.

My body collapsed into itself. The room swirled around us. My vision blurred, I felt lightheaded, as I gasped wet, crackling breaths. Choking, I couldn't speak, couldn't breathe. Tears filled my eyes until I shut them. Until I willed myself away. *The smell of butterfly cakes, enticing and eggy and sweet.*

His strength was too much.

Balmy-baked afternoons sitting, lying, sitting again. Slinking cool sheets snatched from the line. I felt sick. And light, like a feather. *Soft, mohair hugs.* My gasps moved close to wails. *Cow parsley dustings on pine kitchen work tops.* It felt so strong it felt like everything, nothing, everything. *Rose drawer liners, pretty and neat.* It was nearly over. *Hailstones on sunny-streaked mornings.* I could barely breathe. It really fucking hurt. *Tiger-orange bottles on bathroom shelves; their promises. Their agonies. Their promises.* I really fucking hurt.

He released his grip. I hauled desperate breaths, my vision still blurry. He moved away, but I could still feel him. His fingers, his thumbs, his pressure. The pain of it all. The pain of him.

"I'm sorry," he whispered into my ear until it screamed.

Truths cut keen like whetted knives, but deceptions cook slowly, stewing until they rot; and everything rots faster in the heat. We lay in bed that night tectonically shifted. Things would never be the same.

I woke having barely slept, desperate to talk about the secrets we'd been hiding from each other. I no longer knew what was real—within me or around me—like a proper crazy bitch. Like my mother. Hiding in the shadows of shame. Believing what wasn't true, but also, honestly, refusing to believe what was. Though it was still in there somewhere, screaming, demanding my attention—the clawing ferocity of truth. And I had to talk to him. We had a chance to make it right, if I could only talk to him, help him.

When I opened my eyes in the dawn light, he wasn't lying next to me. I grabbed my hearing aids from their charger next to the bed. I lodged them into my ears, but they were dead. Drained of battery, again. I'd switched them on the night before, hadn't I? Maybe I hadn't. I couldn't make sense of it. My head was so confused, foggy with thoughts and memories, days mixed in with nights. *Crazy bitch.*

I charged my aids a little while I got dressed. Then I found him by the edge of the trees, kicking at the litter of leaves, hands clamped under his arms, staring at his feet.

I moved closer. Inhaled. Took my moment. "Aid, I *know* . . ."

He gazed up at me. "What do you know?"

"I know why you're acting so weird here." My voice wavered, but I went on. "Why you've been so distracted . . . I know, Aid. I know about Luisa." The words rushed from my chest.

He stopped then drew back his head. "What are you talking about?"

"I know you were married . . . I know she died."

His face crumpled. Why was he looking at me like that? Like he's so confused.

"I . . ." His mouth collapsed before he composed himself. He scratched his cheek. "I know you know," he said. "Of course I fucking know."

Maia must have told him she told me.

"Maia thought I already knew," I went on. "Why didn't you tell me?" His body stiffened. He rubbed his hands over his eyes, and his mouth fell open. He couldn't speak. "It must have been so awful for you," I said. "The accident."

His head jerked towards me, his eyes widening. He nodded, slowly. I held his cheek, smearing away his sadness. His eyes darted back to me. "Oh, Laelia. I'm so fucking sorry."

"I know . . . I know."

We sat, clutching each other, on a fallen kapok tree. He said he'd been terrified to tell me early on, to open the past back up. And then it got easier to just not think about it, to detach and move on. He told me life was easy with me. "When I met you, I knew I was going to love you so fucking hard." He lit a rollie, passed me one. His nails were dirty, soiled with mud.

I was a wreck of tears. I couldn't speak.

"When it happened, it was horrible," he whimpered, his voice collapsing with the words. "I saw her . . . Underwater. She couldn't breathe. She panicked. She wasn't an experienced diver. She was so nervous before we set out . . . I should have listened to her, told her not to go . . ." He caught his breath, took a drag on his cigarette, wiped his tears away. "They said her mask was broken. The side pin was missing . . . The dive operator was so shit. I should have used the other company. Checked it all properly, but you . . . you don't think, do you? That that's going to happen? To you."

I rubbed at his back. "It's okay . . . it's okay."

"They tried to say she pulled the mask off her face when she was freaking out, that she broke it . . . I don't know. It was all such a blur . . ." He heaved a crackled sigh. "Afterwards, I wanted to forget it all, forget it ever happened. I didn't really talk about it. I wanted to move on. When I found you again, in Brighton, I was so happy. I had this chance to start again. To forget." He stared at me, his voice breaking. "Except you can't forget, can you? Not really."

Smoke stung in my eyes. "I'm sorry." Shadows of branches twisted around us. I stared at the silhouettes across the ground, thinking about how our eyes are attracted to the light though often the shadows have more to say.

"Please, let's not talk about this again," Aid pleaded. "Not to anyone."

"But it might help t—"

"I don't want to." His voice cracked urgently. "I want to get on with my life. I can't keep reliving it. Promise me you won't tell anyone?"

"Okay," I said. "Okay."

He nodded, smiling through his tears. He kissed me. It smelt of earthy rain.

After we had coffee, Aid headed out. I grabbed my phone to call Chloe. When I finally found a bar of service down the driveway, I rang and rang, but she didn't pick up. Tears brewed in my eyes. I saw her last text:

Had to leave early. Major fuckup at work. Managed to get a refund for your tickets. Sorry you didn't want to come. Chlo xx

And the one before that:

I've remembered. Are you sure dad didn't mean Lavender FIELDS?

Everything started spinning in the dawn light, my neck still raging agonies. I felt instantly nauseous, my stomach a knot. I threw up twice before I sloped back inside and collapsed on the sofa.

There was the sound of a truck, then shouting outside the hut. The night before was still stuck in my throat, the whole scene of it, the soured mess of us.

"La-elia . . . !" Henry's voice and a pounding up the veranda steps. "Laelia, wake up . . ."

"I'm awake." I called, rushing to the door. "What is it?"

Henry stopped in front of me, breathless. "The hospital's been trying to get hold of you."

"What?" My voice cracked.

Henry scanned my face. "It's your dad."

Ellis

He feels relaxed here in this place of little pace. It instantly calms his nerves. It feels needfully indulgent, but still indulgent—a holiday from a holiday of retirement in the jungle, lobsters and reggae and beer.

He takes a birthday trip up each year now, to go diving and connect with the old friends he's collected here, the ones who thrive on his eccentricities and embellished stories, who love hearing tales from the heart of a jungle to which they have never been, would never go.

He's staying on the west side of the island—the quieter side, where he can read and write and watch the setting sun, where he can finish off that peer review. Carmen has sorted him a friend's place overlooking the football field near the seahorse sanctuary. It's not too far from the girls' inn on the other side. But then nothing's too far here. A short walk, or a quick bicycle ride. Carmen has sorted that for him, too.

The building was easy to find. BlueBay Cottages: a weatherboarded oblong, turquoise with yellow and orange doors, white balustrades. The apartment is at the top of a flight of baby pink stairs on the first floor—or second here—he still, sometimes, forgets the Americanisms of Belize.

The morning trade winds whisper in as he unpacks in his room. Two pairs of shorts, three T-shirts, two shirts, swimming trunks, a washbag, mask and fins, eight books, his journal, his laptop, his Panama hat, and his pipe. Then he paces.

He's run out of things to do already. His chest feels tight with anticipation—of seeing the girls, of telling them.

He texts Chloe:

Can't wait to see you both. I'm here. Dad x

He takes his cue from them now, from Chloe really.

He sits around the apartment, shuffling his paperwork and shifting himself from desk chair to kitchen stool to desk chair again, going back in to edit his piece for *The Orchid Journal*, cross-checking the references, waiting, thinking, waiting. He rereads the bio he's drafted to submit:

> *Dr. Ellis C. Wylde, OBE, is Emeritus Fellow and previously Sherardian Professor of Botany at the University of Oxford. He has been editor of* The Orchid Weekly *and* The Orchid Review, *and has written and published over 1,500 papers.*

His phone pings. A text back from Chloe, summoning him. He'll tell them today.

He feels the scribbled note inside his pocket with his fingers, checks again he did pick it up from the desk. As he ambles along the dusty track across the island, he recalls the last time he properly saw them, these daughters—taking Tom and Simon for pints at the Onslow Arms while the kids played on the swings. Holding Scarlett for the first time while Chloe ssshhed exhaustedly from her hospital bed. Hanging around in a Travelodge for three days, wondering what to do with himself, what there was for him to do.

There is nothing in England for him now. Grown women have little need for their fathers. They have little need for men at all these days. He has raised pioneers, proudly, and their decisions are no longer his to question. Once the centre of their worlds, their lives have diverged, grown apart, and that's natural. Adaptation. These daughters don't need their old man anymore.

A couple of American tourists pass, yoga mats slung over toned shoulders, shins sleeking in the sun. Ellis catches the blonde's eye until she drops it. She's pretty enough to know she can ruin him with a look. She already has. He feeds his hand back into his pocket. She's younger than his youngest daughter.

Pulling out his scrawled note, he checks the name of the restaurant: Elden's Kitchen, Avenida Hicaco. He's half an hour early. Chloe said it's next to their hotel. He passes the Caye Reef Inn, considers a drink there first. Wonders if the girls aren't still getting ready, though he's not sure what room they're in. He could text Chloe, but he doesn't want to seem too keen, too overbearing. Too useless. But he's angling to get on with it, to tell them.

The patio in front of the U of hotel rooms is a beautiful spot at the cusp of the sea. Palm trees and cabanas, and a gorgeous, inviting pool. Or it would be if it wasn't swarming with baseball-capped guys launching footballs and smug grins.

The beach bar is already teeming with punta rock and rum-fuelled life. Swimsuits sit on submerged turquoise stools downing cocktails under the cohune shade. The bartender whizzes up a rainbow of daiquiris and margaritas. There's a large group of jacked-up Americans, sprawling over one another with endless limbs and laughter and phones. Young, though they're in their thirties, at least. Ellis wonders how Chloe is coping with these unapologetic roommates. He's glad he'd already accepted Carmen's friend's apartment before declining Chloe's lukewarm offer to stay with her and Laelia here.

He only wants a beer. He's desperate for it now, to calm his nerves. After waiting too long at the bar, he decides to make his way to Elden's, grab a quick drink there. He turns to head off and edges past a bronzed, toned couple necking each other like animals. He can smell the pheromones, feel the heat of them. They glow. As if they've fallen to earth from a billboard for French aftershave or American jeans. The man's bronzed hand, blackened with tattoos, grabs at her pert red-bikinied bottom, her dark hair French plaited, skimming the top of her small waist. He is lost in her, as men tend to get lost in beautiful women. Ellis could get lost in her, too.

"Excuse me," he says as he passes, pushing his hat into his chest. Though they ignore him, this old codger, too wrapped up in each other to notice.

The man's other hand, stubbornly inked in tattoos, is draped over her sun-kissed shoulder, clutching a copy of a paperback. One of Theroux's best, Ellis thinks—a classic: *The Mosquito Coast*.

45

Laelia

I slammed the truck into the parking lot, rushed past the reception desk, past the coffee machine. Ran straight into ICU.

"Dad?" I called, gusting into the room. They'd removed the tubes.

Dr. Guevarra glanced up from beside the screen, checking an intravenous line. "He can breathe on his own . . . We're monitoring him closely. It may take some time for him to come back to full conscious after such a long coma, but he's been listening to our instructions, and he's talking a little. He's confused about where he is, but it's normal."

"Dad?" I said again.

No response.

"He's very tired," Dr. Guevarra reassured me. "He'll need to sleep like this most of the time."

After an hour or so sitting with Dad in disbelief, I phoned Chloe and woke her up to tell her.

"Laelia?" she said, yawning. "I've been so worried about you. I tried to—"

"Chloe, not now . . . They're bringing him out of the coma," I shrieked.

"What? That's amazing." I could hear the relief in her voice. She asked me a thousand questions I couldn't answer, and then said, "Tell him I love him." She said she would book a flight back again as soon as she could.

I slept in the chair next to his bed, our roles reversed, watching over him like he was a child. I couldn't sleep, keeping vigilant to any little change—the flicker of an eye, the judder of a finger, the murmur of memory and sound.

"Hel . . . Hel . . . na?" he muttered, wrestling for breath.

"Dad, it's me. Laelia." I stroked my hand across his forehead.

"Helena," he said again, more certain. He began flailing his arms, pulling at lines. An alarm sounded. And another. *Beepbeepbeepbeepbeep-beepbeep.*

"Nurse?" I shouted into the corridor. "Doctor? Is anyone there?"

Dr. Guevarra came rushing down the hallway.

Beepbeepbeepbeepbeepbeepbeep.

"Nooo," Dad blurted as I walked back towards the bed. "Not him." He was thrashing his legs under the sheet.

Guevarra swept into the room. "He is agitated as he's coming to." She was trying to sound in control, but her voice was urgent. Another two doctors dashed in, coats flapping.

"Dad," I said again, trying to calm him. "It's Laelia. Not *who*, Dad? Who's him?"

"Drown . . . Drownon," he mumbled, fainter now. Almost whispering. I could only just hear it.

Dr. Guevarra leaned over him. "Está bien, you're okay . . . You're in hospital." She started checking monitors and assessing graphs, while the other doctors tried to pin him back down. "Oxygen."

"What's he saying?" I asked. "He's trying to tell me something."

"Drowning," Guevarra said to me. "He says he feels like he's drowning."

The alarms kept sounding. Doctors passed signals to one another with acronyms and eyes. Urgent voices pushed me out of the way.

"EEG?"

"Normal."

"Drowning," Dad's voice rasped.

"Unstable blood pressure."

"Arrythmia. BPM one twenty."

"Drowning . . ."

I stood right back, pushed into the wall, clawing it for support.

Ellis

As you age, it starts to rattle in your bones—the truth of death, the biorhythm of life. In that moment when you realise your children are as old now as you still feel in your soul, there's an undeniable melancholy from which you cannot turn away. *Saudade.* There's no word for it in English.

Both girls look relaxed, though Laelia seems older, more tired. Chloe does, too, but somehow, Ellis expected that. Laelia, being the youngest (of the two) and less serious, has always flowered differently, blooming with life. But now she is wilting. This business with Simon must have dragged her down more than he realised. She needs this break, barely ever leaves that restaurant.

They hug, bridging a gulf, then Ellis kisses them each on the cheek. Sensitive to boundaries, he doesn't ask Laelia about the divorce, not yet, not directly.

"How was Mexico?" he asks once they're sat at their table, easing in, before he tells them.

"Oh, it was amazing." Chloe pours another glass of wine. "So relaxing."

"What did you think of it?" Ellis asks Laelia, before swigging his beer.

"It was good. What I needed." Though, like him, he knows Laelia would have been itching to get out of Cancun the moment she saw it, away from the high-rise hotels and low lines of beach loungers, the daylight robbery of it all. That's the trouble when someone else is paying, you can't say anything, can't complain.

Over Laelia's shoulder, Ellis sees that couple from the beach bar, fondling again at their table, locked gazing into each other in the corner. The man's smoking a cigarette, shaking his leg up and down. *The Mosquito Coast* lies on their table like a talisman. They're drinking champagne. She's eating oysters. Gazing at each other like they are the only people in the world. It won't last, though, of course. It never does. Helena and he used to have that same passion once, early on. Like each other was the world.

"Did you dive there?" Ellis asks, still distracted.

Chloe shakes her head. "Laelia did. I was too busy sunbathing."

"Well, maybe we can go here together?" he says, but they don't commit. He takes another sip of beer. A young woman joins the magazine couple at their table, one of the yoga bodies he passed earlier. She's laughing with them. She pulls up a chair and steals an oyster from her friend's plate.

"What are you both having?" Laelia asks, perusing the plastic menu.

"I'm going for oysters then the shrimp kabobs," Chloe says. Laelia and Ellis both choose the steak.

After lunch, they go to the bar overlooking the Split, the narrow rush of sea between the two islands that make up Caye Caulker, though everyone still refers to it as one island. It once was.

He still hasn't got to telling them. It never felt like the right time. Maybe in a moment after a few more drinks.

Reggae thumps from the oversized speakers. Ellis hands his card to the bartender before he starts mixing the drinks, before Chloe tries to pay. She earns so much money, and doesn't mind who knows it, but sometimes an old dad wants to treat his daughters. There's little else he can do for them now.

"You know what? Can you leave my drink?" Chloe asks, and Ellis's first thought is he's offended her, wanting to pay but then he sees she's clutching her stomach. "The oysters."

She heads back to her room to try to sleep it off, leaving Laelia and him alone for the first time together since he doesn't know when—over a decade, at least. And he cannot tell her alone.

They find a parasoled table by the water's edge, settle themselves in overlooking the turquoise. Laelia flicks off her flip-flops to feel the sand under her feet.

In the distance, there's a commotion out in the Split. A person—a man, Ellis thinks—flailing, caught in the current.

"See that?" he asks Laelia. *Yes, a man.* Figures in the shallows are trying to reach him. Ellis spots Carmen in her diving school T-shirt organising them, commanding others to help.

"Oh my God. Is he drowning?" Laelia stands to see better. Carmen gets to the man, pulls him from the deeper water, then swims him back towards the land.

"You've got to be careful with the rips," Ellis tells her.

Laelia sits back down. They don't say anything. She sips with her straw. And Ellis looks at her—his second born, his Snoozy Bug who hasn't slept well for years—divorced and downhearted, irritable and strained. They are further apart than they have ever been. The separation washes over him, the gulf they must endure now, the one he knows he has made.

"It's a shame you girls won't make it down to the jungle." He could have told them there; that would have been better.

"Chloe didn't want to. Thought it was best to stay on the islands."

He takes a sip of beer. "And you can't be here for my birthday."

"I'm sorry," Laelia says. "Chloe couldn't stay any longer. What with work and kids and stuff. But we'll come back soon, I promise."

There's a stilted silence. He remembers then how the Split was formed. Decades ago, the island cut in half by a hurricane, divided by the sea.

They drink their drinks. They watch the world go by. And then Laelia asks him, out of the blue, "What was she like? As a wife . . . ? Mum? I'm nearly as old as she was when s—"

"Oh, Laelia . . ." Ellis tenses, takes another sip of beer.

"You should talk about her more."

He coughs. "I can't . . . I really can't. I'm sorry." And that is all he says, all he can manage.

Laelia looks out to sea. "I miss her. And I never even knew her. Not really. I—"

"I'm sorry." He stands, swilling down the ends of his beer. "I need to get back. Finish up my paper . . . Shall I walk you back to your hotel?"

Laelia squeezes her eyes shut, then shakes her head. "No. No, thanks, Dad . . . I'm going to grab another drink first. I've got my book."

"You know, you're like she was."

Laelia gazes up at him. "Hmm?"

"Brittle roots, but beautiful through and through." He leans in and kisses her cheek.

She pulls out a paperback, dropping it onto the table. "Bye, Dad."

"Bye, Laelia."

The blue eye on the cover pierces out, footprints crying tears. Ellis has never read it but has heard it's very good: Alex Garland's *The Beach*.

46

Laelia

Karl Heusner Memorial Hospital, Belize City
29th April 2023

Dad's heart rate and blood pressure got so unstable the doctors had no choice but to sedate him again. While the children stayed with Falicia, I slept at the hospital, drowning in the utterness of it all, listening to automatic tubes, watching lines keep him alive.

Eventually, Aid and I decided I should get back home to rest, build up my reserves for when I might need to return. I called Chloe and asked her to wait, not to book a flight back out yet.

"I'll come as soon as you need me," she promised. "If there's any change . . . Hey, did you get my text? About lavender fields?"

"What?" My stomach lurched. "Oh God, Chloe. I don't know . . . I can't think now," I said, hanging up.

When I was saying goodbye to Mounia, she promised to phone if there was any change at all. "There's so much I still have to tell him, have to ask him," I told her.

She lifted her glasses up onto her head. "Here," she said, reaching into her bag. "For when you feel like reading them." She passed me a wedge of documents: Dad's Spanish journals, and pages of handwritten translations. "In the end, I got my cousin to translate them. He's better at it than me. I hope they bring you the answers you need."

"Thank you," I said. "For everything. For being here for him. And me."

"Your father isn't perfect, Laelia. But he tried very hard. And he loves you more than anything. His first orchid flower."

We hugged each other tight. Then the tears came. I collapsed like a galaxy into her. Into myself.

The drive home was a soup—a potage of memories, snippets, echoes from the past. Words Dad had said to me, ones he had not. The tinnitus trashed on, louder than ever, hissing and screeching and roaring against the tide of reminiscence. Ragged tired, my bones ached, my ears throbbed. My heart panged.

Aid rang when I was passing somewhere near Bella Vista. "Hey, gorgeous," he said jarringly. "How're you doing?" I felt sick hearing his voice. This person I no longer knew.

"I'm okay," I croaked, my voice breaking. Tears streamed down my face. I didn't know what to do, what to say. Until I had a plan, I needed to keep up some sort of pretence. Some form of self-protection. "It seemed like he was doing so well."

"Falicia's still got the kids at hers."

"Are they okay?"

"They're all right. Ella's upset. When are you back?"

"Half an hour or so."

"Have you eaten?"

I sighed. I couldn't remember when I'd last eaten. "I'm not hungry."

"You should eat . . . I'll make you something. What else do you need?"

"Nothing. I'm fine."

There was a pause. "Nico came by earlier." My heart jumped.

"Oh?"

"He's leaving Stann Creek. Came to say goodbye." Aid's tone was flat, in control.

I tried to catch my breath, my heart racing. "Oh."

"Yeah. He's gone."

He's gone.

47

I swept into the driveway as dusk was fading in, the evening hot and breathless, another storm brewing in the air. My ears ached. Shutting off the Frontier, I pulled the hearing aids out, their batteries dying, zipped them into my bag. I sat inert, staring at the house sign: WITTERING LODGE. His words. His memory. His home. Mine. I didn't want to leave here, this place where I could finally hear myself.

Gathering myself, my grief of bones, I ambled towards the hut. I was exhausted. The smell of sage and thyme and rosemary seasoned the air, and a deeper acrid scent of charcoaled burning. I could still make out the slaughtering hum of cicadas beyond the tinnitus. Then somewhere, a gunshot. Poachers again. But closer this time.

Pushing the door open, I slung my bag down. "I'm home . . ." I choked.

The hut was thick with smoulder, caramelised citrus burning, a background sizzle of cremation. I ran to the kitchen and pushed the pan from the stove, trying to breathe. Two chicken breasts lay blackened, crisped solid, wisping smoke into the air. I shut off the gas.

"Aid?" The table was laid for two. A bottle of wine uncorked. Expectant empty glasses. I flicked back our bedroom curtain. The bed was unmade. Traipsing through the house, I searched for Aid, for Ursula, for some small sign of life. The bathroom was empty. The study, too. On the way to the vegetable patch, I checked the old lodge buildings. The high plastic stench of new paint stung my nose, but everything was stag-nantly still, untouched. There was no-one. "Aid?!" I shouted.

I flung open the storage hut door. The scent of cigar smoke. Specks of blood across the floor. Ursula was cowering next to the spare gas canis-ters, her ears pushed back, panting furiously. Her eyes stared at me be-fore glancing towards the far corner, towards the darkness.

A hooded body sat there tied, grappling, heaving for breath, his T-shirt and tattoos drenched in perspiration, his bare ankles roped to the legs of a chair, his arms pulled taut behind his back.

The "L.F." heart dripped in sweat. Ursula whimpered into a yelp.

"Aid?"

The pillowcase hood flinched. "L lia?" I couldn't hear, hardly any-thing at all, the tinnitus crescendoing into high-pitched torture.

"What the—" I started.

Cold metal pressed hard against the base of my skull. I smelt the stench of body odour, sensed a heavy breathing behind me. I froze, terri-fied of who was there, of what I might find if I turned.

I felt sick, dizzy. Like I might . . .

. . . faint

. . . chatter crisped into the night. A dream. A memory.

Champagne dreams wid lime juice money. Reggae boomed; beachgoers spilled in from the edge of the sand. A throng. A throng of people. A throb. A throb.

I'd almost got the bartender's attention.

Belikins, daiquiris, margaritas.

Champagne dreams with lime juice money.

"Hmm?"

My head throbbed.

48

My wrists burned. Tied behind my back. Tight, too tight. I moved my fingers, my hands, as much as the restraints would let me. Faint fragments of conversation seeped into my ears. Deep, hard voices. American. Belizean. English. Who were they?

"... can't her.... li en   the dog ..."

I couldn't make it out. It was so isolating, this deafening world I was held hostage within. Slowly opening my eyes, paralysed by what I might see, I glimpsed only darkness. Cold black darkness.

My tinnitus raged.

The lights flicked on, searing into my eyes.

Aid stumbled, pushed back into the room. The concrete floor felt hard against my cheek. I was lying on my side, numb, my hips aching. Dad's gardening equipment, garden chairs, and chicken wire rested against the walls. I kept as still as I could, apart from wriggling my wrists, desperate to be free of the restraints. Keeping watch quietly from the corner, I was afraid to be conscious and afraid not to be.

Aid was no longer hooded, the pillowcase removed, though his wrists were still tied, bound tight with turquoise rope, its ends hanging long. Two men followed, one gesticulating wildly, one shoving at Aid, forcing him back into the chair.

Once he was sat, he looked at me, his eyes blue-wild and alert. The dried blood on his eyebrow had darkened, mixed with dust and dirt and fear. He groaned and grunted. Muffled ughmm sounds came but his words remained captive. Not that I would have heard them with my aids back in the kitchen, zipped inside my bag. Aid's mouth was gagged, his chest a bruised and blooded mess.

One of the men was Belizean, the other British. Solid stacks of men. Both short. Both bolstered with thick muscle. One smoked a cigarillo, his filthy fingers tightening around, strangling its last breath. The other wore a bright T-shirt proclaiming TRUTH, the ombré text fading into oblivion. Cigarillo said something, kicked at Aid's bare shins. The chair jumped.

I spotted something hard and black behind the chicken wire. The rifle. Aid had never gotten rid of it. He hadn't listened to me. Was it even loaded?

"Thirty- our thou and," TRUTH spat. His voice was lower, I could just about make out his words. Aid howled behind the gag, his head tipped back, trying to find breath, his chest heaving. His eyes flicked around the room, returned to me. Then he closed them and mustered a sigh, as though willing it all to disappear.

Cigarillo picked up Dad's machete from the corner and stood behind Aid to slice through the back of the gag, flinging the material to the floor.

"Where is it?" TRUTH asked. Aid panted sharp breaths through his mouth, gasping for oxygen. "Where is it?!" *Was this drug money?* I could barely look at Aid.

Cigarillo saw me then, clocked me clocking him. He signalled to TRUTH with a nod of his head. TRUTH turned, stared, started pacing towards me. Grabbing me under my armpits, he dragged me up off the floor.

The door flung open, and a new figure appeared. A rage of recognition flooded through me. I saw his signet ring first.

49

G oin' naked today, sugar?" He spat towards me. I struggled to breathe. I stared at him, his dirt-brown eyes, but didn't say a word. His smudgy thick fingers teased at my earlobes, pulling on the skin.

"Your hearin' aid . . . Not wearin'   ?" Hector laughed. "Your boy Aidrian has   silly   mi ake.   think?" I stood, silent. The air was stifling, the night unbearable.

"You fucker," shouted Aid. Hector looked back at him, back to me. TRUTH hit Aid in the stomach. Hector circled like a buzzard. Then he stopped, swooped in towards me, pushing his face up to mine, his nose an inch away. His breath was damp and claggy, his skin pitted with hard nights.

"How's your daddy doin'?" Hector asked. I felt sick. "CAN YOU HEAR ME?" he mouthed theatrically. I nodded, slowly, barely at all. He roared gravel laughter. Aid continued groaning agonies in the chair.

"You can   ," Hector spoke towards the men. Cigarillo and TRUTH walked outside, taking the machete with them.

Hector's mouth circled into an "O." He began whistling, haunting and low. I could just about hear. "Y'all, we   a little proble ." He took a sniff of cocaine, a bump from his pocket. "Somebody's been stealin' from me."

"Hector, please. Come on," Aid begged.

Hector ignored him, continued at me, whistling on, lost in thought. "I wanna tell y'all a story." I tried to lip-read as much as I could.

He clumpered towards the door, heavy on his feet. Poking his head around the corner, I heard his muffled calling for the men to come back in. I couldn't make out any more. Tears rolled down my face. Hector grabbed me by the arm, pulled me across the room, shoving me into the corner next to Aid. He was whimpering like an animal. His eyes were stunned, leaking tears down his cheeks.

TRUTH appeared back in the doorway, another figure lingering behind him. It was Benny, smirking with curled lips.

Aid yelled, "You bastard," which only served to coax Benny's smile to a laugh. He picked up a folded chair lying next to an old stack of newspapers, flipped it open, and positioned it in front of Aid. TRUTH stood over, watching it all.

"My little story . . ." Hector sat, drawing the chair even closer. "It's legend in these parts." He started whistling again, his eyes fixed on Aid. Benny reached into his breast pocket, pulled out a crocodile case. He dragged out a cigar, snipped at its cap with his cutter, then lit it, passing it to Hector.

"There's a man . . . ," Hector continued. He made pah-pah-pah motions with his mouth. Smoke rings filled the air. "He smokes cigars plays guitar. Funny little fella. The Belizeans, they say he wears animal skins, wreckin' havoc   the jungles. Folks know when he's comin' they hear a whistlin'   ."

Hector pushed his chair back, started towards me, making the same "O" with his mouth again. A smoke ring and then the deep whistle, its melancholy tune.

"Tata Duende, they call him. Old-man dwarf." Hector laughed. "He's three foot high, got a gnarly face . . . Folks say his feet are backwards, deformed and contorted   wrong way round. Ugly little guy."

He stared into my eyes. Closer now, I could hear it all. "He likes to braid horses' manes and little girls' locks." Hector grabbed a section of my hair, corkscrewing it around his thick finger. "Twistin' it all so complicated it will never, ever loosen . . ."

He pulled at the roots of my scalp until I winced, tears trickling down my face. I searched for quick breaths. He untangled his hand, laughing.

"The thing about Tata Duende is . . ." Hector smirked, making his way back to Aid while signalling to Benny, who started pulling something out of his pocket. Benny lifted it high, his black and silver toy, glinting in the light. The cigar cutter. "He has no thumbs!" Hector hacked out a laugh. Aid was furiously shaking his head, pleading with his eyes. "So the poor little fucker's always on the lookout for some more—"

"Hector, please . . . please," Aid begged. "Benny, man, come on."

"Don't . . ." My voice creaked into a wail. Aid spat at Hector. His saliva missed, hit the floor.

"C'mon." Hector smirked. "Let's not be like that."

Benny untied Aid's hands. His whole body was shaking uncontrollably, his breathing bursting in and out. TRUTH wrestled with Aid's arms, then punched him hard in the gut, stunning him into submission. Benny grabbed his wrist. With peals of unhinged laughter, he forced the circle of the cutter down over his thumb.

"Noooo," I screamed, looking away. Aid emitted a loud, deep roar. I looked back too soon. There was the snap of bone, I actually heard it. A severed silence. And then an ear-crushing yowl.

Aid's thumb lay on the floor like a Halloween prop. He was crying, howling coyote yelps. Benny passed him handfuls of rags to stem the blood.

Hector took a glug from his military canteen. "Your boy here   stupid   owes me   money." All for money, dirty money he didn't even need.

"How much?" I screamed, watching Aid bent over himself. Hector pushed Aid's head back, waterfalling liquid into his mouth, but Aid was gyrating and yowling so much, it splashed over his face. "How much?" I asked again.

"Thirty-four grand." I eyed up the chickenwire on the other side of the room, the black of the side edge of rifle peeking out from behind the metallic silver roll. Aid wouldn't have been stupid enough to leave it loaded. "Plus interest," added Hector, wiping his moustache. "A bargain at forty thousand . . . Let's call it fifty."

I'd never shot a gun in my life. Never held one.

"So what's it gonna be?   gonna   pay me back?" Hector paced, grabbing the filthy cotton gag from the floor, stuffing it back in Aid's mouth to quell the screaming.

What would I do with it—the gun—if I could get to it? If it were even loaded. I thought of Dad's money, the stash of bills I'd buried under the tree. My dream of a restaurant. My own small slice of something. A taste of freedom. A flash of future. I stared at Aid, gritting my teeth. My wrists were tied. Even if I could somehow grab the rifle, would I know how to shoot it? They would overpower me, force it back on me. My mind glared to a feeling, an image: me lying slumped and blooded on the floor. Dying before Dad. Without a final embrace. Without apologising to Chloe. Without holding Ella and Dylan, stroking their faces, kissing them some sort of wretched goodbye.

Hector picked up the machete. The metal was dull—deadened with use—though it still glinted terror in the light. The excitement of retribution; its anticipation. He paced, circling like an animal eyeing its prey, then held the knife above Aid's head. He snarled, lifting the metal higher still, catching my eye.

All Aid had done to me, to us. What he'd put us through. It would be so easy to let this moment happen, to watch it play out however it was meant to go down. But he didn't deserve to die. Not now. Not like this.

"I . . . I have it," I cried out.

Hector stopped, turned his whole body towards me. "What'd you say, woman?"

"I've got it . . ." I stuttered. "The money." Sweat trickled down my cheeks, salted into my mouth. "I can get it."

"When?"

"Now. I can get it now."

50

We reached the edge of the forest, the two of us. Hector and me. The others stayed in the shed with Aid, watching him. The sky was dark, threatening. Flashes of moonlight enlivened the gathering clouds as though emblazoning a warning. A sense of an ending. I traipsed like a death march, my thoughts racing, wondering how this was going to end, what they were going to do to Aid, to me, if I shouldn't have tried to grab the gun. Thank God the children were with Esther. Who would tell them? What would they be told? Who would take care of them? Comfort them? If they killed us. Oh God.

I pointed to the ground.

"Under the logwood?" Hector laughed, hacking at its branches with his machete. Dad's machete. "The tree   rich."

I shook my head. "I can't hear you properly."

He laughed. "What's that?"

"I can't hear you."

He got back up in my face again, whispered into my ear. "The tree that made rapin' men rich." He flung fractured pieces of bark to the ground, threw me the shovel. "Dig."

Distant thunder crashed and rolled. I pushed into the soil until it loosened. Levering back and forth, I worked, throwing spadefuls of dirt onto a burgeoning mound. Hector stood over as I kneeled, my hands caked in soil, ploughing through its tiny, weathered rock, its dead rotten plants, its decomposing animals. The thunder boomed through my ears, through my rib cage.

"Come on," Hector shouted, as though I could go any faster. Lightning snapped, illuminating us like a stage as he launched into another soliloquy. "You know, your old man and me, we ain't so different . . ." I flinched with the mention of Dad again. "With all his qualifications, his *ac-a-de-mia*, he reckons he's better than us all. But he ain't no saint. He's as possessed by orchids as the rest of us . . . You know, he sold some once? Took 'em outta the wild and sold 'em to a friend of mine. Couldn't help himself. It's a sick, sick fever. Kinda like an addiction. But there ain't no AA for fuckin' flowers."

The rains came fast, cold, and hard. I threw my head back, tried to take a breath. On the slashed bruise of the tree, deep red droplets formed, little tears of dripping blood.

Water tore, lightning jumped. "Hurry up. C'mon . . ." Rivers of rain ran down the trunk of the logwood, down my arms. The crimson from the tree sluiced down my wrists. Torrents formed in the dirt, glooping it into sticky, gluey mud. The water pelted at my back, my hands tearing into the burnished brown soil. *Please let this be over.*

I saw it then; Benjamin Franklin's eye staring at me from the sludge. I prised the first stack from the soil, lifting it towards the sky. Dye dribbled down over my hands, trickling over my fingers, over the banknotes, staining them like blood.

Hector started digging, pushing me away. He grabbed at the notes, stashing them into his rucksack, counting the bundles as he went. I stood watching on, seeing him take my dad's money in the pouring rain. Fifty-five thousand I'd counted as I'd buried it into the ground that night. I wondered what Dad was planning to do with it, what it would have been for.

Hector seemed calmer, lighter, as we walked our way back, now he had his money. My money. With interest. And more.

I trudged along behind him, rubbing my eyes and trying to blink the dirt, the night, away. "What are you going to do now?" It felt bold—the question, but it was ravaged with fear. Though Hector was so focused on his prize, he didn't notice.

"I'm gonn' go home light a massive fuckin' bong. Count th babies . . ."

The door of the hut was open, sniggering laughter drifting out. The men sat smoking, sharing swigs of celebratory rum. Aid was still tied to the chair. Benny was shoving a cigar into his mouth, mocking his disabled hand, his missing thumb. It lay across Aid's lap, the ragged bloody stump. He broke into soft, conciliatory laughter with them, until it hurt too much, and his face collapsed, and he creased over again in pain. Bloody and battered and raw.

"Well," Hector said, pirouetting towards the rum. "Your sugar done good."

Aid looked at me. I couldn't read his thoughts.

I stared at the chicken wire. At the gun.

Hector propped the machete back down against the wall, then threw the rucksack of money to Benny; told him and the others to leave. They tossed away the ends of their cigars, stole last, parting slugs of rum.

"I'll meet y'all at mine," Hector called after them. "Get Serena to find the bill counter, check it all again."

"Right on," sniggered Benny, waving a goodbye. Cigarillo and TRUTH followed, disappearing out the door. My hand reached into my pocket. I felt Nico's healing stone there. Wondered if it was big enough to crack a skull.

Aid had never looked so helpless, so utterly broken and afraid. His body was slumped. His eyes lifeless.

Hector took a mighty swig of rum. He slimed towards me, teasing his rough hand over my collarbone, dragging it down towards my breasts. I lurched my head away.

Aid pleaded. "Come on. You got what you came for."

"How d'y'all know what I came for?" Hector laughed. One hand still clutching my breast, with the other he teased at my hair, twirling it again between his fingers. His thick, fat thumbs. The strands caught, knotted into a mess. *Ohmygod, ohmygod, ohmygod.* My head pulsed; my tinnitus shrieked.

I shook my head at him, pleading with my eyes. "Please, Hector." But he wasn't listening. He dragged his eyes back down my body, moved his face in towards mine. His hand squeezing tighter, hurting me now.

"Get off her," Aid shouted, wrestling in his chair.

Hector turned, inflamed. He launched towards Aid, grabbing the machete. "Won't you shut the fuck up?"

I eyed up the rifle again. Two metres away, three maybe. I looked over at Aid, his face collapsing into a mess of shock and tears. I could barely breathe.

Hector raised the knife above Aid's head. "If you can't keep quiet, I'm gonna have to help you shut up." My head was a blur. I lurched my body, rushing, not looking back. I pushed the chicken wire over, grabbing breathlessly for the gun without thinking. I spun around, lifting the rifle up onto my shoulder. It was tail-heavy and cumbersome. I struggled to hold it properly, wedging it into the crook of my neck as I swayed, unbalanced by the load. My finger trembled over the trigger, dancing to try and ready itself. I stared through the scope gasping ragged breaths. Hector's eyes pulsed right at me, repulsive. Daring me. I pushed on the steel ever so slightly.

Hector laughed, a deep but uncertain laugh. I lifted my finger and took a breath. He turned away, grabbing the bottle of rum before he spat at Aid, grabbing his crotch, "Next time it'll be all your other digits." I stood frozen, trying to breathe, as Hector walked past me towards the door. He whispered in my ear, "Chicken dinner tonight, Lie-lee-a . . . Your old man there might need help with his fork."

I waited until he was steps away before I dropped the rifle, my sweat dripping over its handle. Rushing over to Aid, I untied him. I could barely breathe.

I collapsed to the ground, shaking, wrapped in terror and relief.

Caye Caulker, Belize
9th January 2020

He's early again, for their final dinner together. A last chance to tell them in person. The girls wanted to meet at their hotel but Ellis's intolerance for the overexcitable young Americans has grown. He cannot bear to wait at the pool bar listening to their superficial conversations and watching their Instagram Lives, so he purchases a Belikin from the bar and heads down onto the sand, to smoke his pipe in peace.

Finding a spot in front of some of the beachfront rooms, he lights up and gazes out across the Caribbean Sea. *Ahhh.* That first hit of tobacco always stirs him up.

They fly back tomorrow, the girls. It has been so valuable to check in with them and spend some time together, even if their old man cramps their style. He can't hide the fact it hurts they're heading off on his birthday. They're leaving so early in the morning; he won't even get to see them before they go for the water taxi. And he has to tell them tonight.

There is a loud banging behind him. One of the inside doors in one of the rooms, presumably, getting slammed. He takes another sip of beer, another inhalation from his pipe.

It's unfortunate Chloe got so sick with those oysters, a disappointment they weren't able to go diving. And Laelia wasn't feeling it either, wanting to lie low. It didn't bother him—not really—the girls not wanting to hang out so much. He isn't far off his seventies, and they don't have much in common to talk about, not anymore, their lives so different now.

It's bittersweet—the betrayal of children, daring to grow up and become themselves.

It has meant he got to finish up his *Orchid Journal* piece. At least he can turn it in early now. The title needs reworking, of course. "A Review of the Implications for Conservation in the Central American Orchid Trade" requires some finessing, but he's completed it and the references are done, and he'll be able to submit it well before the deadline. He'll have to go diving on his own, maybe with Carmen in a few days' time, once the girls have flown home.

Another bang from behind, and then someone's voice, a man's voice, North American, shouting, "You fucking kidding me?"

"Well, it's not mine." A woman's voice now, feeble, East Coast maybe. The walls are so thin, Ellis can hear almost every word.

"They're the maid's," the man argues back.

"D'you think I'm stupid? Maids don't wear heavy jewellery like that."

Ellis turns to check out the doors, to work out which room the brouhaha is coming from. The curtains are all drawn. He feels a little awkward sitting here, so British, listening to this. He wonders if he shouldn't say something, or maybe get up and leave, though he had staked out this position before they even started arguing. It's not like he's purposefully listening in.

"I haven't fucked anyone else," the man shouts now.

Oh. Of course. They must be with that group of dissolute youngsters by the pool.

"Oh my God." She is breathless, uncontrollable now. "Was it the Englishwoman . . . ? The other night? When me and Maia had those bad oysters?! When I was staying in with her?"

It's a little like he's eavesdropping. Though, of course, he was sat here first, before all of this began. Ellis usually loves sitting by the sea at this time of the night, while the sun sets on the other side of the island, seeing the oranges streak across the sky. He takes another draw on his tobacco.

"Was it?" The woman cries. "What d'you think they're all gonna say? Rich and Kadeem and Maia and everybody, when I tell them what you've done? How you've fucked up their vacation as well as your marriage?"

Smack. The stinging sound of skin on skin.

And then a woman's scream.

"I'll call the police," she says.

"Don't ever scratch my face," he shouts.

Christ, they're both at it. She's giving as good as she's getting. They're passionate, as bad as each other.

"Get off me," the woman says, strained, her voice a little muffled. "Get off."

Ellis checks on his watch as he finishes his beer. They'll make up and make love soon—Helena and he always did, eventually. Time to meet the girls. He takes a final draw on his pipe, steadies himself up to standing, and heads back across the sand. Best leave them in peace.

51

Laelia

Wittering Lodge, Stann Creek District, Belize
30th April 2023

The images of the night still too raw, we were both too wired to sleep. We collapsed onto the sofa, Ursula at our feet, staring into nothing; negotiating the bruises and the cuts, processing our thoughts, unable to speak. Aid told me later the rifle wasn't loaded. He'd hidden the cartridges because he knew I hated guns, insinuated it would have been my fault if things had ended differently, if they had shot us both dead.

He wouldn't go to the hospital—said they wouldn't be able to save his thumb. It wasn't worth it. Not in this heat, and not with all the questions they would ask. I placed it at the back of the freezer, wrapped in plastic like a cocktail sausage. His cold dead digit.

I still felt sick thinking about the cigar cutter. The torment. The noise.

"We could go to Kantun?" I suggested. "See if he can sew—"

"It's gone, Laelia," Aid snapped, like he'd already given up, like he wanted to feel the punishment, like I needed him to feel it, too. Together, weeping wordlessly, we bandaged his hand, hid the horror away.

"I'm sorry" was all he could say, over and over again. "I'm so sorry." He necked painkillers and whisky and rum. I necked them, too, to numb the pain.

"Was it drugs?" I asked, finding him in the kitchen eating bread and downing glasses of water. "Were you shipping drugs?"

He glared at me. "No, it wasn't drugs." The bruises on his rib cage burst like watercolour clouds.

"What was it for then, the money?"

"A misunderstanding. I sold some of Hector's orchids. Didn't get him all the payments back." I wondered if he'd had more energy, if Aid wouldn't have been shouting at me now, livid at my interrogations. But maybe he thought he owed me this at least—an explanation, after everything, after last night.

"Is that who they were from? The notes? The turquoise rope around Ditsy's neck, it was their rope, wasn't it?"

"I guess so."

"I thought it was you. Leaving them to scare me. Drive me mad." He didn't react. "And the gunshots? Were they a warning?"

"I don't know, Lil. Maybe."

"You told me you'd stopped working for him."

"I did . . . I . . . It was Benny. He and a friend persuaded me to go in with them, getting orchids to rare collectors. He didn't tell me they were Hector's plants he was siphoning off."

"Was it all bullshit, you working at Maya Beach?"

"No, that was real. Benny came up with this plan while we were there: start doing our own orchid trades, undercut the competition." Thunder rolled outside. "He didn't want Hector knowing, but I didn't think it was because they were his fucking flowers."

"I don't want to leave." The sound of a helicopter thrummed in the distance.

"We don't have to," Aid said, fumbling to open the butter with his good hand. "They won't come back. Hector's got what he wanted."

"We can't stay. Not with him so close. Not with the kids." Something like scorn was growing inside my gut. How this man could make me feel like this, make me want to leave this place, my place. But more than anything, I wanted him to leave. "What did you do with it?"

"With what?"

"The money?"

Aid shook his head, trying to butter his bread one-handed, pushing it about the plate. "I don't know, Lil. We spent it, I guess."

"On what?" I stifled a laugh. A disorientating stream of air breezed in from outside, a patter of rain starting up. "You know, I was going to open a restaurant . . . make a life here for us. For the kids. Really make a go of it . . . and I've been scrambling about, scrapping for dollars to get started, to afford some ovens and fridges and basic equipment, to set it all up. I wanted to do something for me, for us . . . I'd worked out a business plan, started saving, dared to dream it could be real. And it felt so right . . . an outdoor kitchen, a place where I can hear myself working. And all this time . . . all this time, you've been snorting coke and flogging orchids and pissing our money up the wall." I stopped for breath. "I can't take it anymore." The helicopter juddered right overhead.

"I'm sorry, Lil. I'm so fucking sorry." He couldn't steady the roll on his plate. His knife slipped, and the bread fell to the floor. He stooped to pick it up.

"It was my dad's money. Did you know that?" I drank some water, trying to calm down. "What am I going to tell him?"

"Laelia, your dad's not going t—"

"Shut up," I spat, glaring at him.

He paused as he came back up, holding the knife midair. He turned to look at me, his eyes pulsing red. "What did you say?"

I grabbed the knife from his hand, smeared the dirty roll in butter, and pushed the plate towards him. "I said, shut up."

I ditched the rest of his cocaine while he slept; emptied out the drawers, his pockets, the glove compartment in the truck. I dumped it all into the outside bin, watching as dust drifted up into the forest like ghosts into the breeze. I didn't know if the money was just about the orchids, or if it wasn't also about the drugs. It didn't matter. None of it mattered anymore. It was over. It was done. *I* was done.

As I balanced the lid back on the bin, I saw her. Something. In a shadow of trees at the hem of the forest. A flash of piercing green eyes.

I shook the image away and looked again, but whatever, it was gone. If it was ever there. Seeing X'tabai like Aid had. *You fucking crazy bitch.*

I started packing bags, terrified of retribution, of what Hector might do next; what devastation he could reap now, where all this might end.

While I loved the jungle—this place I felt closest to Dad—I had to leave. I had to get away from him, from Aid.

As I shoved T-shirts and trousers into a case in the kids' bedroom, Aid appeared in the doorway. He was holding his phone; a look of total devastation overtook his face.

His eyes were a sea of sorry. "The hospital." I took a breath. He pursed his lips. "It's your dad, Laelia. He died."

PART FIVE

Ashes

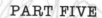

Swietenia macrophylla. Mahogany, *chiculte* (Maya), *punab* (Yucátan, Maya), big-leaf mahogany. A species of the Meliaceae family native to Southern and Central America. Its leaves are large and shining. Along with only the *Swietenia mahogani* and *Swietenia humilis*, it yields mahogany timber and is semievergreen, losing old leaves as new leaves begin to grow.

52

Laelia

Maya Beach, Stann Creek District, Belize
2nd May 2023

Dad slipped away like a jaguar, back into the night before I got back to see him, before Chloe's flight had even taken off.

After all the hospital bureaucracy, he was moved to a funeral home Chloe and I chose together. Aid and Tom waited outside with the children, consoling each other, finding things to look forward to again. There was a calmness about Aid now, some sort of understanding. Or at least, a little respect.

We sat with Dad—Chloe and I—in the stale-aired Chapel of Rest, clutching each other's hands, unearthing forgotten memories through staggering gusts of grief. So many busy upholstered fabrics. Plaques dedicated to Jesus. Crosses enshrined in wood.

"Can you forgive him?" I asked, the tinnitus screaming in my skull. I thought about the toxic illicitness of secrets, the power they have to take refuge in your soul. To become you.

"For the affair?"

"For the affair . . . For not being there for Mum."

"He left his orchids, gave up this place to come back for us. That can't have been easy." Chloe wiped a tear from my cheek, from hers.

"Do you remember he hit her? Or he did once."

"They argued a lot," she said. "I remember that."

"I can't forget that."

"I think there's lots we can't ever forget. But there's lots we can. I want to forgive him." She tried a smile.

"Do you ever think like her?"

"How do you mean?" Chloe's voice creaked.

"I don't know . . . I sometimes think I'm going . . . In my head. I'm sorry," I told her.

"What for?" Her lips were trembling, her hand clutching a screwed-up ball of toilet paper.

"For not listening to you. For being so wrapped up in my own shit . . . For not being a good enough sister."

"Fuck off, Laelia. You don't know how good enough you are."

My breath was jagged and raw. "I've messed it up."

"What?" she asked. "What could you possibly have messed up?"

"All of it . . . My chance to start again. Here."

"What do you mean?"

"I want to stay. At Dad's. I want to be here where he wanted to be. Make him proud."

"Why can't you?"

I paused. "Do you know why I lost my job?"

She frowned, tears in her eyes, shaking her head.

"I lied," I said. "I was ashamed, too proud to wear my hearing aids, too embarrassed to wear them, not with my hair up . . . And then one day, I didn't hear Tris telling me about a shellfish allergy." I wiped a tear from my cheek. "I could have killed them."

"That's not your fault."

"I couldn't even tell Aktar why it happened." I cleared my throat, took a deep breath. "You know, I had this stupid fantasy of setting up a restaurant here, an outdoor cantina where I could actually have heard properly—"

"Laelia, when are you going to start trusting yourself? Listening to that beautiful gut of yours?" I felt the butterflies again, the blue morphos flitting about my stomach. "You've all the answers you need already," she said. "You always have." *The body has a way of knowing before the mind ever catches up.* Chloe moistened her lips, took a breath. "You know." Her voice cracked. "When we were young, I was so jealous of you."

"What? Why . . . ?"

"You always knew who you were, what you wanted to be. You mastered that kitchen, way beyond your years, finding ingredients, making up recipes . . . I got bogged down trying to be responsible, looking after you. Taking Mum's place, I suppose." She grabbed my hand, held it in hers. "They say trauma isn't only the shit that's happened to you. It's the shit that didn't happen when you needed it to; the love you missed."

"We were loved."

"But we missed a lot, too. And she did . . . I don't think Mum had the courage; she didn't know how to listen to her heart." Chloe pulled me close for the tightest hug we'd ever mustered. "We always used to say you were most like her," she whispered in my ear while my hearing aid crackled. "But you're not . . . You know how to be brave; I know you do. You've just forgotten."

We gathered at a restaurant down the road from the funeral directors, eating pizzas and drinking whiskys while the kids played in the sand. Dylan asked Aid if he'd play volleyball with them under the beach lights, but he shook his head, "Not now." He said he was too tired after the long day, unable to hide the frustration in his voice.

Dylan was unable to hide the disappointment in his. "But you said you would—"

"He can't, darling," I said. "Not with his hand."

"Dude," Aid said. "I'm sorry. Let me have a drink." Dylan looked so much like Simon then, I had to turn my head down and away.

Aid wasn't drinking, only icy Cokes. Since that night with Hector, he'd stopped. Cold turkey. It made me wonder why he'd never managed it before.

"I'll play with you," I said to Dyl, pushing back my chair. I was drunk and exhausted but able to punch a few solid balls back over the net.

At sunset, I managed to catch Ella for a moment, sitting in the sand. My throat burned with alcohol and happiness and regret. That bittersweet feeling is the strongest of them all. It gusts through your heart and your soul like no other, a longing stronger even than the force of shame. *Saudade; is that what they call it?*

"I'm sorry," I said after a while, my throat closing up.

She didn't turn to look at me. "I want you to be happy, Mum. You deserve to be happy."

"Don't you worry about me. It's you I care about."

She nodded, tears in her eyes.

"Don't you ever worry about me," I said again. "I've got it."

"Promise?"

I didn't hesitate. "I promise."

"I miss Paw-Paw so much."

"I know, sweetie," I said, hugging her tight.

When Ella strolled back for dessert, I sat watching the sun disappear, listening to the gentle lap of the waves. The sound was as continuous as the whoosh in my ears, enveloping me in calm. It would always be there. A beautiful part of it all, a part of me I no longer tried to fight.

I joined them all for cheesecake, and we toasted Dad with rum and Cokes, sharing snippets and family folklore.

"So, you cut your thumb with a saw?" Chloe asked Aid again after the kids left the table. She could smell bullshit like chocolate. *It was my fault*, I almost said, but didn't. I took a sip of my drink instead. *I interrupted him doing DIY*, I could have said. *He looked up and then he slipped*. I could have made excuses for him, for his choices. For mine. But I kept quiet, let Aid answer on his own. "Yeah" was all he said.

"Easily done," said Tom. He *ate up* bullshit like chocolate. Chloe gave me a look, a knowing stare. Sisters are like mirrors; they shine the truth back at you. If you can bear to look.

She grabbed me later, alone, when I went to pay the bill. "I want to give you the money," she said.

"It's fine. I've got it."

She shook her head. "No. For your restaurant. I want to give you the money."

"What?"

"And it's not a loan, and it's not a favour. It's a gift. From me. And I want you to have it."

"I can't—"

"I want to, Laelia. There's no shame in taking it. And I won't tell Aid. I won't say a word . . . I know you've got this." The way she said that, like she knew.

I smiled and said, "Thank you." It was all I needed to say.

In the taxi on the way back to the hotel, drunk and sleepy, we caught the end of a news bulletin. "Dion Zabaneh, who police have been hunting for several months, was last night shot dead in the Stann Creek District during a G-Thirteen drugs raid at the home of American entrepreneur Hector Hicks, who was also killed in the incident. Several others have been detained."

Aid squeezed my leg and leaned to whisper in my ear. "It's over, Lil."

53

It was a clear day, the day we scattered his ashes; the sun searing bright, the cicadas throbbing strong.

We left him where he'd wanted, where his heart was, and would always be—under the shade of the mahogany, the black orchid clinging to it like an infant, thriving like an everlasting jewel. *Sub umbra floreo.* Flourishing forevermore in the jungle by the lagoon.

Jonas burned copal resin as we grasped each other and said our final goodbyes, Ursula propped at our feet. Dylan recited "The Lake Isle of Innisfree," which he'd learned from one of Dad's poetry books. Mounia poured cashew wine. I refurbished precious memories from childhood of a dad who was our champion of unconditional love: his baked bean lasagnes, and poetry nights, and Ursula Le Guin; the Latin plant names he'd drill into us, and the nineties pop songs we'd drill into him.

When Chloe was saying her piece—how much she would miss his letters, his phone calls, his hugs—I couldn't stop my mind from flashing to a time when he wasn't there, when I was still so young but still picked up on things, still remembered. Mum a shadow, clouded with sadness. I felt it rather than saw it—her hugging me overly tight, weeping unspoken tears.

A haze of recollections. I remembered Aunty Penny dropping us home and going in through the back patio door, not the front. It was drizzling. The television blaring to an empty room, a rugby match. She left

Chloe and me in our anoraks on the sofa. We were arguing over Hungry Hippos when she came back in the room, I remembered that. She picked me up from the carpet, hugging me. "Your Mummy's not well," she must have said, or "Mummy's sleeping," or "She got held up at the shops," or something like it; I couldn't recollect, and sometimes it's better to forget. I remembered the clouds, though—the three of us walking back to her house through the rain, hand in hand in hand—the sky such a gloomy gunmetal as though it had never known blue; as though it never would again.

I blinked the thoughts away, took another sip of wine, sweet and tart on my tongue. Ella began singing "My Hero" and strumming her guitar, her raspy voice ghosting through the breeze.

Out the corner of my eye I saw a figure standing under the kapok tree, watching on, elbows gathered in her hands, dark hair cascading, tears streaming down her face. Stark green eyes. The woman from the hospital. *From the trees?* Aid froze, eyes wide in recognition. He grabbed at my arm.

Mounia said her name first. "Cattleya?"

She was warm, and beautiful. She had Dad's mouth, and his smile, his way of gazing into the distance as she talked. I thought she looked more like Chloe than me; they had the same eyes, the same full, thick brows.

"I didn't know if I should come," Cattleya said as Mounia poured tea. "What you would think."

"Of course," Chloe said. "Of course you should have."

"I didn't know if you would know who I was, if he ever told you."

"We thought you'd died . . ." I said, my voice shaking. "Dad thought you died."

"When your mama passed," she said gently, "my momma decided to tell him I was stillborn. To make it easier for him to go back to England, to be with you. So he didn't have to make the hardest choice."

"When did he know the truth?" Chloe asked. "Did he ever?"

"Four years ago. When my mother was dying of cancer, she wrote him a letter. She passed away before she ever sent it, but my aunty Aapo found it and posted it to him."

"He wanted to tell you," said Mounia. "He tried to a couple of years ago. He wanted you to know. But he couldn't easily find the words. He carried a lot of guilt."

"Did you know?" I asked her.

"He wanted to tell you both so desperately. It was not my secret to share."

"He loved her," I said to Cattleya. "Your mother."

"She named me after an orchid, for him." She showed us a faded photograph of them—her parents together, on horseback, Agapita's arms wrapped around my father's thick waist. They looked so happy, so carefree. "She would have been pregnant then, with me."

"Did your mother forgive him?" I asked.

Cattleya took a sip from her cup. "Momma used to say forgiveness is the scent of a crushed orchid. I think that came from our papá." *Our papá.* "She never meant to fall in love with him. She never knew he was married. It wasn't until he heard the news about your mama's death that he even told my mama about her. She knew then he had to go home to you girls. You had no-one. It wasn't a question in her mind."

Agapita fell in love again and married a local man. She had two more daughters and a son. They lived together on the family cacao plantation, which Cattleya now ran, exporting to bean-to-bar manufacturers in Europe. She travelled there a lot. Agapita never saw my father again.

"It must have been hard for you," I said. "Growing up not knowing him."

Cattleya shook her head. "I was surrounded by love. My *abuela* felt shame I was born out of matrimony. We moved away. To Distrito de Toledo, not far." She smiled reflectively. "I understand why she did it, why my mama never told anyone until the end. The sacrifices she made."

Mounia smiled. "One person can keep a secret, but a secret woven between two, that's a heavy burden."

Cattleya sipped on her tea. "Momma used to say another thing . . . A flower cannot blossom without sunshine, and most need a little bit of shade."

The hairs stood up on my skin.

We shared photos and memories and scars while the sun set, then we swapped details and hugged heartfelt goodbyes, Cattleya promising to stay in touch. She invited us down to Toledo, said she'd supply me with cacao for my restaurant, if it ever took off. Aid glared at me the whole time.

We waved the kids off with Falicia for the night. She insisted upon it, told me to rest, enjoy the peace and calm. Mounia came to find me to say goodbye. She wiped a tear from my cheek, a tear from hers. "You know, warriors are hard as avocado stones, but they're also soft as flower petals." I broke into a smile and embraced her tightly.

I begged Chloe to stay, a final night together before she flew home. Most of the lodge rooms were finished so she could have a proper bed. I didn't think she would, but she relented. "I'd like that," she told me. "For old times' sake."

"Let me do the chickens," I said. "Then I'll bring over a bottle of wine. We can put the world to rights."

When everyone else had peeled off or gone to bed exhausted, I took out my hearing aids and put them on to charge. Aid was lying asleep, wrapped in our sheet, his bandaged hand resting on his chest. I stood staring at him, remembering how we used to be. The trail of lust we left wherever we went. The smiles we shared. The forgiveness. And then I remembered the pain of us. Our unravelling. Our hurt. *You stupid, crazy bitch.*

I pulled on my nightclothes, made my way down to the chickens. After I closed them up, I walked up the drive to check the post. Nobody had looked in days. Slung below the box was a parcel wrapped in brown paper, the "i" in my name heart-topped, set out in purple print. Inside there was no letter, no note. No need for one. I cried laughter and tears when I saw them. A pair of gold kitten heels.

Heading back into the forest, it was still not quite sunset. I walked back to the mahogany tree and stood, stroking at the black orchid's leaves. "Strength and determination and rebirth," Dad had told me it symbolised. Tears rolled down my cheeks. I crushed the deep purple petals in my hand and breathed the scent of them in.

I forgive you, Dad. And I'm sorry. For not listening to my heart, for lying, for forgetting how to be me.

Before I went over to meet Chloe with the rosé, I slipped back into the bedroom to grab a cardigan. I saw Aid up, awake, hovering over my hearing aid charger, flicking off the switch.

I found Chloe on her balcony, crunched up on a chair, rubbing night cream into her face. "Are you okay . . . ?" she asked. "You look like you've seen a ghost."

"I'm fine . . . it's a lot to process, you know? Nothing quite what it was."

She poured wine into our glasses. "I can't get my head around the fact we'll never see him again."

"Hmm?"

"There's so much he never said."

"Sometimes the truth can be too overwhelming, I guess . . . I know we loved him. But his journals . . ."

"What about them?"

"He was so hard on Mum . . . They were awful to each other. When she was losing her mind."

Chloe gazed into her wine glass. "I can't believe he kept so many secrets. It must have haunted him, all that deceit."

"The world is full of cowardly men. Trapped in armour of their own making, but we all pay the price."

"We're not his actions." She stared at me. "You know that, don't you? We couldn't change him. We can't change anyone; sometimes you have to let them go."

I took a large sip of wine.

"Hey," she said. "Did you ever work out what Dad meant by the way? Lavender fields?"

"What? Er . . . no."

"You know what it is, though, right?"

I shook my head, running my finger around the rim of my glass.

"It's what Dad used to say to us as kids . . . Even in the most beautiful lavender fields—*especially* in the most beautiful lavender fields—you still have to keep your wits about you because that's where snakes hide best." She lowered her brows. "He was trying to warn you about something, someone . . . When did he say it again?"

54

Aid brought the final stack of old newspapers into the last lodge room from Dad's shed. Together we lay page after page across the floor. I peeled that morning's paper down, too, the one that told me the night Dion Zabaneh was apprehended when Hector and Benny were killed, two Belizeans were also arrested: Moses Williams, thirty-six, originally from Brixton, and Jamal Fernandez, forty-four, from Belmopan. TRUTH and Cigarillo. Moses and Jamal. I stared at their photos over the last of my coffee while Aid went to get more drinks. Police were still searching for Serena Perez, who they believed had fled, crossing the border to Mexico. Part of me hoped she'd managed to get out with the money. Good luck to her. She'd made her escape. One of us got away.

Dragging the stepladder across the old newspaper sheets towards the furthest untouched corner, I poured out the last of the paint.

"Hey," Aid said from the doorway. "Almost done?"

"Nearly."

He passed me a lemonade. The ice clunked in the glass. "Your Dad would have loved this. How much longer you gonna be?"

"I want to get it done before the kids are back tomorrow. It's just that bit by the window."

Aid rubbed the back of his neck. "I was thinking, we should call a Realtor. Get some idea of how much we'd get."

"What?"

"Now your dad's gone, there's no reason to stay."

"I don't want to leave."

"Lil, there's nothing for us here."

"I want to stay."

"Why?"

"Because I love it here. I can be myself. I can hear myself think."

"And what about me?" he said, raising his voice. "After everything, what about what I want?"

I balked, and when he saw me, he stopped himself, took a breath. His moods were still so up and down. I think he thought, after everything, after he'd shared the truth about Luisa, he'd be better. We'd be better.

"I'm sorry . . . I'm sorry." He sidled over and dragged his hands around my waist, pulling me close. "Let's go for a walk when you're finished . . ."

"Oh, Aid. I'm exhausted."

"A quick walk before dinner." He let me go, started towards the door.

"Okay. Okay." I waved the paintbrush, pointing at the wall. "You could help . . . I'd be done sooner."

"You don't need me," he said with a laugh. "I'm heading out to grab some bits. I'm cooking tonight, my treat . . . I'm gonna spoil you sense-less." My stomach lurched. He shut the door, left me inhaling the paint fumes.

The lemonade was sweet and icy and strong. As I placed the glass on the floor of old newspapers, a headline caught my eye: *Construction Worker Falls in Belmopan*, then another: *Man Arrested for Murder over Blue Hole Drowning*.

Picking up the sun-faded copy of *Amandala*, I gazed at the text, staring at the date. I read it again. And again. And again.

My eyes blurred.

"Aidrian Lynch is being questioned for murder . . ."

My heart sped.

". . . initially thought to have been an accident."

My head spun.

". . . A postmortem examination concluded bruising injuries evident on the victim's neck were consistent with possible strangulation. Police are looking into the possibility Ms. Farrante may have suffered a delayed fatality following an earlier incident. The victim had approximately nine individual bruises to the front of her neck." I felt sick as I rubbed my throat. "These types of injuries are in keeping with manual gripping such as strangulation."

I glared at the photos. One of Aid, close up; it was definitely him. And a second. A library shot of the Blue Hole taken from above. Another of the dive boat *The Kraken*. And a final photograph of two police officers in conversation with a gesticulating man. A man in a Panama hat.

In Dad's study, I started rifling through his things. I couldn't remember where I'd put them. I flung papers out, threw notebooks on the floor. Eventually, three drawers later I found them: Mounia's translations. I skimmed through the pages, tracked to the dates I was looking for. 12th January 2020. Caye Caulker. And read it all.

Dad's voice echoed in my head. *Lavender fields.*

55

I ran so hard back to the house, shaken by the revelations. *Was it really true?* Storming in, I started ransacking the drawers, pulling out sunscreen and keys, notebooks and cables, throwing them all to the floor. Eventually, I found it: Dad's iPhone Mounia had given me for safekeeping.

Pushing the On button, nothing happened. No battery. I fell to my knees, sorting through the fallen detritus. I checked one cable, but it wasn't right. Then another, forcing it into the jack. Plugging the phone in at the wall, I sat watching, waiting, until the phone flashed into life. I found Dad's photographs. Searching through, I felt nauseous, sick to my stomach. Dad with Mounia, a chicken, a boat, an orchid, a tree. I switched to year dates, furiously scrolling back through. 2022. 2021. 2020. January. A photo of Chloe and me, arm in arm, a plate of oysters in front of her. White wine. Elden's restaurant sign. The view over the dock at Caye Caulker. Sunset. Carmen in her dive T-shirt. I flicked through further. Dad in his wetsuit, mask in his hand. A picture on the boat, *The Kraken*, a sea of people squashed in together. And in the background, a couple.

I zoomed in, enlarging their faces. Aid. And her. It was her. Emerald eyes. Lustrous dark hair. His wife. Luisa. Thoughts and memories converged, clashing echos in my mind.

I'd seen her before. *I'd seen her before.*

I remembered it so clearly now.

Faint chatter crisping into the night. Reggae booming, beachgoers spilling towards the bar from the sand. It thronged like we were inside, there were so many people. It was electric. I'd almost got the bartender's attention amongst a choppy sea of drinkers.

But then she appeared, ghosting in as if from nowhere. She was about my age, perhaps a little younger. She was clutching a fistful of dollars, a see-through kimono floating behind as though it was skimming an angel. She was dressed ready to party, for day into night and probably back into day again: gold hoop earrings and bangles circling long, lean arms; dark waves brushing the crimson bikini top that encased lush, plump breasts. She moved like a movie, her eyes smiling until her lips followed. The entire bar's attention drifted towards her, and she barely even noticed, the woman with the emerald eyes.

"Five Belikins, four daiquiris, three margaritas, and twelve tequilas," she said. Or something like it. Her words purred, I remembered that; the huskiness of her East Coast accent gliding over the music. The bar guy set to work, stirring, shaking, salting with divine intention while she lined up crisp notes along the bar. Each time she flicked her wrist to peel back another bill, her bangles jangled a tinny accompaniment, her cactus tattoo blurring.

"Champagne dreams," the barman hollered.

"Hmm?" she replied.

He grinned. "You're gonna need more than a hundred twenty."

She rolled her eyes, pushing the notes across the bar. "Take this, and I'll go get some more."

The barman was still rolling his eyes and shaking his head when he turned to take my order. "You see that? Champagne dreams wid lime juice money . . . ! What do you want?"

I ordered my daiquiri and picked up *The Beach* again.

Ellis

The waves crash gently across the sand. The party is pounding, "Come on Eileen" in full swing. Ellis's head is pounding, too. He feels nauseous. Now the girls are here, it would be a good time to tell them; about Cattleya, about Agapita, about his betrayal and his regrets. He will have to grab them both later, or maybe tomorrow when he can get them alone. He's always been sure he wants to tell them in person, not leave it to a letter. He's tried to pen it a dozen times over the past couple of years, but then abandoned it. They need to hear it in person, be able to ask questions about the mistakes he has made, and the ones he didn't.

He's left his whisky inside, but part of him wants it now. The beach is empty, save for one lone soul slumped by the firepit back there. *Young women shouldn't drink so much*, Ellis thinks to himself.

"I love this song," Aidrian says as they make their way across the sand. His small talk belies his discomfort. At the bar before, it was just a feeling—a sense, really, that maybe he'd seen this man before, met him perhaps, one time or other. Ellis couldn't put his finger on it, not right away. And it wasn't a father's natural overprotectiveness—God, if it was that, he would have stopped her from marrying that arsehole Simon, kept her away from all of that hurt. No—decades of following his instincts must have taught Ellis something because he knows well that, just as the jungle demands vigilance—hiding its dangers like secret lessons—so does life.

When he asked Aidrian to go with him to get some air, he wanted to probe him a little further, to see. Now though, he has more of a sense of it, more a feeling; they've definitely met before.

"So you say you lived here before? In San Ignacio?" The neuralgia in Ellis's skull is crushing now. Should he feel quite this dreadful? He's only had a couple of drinks.

Aidrian stands next to him, hands in his pockets, staring out to sea. He is calm, compliant. "Yeah. I worked at the Botanic Gardens."

"By the Macal River. Beautiful."

Aidrian is kicking his feet in the sand—something to do while he humours me, Ellis thinks—his girlfriend's tiresome father, and it feels to Ellis like he is kicking at his head. "Come on Eileen" changes tempo, executes its key change. Drunk party guests sing out inside.

Ellis straightens his back as the memories return. "It used to be paradise here . . . At least, that's how I remember it, how it was before, back in the eighties—idyllic and out of time. But we ruined it, or maybe it ruined us. With its sugar sands and crystalline waters, its feathered palms." He takes a breath. "I don't believe you, by the way."

"Sorry?" Aidrian turns to him, his eyes piercing blue even in the moonlight.

"I don't believe you haven't been married."

"What . . . ?" Aidrian feigns incredulity. "What are you talking about?"

It comes to Ellis more clearly now. "I remember you . . . The newspapers, they said you were married. Elden's, I think it was called, the restaurant where I saw you . . . It's not there anymore." Aidrian cocks his head, rubs at his brow as Ellis goes on. "Food poisoning, wasn't it?" As Ellis speaks, the images flood back to him. He can almost feel himself sitting on the beach again, along from where they now stand. He recalls the sounds of it all, outside the hotel room door: the fighting, the screaming, the hit. "She had oysters at dinner that night, your wife. Chloe had them, too. I should have told her. Oysters here are so hard to come by, they were probably frozen, bound to be a risk."

"What are you talking about?" Aidrian says again, his voice cracking.

"She said she moved rooms, your wife. Shared with a friend of hers . . . I can't remember her name." Ellis's eyesight is blurring. He can't be this drunk, surely. "I was there . . . I was there at the Blue Hole that day. When your wife . . . What was her name?"

"Luisa," Aidrian says weakly. Even in the darkness, his eyes shine so strong.

"Luisa, that's it." Ellis gives him a moment. "I was there when they brought her up out of the water." Aid flinches, looks to the sky. "The police spoke to me at the scene. I tried to tell them, but they were only interested in what happened in the water. They didn't want to hear much else. They barely took any notes when I told them about her black eye—"

"You—"

"About the marks around her neck, about what I overheard outside your hotel room . . ."

"You're wrong," Aidrian protests.

"They closed the case so quickly. I read they did arrest you. I phoned the police again. Told them what I'd heard, what I'd seen . . . but they said the case had been dropped. They didn't have enough evidence. Said the marks on her neck could have come postmortem. I couldn't place you," Ellis says, feeling so hot now. The headache is intense, like nothing he's ever felt before. He tries to loosen his collar. "I had a sense just now I'd met you before." Ellis thinks suddenly, out of nowhere, of the beauty of nature, the violence of it. "Your wife . . . I overheard her. She said you'd slept with someone else . . . 'the Englishhhwoman,' that's what she said . . ." Ellis slurs his words, his vision fuzzing.

"You've got it wrong," Aidrian says again.

"I ssshould call the police again. Get them to . . . re . . . reinvestigate." And then it dawns on Ellis—who it could have been, who it must have been. Who it was. The Englishwoman. *Laelia*. His head screams in pain and his brain . . . his thoughts . . . are so confused. He can't think straight. He feels like he's going to throw up.

Aidrian's looking at him strangely, grabbing at him now, the tattooed hands pushing at his chest.

They struggle into the water, the sea snaking at their ankles.

Cold. Ellis is so cold. He feels horrendous. Is he trying to hold him up? Help him? Push him down?

"No . . ." Vomit collects in Ellis's throat.

"Ellis?" Aidrian grabs at his collar.

"Aid?" A female voice calls from the distance. The hands on his chest release.

Everything's hazy now, fuzzy. Cold. So cold. A dark figure is walking towards them across the sand. In the moonlight. *Laelia? Is that Laelia?* He wants to tell her. Wants to warn her, properly this time. But his mouth is trembling, and he cannot speak. There's so much he hasn't told her.

But Ellis can't think of anything then apart from the eyes. It was his eyes; the bluest blue he has ever seen, the last things he sees.

Laelia

Wittering Lodge, Stann Creek District, Belize
9th May 2023

Aid ambled back through the door as I was finishing the final strokes by the windowsill: Mountain Salt, with undertones of sage and violet. "Ready for that walk?"

I nodded, throwing the brush down into the tray. Peeling off my overalls, I caught him giving me that look. His look. With those eyes. Water reed crinkles, harder now. *What he wants to do to me.*

"I need to change," I said, dropping my gaze, busying myself collecting paint pots and rollers, heading towards the door as he followed on behind. *What I want to do to him.*

I waited until we were deep into the jungle, its clamour of leaves and roots and vines, until the dark greenery had calmed my nerves—just a little, just enough. Verdant light kaleidoscoped, dancing over Aid's skin, his tattoos eddying and whirling over his sleeves and across my mind. Birdsong pulsed its backdrop. A screech owl tremored in the distance. *Gogogogogogogo.* History has a way of casting deep shadows; the past disfiguring the present, entwining it like bindweed, so slowly, so gradually, so you don't even feel its stranglehold until it's too late.

We stopped by a fallen mahogany, throwing our rucksacks to the ground. Aid rummaged in his bag and pulled out a flask. A butterfly—a blue morpho—flitted before settling on a leaf, its iridescent wings shining like a prism.

I took a deep breath, and then another. "When did it happen?" I asked, gripping my machete tight.

"When did what happen?" He smelt of moss and stale tobacco, the scents catching in my throat. His eyes were rough seas. I edged away from him.

"The diving incident." Not accident, I didn't say accident. "With Luisa."

"What?" His eyes flashed around before he took a swig of water. "I said I didn't want to talk about it."

"No, but I do. I think you owe me that much . . . Was it when we first met? That January?"

He hesitated, collecting his thoughts. "What?"

"I was there, wasn't I? On Caye Caulker. Your wife had food poisoning like Chloe. We ate at the same restaurant. They both had oysters." His face dropped. "It's all in Dad's journals."

"In his journals? What are you talking about?"

"She moved to Maia's room . . . and then you found me. You fucked me behind your wife's back, and you never even told me. Or her. But she found out."

He shook his head. "Lil . . ." He couldn't speak. I didn't need to hear him anyway. His look said it all.

"The dive to the Blue Hole. You did that a few days later, when she was feeling better, once I'd left. Once you'd planned your escape."

"Lil—"

"Aid, stop lying . . . I know. I know you slept with me when you were married. I know Luisa found out." My voice broke a little now, but swelled again with momentum, a surge of adrenaline. "I know you throttled her . . . My dad was there, on that dive trip. That's why he recognised you. He couldn't place you at first, just had a sense that he knew you. But he worked it out later that night. At his party. Did you recognise him?"

Aid was still shaking his head, staring wildly, running his hands through his hair. "One thing I don't understand . . ." I steadied myself against a kapok. "Why did you say that before, after River Day? You said you were scared about what I might tell Nico . . . What would I tell him? About the orchids . . . ? But he knew about the orchid trading, didn't he?"

Aid laughed. He actually laughed. "Oh, Laelia. You're so fucked in the head . . . You *knew*. You've always known." He rested his hands behind his neck.

"Known what?"

"You *met* her. Luisa. You saw her at the bar, the night before we slept together . . . You knew I was married."

"What?"

"You told me to leave her."

"*What?*"

"You were joking, of course, sort of. But it planted a seed." He squeezed his eyes shut. "You know all this. Or you knew it. You knew everything." He laughed. "It was your idea. You asked me to be with you . . . without her. You kind of willed it into being." A flicker of a memory. Emerald eyes.

I couldn't breathe.

"Your mind's so fucking addled, though . . ." He laughed as if he was taking great pleasure in all of this. "You've managed to forget."

"You're lying."

"No, Laelia." A flash of dark hair, drifting like unravelling ropes. "You're the one who's been lying. All this time you've been lying to yourself, telling yourself whatever you need to forget. You put the idea in my head . . ."

"What?"

"You wanted to forget. And I let you. I told you about it afterwards, in Brighton. . . . About how I lost my temper with her that night." *Oh my God. Oh my God.* "About how it got rough after she'd found your earring. You fucking idiot, that was definitely your fault . . . I didn't mean to hurt her that bad, I didn't . . . The next day, the marks on her neck were so obvious, I was worried she was going to say something, tell someone. But she didn't. Then, when we were underwater, she panicked. And she couldn't breathe. And . . . I don't know, I froze."

Like with Dylan.

"You're lying." I felt like I might throw up. I dropped my machete, and it hit the forest floor with a thud. "Wha . . . What are you talking about?"

My head was spinning. *I knew?* I didn't know. I didn't. Surely he was lying to me, still? *Stop lying.* "Stop lying."

"It was you who wanted to forget . . . who pushed the memories away. And I let you, because I wanted to protect you. Because I love you . . . I *love* you."

I pictured her. Like I must have pictured her in my mind's eye then, when Aid first told me what he'd done. Her emerald eyes; her panic-stricken eyes. Her dark hair like tentacles floating underwater.

I cupped my hands over my mouth, trying to breathe, trying to push the mosaic of memories away. My stomach dropped. "This isn't on me. It's not—"

He sat down on the mahogany trunk.

"Aid . . ." My voice caught itself against some deep knowledge. I shook my head, stealing shallow breaths. *I knew? All this time. I knew her? I knew he was married. I knew that she drowned.* I closed my eyes. I couldn't breathe. I knew he strangled her? A tidal wave of images crashed around me. I knew he strangled her. *I've known all along.* I heaved, bile lacing my throat.

They weren't memories of Luisa, not really; they were memories of nightmares. Nightmares I must have had. Warped dreams she'd inhabited, back then, when he told me. Imaginings of how it must have gone down, of what happened, of what he did. Before I blocked it out.

Thoughts ricocheted about my mind. "I . . . I should go to the police," I said, my voice quavering.

Aid let out a guttural laugh. "Don't be crazy, Laelia . . . Go to the police? That's what your dad said."

"What?"

"It's what your dad threatened me with."

"When he collapsed? He— He was confronting you?"

"Lavender fields," I mumbled. *He was trying to protect me.*

"What?"

"Lavender fields."

"What the fuck are you on about?"

"I need to go to the police, tell them what happened."

"Don't be fucking stupid," Aid spat, venom in his voice. "You're implicated, Laelia. You've known all along. You might have forgotten it, you might have managed to push it down, pretend it never happened. But you knew."

"You're a liar." My voice cracked.

"I'm not lying, you stupid, stupid bitch."

"In the water, with my dad . . ." I could barely speak. "You didn't help him . . . Not until you saw me. You want . . . you wanted him dead."

Aid screamed. The most bestial scream I ever heard. He grabbed at his calf. Groaning in agony, he tried to stand up. An unmistakable rattle. So loud. Out the corner of my eye, I saw it: the crisscross yellow-brown tail of a fer-de-lance sliding under the trunk.

His eyes widened. "Laelia!" I stood staring at the puncture mark on his leg as he flailed in pain. "Help!" Unstable on his feet, grappling for balance, he grabbed for the cedar tree. "Laelia . . . ? Please!" He ripped at the *Cattleya*, pulling its bloom from its leaves. He was writhing like an animal, howling like a wolf.

My hand felt into my pocket, rubbing at the leaves I always carried— the mother-in-law's tongue, nature's analgesic—that would buy him more time. Enough time I could fetch help or call for an ambulance. Or I could stand and do nothing at all. Leave him here, with his sharded memories, our fucked-up lies, the truths only he and I knew. The stories we'd told ourselves, told others, that no-one ever need unknow.

"Please . . ." Aid begged, his eyes pulsing. "Have you got the leaves?"

My fingers stroked at the roughness of them, the beautiful secret of them, deep in my pocket. I stared at him, so close but a world away. I'd been lying to myself; I could admit that much—believing we were some-how different, invincible and unshakable and passionate beyond belief. But we'd lost ourselves into each other, into ourselves, and he had kept the maps.

"There but for the grace of God go I." I almost smiled. I think I smiled.

"Laelia . . . please." He spat fear, like he was about to be fed it. "Hel . . ." The words died in his throat.

"I can't hear you, Aid," I said, pointing at my hearing aids.

He rolled his head back and forth, thrashing his body. "Plea . . ." He was rocking back and forth in helpless agony, the fingers of one hand grabbing at his skin, gripping onto the "L.F" heart, and with the other, his thumb-stumped hand, his four remaining digits caged around the orange orchid, trapping it in his grip.

Tossing the plant leaves to the ground, I turned away. A vulture glided and circled overhead. I smiled, only to myself, revelling in the roaring power of nature and the might and miracle of the jungle, the most powerful leveller of them all.

It was a sweet and balmy night—that magic moment of twilight, after the day is done before dusk dissolves in. The festoon bulbs skimming the gazebo were starting to glow, illuminating a natural gallery of orchids, their lush pinks and lemon-limes. The Wittering Lobster bustled with customers, hopeful diners snaking out the door. We'd had a few buzzing reviews that had garnered attention, all of them homing in on our focus on the senses. Acoustic synaesthesia. Eating to the noises of the jungle, understanding how sound (the forgotten flavour sense) influences taste. *Time* magazine said, "It's a genius point of difference," and praised the girls' scholarships we fund in my mother's name. Mounia's set up a shop out front, where the cooperative sells their ceramics and baskets and clothes. Travellers flock for hours to say they've been. I encourage them to stay for days and days, to visit the local villages, and take the tours with Henry; to soak up, and give back, to this homely paradise.

Over my tinnitus, so much softer now—a part of me—I could hear the laughter, no longer drowned by shame. In between sparkling giggles and lemonade, Ella and Jonas showed couples to their tables; Dylan folded napkins at the counter—weighing them down with the aquamarine stone as he added to the stack—Ursula wedged at his feet. They were more at home with themselves now than they had ever been.

There's a guy who comes in sometimes, always sits at table seven. When I saw him the first time, it chilled me like a ghost, the way he smoothed his tattooed hands up through his hair, smiling like a secret, eating me up with his eyes. He doesn't truly look like him, not really, but in a certain shadow, in the half-light, I sometimes have to do a double take.

I often get to thinking of all the things we'd been through here: the emotions still roiling in my stomach; the fragments of lust still glittering at my heart; the lies we had to tell ourselves to survive. I sometimes wonder if the notes weren't from Aid all along, staged to mess with my mind. But you cannot question things too much. It's enough to drive you mad. I told the children about him. Not everything. But enough. I would no longer hide behind my shame, not let the lies carry on. I told them that he hit me, that he was a coward, that I had been too but now it was over, and he was gone. He was gone.

"Laelia," the new sous-chef called, carrying a bowl of limes. "There's someone at the side door asking for you . . . Says he hasn't seen you in months." My heart started hammering. *Water reed crinkles.* Sweat prickled over my skin. *A flash of machete. A gold signet ring.* I pushed the thoughts from my mind. *They are dead. He is gone.* "Laelia?"

They cannot hurt you now.

Turning up my hearing aids, I nodded. I gave the chowder a stir with Mum's wooden spoon. Edging through the kitchen, past the clatter of cutlery, the din of dishes, my body tightened. I pushed open the door. He was holding armfuls of lionfish. He looked older, rugged. But his eyes were gentle still.

ACKNOWLEDGMENTS

I'd planned to keep this short, but too many incredible people have helped me along the way. . . Firstly, I am indebted to my astounding agent, Madeleine Milburn, who is just THE best. You understood so wholeheartedly from the beginning what I wanted to achieve. Thank you to the whole team at MMA, especially Hannah Kettles, Valentina Paulmichl, and Saskia Arthur. I'm so grateful to my amazing editors, Sara Nelson and Charlotte Brabbin, for believing in me and for helping me machete my way through the manuscript when I could no longer see the wood for the trees. Big thanks to everyone at HarperCollins and Harper Fiction for bringing this novel out into the world, especially Edie Astley, Lydia Weaver, Alice Brown, Olivia McGiff, Elina Cohen, Nina Shchavielieva, Megan Smith, Ellie Game, Lipfon Tang, Libby Haddock, Samantha Lubash, Maya Baran, Lynne Drew, Holly Martin, Harriet Williams, Ruth Barrow, and Angela Thompson.

Huge gratitude and love to the formidable Joey Garcia, who provided such brilliant notes and wise counsel, ensuring I capture the culture and beauty of Belize as accurately as possible. I am so grateful for your input. Thanks also to Neville Evans for his botanic garden insights, Campbell Munn for his expertise on vultures (and their pissing habits), Dr. Hannah Dawe for not laughing (too much) at all my ridiculous medical questions, Magdalena Viehl for helping me fall in love with diving again and adding detail to those sections, Katie Willis and Phil Cornwell for answering my audiology questions, Silvanna Udz for her Kriol language teachings, everyone at Sweet Songs Lodge in San Ignacio, especially Erminello Tec for showing me the jungle plants and medicinal herbs and water straight from the vine, healer Aurora Garcia Saqui, Michelle Little for your insights into Belize, Clarissa Rudd and Rupert Hall for answering my cheffing conundrums, and to my oldest, dearest friend, Dr. Amanda Jones, for academic insights and ongoing support. Any errors on the page are mine alone.

Susan Orlean's fantastic book, *The Orchid Thief* was a great inspiration for my Ellis sections. A heartfelt thank-you to Mary Ruefle for allowing me to use her beautiful poem "Voyager" as an epigraph. I cannot imagine a more fitting verse.

Huge thanks to my early readers: my writing wife, Esme Hall, for always encouraging me to stab the udder, Julian Morgan, Jo Furniss, Diane Stevenson, Beth Miller, Mary Murray-Brown, Louisa Moss, Lucy Waverley, Laura Daniels, Patricia Holland, Alex Dey, Claire Chamberlain, Clare Collins, Julie O'Sullivan, Elizabeth Rutherford-Johnson, Leslie Theibert, and all the Cheshire Cats, as well as to Emma Cowing, Natalie Gregory, Claire Allen, Zee Y, Leona Farquharson and Anna Brewer, and to my oldest friends, "Lovely People" and Jemma Hardelle—thank you for following my dreams with me.

I'm indebted to so many other supporters along the way, including Hove Writers (Tam and Beth especially), Real Writers Circle, the Faber Academy and Rowan Hisayo Buchanan, the Arvon Foundation (James Spackman and Suzie Dooré) and Curtis Brown, Alice Lutyens, Amanda Harris, and Luke Speed. John Niven for your little boost of confidence ("fucking good title, that"), Jennie Godfrey for your online support (we will meet someday!), and Will Dean for your openness and encouragement of debut novelists everywhere. Also, thanks to Chris Pitsillides for your patience. I am eternally grateful to Sara Cox and the Cheshire Novel Prize for their ongoing support and enthusiasm for this story, as well as Lisa Milton and the Primadonna Festival. Without you, I'd still be stuck at 40 percent.

Thank you, Jill Dawson and Gold Dust, for your wise counsel (and the margaritas). You have showed me such wisdom, generosity, and ongoing magic. And to Chloe Timms—your spirit and positivity have been hugely inspiring. A special mention to the unbelievably gracious and insightful Eleanor Dryden who was my biggest early cheerleader right when I thought I might possibly, hopefully, have a shot at taking my manuscript somewhere. Your kindness and support have kept me going. You are exceptional.

I would never have got to this place without the early encouragement of an unorthodox but eternally inspiring English teacher, the late Mr. Alun Pinkus. At the lowest moments, I imagined you there telling me to "just fucking get on with it." I wish you were here to see me now. Thanks to Lucy and Paul for your ongoing support and help with everything else going on in my life and to the rest of my family, Simon, Clare, Eve, and Tom, but most especially Mum and Dad for always encouraging me to strive high and work hard. Tenacity is a precious gift.

To my biggest (and loudest) cheerleaders, Jackson and Charlie. My boys. My world. My heart. JackJack, I followed my eight-year-old's dream because, when you were age eight, you showed me how to follow yours. This couldn't have happened without you. Thank you for encouraging me always. I cannot wait to visit Belize again with you both soon. And finally, to my husband, Will, who always believed I would write a novel and kept me going when I didn't think I could. I love you. Thank you for everything.

I owe you all a thousand lime daiquiris (Jackson and Charlie, you'll have to wait a few years for yours . . .)

Thank you, dear Reader, for coming on this incredible journey with me too.

AUTHOR NOTE

Belize is rich in kindness, culture, and fantastic literature. If you've enjoyed reading this, I encourage you to explore brilliant Belizean authors such as Joey Garcia, Zee Edgell, and Zoila Ellis, all of whom have been inspiring to me. You can also check out my playlist on Spotify which I listened to ad infinitum while working on this novel: http://bit.ly/3PYOODi

Find out more about my writing and forthcoming novels at jomorey.com

ABOUT THE AUTHOR

JO MOREY studied English literature and French at the University of Leeds, and is a graduate of the Faber Academy and the Curtis Brown Disability Mentoring Scheme. *Lime Juice Money* came second in the Cheshire Novel Prize, was finalist in the Killer Nashville Claymore Award (Literary), and was shortlisted in both the Plaza First Pages and Page Turner Awards. Jo won the Claire Mannion Prize at the Primadonna Literary Festival and was shortlisted in Leicester Writes Short Story Prize. Jo lives in Sussex at the foot of the South Downs with her husband, two boys, and two Portuguese water dogs. *Lime Juice Money* is her first novel.